Carla Cassidy is an award-winning, *New York Times* bestselling author who has written over 170 books, including 150 for Mills & Boon. She has won the Centennial Award from Romance Writers of America. Most recently she won the 2019 Write Touch Readers' Award for her Mills & Boon Heroes title *Desperate Strangers*. Carla believes the only thing better than curling up with a good book is sitting down at the computer with a good story to write.

Janie Crouch writes passionate romantic suspense for readers who still believe in heroes. After a lifetime on the East Coast—and a six-year stint in Germany—this *USA Today* bestselling author has settled into her dream home in the Front Range of the Colorado Rockies. She loves engaging in all sorts of adventures (Triathlons! Two-hundred-mile relay races! Mountain treks!), travelling and surviving life with four kids. You can find out more about her at janiecrouch.com

Also by Carla Cassidy

A Bayou Investigation
Murder in Dark Waters

Marsh Mysteries
Stalked Through the Mist
Swamp Shadows
Hunted in the Reeds

The Scarecrow Murders
Killer in the Heartland
Guarding a Forbidden Love
The Cowboy Next Door

Also by Janie Crouch

Warrior Peak Sanctuary
Protective Assignment
Protective Lawman

The Risk Series: A Bree and Tanner Thriller
Constant Risk
Risk Everything

Omega Sector: Under Siege
Daddy Defender
Protector's Instinct
Cease Fire

Discover more at millsandboon.co.uk

KIDNAPPED IN DARK WATERS

CARLA CASSIDY

PROTECTIVE REFUGE

JANIE CROUCH

MILLS & BOON

All rights reserved including the right of reproduction in whole or in part in any form. This edition is published by arrangement with Harlequin Enterprises ULC.

This is a work of fiction. Names, characters, places, locations and incidents are purely fictional and bear no relationship to any real life individuals, living or dead, or to any actual places, business establishments, locations, events or incidents. Any resemblance is entirely coincidental.

Without limiting the exclusive rights of any author, contributor or the publisher of this publication, any unauthorised use of this publication to train generative artificial intelligence (AI) technologies is expressly prohibited. HarperCollins also exercise their rights under Article 4(3) of the Digital Single Market Directive 2019/790 and expressly reserve this publication from the text and data mining exception.

® and ™ are trademarks owned and used by the trademark owner and/or its licensee. Trademarks marked with ® are registered with the United Kingdom Patent Office and/or the Office for Harmonisation in the Internal Market and in other countries.

First Published in Great Britain 2026
by Mills & Boon, an imprint of HarperCollins*Publishers* Ltd
1 London Bridge Street, London, SE1 9GF

www.harpercollins.co.uk

HarperCollins*Publishers*
Macken House, 39/40 Mayor Street Upper,
Dublin 1, D01 C9W8, Ireland

Kidnapped in Dark Waters © 2026 Carla Bracale
Protective Refuge © 2026 Janie Crouch

ISBN: 978-0-263-42027-2

0426

Printed and Bound in the UK using 100% Renewable Electricity at
CPI Group (UK) Ltd, Croydon, CR0 4YY

KIDNAPPED IN DARK WATERS

CARLA CASSIDY

Chapter One

Mystique's Magic. The large purple lettering danced across a seafoam-green background on the sign above the front door of the store. A white banner hung just below it, with big red lettering announcing the grand opening.

Dominique Santori stood in a line of women waiting to get into the interior of the new, small store. The store was her older sister Angelique's lifelong dream, and a deep sense of pride filled Dominique at her sister's accomplishment. However, the pride and happiness she felt for her sister was tempered with a healthy dose of sadness and grief.

The store had been named after their mother, Mystique Santori. She'd been viciously murdered a little over two months ago and so far, there hadn't been any arrests for the crime.

She now smiled as she saw Monique, her younger sister, approaching where she stood. "Sorry I'm late," Monique said.

"When aren't you late," Dominique replied teasingly.

As usual, Monique looked sharp. She was clad in a long black-and-white-striped skirt with a ruffled white blouse. Her long, black hair was caught at the nape of her neck with a silver clasp and dainty silver earrings danced from her ears.

"Looks like she's got a good crowd," Monique said, obviously ignoring her sister's jab about always being late. "Have you heard anything from the women leaving the store? Any early reviews?"

"Not really, but I've heard snatches of conversations from the women standing in line behind me." Dominique released a deep sigh. "Some people apparently believe Angelique is setting herself up to become the next voodoo queen, since Mama is gone."

Before her murder, Mystique Santori was known as a voodoo queen both in the swamp and in the small town. People came to her under the cover of darkness to her shanty deep in the wetland that half surrounded the small Louisiana town of Dark Waters. It was whispered that she had dabbled in black magic, and most people in the town and swamp had been afraid of her.

"Well, that's just ridiculous," Monique scoffed. "Especially now that she's moved in with Daniel."

A little over a week ago, Angelique had left the swamp behind and moved in with the chief of police, Daniel LeCroix. The two had found love as Daniel had worked on solving their mother's murder. There might not be anyone behind bars yet, but Dominique knew Daniel was still hard at work trying to find out who took her mother's life.

"But you know how people love to talk," Dominique replied. "Still, it's an exciting day for Angelique and I hope she sells a ton of items today."

"I intend to buy something from her, but I'm just not sure what." The two women took several steps forward as the line moved closer to the door.

The two sisters small-talked and then they reached the

shop door and went inside. The interior smelled appealingly of a variety of florals and spices. On one side of the store were candles, bath salts and an assortment of other items for self-care.

On the other side was why Angelique had wanted to open the store in the first place. Shelves held a variety of poultices and tinctures and teas made from the healing plants and flowers from the swamp.

Angelique greeted both of them with hugs. "Thanks for coming in," she said, her face flushed with excitement. She was dressed in a pair of black slacks and a purple T-shirt with the store logo on the front. Her long black hair was in a high ponytail and tied up with a purple ribbon.

"We wouldn't have missed it," Monique said.

"How's it going?" Dominique asked.

"Better than I could have ever imagined. I've sold so much of the swamp-based items I'll need to head out to restock in the next day or two," Angelique replied.

"That's terrific," Dominique said. "We're here to shop, so we'll just look around while you take care of other customers."

Minutes later, Dominique paid for a candle and Monique bought some scented body lotion, and then together the two said their goodbyes to their sister and they left the store.

"Are you working today?" Monique asked once they were outside again.

"Yes, I'm on lunch duty today so I'm working from eleven to four," Dominique replied. "What about you?"

"I'm going in to work at five and I'll be there until close," Monique replied. "A new shipment is supposed to come in sometime this afternoon so at least I'll have something to do. I always love to unpack, inventory and then tag and hang new clothes."

"And you love to spend half your paycheck on the clothes you unpack," Dominique teased.

Monique laughed. "You aren't wrong."

"Then I guess I'll see you sometime tomorrow," Dominique said, eager to get into her car and out of the early August heat.

"Okay, sis. See you later," Monique replied.

Minutes later Dominique was in her car and headed home. She had a little less than an hour to get ready for her shift at the Dark Waters Café.

It wasn't long before she pulled up in front of the swamp's main entrance. She parked in the area where most of the people who lived in the swamp parked their cars and then she got out and headed into the thick tangle of greenery.

She half ran along the narrow path that would take her to the shanty where she'd grown up. Until a week ago, Angelique had lived there, but when Angelique had moved out, Dominique had moved in. The shanty was far bigger than the one where Dominique had been living and it filled her with the comfort of feeling as if she was home.

The shanty was one of the largest in the swamp, with three bedrooms, a bathroom, a living room and kitchen area. It was high on stilts above the water that half surrounded it. Tupelos and bald cypress trees rose up majestically around it.

Her mother had slept in one of the bedrooms, with all three girls in another. The third bedroom was where the 'voodoo queen' met her clients.

Once there, Dominique went into her bedroom and quickly changed out of the red blouse she'd had on and into the pink T-shirt that had Dark Waters Café printed across the front. Thank goodness she could wear her jeans to work.

Her bedroom was done up in the colors of a sunset. Her spread was in shades of deep pinks and oranges and matching curtains hung at the single window in the room. She loved this room, which had once been the bedroom she'd shared with her sisters. She'd always felt safe in here.

She pulled her long, dark hair into a high ponytail, sprayed on a spritz of her favorite perfume and then she was ready to go once again.

However, before she left, she walked to the door of her mother's bedroom…the room where her mother's body had been found by Angelique. Mystique had been in bed and her throat had been slashed.

Dominique opened the door of the room as a deep grief clutched at her heart. The bed was bare, but many of her mother's items were still there. At some point they all needed to be packed up or given away.

Her mother would never be there again to spray on her favorite perfume or read one of the books in the bookcase near the bed. She would never be there again to pull Dominique into a hug or share conversations about anything and everything. With a heavy sigh, Dominique left the room and headed for the front door.

It was time for her to get to work. Once again, she hurried down the narrow paths that would take her back to her car. Minutes later as she drove back into town, she shoved thoughts of her mother's murder away and instead focused on the workday to come.

Since it was Saturday, the café would be packed. But she didn't mind. She loved being a waitress and had a bunch of regular diners who always sat in her section.

She made good money in tips and couldn't imagine doing anything else.

She found a parking space in the lot at the back of the café and then went in through the back door. The people working in the kitchen all greeted her as she walked through to the small break room.

"Hey girl," Sunny Herbert, one of Dominique's good friends and coworker, greeted her. "Ready for another day in the trenches?"

"Always." Dominique placed her purse in one of the small lockers in the room and then pocketed the little key.

"I went into your sister's new store this morning. It's awesome. I bought a tea that's made from plants from the swamp and is supposed to help with cramps."

"Angelique is really into the plant and flower cures from the swamp," Dominique replied. "She's studied all about them. And now we'd better get out on the floor or Annie will have our heads."

Annie Fulbright was the owner of the café. She was in her mid-sixties and was a fair—but tough—boss. She had high standards and expected her staff to meet those standards.

The café was very attractive, with three of the walls painted by a local artist. The first wall was of pink bougainvillea flowers and the second was of majestic tupelo and bald cypress trees rising out of sunlit dark waters. Finally, the last wall was of the colorful storefronts that lined Main Street.

Within minutes, Dominique was busy taking orders and delivering food. She grinned as she greeted a man seated alone at one of the two-top tables. "Hey Burt, how are you feeling today?" Burt Stanfield was one of her regulars. The fortysomething man worked for the city in the maintenance department, and he was a widower. His wife had passed away two years before due to an advanced case of breast cancer.

"Fine as a fiddle, what about you?" he replied with a big smile.

"I'm doing just fine. So, what can I get for you today, Burt?" she asked.

"I'd like some coffee and the number three special. And even though it's a bit early, give me a slice of sweet potato pie. I've had a hankering for pie since the moment I woke up this morning."

"Then I'll make sure you get the biggest piece there is," Dominique replied. "You know I always take care of you, Burt."

"That's why I'm so crazy about you, doll," he replied with another one of his big smiles.

Dominique laughed. "I'll be right back with your coffee." She wished all her customers were as pleasant as Burt.

The next regular she waited on was Austin Colbert. Austin was in his thirties and was the town librarian. He always came in with a book and would read while he ate.

"Austin, how are you doing today?" she greeted him.

"Good now that I've seen your beautiful, smiling face," he replied.

"My goodness, Austin. You'll turn a girl's head with your shameless flirting," she replied with a laugh. "So, you want the usual?" The usual was a cheeseburger, fries and a diet cola.

"The usual is exactly what I want," he replied.

"I'll have that out to you in just a few minutes," she said and then left his table.

It was half an hour later when chief of police and future

brother-in-law Daniel and two of his men sat in a booth in her section. Dominique knew how hard the lawmen were working to solve her mother's murder, but so far it hadn't happened.

"Hi, Daniel," she greeted and then smiled at Luke Madison and Clay Caldwell. She had a bit of a crush on Luke, who she found ridiculously handsome, but she really didn't know him at all.

"Hey, Dominique," Daniel replied. "Your sister had a big morning."

Dominique smiled. "Yeah, I was at the store earlier. It appeared to be a huge success."

"It was, and Angelique is beyond thrilled," he replied. When he said her sister's name, his love for her was evident in his voice. Someday, Dominique would like to find a man who said her name with a wealth of love.

She took their orders and by the time they ate and left, the lunch rush hour was over and Annie sent her on a break. Instead of going into the break room where she usually took her breaks, she went out the front door, wanting to see her sister's store again.

From the café she could see Mystique's Magic in the distance. As she watched she saw two women walk out with shopping bags in their hands.

She was so proud of her older sister for working for and finally realizing her life's dream. Dominique's life's dream was far less spectacular. Eventually she wanted to be a wife and a mother. But she wasn't even dating anyone at the moment.

In fact, it had been almost a year since she'd had a relationship. At that time, she'd gone out on a couple of dates with Oliver LeBoeuf, who lived in the swamp and was a fisherman.

It hadn't taken her long to recognize that she liked Oliver a lot, but there were no real romantic feelings for him, so after about half a dozen dates, she'd broken things off with him. Since that time there hadn't been anyone.

She turned her gaze in the other direction, looking down to the popular dress shop, All That Jazz, where her younger sister Monique worked. And then she saw him. He was walking down the street toward the café.

Pierre Guidry. He had been her mother's on-again, off-again lover for years, and he was the man Dominique believed had murdered her mother. She also knew that according to Daniel, he was the number one suspect in the case but so far there wasn't any evidence to arrest him.

But Dominique had a plan to get the evidence required to get him under arrest. It would be dangerous, but she didn't care. She was determined to get her mother's murderer in jail and she would do whatever she could to make that happen, no matter how dangerous it was.

LUKE MADISON SAT in the small interview room that had been designated the murder room. Everything inside was dedicated to Mystique Santori's murder. His boss and good friend, Daniel LeCroix, was there along with Luke's other good friend and coworker, Clay Caldwell.

The three of them had worked almost exclusively for a little over two months to find Mystique's killer and get him behind bars. Their frustration with the case hung heavy in the air.

"I still think Pierre Guidry is the killer," Clay said. "It's the only thing that makes any sense. He went there on the night of the murder to get back together with Mystique. When she refused, he lost his temper and a fight ensued that resulted in him slashing her throat."

"Knowing and proving are two different things," Daniel reminded them.

They had interviewed everyone they could find who'd had dealings with the "voodoo queen," and they'd come up with two suspects... Pierre and a man named Charles Lathrop. Charles had come to Mystique for a love spell and when the spell hadn't worked, he'd been very angry with Mystique. But had he been angry enough to slash Mystique's throat? Pierre was by far the more likely suspect.

"So, where do we go from here?" Luke asked.

Daniel frowned. "We have no place to go. The case has stalled and unless somebody comes forward with some new information or the guilty party confesses, we're at a total standstill."

"How's Angelique taking it?" Luke asked. It had to be tough to be romantically involved with one of Mystique's daughters as the case grew cold.

"She's okay. She's frustrated as we all are, but she knows we're doing everything possible to catch her mother's murderer," Daniel replied. "Of course, she has her new store to focus on, which has helped."

"From the traffic going in and out, it looks like her grand opening was a huge success," Clay said.

"It was." Daniel looked at his watch and then back at his two officers. "And now it's time for you two to get out of here," Daniel said as he stood.

Luke and Clay got up from the table as well. It was just after five and time to head home. The men all said their goodbyes and then Luke walked down the long hallway that would take him out the back door.

The early August sun was hot on his shoulders, and now that he was off duty, he was eager to get home. Home for Luke was a two-bedroom suite in the Cypress Apartments.

He'd been lucky to get a place in the fifteen-unit building. He'd been there for almost two years.

Eventually, he wanted to find a wife, buy a house and build a family. But so far, he was stuck on the *find a wife* part. He wasn't even dating anyone at the moment. In fact, it had been a little over a year since he'd had a relationship.

The apartment complex was only minutes away from the police station. When he reached it, he parked in his assigned spot and then got out of the car and went to apartment 107.

He went inside and walked through the living room and into the kitchen. He dropped his keys on top of the counter and then stripped off his gun and holster and placed them next to the keys.

He then headed down the hallway to his room. The neatly made-up queen-size bed was covered in a navy-blue spread, and matching curtains hung in the window. There was a dark walnut dresser and two matching end tables with small silver lamps on each one.

It took him only minutes to undress and get into the shower. The warm water didn't even begin to wash away the frustrations of Mystique's murder case. More than anything, they all wanted the guilty party to be caught and placed behind bars.

Once he got out of the shower he dressed in a pair of jeans and a gray T-shirt and then he went back to the kitchen. He grabbed a chicken dinner from the freezer and popped it into the microwave.

As he waited for it to cook, he sank down at the table. Lately, the silence in the evenings really pressed in on him. It was in the evenings that he wished he was married and had somebody to talk to…somebody to share his day with. So far, at thirty-one years old he hadn't found that special woman.

The microwave dinged and he ate. After cleaning up the kitchen, he went into the living room and sank down in a recliner chair.

It was Saturday night and time for him to call and check in with his brothers. Jerry was twenty-six years old and Brandon was twenty-four. Growing up, their father hadn't been in the picture and their mother had been a raging alcoholic. Luke had wound up being both mother and father to his two younger siblings.

Jerry now lived and worked in a warehouse in Shreveport and Brandon lived in New Orleans and worked as a waiter in a high-end restaurant. Their mother had passed away four years ago from acute alcoholism.

Luke made the calls, pleased that both of his brothers were doing well and sounded happy. Once that was done, he turned on his television. He tuned it to a crime drama and figured he'd watch a couple of episodes before going to bed.

He'd only been watching for a few minutes when a knock fell on his door. He frowned, wondering who it could be. Daniel used to drop by occasionally for a beer, but now the chief spent all his evenings with Angelique, the woman he loved—and Luke certainly didn't blame him.

He got up from his chair and went to the front door. When he opened it, he was surprised to see Dominique Santori. As always, she looked positively stunning. She was clad in a pair of jeans that hugged her long legs and a fitted pink blouse that enhanced her dark eyes and hair and showcased her slender waist and full breasts.

"Uh... Miss Santori, what can I do for you?" he asked curiously.

"Hi, Officer Madison. Could I come in and talk to you for a few minutes?" she asked.

"Of course, come on in." He held the door open wider to allow her inside and as she swept past him, he caught a whiff of her perfume. She smelled slightly mysterious and spicy, a scent he found very attractive. "Please have a seat." He gestured toward the sofa.

Once she was seated, he sat back down in his recliner facing her. She must have questions about the investigation, he thought. Before now, Angelique had always been the point person they all spoke to about the case. Maybe with Angelique busy with her new store, the sisters had decided Dominique would be the point person. Still, if that was the case, he wasn't sure why she'd ask him questions instead of going to Daniel.

"Uh…would you like something to drink? Maybe a soda or some iced tea?" he offered. Her black hair was loose and fell over her shoulders and down her back. The silky-looking strands only added to her attractiveness.

"No thanks, I'm fine," she said.

"What can I do for you, Miss Santori?"

"Please, make it Dominique." She smiled at him and the power of her beautiful smile formed an unexpected ball of warmth in the pit of Luke's stomach.

"Okay, Dominique, what can I do for you?" he asked, definitely intrigued by the unexpected visit.

"It isn't what you can do for me, but rather what I can do for you," she replied, intriguing him even more. She leaned forward, her chocolate-colored eyes flashing brightly.

"I think everyone is in agreement that Pierre Guidry killed my mother, and there just isn't enough evidence to arrest him," she continued. "We also believe that whoever killed my mother stole the notebook she kept of her clients."

"Yeah, but we checked out Pierre's shanty and we didn't find the notebook there," Luke replied.

"Pierre is no dummy," she scoffed. "He wouldn't keep the book in his shanty where a police search would easily find it. He's smarter than that."

"Then where would he keep it?"

She sat back on the sofa. "He'd bury it. He once told me he buried all his important things all around the swamp. I believe he has my mother's book and he's buried it someplace. I also believe if I tail him, he'll eventually lead me to it."

"Whoa." Luke stopped her in alarm. "What do you mean by tailing him?"

"I'll secretly follow him when he's out of his shanty at night," she replied.

"Are you totally out of your mind?" Luke stared at her, appalled by what she apparently intended to do. "Pierre isn't some cream puff. He's a tough, strong gator-hunter and if what we believe is true, he's also a stone-cold killer."

Her cheeks flushed with color. "I know what he's capable of. I grew up with him in and out of our shanty. That's why I said I'd secretly follow him. I can move through the swamp like a ghost when I want to."

"Miss Santori—Dominique—I know how frustrated you must be with how long it's taking us to get your mother's killer behind bars, but the last thing you need to do is try to take the law into your own hands," he said.

The woman must be completely out of her mind to even think about doing something like this. "You could be hurt or even killed," he added.

"That's why I'm here. I thought maybe you could act as my backup."

He stared at her in disbelief. "Why me? Why didn't you take this idea to Daniel?" Luke asked.

She flipped a strand of hair over her shoulder and frowned. Even with a scowl on her features, she was still quite lovely.

"I didn't go to Daniel because he would tell Angelique about my plan and I don't want to have a big fight with my sister." She leaned forward once again. "So, are you going to help me?"

"No, and I don't want you following through on this crazy plan," he replied. "Seriously, Dominique, if Pierre is guilty, then we'll eventually get him without you doing something so risky. Go home and leave the investigation to us."

"Are you sure you aren't going to help me?"

"Positive," he replied firmly.

"Then I guess I'm done here." She stood, her features radiating her unhappiness at his words. He got up from his chair and together they walked to his front door.

When they reached it, he opened it and then turned to her. "Good night, Dominique."

She nodded and swept past him and then turned back to gaze at him once again. "So, you won't help me," she said, and then offered him a small smile. "But I wouldn't be breaking any laws, so you also can't stop me, either." With that, she turned and headed toward the parking area.

"Dominque...wait," he called after her. But she didn't stop. She quickly disappeared into the twilight shadows of the night. Luke closed his door and returned to the recliner where his thoughts filled with what had just happened.

He'd always found Dominique to be incredibly beautiful with her long black hair and big brown eyes. He just hadn't known she was reckless, for that was the only explanation as to why she would possibly think tailing a potential vicious murderer in the darkness of the night was a good idea. Hell, Pierre could kill her and bury her body someplace in the swamp and nobody would ever be able to find her.

He leaned his head back and tried to relax, but relaxation was the last thing that was happening. He didn't know Dominique well. Had this idea of hers only been an attempt to motivate him and the team to work harder on the murder case? Or did she really intend to follow through on her harebrained scheme?

Chapter Two

There was no question that Dominique was disappointed that Luke wasn't going to help her, but she certainly didn't intend to let that stop her. Both of her sisters had always teased her about being impulsive, but this idea had been brewing in her head for the last two weeks or so. It was not an impulse…it was a plan.

She knew Pierre had a bad temper. She had grown up hearing the many fights Mother and Pierre would have. However, the arguments had never turned physical, at least not that she knew of. The two of them would fight and then make up, a pattern that had gone on for years.

When she and Pierre were off, then her mother would take another lover or two. However, she always wound up getting back together with Pierre.

But at the time of her murder, her mother had decided she was finished with Pierre for good, and Dominique believed that's what had driven him to kill her. But Dominique had no doubt that Pierre had loved her mother deeply.

She believed he'd taken her mother's client book in order to have a piece of her after death. And Dominique believed he would occasionally dig up the book and hold it tight against his chest as he mourned for the woman he had loved...the woman he had killed.

All she had to do was be there when it happened. Then she could tell Daniel about the book being in Pierre's possession and that would be enough to get him behind bars. It was a good plan.

When she got home from Luke's, she started her generator and then plugged in her phone to charge. She also got out a two-burner electric stovetop and for dinner she fried up a couple of pieces of fish and made a salad.

As she sat down to eat, an electric energy surged up inside her. It was very possible that tonight she could solve the crime and see Pierre arrested. That's all she wanted. Justice would be served and her mother would finally be able to rest in peace. And Dominique and her sisters would finally be at peace, as well.

By the time she finished dinner, she was wired for the night's events to come, but it was still a bit too early for her to get into place.

From years of knowing Pierre, she knew he did his gator-hunting and fishing a couple of hours after darkness had fallen each night.

While she waited for it to be time to leave, she changed into a pair of black slacks and a black T-shirt so that hopefully she could blend into the night without being seen.

Once darkness had completely fallen, she grabbed the pink-handled knife she carried for self-protection, then turned off her cell phone and slid it into her back pocket. Finally, she lit several of the battery-operated lanterns around the living room and then went out and turned the generator off.

It was time to go. Her heart beat a rhythm of nervous anticipation as she left her shanty. Just as she'd told Luke, she moved silently through the marsh. She'd grown up running these trails and knew just where to step and where to jump to avoid the pools of water that occasionally obstructed her way.

Spanish moss laid ghostly, delicate fingers on her as she ducked under it and small nocturnal animals scurried along the brush on either side of her.

She finally reached Pierre's shanty, where she crouched down behind some thick brush in front. Light flowed out from the single window and she saw movement inside, letting her know he was still there and hadn't already left for his nighttime activities.

Her heart still beat quickly. This had to work. It had been too long with no closure in her mother's case, no closure for the three daughters who had loved Mystique so much.

Angelique had told her and Monique that the investigation had stalled. Hopefully in the next few nights, Dominique would be able to unstall it.

The moon was full overhead. It would let her see Pierre more clearly, but she was also aware that the silvery light would make it easier for her to be seen as well.

Her heart banged against her rib cage as Pierre's door flew open and he stepped outside. He was clad in jeans and a white T-shirt, and carried with him a snagging rod...a harpoon-type tool that was popular with all the gator-hunters. He also had a fishing pole and a large tackle box.

He probably had a gun as well. Dominique had grown up around enough of the tough men who made their living by catching gators to know it was a matter of pride to get one of the big beasts without having to shoot it. However, most of them carried a gun in case one of those big beasts needed to be killed quickly in order to save the hunter's life.

Angelique had told her that during one of Pierre's interviews with Daniel, he had mentioned that he had a sweet honey hole full of fish and one particular large gator that he was eager to catch. She figured that's where he was headed now. And it sounded like that would be a good place to have hidden the book he took from her mother on the night she'd been murdered.

She rose slightly from her position and nearly screamed as a hand clamped down firmly on her shoulder. She whirled around and in the moonlight she saw Luke, his brilliant green eyes burning with an anger that nearly stole her breath away.

He removed his hand from her shoulder and then gestured with a curt nod of his head for her to follow him. She looked back to see that Pierre had disappeared into the darkness of the night and she had no idea in what direction he'd gone. Damn, there was nothing more she could do than follow Luke as they made their way back to her shanty.

What was he doing here, anyway? Had he changed his mind about working with her? Doubtful. His gaze hadn't exactly radiated with "good partner" energy.

As she followed behind him, she couldn't help but notice his broad shoulders and slim hips. She'd always found him handsome with his slightly shaggy black hair, piercing green eyes and chiseled facial features. But she wasn't looking for a date, she was looking for a cohort to help her catch her mother's killer.

They reached her shanty and neither of them spoke as she unlocked the door and then allowed him inside. She sank down on the sofa while he remained standing.

"I really didn't think you would follow through with it," he said, his eyes still blazing with anger. "I was sure you would come to your senses and realize just how dangerous this idea of yours was."

"Then why are you here?" she asked.

"Because I also worried that there was a chance you wouldn't come to your senses," he replied. Some of the fire in his eyes dissipated a bit. "Seriously, Dominique, this is far too risky for you to do." He blew out a deep breath and sank down in the recliner facing her.

"This is necessary to get the evidence you need to arrest him. I truly believe that if he has it, he'll lead me to the book and that will be all the proof you need to get him behind bars," she replied fervently.

"We'll get the evidence we need without you putting your life in danger," he replied.

"When?" she shot back. "It's been a little over two months and you and I both know the case has stalled. It's on its way to becoming a cold case. Somebody has to do something."

"Well, it can't be you...not this way." He raked a hand through his hair, his frustration with her obvious. He drew in a deep breath and then released it slowly. "Dominique, I don't want to see you get hurt...or worse."

"That's not going to happen. I'm smart, Luke. I'm smart and I'm fast, and I'm quiet. Pierre will never know I'm following him."

He gazed at her for a long moment. "Is there nothing I can say to make you not do this?"

"Probably not," she confessed. She truly believed this was the only way to get the evidence necessary for the case. She had sat on the sidelines and allowed law enforcement to do everything they could and now it was time for more drastic measures. She truly believed she had a good plan that would lead to Pierre's arrest.

"Would you at least promise me that you aren't going to head back out there the moment I leave here tonight?" he asked.

"That I can promise you," she replied. There was no point in her trying to go back out tonight. The swamp was vast and she wouldn't have a clue where to find Pierre now.

He stood and she got up as well. Together they walked to her front door. He opened it and then turned back to her. "Can I get your promise that you'll put this idea away and wait for law enforcement to take care of things?"

"That I won't promise you," she replied. Standing this close to him, she noticed his scent. It was woodsy with a note of cedarwood and it was very appealing. "I'm sorry, Luke, but I have to do what I have to do for my own sanity. As long as my mother's killer is free, I can never really heal."

He frowned. "I know how hard this time has been for you and your sisters, but it would be a real tragedy if something happened to you. I'm sure your sisters don't want to see you doing anything this dangerous."

"It doesn't matter what my sisters think. This is my decision and mine alone," she replied. "Now, I'll just say good-night to you."

He frowned once again, the gesture doing nothing to take away from his handsomeness. "I still wish I could change your mind."

"Well, you can't," she replied firmly. "And if you were really worried about me, then you'd be my backup."

"I am concerned about you, but that doesn't mean I intend to be your partner in this foolish scheme. So, I guess this is good night." With that, he walked out of the door and quickly disappeared into the darkness outside.

Dominique closed and locked the door behind him, her thoughts scattered and disjointed. For a moment when he had grabbed her shoulder and she'd seen him, she'd hoped he was there to help her in her quest.

Was her idea really that crazy? She grabbed hold of one of the lanterns and went into the small third bedroom. This room held a compact round table and two chairs. It was here her mother would meet the clients who would come to her at night, seeking a spell or something else to heal them or somebody they loved.

One wall was covered with a dark blue scarf with the sun and the moon on it. A dark purple scarf also covered the top of the table. A bookcase held bottles and poultices, pieces of swamp plants and flowers and a variety of other items Mystique had used in her spells.

There was no question that her mother sometimes liked to play up her role as the voodoo queen, but her real power was in her knowledge and understanding of people and what they needed to feel better.

Dominique sank down at the table where her mother used to sit and a new, deep grief filled her. At the time of her death, Mystique was in perfect health and should have lived another thirty or forty years. She should have been at her daughters' weddings and held her grandchildren. Dominique and her sisters had been robbed of their mother's presence…of her love and support.

Mystique had been a spontaneous, free-spirited kind of woman. She was not a traditional parent, but she'd still been a wonderful mother who had always told her daughters how much they were loved by her. The only way Dominique knew to keep her mother alive in her heart was to live her life just like her mother had.

The grief suddenly transformed to a deep anger. She

wasn't about to give up on her quest to see Pierre behind bars. She had promised Luke she wouldn't go back out tonight to trail the man she believed killed her mother.

However, tomorrow night she would be back out there again, shadowing the gator-hunter in the darkness of the night.

"WE HAVE A big problem," Luke said to Clay and Daniel the next morning. The three of them were once again seated in the murder room.

"What kind of a big problem?" Daniel asked.

"A Dominique Santori problem," Luke replied, and then proceeded to explain to the others about Dominique coming to his apartment the night before and the discussion she'd had with him.

"I told her it was a dangerous idea and that she should leave the investigation to us, but I knew she wasn't listening to me." He continued to explain about going out and finding her crouched down in the darkness in front of Pierre's shanty.

"Damn, something like that could get her killed," Daniel replied with a deep frown. "If you recall, initially Angelique tried to meddle in the investigation."

"Yeah, but all she was doing was questioning potential suspects and you got her to stop. I'm not sure if anything will stop Dominique," Luke replied with frustration. "I tried to reason with her, but she's adamant that her plan will get us the evidence we need to get Pierre behind bars."

"We aren't even a hundred percent sure that Pierre is the killer," Daniel replied.

"Dominique is certain," Luke replied. "And she's also certain at some point in time he's going to dig up the book that he presumably stole and that will be the proof we need to arrest him."

"Well, we need to figure out a way to stop her," Daniel said.

"Good luck with that," Luke replied drily. "I got her to promise she'd stay in last night after I left her place, but I'm afraid she'll be back out there again tonight."

Daniel reared back in his chair. "The first thing I'll do is have Angelique talk to her. Maybe big sister can get her to stop with this crazy idea of hers."

"And if that doesn't work?"

Daniel eyed him for a long moment. "Then maybe you should partner up with her and see if you can keep her out of trouble and alive."

Luke stared at his boss in stunned surprise. "You're kidding me, right?"

"I'm not kidding. I would never forgive myself if something bad happened to my soon-to-be sister-in-law. Legally, we can't stop her from doing what she's doing, so the next best thing we can hope for is with you by her side she won't come to any harm," Daniel said.

Luke's head reeled as he considered what his new assignment would entail. "It's going to be difficult for me to be up half the night with Dominique and then show up here in the mornings for my normal shifts."

"We can arrange your shifts differently," Daniel replied.

Luke frowned thoughtfully. "I've got two weeks of vacation time coming to me. Why don't I just take it now so I can devote whatever time necessary to keep up with Dominique's nighttime activities?"

"I don't expect you to take your vacation time to work," Daniel protested.

"I don't have anything else planned, so I'll just take it

and do a little bodyguard duty." The worst thing about this was the knowledge that he would have no set schedule. Normally, he was a stickler for structure but most of that would have to go out the window for now.

"Hopefully, Angelique will be able to talk some sense into Dominique and none of this will be necessary," Daniel said.

"Let's hope so," Luke replied. If Angelique couldn't turn her sister around, then Luke would be spending his vacation time babysitting a headstrong woman...albeit a beautiful one.

"I'll speak with Angelique as soon as I get back to my office and we should know how the wind blows soon after that," Daniel said.

"What do you really think about all this?" Clay asked him the minute Daniel had left the room.

Luke released a deep sigh. "I'm not sure what to think. On the one hand, I just want to do my normal job with the normal hours, but on the other hand, I don't want to even think about Dominique being out there in the dark all alone spying on a potential killer."

"Sounds to me like the Santori sisters are definitely a headstrong trio of women," Clay observed.

"I don't know about Monique and Angelique, but I can definitely say that Dominique is willful. I tried and tried to talk some sense into her last night, but she was having nothing to do with it."

Luke couldn't help but think about how beautiful she had looked the night before, with her dark brown eyes flashing and her chin thrust upward in stubborn defiance.

"At least her idea isn't a bad one," Clay said. "If we can tie that missing book to Pierre then that would be enough evidence for us to make an arrest and get him prosecuted for the crime."

"It might not be such a bad idea, but she definitely shouldn't be the one out there in the dark with a potential killer," Luke said.

Daniel returned to the room and sank down. "Okay, so I spoke to Angelique, who was positively appalled by her sister's plan. She was going to call Dominique the minute we hung up."

It was twenty minutes later when Angelique called back to tell Daniel that she'd been unable to make any headway with her sister.

When Daniel hung up from that call, he looked at Luke once again. "I would suggest you take off now and get some sleep before your bodyguard duties begin."

It was definitely a duty Luke didn't particularly want, but he would do it to the best of his ability, knowing that a woman's life could be at risk.

He got up from the table. "Then how about I officially take my vacation time starting now?"

"You know you don't have to do that," Daniel protested.

"I know, but it will actually make things a little easier on me," Luke replied. This way he wouldn't have to worry about working sporadic hours during the day. Hopefully, he would still be able to keep a routine of sorts. After the chaos of his childhood, routines were very important to him.

Minutes later, Luke left the police station and headed back home. Once there, he sank down in his recliner with the intention of catching a nap, but sleep was the furthest thing from his mind.

Instead, it was Dominique who took up residence in his thoughts. The woman was not only beautiful, but she'd smelled amazing, too. Her scent was one of mysterious spices and hints of florals. He had found it extremely attractive. He'd always thought she was gorgeous but he'd never asked her out on a date. He'd instinctively known she wasn't the type of woman he would want as a wife, so what would be the point in dating her?

He must have nodded off, for he awakened just before four. He stripped off his uniform, took a shower and then changed into a pair of jeans and a navy-blue T-shirt.

At six he fixed himself a sandwich with a handful of chips for dinner, and by six-thirty he was ready to leave the house and head to Dominique's shanty. It was plenty early enough that he knew she wouldn't have left for her spying duties yet.

Maybe it was possible he'd be able to distract her with conversation long enough that it would be too late to shadow Pierre. That might work for one night, but it certainly wouldn't work every night.

Perhaps she'd tire of this. After all, surely an attractive woman like her had better things to do with her time in the evenings. He had no idea if she was dating anyone, but if she was, undoubtably that person wouldn't want her out there putting her life at risk.

It didn't take him long to get to the area where the people living in the swamp kept their cars. He parked and got out. The swamp entrance itself was like a giant maw of dark greenery and tangled brush. It did not look inviting, but rather appeared forbidding.

Luke headed in. He carried with him a flashlight, although at this time of the evening it was unnecessary. He wore his shoulder holster and gun but he hoped he wouldn't have to shoot anyone before the night was over.

He walked quickly on the narrow path, dodging low-hanging tree limbs and Spanish moss. The air grew slightly cooler as he went deeper in where the sun couldn't shine through the thick leaves overhead.

Finally, Dominique's shanty came into view. He went across the bridge and then knocked on the front door. She answered the door and gazed at him in obvious surprise.

"Luke...what are you doing here?" she asked.

He forced a smile to his lips. He suddenly had a very bad feeling about all this. "You asked for a partner, so here I am."

Chapter Three

Dominique stared at him in surprise. He was the very last person on earth she'd expected to see this evening. "Are you going to let me in?" he asked.

"Oh, of course." She opened her door wider and as he swept past her, she caught a whiff of his delicious scent. "Would you like anything to drink?" She gestured him toward the sofa.

"No thanks, I'm good."

He certainly looked good. His jeans fit his long legs perfectly and his navy-blue T-shirt stretched taut across his broad shoulders and chest. His black hair was shiny and his green eyes were bright and alert. The shoulder holster and gun he wore made him look hot and slightly dangerous.

"Am I interrupting your dinner time?" he asked.

"I don't really have a specific dinner time and no, you aren't interrupting anything." She sank down in the chair facing him, still surprised by his presence. "So, are you really here to help me?"

"That's the plan. Daniel thought it was a good idea that I make sure you don't get yourself killed and I agreed with him."

"By the way, thanks a lot for getting Daniel involved in

this," she said with a touch of irritation. "My sisters paid me a visit this afternoon and practically took my head off. They couldn't believe what I intended to do, and tried their best to talk me out of it."

"Were they successful?" he asked, an obvious hope in his tone.

"No. Nothing and nobody is going to deter me from doing what I believe will prove that Pierre killed my mother." A wild grief shot through her. "You don't understand what it's like to know somebody is guilty and yet see them walking around freely and continuing to enjoy their life while the person they killed is dead and gone forever."

"I'm sorry, Dominique. I'm really sorry we haven't been able to get the justice you need for your mother." His gaze was so soft, and she wanted to fall into the green depths. He definitely had beautiful eyes. And for just a brief moment she wanted to be held in his big, strong arms as she grieved for the mother she had loved…the woman she had lost to a heinous crime.

"But we will get that justice for your mother and for you, if you could just be patient a little longer."

"I've been patient long enough," she replied and swallowed hard against her grief. "I know how diligently you all have been working on this, but you have to admit the investigation is going nowhere now."

"We are at a standstill at the moment," he slowly admitted. "But have you considered the possibility that maybe Pierre isn't guilty?"

"Yeah, I considered it and then completely dismissed it," she replied. "Pierre being the killer is the only thing that makes sense, and I know that he's your number one suspect, too."

"What if you follow him for days and days and he never

digs up the missing book?" He leaned forward, his gaze once again intent on her.

"Then the only thing I'll lose is time and time is something I've got plenty of." She was aware of her chin shooting up in a tenacious fashion.

His gaze appeared to attempt to pierce through to her very soul. "Have you always been so stubborn?"

A small laugh escaped her. "If you asked my sisters, they would probably tell you yes. But I'm not stubborn, I'm determined—and there's a difference." She pushed a strand of errant hair behind her ear.

"I would beg to differ," he said.

"What would you know? You don't know anything about me or my life," she replied.

"Then tell me about you," he said.

She looked toward the window where twilight was falling, then looked back at Luke. Was one of his goals to distract her enough with conversation that she would miss the time to go out to tail Pierre? Well, that certainly wasn't going to happen.

There was no question he could be a big distraction if she allowed him to be. She couldn't remember when she'd last spent any time with a man, especially one as handsome as Luke.

"Do you have a special somebody in your life?" he asked.

"No…what about you?" If he was going to be her backup, then it wouldn't hurt for her to know a little bit more about him. Or so she tried to tell herself this was her only reason for asking.

"No, there's nobody in my life at the moment," he replied.

For some crazy reason that pleased her. Surely it was

just because it meant he would be available every night without having to answer to anyone at home.

"I know you waitress at the café. Do you like your job?" he asked.

"I love it. I really enjoy people and working at the café gives me an opportunity to visit with a lot of the townspeople I wouldn't ordinarily get to know."

"How are you going to be able to be awake for half the night and still work at the café?"

"I'll manage," she replied. Thankfully, there were many days when she worked the mid-shift, allowing her to sleep in a little bit in the mornings. "What about you? Why did you go into law enforcement?"

"A large part of the reason was Daniel. We've been friends since he and his dad moved here when Daniel was about eight years old. When he got the job as chief of police, he urged me to join the force. At the time I was kind of drifting and I didn't know what I wanted to do, so I wound up becoming a cop and I love it. It was the best thing I could have done for myself. I love the structure of the job and knowing the rules that need to be followed."

He sat back and frowned. "Sorry, that was probably way more information than you needed or wanted to know."

"Please don't apologize," she replied. "You know I have two sisters. What about you? Do you have any siblings?"

"Yeah, I have two younger brothers. They've both moved away from Dark Waters, but we're still very close," he said. "We talk to each other on the phone at least once a week."

"That's nice. Even though there are times they drive me crazy, I don't know what I'd do without my sisters. The three of us are very close." Once again, she looked toward the window, aware of time ticking by.

"You three are very close in age. Was there ever any sibling rivalry?" he asked.

She wondered if he was really curious or simply trying to pass the time. "Never," she answered. "We have always been best friends and there was never any sibling rivalry between us. What about you and your brothers?"

"No, but I'm quite a bit older than them. I pretty much raised them when we were all growing up," he replied.

"Why is that? Where were your parents?"

"Oh, it's a long story and not all that interesting," he replied, obviously not wanting to share. "I've learned a lot about your mother during our investigation. Where is your father?" he asked, obviously changing the subject.

"The real question would be who is my father and I don't know. My mother never wanted to discuss the subject with us. We don't even know if the same man fathered all three of us, not that it ever mattered to us."

It had never really bothered Dominique that she didn't have a father in her life. "My mother was such a huge presence we never missed having a father."

She might be enjoying her conversation with Luke, but she remained aware of two things. The first was that he wasn't here to socialize with her. He was here because Daniel had probably ordered him to be here. This was a job to him and nothing more.

The second thing she remained aware of was that she wanted nothing more than for him to keep her safe as she hunted down the man who killed her mother.

"Even though a lot of people were frightened of your mother, I have spoken to a lot who sang her praises," he said. "From what we've learned, she helped a lot of people with her spells and chants and the natural medicines she gave them," Luke continued.

Dominique smiled, her heart greatly warmed by his words. "That's all Mama ever wanted to do. Despite the fact that a lot of people believed she used black magic and could curse people, they came to her because they needed some kind of help they weren't getting from anyplace else."

The warmth his words had evoked inside her faded away as the familiar emotion of grief and anger took over. She stood. "It's time to go."

Luke looked at her with obvious disappointment. "Oh, and we were having such a nice conversation. Why can't we just stay here and continue to get to know each other better?"

"Officer Madison, this isn't a date. It isn't a social visit at all," she said. "You can either sit here and talk to yourself or you can come with me. The chitchat was nice, but it doesn't change my plans."

He stood as well. "I know from experience that I can be quite boring when I talk to myself, so I guess I'm going with you...and make it Luke."

She gave him a curt nod as her heartbeat quickened with thoughts of following Pierre. They left her shanty and stepped out into the bright moonlight. She turned to face him. "I'm going to be moving fast, so try to keep up—and for God's sake, try to be as quiet as possible."

With that, she turned back around and then took off down the narrow path.

LUKE FOLLOWED HER, grateful for the moonlight that illuminated the path they traveled. She hadn't lied—she moved quickly and with a confidence he certainly didn't feel. It was obvious she was quite comfortable traversing through the wooded junglelike landscape.

Tension kept his muscles taut as adrenaline rushed

through his body. He kept his eyes on her black-clad body and tried to move as quietly as she was. Still, he couldn't help but notice that she looked very hot in the skintight jeans and black T-shirt.

It wasn't in his job description to enjoy her company, but he had enjoyed the conversation they'd been having before they'd left the shanty. She'd waited on him often at the café and he'd always found her pleasant, but tonight she had revealed a lot more of herself to him.

Of course, she was nothing like the woman he eventually wanted to find for himself. She was far too...too spontaneous for him. She was right—his being here with her wasn't a date or a social event at all. His sole job was to keep her alive during her nightly activities.

They finally reached the area in front of Pierre's shanty where she crouched down behind a large thicket of brush and he crouched just behind her. It had been a very long time since he'd been with a woman and being so close to her awakened parts in him that had been dormant for far too long.

Her body heat radiated toward him and he could smell the heady scent of her. A couple of strands of her silky hair moved with a small breeze and caressed the side of his face.

He tried to stay focused on the shanty they were watching instead of the woman so close to him. Lanterns were lit in Pierre's shanty and moving shadows indicated that the gator-hunter was inside.

If Luke was lucky, Pierre wouldn't leave tonight. It would be far easier to keep Dominique safe if she wasn't trailing the man who might hear them or see them and react in a dangerous fashion.

If what they believed about the man was true, then he

had already killed a woman in a vicious way by slicing her throat. What lengths would he go to in order to save himself from prison?

Unfortunately, after about twenty minutes of waiting, the man left his shanty. He carried with him a long spear-like tool, a fishing pole and a large tackle box. He headed down a path to the right of his house and Dominique and Luke quietly followed.

They kept bushes and thickets and some distance between themselves and Pierre. Thankfully, he didn't seem to be worried about how much noise he was making as he walked and so Luke figured it was less likely that he would hear their quiet progress behind him.

The going grew more difficult as Pierre continued on and the swamp became thicker and more challenging to travel. Luke lost track of time. There was only Dominique and the swamp and the man they were tailing.

Finally, they came to a large pool of water where Pierre set his things down and uncovered from the nearby brush a large pirogue. He put the shallow boat into the water, grabbed his items and added them, then he jumped in and took off, using the long tool to help him move away from the shore.

"Where are you, you bastard? I intend to get you tonight," Pierre yelled into the night.

Within moments he was out of their sight.

"What do you want to do now?" Luke whispered, hoping this would be the end of their nightly activities.

She turned to look at him, her dark eyes shining brightly in the moonlight. "To wait. Eventually, he'll come back to shore. If you want to go on and leave, I won't blame you."

"I'll stay," he replied.

So, they waited. Small animals rustled through the

brush all around them. Mosquitoes and insects buzzed and whirred in the air and a bullfrog croaked his deep-throated song. Fish jumped in the nearby water, and occasionally from the distance they could hear Pierre curse.

Minutes ticked by. Occasionally, they would change positions to be more comfortable. An hour passed and then another one. Although Luke felt like this whole idea of hers was a wild-goose chase, he couldn't help but admire her resolve in seeing it through.

They didn't talk while they waited. Having any kind of conversation would be a risk. What he was finding the most difficult was remaining so close to her. There was no question he was physically attracted to her and it was an attraction he hadn't expected to be so strong.

It was about two hours later when Pierre finally came back to shore. He got his items out of the pirogue and then hid the boat in the brush once again. He had a stringer full of fish and he immediately headed back to his shanty.

They followed some distance behind him. He made no stops and when he reached his shanty he went directly inside. As Luke followed Dominique on to her home, he could feel the disappointment that radiated from her.

When they reached her shanty, she turned to gaze at him. "Okay, so tonight was a big bust," she said.

"I'm sorry we didn't get what we needed tonight," he replied. He wasn't without sympathy for her. And of course, if she was successful in this quest, they would all get what they wanted…an arrest for the murder.

"Do you want to come in? I'm going to fry up some eggs and make some toast. You're welcome to come in and eat with me," she said.

"You're going to eat now?" he asked in surprise. "But it's the middle of the night."

"It doesn't matter what time it is. I'm hungry and so I'm going to eat."

"Thanks for the invitation, but I always eat my dinner at around six each evening," he replied. "So, I'll just see you at the same time tomorrow night?"

"That's up to you," she replied. Her big brown eyes threatened to pull him in as the moonlight caressed her delicate features. God, she was so beautiful and for just a moment he wanted to pull her into his arms and take her lush lips with his.

The impulse shocked him and instead, he took a quick step back from her. "I'll be here tomorrow so don't leave without me," he said.

She half smiled at him. "Then don't be late."

He returned the smile. "I'm a punctual kind of guy. Good night, Dominique."

"Good night, Luke." With that she went into her shanty and he turned to leave.

As he headed back toward the entrance where he'd left his car, his thoughts were filled with the woman he had just left. Maybe she was right. It wasn't so much that she was stubborn, but rather she was determined.

No other women he knew would sit in the swamp for two long hours waiting for a killer to dig something up. He felt the weight of the investigation on his shoulders. If only the police could come up with the evidence they needed, then she wouldn't have to be out in the swamp waiting for a killer to make a mistake.

By the time he got to his car he was exhausted. Thank God he didn't have to show up early the next morning at the police station for his shift. He'd go in about noon to check in with Daniel and let him know about tonight's events.

He certainly wouldn't share with his boss or anyone else how physically attracted he was to Dominique. There was no reason for anyone else to know that. After all, nothing would ever come of it.

THE NEXT MORNING, Luke got up at eight and took a long, hot shower. He couldn't remember the last time he had slept this late. He dressed in a pair of jeans and a dark green polo shirt and then left his place and headed to the police station.

His plan was to check in with Daniel and then eat lunch at the café around noon. He had no idea if Dominique would be working or not, but he was vaguely surprised to find himself looking forward to seeing her again.

Daniel was in his office and after knocking on the door, Luke entered. "So, how did it go last night?" Daniel asked.

"It went." Luke sank down in the chair across from his boss and then shared the events of his time with Dominique. "I'll say this, she's unlike any woman I've ever met before. She's very strong-minded."

"I have a feeling all three of Mystique's daughters are strong-minded. I know Angelique is. I think they all had to be in order to grow up with their mother's reputation hanging over their heads," Daniel replied.

"Yeah, it had to have been tough for them," Luke replied. He certainly knew how it was to grow up with people gossiping about a parent. He'd known from a very young age the terrible reputation his mother had around town.

"I know this isn't a duty you wanted, but I appreciate you going full speed ahead with it. The last thing I want is another dead body and I really don't know what Pierre is capable of if he were to catch Dominique spying on him."

"I don't want to find out," Luke replied darkly. "Anyway, I just figured I'd check in and let you know how it went last night."

"All I can say is keep doing what you're doing," Daniel replied.

"That's what I intend to do. I'll spend however much time in the swamp I need to in order to keep the lovely Dominique Santori alive."

"'The lovely'?" Daniel raised a dark eyebrow.

The heat of a flush filled Luke's cheeks. "I think we can agree that all the Santori sisters are quite lovely."

Daniel grinned and shook his head. "Take note, my friend. First, you notice how beautiful they are and then before you know it, they have you wrapped up in love knots and you can't imagine being without them."

Luke laughed. "That's not about to happen with me. Dominique is nothing like the woman I intend to eventually marry. She's just a job to me and she'll never be anything more."

Chapter Four

Dominique sat at a booth next to a window in the café. It was her day off and Angelique was supposed to be meeting her for lunch. Dominique was grateful that she didn't have to work that day because she was tired after the very late activities of the night before.

Sunny appeared at the booth. "So, who are you meeting for lunch today? I hope it's a very hot man who is madly in love with you."

"Don't I wish," Dominique replied drily. "You know there's no man in my life right now."

"And I also know how much you'd like to change that," Sunny replied.

"Yeah, well I'd also like to change my brown eyes to blue, but I don't see that happening anytime soon," Dominque said, making her friend laugh. "I'm actually meeting Angelique for lunch, but she's apparently running late."

"While you wait for her, would you like me to bring you something to drink?"

"A diet cola would be great."

"I'll be right back with it." Sunny left the booth and Dominique looked at the clock on the wall. Angelique was fifteen minutes late, which was unusual because normally she was quite punctual.

She looked out the window where the early August sun was bright in the sky. But she knew from reading the weather on her cell phone that the sunny skies weren't supposed to last and rain would move in later. She hoped the weather didn't interfere with her plans for the night.

Sunny returned with her drink and at the same time Dominique's phone rang. It was her sister. "Dominique, I'm so sorry, but I'm not going to be able to make it for lunch," she said.

"Is everything okay?" Dominique asked.

"Everything is fine except the girl I hired to run the store today didn't show, so I can't leave. Again, I'm so sorry."

"You don't have to apologize, sis. We can meet for lunch on another day."

"Yes, but I really wanted to talk to you today," Angelique replied.

"If you want to talk to me about my nightly plans, then you might as well hold your breath. I'm doing what I'm doing and no matter how much you try to change my mind, that isn't going to happen."

Angelique's deep sigh was audible. "Okay, then we'll just plan lunch for another day."

The two sisters said their goodbyes and Dominique hung up and then motioned to Sunny. "Looks like I'll be eating alone today, so I'm ready to order."

"Your sister couldn't make it?" Sunny asked.

"No, she can't get away from her store. The girl who was supposed to come in didn't show."

"Ah, business owner dilemmas. So, what can I get for you?"

"I'll take a club sandwich with french fries," Dominique said.

"You got it," Sunny replied and then once again left the booth.

Once she was gone, Dominique looked around. As usual, the café was busy and most of the seats were filled.

She waved at Burt and Austin, who were seated alone at different tables. They were definitely her favorite regulars. They were not only kind and respectful to her but they tipped generously, too.

She also nodded with a friendly smile at Oliver LeBoeuf, the last man she'd dated, who sat with two other men she knew were fellow fishermen.

He returned her smile with one of his own. Thank goodness after she broke up with him, they had managed to maintain a fairly friendly relationship.

As she gazed toward the entrance of the café, Luke walked in. He looked around and, spying her, headed toward her table.

He looked ridiculously handsome in his jeans and a dark green polo shirt that she knew would match his green eyes. "Hi, Dominique," he said as he reached her.

"Hi back at you," she replied. Despite all the scents in the café, she could smell him. The woodsy cologne he wore was exceedingly attractive.

He gestured toward the empty space in front of her. "Are you expecting somebody?"

"I was, but I'm not anymore," she replied. Why did her heartbeat always quicken when he was around? She wasn't even sure she liked him yet.

"Mind if I join you?"

She was vaguely surprised by his request. He would

be at her shanty tonight. Why would he want to spend his lunch time with her?

"Knock yourself out," she replied.

He slid into the booth and offered her a smile. "How is your day going?"

"It's going," she replied. "It's my day off and so far, I've been as lazy as a gator on a sunlit log."

He laughed, the sound low and pleasant. "I've been a bit lazy myself today."

Sunny appeared at the booth. "Hi, Officer Madison. Are you staying here and eating?"

He shot a quick look at Dominique and then looked back at Sunny. "I'm staying here and eating," he replied with one of his gorgeous smiles.

"Then what can I get for you?" Sunny asked.

"I'll take a cheeseburger and fries and an iced tea," he replied.

"I'll be back with both your orders." She gave Dominique a pointed look. "And we'll talk later."

"Why on earth would you want to sit with me?" she asked once Sunny was gone. "Didn't you get enough of me last night?" This close she could see that his green eyes had tiny flecks of gold in them. Definitely attractive.

"Why wouldn't I want to sit with you? You're beautiful and smart and I enjoyed your company last night," he replied.

She stared at him and he laughed. "Stop, you're looking at me like I'm a species from another planet," he said.

"I'm trying to figure out what kind of a man enjoys crouching down in a swamp for two hours," she replied.

He laughed once again. "Okay, I'll admit, I kind of hated that part of the evening, but before that I enjoyed the conversation we had."

"What're your plans for the rest of the afternoon?"

"I don't really have any. I hate not having a schedule. I like routine and structure."

It was her turn to release a laugh. "Then you're dancing with the wrong partner. The only schedule I keep is my work schedule. Other than that, I have no structure. Don't you have to go in to do regular police work?"

"I took two weeks of vacation time, so no, I'm not working my regular job at the moment."

She stared at him once again. "You took your vacation time so you could sit in the swamp with me every night?"

"Daniel and I figured it would be easier that way," he replied.

"Now I feel really guilty. Surely you had better things to do on your vacation."

"Actually, I didn't have any plans at all for it, so please don't feel guilty about a decision I made," he replied.

At that moment Sunny returned with Luke's drink and their food. "What else do you do with your time when you aren't waitressing or hunkering down in the swamp?" Luke asked. His beautiful green eyes pulled her in.

"I like to read and spend time with my sisters. I enjoy visiting with people and sometimes I have little gatherings of friends at my place, although I haven't done that since the murder."

As always, her heart squeezed tight with grief as she thought of the mother she had lost. "When Sunny and I are off at the same time we like to shop together. What about you? What do you do in your time off?"

"I also like to read, and occasionally me and a couple other men get together and have a beer at Jake's Place." Jake's was a small bar on the north side of town.

"I've never been there," she replied. "My sisters and I

always enjoyed going to the Voodoo Lounge." The Voodoo Lounge was a large bar with a big dance floor where lots of single people gathered on Friday and Saturday nights.

"Jake's is your typical dive bar. The drinks are strong and the food is greasy, but it's a good place just to unwind and talk. If you want, I could take you there one night."

"That might be fun," she replied. What exactly were they doing? They were talking as if they were a couple and that couldn't be further from the truth.

As they began to eat, they small-talked about things going on in the town and the people they both knew. Dominique found herself enjoying his company. He was not only easy on the eyes, but he also had a good sense of humor. He was very easy to talk to and then there was the simmering burn of physical attraction she had for him.

She had to keep reminding herself that she was just a job to him. He was probably cozying up to her in hopes he could talk her out of her plans with Pierre.

Well, that certainly wasn't going to happen. Until the police had somebody under arrest for her mother's murder, she intended to continue to shadow the number one suspect in the case.

"What are you doing after lunch?" he asked when they were finished eating and waiting for Sunny to bring their tabs.

"Going home and I think a nap might be in my plans," she said. "What about you?"

"Same," he replied.

At that moment, Sunny appeared. Luke tried to pay for Dominique's lunch, but she wouldn't allow it. Minutes later they walked out of the café together.

"This was pleasant," she said.

"It was very pleasant," he replied, his eyes sparkling brightly. "Then I guess I'll see you tonight."

"Same place, same time," she replied. "I'll see you then."

They parted ways to go to their cars. As she drove home, her thoughts were filled with the very handsome man she had just shared lunch with. Luke Madison. She hadn't expected to like him as much as she did.

She was definitely in the market to find that special man who she would love and who would love her. She wanted a husband and she wanted babies, but she knew Luke was nothing like the man she eventually wanted to be with forever.

Just from the brief conversations they had shared, she knew Luke was far too uptight for her. He was wed to structure and routine and she definitely wasn't. She wanted a man who could roll with her and be spontaneous. She intended to remain free-spirited and spontaneous as her mother had been.

"You're overthinking it all," she murmured to herself as she parked at the swamp's entrance. It had just been an unplanned lunch together.

She reminded herself that she was a job to him and he was nothing more than a bodyguard to her. They weren't dating. There was really no relationship except an odd sort of budding friendship between them.

She hadn't lied about a nap. That was definitely her plan for the afternoon. After that she would be ready for the night ahead and maybe this would be the night Pierre would dig up her mother's book and the case would finally be over.

She got out of her car and headed in to her shanty. The walk seemed unusually long today. The late hours of the night before were definitely weighing on her, although she would never admit that to anyone.

Despite her exhaustion, the surrounding swamp comforted her with the fragrances and look of home. It smelled green with the underlying scents of various flowers in bloom. There was also the rather unpleasant smell of decay, which she had gotten used to a long time ago.

The white piece of paper on her front door was visible from the bottom of her bridge. What on earth? She approached her door and pulled the note off. It read YOU WILL BELONG TO ME.

The letters were written in bright red with the word *will* underlined several times. A shiver crawled up her spine. She quickly shot a look around. Who had left it for her? She didn't see anyone lurking around.

She stared down at the note once again. What did it mean? With a chill flooding through her veins, she opened her door and quickly went inside. She locked the door behind her and then sank down on the sofa with the note still in her hand.

You will belong to me.

Even though the words themselves weren't exactly violent, it felt like a prophecy of danger.

AS LUKE DROVE HOME, his head was filled with thoughts of Dominique. She had looked so attractive in a brown sundress that was the exact chocolate color of her eyes. Her hair had been pulled back at the nape of her neck, exposing gold hoops at her ears. A gold necklace with a small locket had looked lovely against her medium skin tone.

There was no question that he had a smoldering desire for her. He hadn't expected that he would like her as much as he did. She was very easy to talk to and he found many things about her so interesting. She was like no other woman he'd ever dated before.

He pulled himself up short at this thought. But of course, he wasn't dating Dominique, and he would never be interested in dating her. He liked structure and routine, and she had said she had none. He couldn't imagine what it would be like to live with her. All he knew for certain was she was definitely the wrong woman for him.

He got back home and decided to take a note from her book and catch a nap. If last night was any indicator, the night to come would be long and probably frustrating.

He went into the kitchen and set his keys next to his holster and gun and then went into the living room and got into his recliner chair.

It didn't take him long to drift off to sleep and into dreams of his childhood. The dreams were snippets, moving quickly from one vision to another. His mother passed out on the living room floor…his brothers crying with hunger when there wasn't any food in the house. Angry banging on the door with the landlord wanting rent.

He woke up two hours later, surprised by the dreams that had tortured his sleep. It had been years since he'd had those particular visions while sleeping. What had brought them all back to him now?

Once he was awake, he spent the next hour seated at the table while he cleaned his gun. It was a task he didn't mind and one he did regularly. It hadn't been that long ago that he'd had to shoot a man.

When a suspect in Mystique's murder case was caught with meth-making materials in his shanty, he had wound up shooting Daniel and then Luke had shot him. Thankfully, Daniel had only been grazed in the shoulder and Luke had shot the suspect in the leg, making it an easy arrest and nobody had died.

Once the gun was clean, it was dinner time. He pulled a frozen Salisbury steak dinner out of the freezer and popped it into the microwave. Not exactly a delicacy, but he didn't feel like cooking anything else.

When he was finished eating, he put on a clean pair of black jeans and a black T-shirt. Surveillance clothes, he thought with wry humor, although there was nothing humorous about what Dominique was doing.

By that time, he was ready to leave for Dominique's. Even though he had spent his lunch time with her, he still looked forward to seeing her again.

While he'd been inside, the skies had become angry looking. He hadn't heard the latest weather report, but it looked as if it might rain at any moment. Which wasn't all bad.

He would assume if it was raining then the night's activities would be canceled, and he could definitely live with that. It would be one less night he had to worry about Dominique's safety.

It still wasn't raining when he got out of his car at the swamp's entrance, but the air smelled like fresh ozone, letting him know the rain was coming very soon. The dark clouds swallowed up any twilight that might have occurred.

He turned on his flashlight to traverse the narrow paths, eager to get there and get inside before the skies opened up. When he reached the shanty, he knocked on the door.

"Who is it?" her voice called out.

He frowned in surprise. Last night she'd opened the

door without checking who it might be. "Dominique, it's me... Luke."

He heard the sound of the lock and then the door opened and she gestured him inside. Once he was in, she immediately locked the door after him.

She looked gorgeous in a billowing pale blue sundress. Apparently, she hadn't changed yet into her night-stalking clothes. Unlike last night, there was no smile on her face as she gestured him toward the sofa.

"Is everything all right?" he asked with concern.

"I'm not sure. Would you like something to drink?"

"No, I'm fine. Sit here next to me and tell me why you aren't sure that everything is okay." He patted the seat next to him.

She walked over to the bookcase in the room and picked up a piece of paper, then sat next to him on the sofa. "This was taped to my door when I got back here from lunch." She handed him the piece of paper.

He read it and a bit of concern washed over him. He set it down on the coffee table and then gazed at her. "You don't have a clue who might have left it for you?"

"Not a clue," she replied. "And I didn't see anyone around, either. I don't know if I should be afraid or not."

"It could be a threat," he said slowly. "It's also possible it's just a note from a secret admirer who plans to win your heart."

A frown furrowed her brow. "Then I don't like secret admirers."

"If that's all it is, do you have any idea who it might be?"

"I have no idea," she replied. "I've never understood the whole secret admirer thing. If somebody is into me, then step up...be a man and talk to me in person." Her eyes held his gaze. "This reminds me of what my sister went through."

Less than a month ago, Angelique had gotten a frightening note on her door. Then she'd been attacked by a person wielding a knife. The first time she'd managed to escape with just some wounds on her arm.

However, she had been attacked once again with near deadly results. The attacker had been Angelique's ex-boyfriend's new girlfriend. It had been solely based on jealousy and the belief that Angelique needed to die so the new girlfriend wouldn't have her as competition.

Luke reached out his hand and took Dominique's in his. "This is nothing like what happened to your sister, so get that idea right out of your mind."

Her cold fingers twined with his, as if she was seeking his warmth and support. "Just tell me...should I be afraid?"

With her big, doe-like eyes staring into his and her hand so small in his own, he wanted to promise he'd keep her safe forever. Instead, he really considered the situation before replying.

"I don't think you need to be overly frightened exactly, but I do think you need to be extra aware of your surroundings when you're out and about. This might be nothing more than a love note of sorts."

"Well, I'm not loving it," she replied drily.

"Could you get me a baggie big enough to hold the note? I'll take it into the station and see if we can lift some fingerprints off it. Hopefully that will tell us who left it."

"Sure, I'll be right back." She got up from the sofa and disappeared into the kitchen area. She returned a moment later with the baggie in hand. He carefully slid the note inside it and then set it back down on the coffee table.

"Now, on to more pleasant things," she said when he was finished. "Tell me what you did this afternoon."

"Nothing too exciting. I took a nap and then I cleaned my gun," he replied.

She raised one of her perfectly arched dark eyebrows. "Are you expecting a gunfight sometime soon?"

He was pleased that she appeared a little less tense than she'd been when he'd first arrived. "God, I hope not," he replied. "There's nothing a police officer hates more than having to shoot his gun."

"That is comforting to know," she replied. "I'm sure you all wish every conflict could be resolved easily and without violence. Speaking of conflicts, has anything happened in the investigation into my mother's murder?"

"Unfortunately, nothing has changed. However, it looks like it might pour rain at any minute. If it's raining, do you still intend to watch Pierre?" he asked.

"No. He won't go out if it's raining and so I think you're probably going to be off duty for the night," she replied. "And don't look so darned pleased about it," she added.

He laughed. "I can't help it that I'm not upset that we aren't going out to sit in a swamp for three hours or so."

"You know you don't have to do this." Once again, her gaze held his intently. Her eyes were so beautiful with their rich color and long dark lashes.

"Oh, but I do have to do this," he replied.

"Why? Because Daniel is making you?"

"Dominique, my need to go with you on your potentially dangerous nightly travels has nothing to do with Daniel. It has everything to do with the fact that I like you and don't want to see any harm come to you."

She offered him a small smile. "I like you, too."

Warmth swept through him, a warmth that enhanced the

smoldering physical desire he felt toward her. He shoved the desire away as best he could. "Since you have no plans to go out tonight, I assume you're ready to kick me out of here."

Once again, she smiled. It was an impish grin that he found enchanting. "I could put up with your company for a little while longer if you want to stay."

He grinned back at her. "Then I guess I could put up with your company for a while longer, too." To make his point, he leaned back on the sofa.

"Tell me more about your family," she said. "You mentioned before that you have two younger brothers, but you said nothing about your parents except to tell me it was a long and boring story. We have all the time in the world tonight for a long story. So, are your parents still alive?"

Did he really want to talk to her about this? Maybe if he did, she would understand him a little bit better. "Like you, I didn't know my father, and my mother passed away four years ago."

"Oh, Luke, I'm so sorry," she said, genuine sympathy shining in her eyes.

"Don't be, it was a long time ago." He decided at that moment to tell her the whole ugly truth about his childhood. "My mother was a raging alcoholic who should have never had kids. I never knew where I'd find her. She'd pass out in the front yard or in the living room or in Swamp's End where somebody would eventually bring her home and dump her on the sidewalk."

Swamp's End was the third bar in Dark Waters. It was a small hole-in-the-wall that catered to a rough crowd.

Luke spoke fast, the words bubbling out of him as he recalled his childhood trauma. "She'd often forget about us and there wouldn't be any food in the house, or she'd bring home some random man who usually didn't want to see or hear me and my brothers. I did my best to take care of them, stealing food for them to eat and trying to hide them from those random guys. I'd get them cleaned up and dressed each morning and would walk them to school."

He drew in a deep breath and then continued. "It was a childhood of utter chaos. We never knew what to expect from one day…one minute to the next. The saddest part of all was when I heard she'd passed away, I felt nothing except the tragedy of a life wasted."

It was her turn to reach out and take his hand in hers. "Oh Luke, I'm so sorry you had to live through all that," she said softly.

He smiled. "It's like the old saying goes, something that doesn't kill you, makes you stronger. I now know what I'll do for my children to make them always feel loved and safe."

"So, you want children?" She released her hold on his hand.

"Eventually I'd like to have a couple, but only if I have a loving wife by my side. What about you? Do you want children?"

"Absolutely, but only if I have a loving husband by my side," she replied. "Right now, I'm not even dating anyone, so finding the man of my dreams might take a minute."

"I'm not dating either, so right now I'm stuck on the get-a-wife part," he replied.

She looked at him curiously. "Why aren't you dating? You're smart and have a good job, and you aren't hard to look at. I would think women would be clamoring for a date with you."

"I could say the same about you. You're obviously bright and witty and you are *definitely* not hard to look at. I would think there would be a long line of men wanting to date you," he replied.

"I've had a few men ask me out in the past, but they aren't men I'm interested in so I haven't gone out with them," she said.

"And I haven't met any women lately who I'm interested in going out with," he said.

At that moment the sound of the rain began to patter on the windows and roof. "The rain is upon us," he said.

"I love the rain," she replied. "I love the sound of it against the windows and the feel of it on my face. In fact, there's one thing I really like to do." She reached out and grabbed his hand and then stood and pulled him up with her. "Come with me," she said, an eager anticipation lighting up her features and sparkling in her eyes.

He let her lead him, curious as to what she had in mind. She unlocked and opened the front door and he gasped as she pulled him out into the rain.

"Follow me." She released his hand and ran down the bridge. He hurried after her. At least it was a cool, not cold, fairly gentle rain, but immediately he was soaked.

She reached the small clearing at the foot of the bridge and then turned back to face him. She laughed with what sounded like sheer abandonment. "I love to dance in the rain," she said. "So, let's dance."

She twirled around, a beautiful blue-clad nymph. She placed both her hands on his chest and smiled up at him. Her eyes glowed with pleasure. "Come on, Luke. Dance with me."

He was already soaking wet and her winsome plea resonated deep inside him. He took hold of her hands and they danced. They twirled and two-stepped and laughed with the sheer exuberance of it all.

He wasn't sure how long they had been dancing when she wound up pressed tight against him. The combination of the rain and her scent half dizzied him and her lush lips beckoned him as she gazed up at him. Suddenly, he couldn't help himself. He took her lips with his.

Chapter Five

She hadn't expected the kiss, but she welcomed it. She raised her arms around his neck and leaned into him. She opened her mouth to allow him to deepen the kiss. Their tongues swirled together and even the cool rain couldn't staunch her desire for him.

His lips were soft, yet held a masterful demand that was intoxicating. She could have kissed him forever, but after several minutes lightning slashed the sky, followed by a loud clap of thunder.

He pulled his lips from hers and instead grabbed her hand. "Come on, that's our cue to get back inside," he said.

He continued to hold her hand as they ran up the bridge and back into the shanty. Only then did he drop her hand from his. "Towels," she said. "Stay there and I'll be right back."

She disappeared into the bathroom and returned carrying two large fluffy red towels. She handed him one and for a moment they dried off.

He ran the towel over his hair and clothes. "What do you want me to do with the towel?" he asked.

"I'll take it."

She took it from him and then went back into the bathroom. "I'm sorry I don't have a dryer to take care of your wet clothes," she said when she came back into the living room.

"It's okay. I'll just head on home and throw them in mine," he replied.

"Thank you for dancing with me, Luke," she said with a wide smile.

"I've never done anything like that before in my life," he replied. "I've never even thought about doing anything like that before."

"Tell me the truth—it was fun, wasn't it?"

He laughed. "I'll admit, it was fun and now I'll just say good-night and I'll see you tomorrow." He walked over to the coffee table and picked up the baggie holding the note and then he disappeared out the front door.

It was only after he was gone that she thought about the fact that he hadn't mentioned their kiss. Had it meant nothing to him? She didn't even know what it meant to her. All she did know was it had been an awesome kiss.

She went into her bedroom and took off the wet dress and underwear and pulled on a navy-blue nightshirt. She walked back into the living room and sank down on the sofa, the kiss still very much on her mind.

She couldn't know what he thought about it, but for her it had been absolutely magical. His lips had been so warm and inviting on hers and she couldn't wait for an opportunity to kiss him again.

Her gaze dropped to the coffee table as she thought about the note that had been on her door. *You will belong to me.* Who had left it for her? And what exactly did it mean?

Was it really just an odd love note of sorts or something more ominous? How afraid should she really be? She definitely intended to be more aware of her surroundings and not let anyone get too close to her.

Her thoughts jumped to those moments when Luke had shared the tragedy of his past. It had broken her heart for him as she'd heard about his mother. It had also shown her what kind of a man he was to take care of his younger brothers' needs above his own.

He was a special kind of man, but he wasn't her special man. She might have gotten him to dance in the rain with her, but she had a feeling he was too uptight...too regimented in his day-to-day life to be a good fit for her.

She double-checked that her doors were locked up and then got into bed. The rain still pitter-pattered on her window, the sound lulling her to sleep. She fell into dreams of dancing in the rain with Luke.

THE NEXT MORNING, the plan was to go to breakfast with her sisters. She was on the dinner shift and Monique was working later that afternoon at the dress shop. Hopefully, Angelique could get away from the store to meet with them. It had been a minute since the three of them had gotten together.

The first thing she did was drape all the wet things from the night before over her railing outside. There was no sign of rain today and the sun was nice and bright and would dry the towels and her sundress in no time.

She dressed in a pair of jeans and a red-and-blue blouse. She pulled her long hair back and tied it at the nape of her neck with a red ribbon. She applied a little makeup and then spritzed on her favorite scent.

At the last minute, she got the knife she carried at night and put it in her purse. Hopefully, she wouldn't have to stab anyone. However, as she thought of that note, she wanted to have something for her own protection in case somebody came at her sideways.

As she walked through the swamp, she kept her gaze shooting all around and listened to make sure nobody was sneaking up on her. She breathed a sigh of relief as she broke into the clearing where her car was parked.

Monique was already there. Clad in a pair of jeans and a turquoise blouse, she looked absolutely beautiful. "Hey, girl." Monique greeted her with a big smile.

"You look very pretty," Dominique said.

"Thanks, sis," Monique replied. "So do you."

The two of them got into Dominique's car. "Have you heard anything from Angelique this morning?" Dominique asked as she started the engine.

"I spoke to her about twenty minutes ago. She was at her store, and the new girl who started working for her was also there so she said she would meet us at the café," Monique said.

"Good. Last time she was supposed to meet me, she didn't show because of staffing issues." Instead, she had enjoyed her lunch with Luke. "I've missed the three of us getting together."

"Yeah, me too. But with all of us working different hours, it's hard to coordinate," Monique replied.

"Speaking of work, how are things going at the dress shop?"

"Really well. Debbie has stepped away and rarely comes in anymore. I think she's about to make me a full-time manager." Debbie Waltrip, a woman who was retirement age, owned the All That Jazz dress shop.

"That's exciting. Are you ready for all the responsibility that would come with that?"

"Definitely. It's nice that I love working there so much," Monique replied.

"Debbie is lucky to have you. I'm sure you're her top seller. You are so good with the customers."

Monique laughed. "If you're trying to make me feel good about myself this morning, it's working."

"Yeah, just don't get a big head," Dominique replied, making Monique laugh once again.

They chitchatted for a few more minutes until they reached the café. Dominique parked and it didn't take them long to be seated in a booth.

Sunny approached them. "Good morning, ladies," she said brightly. "What can I start you off with? Coffee? Juice?"

"We're waiting on Angelique, but in the meantime, I'd love a cup of coffee," Dominique said.

"Make that two," Monique added.

"I'll be right back with those." She left the booth and before she could deliver the coffee, Angelique arrived. She slid in next to Monique and greeted them. She was dressed in a pair of black slacks and one of the purple T-shirts with her store logo on the front.

"Glad you could make it," Dominique said.

"I finally have a nice, responsible young woman working for me," Angelique replied.

"That's good because you occasionally need to get away from the store and have breakfast with your sisters," Monique said.

Angelique grinned with good humor. Within minutes all three had coffee and had ordered their food. As they waited, they talked about the things going on in their lives.

Dominique hadn't decided yet if she was going to share the note she'd received. The last thing she wanted to do was worry her sisters. They were already worried enough about her shadowing Pierre at night, although they were pleased that Luke was going with her when she went out to catch their mother's killer.

She looked around the café. Was the man who left the note for her sitting in here right now? She didn't see anyone paying any particular attention to her.

Sunny arrived with their food. Dominique had ordered pancakes this morning while Monique had ordered an omelet and Angelique the French toast. They were definitely different when it came to their favorite breakfast meals.

As they ate, they continued to catch up with each other. What they didn't discuss was their mother's murder or the investigation. There was nothing more to say about either subject as they all just hoped an arrest would be made very soon and the killer would finally face justice.

There were still days when Dominique's grief over the loss of her mother would rear up and threaten to consume her, but those days were coming less frequently now. Time truly was a healer.

"Girls, it's so nice to see you all three together." Nola Fontenot stopped by the side of their booth. "Your mother must be smiling down from Heaven knowing the three of you are all together," the plump, brown-haired woman said.

Nola had been Mystique's closest friend and was like a favorite aunt to the sisters. "How are you doing, Nola?" Dominique asked.

"Oh, you know, I still have days of grief. I miss your mother like crazy," she replied.

"We all do," Angelique said.

"I just wish Daniel would get that damned Pierre under arrest, because I truly believe that man is responsible for her death." Nola grimaced. "I don't know what's taking him so long."

"Daniel is doing the very best he can to catch Mama's murderer." Angelique quickly jumped to her lover's defense. "Right now, he lacks enough evidence to arrest Pierre, but trust me, he and his men are working hard on the case."

"I just hate seeing that man walking around like he doesn't have a care in the world. I guess I'm just an impatient ninny," Nola said with a small laugh. "And now I'll just let you all finish your breakfast."

She left their booth and headed to the other side of the café, where two women awaited her at a four-top table. "She's as anxious as we are to get this case solved," Angelique said and then looked pointedly at Dominique. "That doesn't mean I want my sister out there watching Pierre in the dead of night."

"I'm perfectly safe in what I'm doing with Luke by my side," Dominique replied. "He's a very good bodyguard and last night I even got him to dance in the rain with me."

Both her sisters stared at her in obvious surprise. "You got Luke Madison to dance in the rain with you?" Angelique shook her head and released a small laugh. "From what I've heard, that man is so uptight he squeaks when he walks."

"You like him," Monique said.

"I do like him," Dominique replied.

"No, I mean you really like him." Monique held Dominique's gaze.

"I suppose you could do a whole lot worse than Luke," Angelique added.

Dominique laughed. "Luke is a likeable guy. He's my partner and nothing more. He is too regimented for me, and I'm too spontaneous and free for him. If we were romantically together, we'd probably kill each other within twenty-four hours."

"You're probably right about that," Angelique said.

They all finished eating and paid, and within minutes Angelique was headed back to her shop and Dominique and Monique were back in the car and heading home.

"This was nice," Monique said. "I always like it when the three of us get together."

Dominique shot a quick look at her sister. Her younger sister was the softest of the three. She often kept her thoughts to herself. She was rather shy and quiet unless she was at work or on the dance floor at the Voodoo Lounge. Dominique might have danced in the rain last night with Luke, but Monique definitely came alive when she was dancing.

"When are you going to find some nice man to date?" Dominique asked.

Monique laughed. "Remember, I'm younger than you so I'm in no real hurry to find a nice man."

"You're only a little over a year younger than me," Dominique replied.

Monique grinned at her and then sobered. "Seriously, Dominique, I have my work and right now that's enough for me. I know you and Angelique worry about me, but really, I'm doing just fine. However, I'll be better once Mama's killer is behind bars and there's true closure to the case. Right now, it's just a festering wound."

"I think we'll all do better after that happens," Dominique agreed. They arrived at the swamp entrance, got out of the car and headed in.

When they reached Monique's shanty, they said their goodbyes and hugged and then Dominique continued on her way. Just as she had when she'd left, she kept an eye out for anyone else who might be on the path with her.

As she walked, her thoughts went to the brief conversation they'd had about Luke. Immediately, the memory of the very hot kiss she'd shared with him warmed her from head to toe.

Surely, Luke's kiss had seemed unusually hot only because it had been a very long time since she'd kissed a man. Oliver LeBouef's kisses sure hadn't been as hot... as wonderful as Luke's had been.

Would he kiss her again tonight? A shiver of sweet anticipation shot through her. She entered her shanty and shut and locked the door behind her.

What in the hell was she doing? Why would she want a man who was definitely all wrong for her to kiss her again?

THAT KISS...THAT VERY hot kiss with Dominique had been on Luke's mind from the moment he had gotten home from her place last night and still teased and tormented him long after he'd awakened that morning.

She had tasted of sweet, hot desire and if that lightning bolt hadn't slashed the dark skies overhead, he had no idea where the kissing might have led.

Now that he'd tasted the sweet heat of her mouth, he was definitely tempted to kiss her again and again. But that couldn't happen.

Nothing good would come of kissing her, except it would feed his physical desire for her and he couldn't allow that to dictate where their relationship went. They had no real relationship except they were friendly with each other and he had the task of keeping her alive.

The other thing that had been on his mind was the note that had been left for her. Did it indicate she was in danger?

His gut instinct told him no, that it probably was the work of a secret admirer. But could he trust his gut instinct?

Still, he intended to remind her that night when he saw her again that she needed to stay aware of her surroundings. There was no way to know what the note writer had in mind, so it was best to err on the side of caution.

At the moment, he was on his way into the police station to do a check-in with Daniel. It was just after lunch time and there was no hint of the rainstorm that had swept the area the night before.

If anyone would have told him that there would come a night when he would dance in the rain with Dominique Santori, he wouldn't have believed them. It was so far out of character for him and yet he had to admit it had been exhilarating and more fun than he could remember enjoying in a very long time. The truth was he had to admit there wasn't much fun in his life.

He pulled up behind the police station and parked in the lot, then entered through the back door. He didn't see any other officers as he walked down the long hallway toward Daniel's office.

Most of them would be out on patrol, except for Gus Smith. The older officer was near retirement age and also suffered from severe arthritis in his hips. He worked the day shift as the receptionist.

Luke went into the murder room and set the baggie-clad note on the table and then continued on down the hallway.

When he reached Daniel's office, he knocked on the door. Daniel immediately called out for him to enter and Luke did just that. "Hey, boss," he greeted Daniel.

"Luke, how are you doing?"

Luke sat in the chair in front of Daniel's desk. "I'm doing all right. I just figured I'd do a quick check-in even though I don't have anything to report. Thankfully, the rain kept Dominique from trying to follow Pierre last night."

"Yeah, Angelique had breakfast with her sisters this morning, and Dominique shared with them about your night activities." Daniel raised a brow as a wry smile curved his lips. "Dancing in the rain, Luke? I didn't know you had it in you."

The warmth of a blush filled Luke's cheeks. He hadn't intended sharing that fact with anyone, especially Daniel. "Yeah, I didn't know I had it in me, either. It started to rain and she grabbed my hand and pulled me outside and before I knew it, we were dancing."

The smile on Daniel's face fell away. "A word of advice, Luke. Remember, she is just a job. I've known you for years, and I really don't think she's the type of woman you need in your life."

"I'm not looking at being a lifelong partner with her, and believe me, she really is just a job to me, although we are friendly with each other." At least, thank God, she apparently hadn't shared the fact they had kissed.

"There is one other thing that happened to her yesterday." Luke told Daniel about the note she had received. "It sounds to me like she's picked up a secret admirer, but I did tell her she needed to stay aware of her surroundings and who she allows to get close to her. I also brought the note in to see if we could lift any prints from it. I left it on the table in the murder room."

"I'll have Clay grab it," Daniel replied. Clay was their number one expert in fingerprint retrieval. "In the meantime, there isn't much we can do about the note, however, you were absolutely right to tell Dominique to watch her surroundings and hopefully the writer of the note is nothing more than a lovesick individual who means no harm."

"Let's hope," Luke replied. "Anyway, that's my report for the day. Anything new on Mystique's murder case?"

Daniel frowned. "Unfortunately, no. We still have no leads to follow at the moment."

"If I really see Pierre dig up the missing client book, do you want me to make an arrest right then and there?"

"No, I want you to call for backup and then we'll take him down," Daniel replied.

"Got it. And on that note, I'll just get out of here." Luke stood.

"Any plans for the afternoon?" Daniel asked.

"Yeah, a nap. I don't think it's going to rain again, so Dominique will want to follow Pierre again tonight."

"Then have a good nap. I imagine you'll need it," Daniel replied.

"Thanks, and I'll see you tomorrow." Luke left the office and walked back out of the building and into the summer heat. As he drove home, his thoughts were a jumble.

His physical desire for Dominique battled with his sense of duty. Then there was the note she received that might or might not portend some sort of coming conflict.

If it truly was from a secret admirer, when they made themselves known to her, would she be thrilled about the person's identity? Would it be from someone she was excited to date? That thought sparked a surprising touch of jealousy inside him...a jealousy that had no place in his thoughts or in his relationship with the beautiful woman.

By the time he was home, he was ready for a nap and it didn't take him long to fall asleep in his recliner. He slept with no dreams and awakened about two hours later, just in time to make dinner.

He had decided to cook tonight, and had a nice steak

marinating in his refrigerator. That along with a baked potato was dinner.

After eating, he cleaned up the kitchen and then went to his bedroom to change into his night-stalking clothing. Once he was dressed, he left the house to head to the swamp. It was a bit earlier than usual. However, he'd rather wait for night to fall at her house with her company instead of sitting in the silence of his own place.

As he drove, a sweet anticipation filled him at the thought of spending more time with her. *She's just a job*, he reminded himself. But he'd never enjoyed a job as much as he was enjoying this one.

She fascinated him. She was so different from any other woman he'd ever known. He was interested in knowing everything about her. That didn't mean he was entertaining any real feelings for her except a deep curiosity.

He reached the swamp entrance and parked and then got out of his car and headed in. The sunlight was still fairly bright overhead but it wouldn't be long before twilight fell.

He walked briskly, more comfortable since he'd become more familiar with the path to her place. As always small animals scampered in the brush and insects buzzed and whirred in the air.

Maybe tonight would be the night she would give up this dangerous job she'd set for herself. What if Pierre hadn't buried the book? Luke still didn't understand why the man would have wanted Mystique's client book to begin with, but the facts indicated the book had been stolen on the night of the murder. And Luke did believe Pierre was their murderer.

He shoved all these thoughts out of his head as he reached her front door. He knocked. "Dominique, it's me."

He heard her unlock her front door and then she opened

it and gestured him inside. As usual, even though she was once again clad in the tight black jeans and a black T-shirt, she looked stunning. Her hair was pulled back at the nape of her neck, emphasizing her high cheekbones and beautiful features.

"Hi," he said as he walked over to the sofa and sat.

"Hi yourself," she replied and sat next to him, bringing with her the wonderful scent that he now identified as hers alone.

"How was your day?" he asked.

"It was okay. I had breakfast with my sisters, which is always nice. After that I worked the lunch shift at the café and I got back here just after four. How was your day?"

"Fairly quiet. I spent the morning doing a little cleaning and then this afternoon I went into the police station and spoke with Daniel. I also dropped off the note you got for fingerprinting."

"Hopefully they'll find some. Still no movement on my mother's case?" she asked. Her beautiful eyes held his gaze and he wished he could tell her something, anything that would take away the haunting he saw in the depths there.

"Nothing," he finally replied. "But that doesn't mean something couldn't break loose at any time."

Her gaze turned skeptical. "And tomorrow gators will learn how to speak English."

"My scenario is much more realistic than yours," he replied with a small laugh.

She grinned at him, that impish smile that always charmed him. "Let's hope you're right."

"The day that gators speak English, I'll jump in the swamp and eat only insects."

She laughed. He loved the sound of her laughter. It was

low-pitched and musical. For the next hour they small-talked. He learned several more things about her.

Her favorite music was old rock and roll, the same kind he liked. She loved shrimp while he preferred a good burger. She believed in UFO's, and he wasn't sure he believed in extraterrestrial beings.

All too quickly, she was ready to leave the cabin and head out to Pierre's shanty. "I wish you didn't believe this was necessary," he said as they walked out into the darkness of the night. She paused at the top of the bridge and turned to him.

"But I do think it's necessary," she replied softly. Her eyes glowed in the moonlight. "It's been over two months since Angelique found our mother dead...murdered in her bed. Over two months with no closure. Over two months with no justice. Luke, I have to do this, otherwise I'd go crazy just sitting and waiting around for something to happen."

"Then let's go," he said gently. She smiled at him gratefully and together they went across the bridge and into the tangled greenery of the swamp.

He followed her on the path to Pierre's place. When they reached it, they crouched down behind the bushes where they had hidden the last time.

Lantern light spilled out of Pierre's window and shadowy movement let him know the gator-hunter hadn't left yet. Like the last time, as they waited for Pierre to make a move, he couldn't help but be far too aware of Dominique's nearness.

His physical desire for her reared up and he had to consciously tamp it down. It had no place in their relationship. They were merely friends doing a job together, and that was all. He just had to keep her from harm, and that was the beginning and the ending of their relationship.

It wasn't long before Pierre left his shanty. He carried the same items he had before and he seemed to be in no hurry as he took off down a path.

Luke and Dominique followed him closely, keeping brush and trees between them. They hadn't gone far when Luke accidentally stepped on a dead tree limb that snapped loudly.

Pierre stopped in his tracks, his head swiveling slowly from right to left. *Damn*. Luke froze in place, as did Dominique as the gator-hunter seemed to look right at them.

Chapter Six

Dominque's breath caught in the back of her throat. The snapping limb had sounded like a gunshot in the relative quiet of the night. It had certainly drawn the unwanted attention of Pierre.

Her heartbeat thundered as Pierre stared in their direction. Could he see them? The moon was fairly bright overhead. Fear kept her half breathless and utterly motionless as she waited to see what was going to happen.

A rush of intense relief shuddered through her when his gaze tracked past where they were hidden. He gazed around for another long minute and then continued on his way.

She felt the sigh of relief from Luke on the back of her neck. Thank God Pierre hadn't decided to come and investigate the source of the loud sound.

They continued to follow Pierre. He wound up at the same area. He uncovered the boat, got into it and then disappeared in the darkness.

Luke remained hidden with her and thankfully didn't speak as they didn't know the exact location of the gatorhunter. She was still shaken up by the close call they had had.

If Pierre found them spying on him, what would he do?

Would he just scream and yell at them? Or would he try to kill them? There was no way of knowing and in any case, she didn't want to find out.

This time, Pierre was only gone about an hour. He returned to the shore, unloaded the boat and hid it, and then began the trek back to his shanty. Apparently, the fish and gators hadn't cooperated with him tonight because he'd come back empty-handed.

Once he was back in his shanty, she and Luke returned to her place. When they got inside, she collapsed on the sofa and drew several long, deep breaths.

Luke sank down next to her. "God, I'm so sorry," he said.

She immediately knew what he was apologizing for. "There's no need for you to apologize. It could just have easily been me who stepped on the branch and snapped it."

"Damn, it was so loud and I was sure Pierre was going to find us."

"All's well that ends well, right?" She drew another deep breath and felt herself finally relaxing. "Do you want to eat something?"

"No, thanks. I always eat—"

"I know, you always eat around six o'clock each night." She looked at him curiously. "What would happen if you ate at seven or midnight? Would you suddenly go mad and bay at the moon?"

He laughed. "No, nothing like that." He sobered thoughtfully. "I'm the first one to admit that I'm tied to my schedules and routines. Rationally, I know it's baggage from my childhood. But I'm working on it. After all, I did dance in the rain with you."

She smiled at him. "Yes, you did." Her head filled with the memory of being held in his strong arms and dancing as the rain came down to caress them. Then he'd kissed her and she wanted him to kiss her again right in this moment.

She leaned toward him as their gazes remained locked. He angled his body to her and a hot anticipation simmered inside her. Closer and closer he came toward her and then he suddenly snapped back and straightened up.

"I'll just get out of here and head home," he said as he rose from the sofa.

Disappointed, she got up as well. She'd been so sure he was going to kiss her again, but it hadn't happened. She walked with him to the front door.

"Good night, Dominique," he said as he opened her door. "I'll see you tomorrow night."

"Good night, Luke." As he walked out into the night, she closed and locked her door behind him.

She could have sworn he'd wanted to kiss her. She had seen a flame of desire in the depths of his green eyes. What had stopped him? Had she misread the desire? With a deep sigh, she turned off all the lanterns in the shanty except one, and that one she carried into her bedroom.

She'd thought she was hungry, but she decided just to go to bed instead. It was late and she was on duty at the café for breakfast the next morning.

It wasn't long before she was in bed and asleep, and having dreams once again of dancing with and kissing Luke. Her alarm blared its wake-up call early the next morning and she got out of bed, dressed and got ready to go.

As she drove into work, she couldn't help but think about that moment when she'd thought Luke was going to kiss her again. There was no question that she was physically drawn to him and she believed he was to her, too. She saw it in his eyes when he gazed at her and felt it in his very touch.

Was she mistaken? She didn't believe so. She truly believed his desire for her matched her desire for him. Would it be so awful if they acted on it and slept together?

She smiled to herself and wondered where on his schedule making love fit in? The man couldn't even adjust the time he ate, for crying out loud. And that reminded her of why he would never have a place in her future.

If they did fall in bed together, it wouldn't be making love. Rather, it would just be an act of physical desire. Passion could come without love, right?

As she pulled up and parked behind the café, she shoved all thoughts of Luke and passion out of her head. It was time to go in and serve the good people of Dark Waters.

"Hey, girl, long time no talk," Sunny said as Dominique walked into the break room.

"I know. I've just really been busy lately," Dominique replied.

"Yeah, busy with the handsome Officer Madison. What is going on between you and Luke?" Sunny gazed at her with open curiosity.

Dominique opened a locker and put her purse inside before replying. "Luke and I are just friends. He's…uh… helping me out with a personal problem."

Sunny's gaze turned sardonic. "It sure didn't look like just friends when the two of you had lunch together the other day. That man looked at you like he wanted to eat you up."

Dominique laughed. "He was probably looking at me as if I was an alien being. The two of us are very different."

Sunny shook her head. "Nope, that wasn't it, but obviously you're being tight-lipped about your relationship with him. I get it if you're not wanting to share it with me right now."

"Sunny, I promise you there is nothing to share and you know I'd tell you if there was anything," Dominique said with a small laugh. She slammed the locker and pocketed the key. "Now, it's time to get to work."

Minutes later, Dominique was taking orders and delivering food to the people in her section. There were several of her regulars there, including Burt and Austin.

"Hey, Jacob. What can I get for you this morning?" she said, greeting another one of her regulars. Jacob Benoit was a fisherman. He was single and rather attractive, and often blatantly flirted with Dominique.

"I'll take a serving of you on a silver platter," he replied with a bright twinkle in his dark eyes.

"Sorry, Jacob, unfortunately we are all out of our silver platters this morning," she replied.

"Damn," he replied with a grin. "Then I guess just give me my regular number two breakfast special. Hopefully, tomorrow morning there will be some silver platters in the house."

She laughed. "We'll have to see about that."

"Maybe you could save one for me," he replied.

"Sorry again, but we aren't allowed to save the silver platters."

"Oh, Dominique, you're absolutely breaking my heart," he said with mock melancholy.

She laughed once again. "I'm sure eating your breakfast will heal it right up. I'll be right back with your food."

She was still smiling as she moved away from his table. She had to admit, she enjoyed some of the teasing and flirting as long as it didn't go too far and get creepy. It was all in good fun.

She also enjoyed it when the café was busy. Although it kept her on her feet, running from the pass where she picked up the food and then carrying it to tables to be served, it also made the time go very quickly.

Before she knew it, it was three o'clock and her day at work was finished. She couldn't wait to get home and take a shower. She always felt like she smelled of fried onions when she left work. Since it was a hot day with the sun bright overhead, she knew the rainwater she showered in would be nice and warm.

It didn't take her long to arrive at the swamp's entrance. She got out of her car and then began the walk in toward her shanty. As she walked, her thoughts were a jumble with Luke at the forefront.

How long would he be willing to continue backing her up at night when she shadowed Pierre? He'd mentioned that he was on vacation. When his vacation time was over, would he still continue the nightly quests with her? More concerning was without his presence as backup, would she be willing to do it all alone?

All of a sudden, from behind her a burlap bag fell over her head. She instantly stiffened as abject fear torched through her. What? Dear God, what was happening? She couldn't see and danger screamed in her head.

The person behind her attempted to pull the large bag farther down her body and she knew if he managed to do that, then she would either be dead or she would never be seen again.

LUKE PUSHED BACK in his recliner. The plan was to get a short nap in before meeting Dominique later that night. It was just after three so he should be able to sleep for about an hour and a half, and then get up and fix himself some dinner.

He thought about the brief conversation he'd had with

Dominique about his meal times. Logically, he knew the world wouldn't explode if he ate at a different time. But emotionally it was difficult to give up on the schedules that had made him feel safe and in control after his tumultuous childhood.

He closed his eyes and tried to empty his mind as he sought sleep. But a vision of Dominique danced through his brain. She had wanted him to kiss her the night before.

She had leaned toward him, her lips parted in open invitation as her scent eddied in his head. Damn, he had wanted to kiss her again but was now thankful that he'd managed to keep his control. Kissing Dominique was dangerous because he knew it would only make him want to kiss her again…and again. Even though it would be wonderful, it wasn't appropriate for their relationship as friends.

He had just drifted off when his phone rang. He grabbed it from the end table next to him. "Madison," he answered.

"Luke…it's…it's me. I… I need you to come to my shanty." Her voice was shaky and it sounded like she was crying.

"Dominique, what's wrong?" he asked, all lingering vestiges of sleep falling away.

"Please…just come here as soon as you can," she replied and then hung up.

He jumped up from the chair and shoved his cell phone into his back pocket. He then hurried into the kitchen where he strapped on his shoulder holster, grabbed his keys and then raced out of his apartment.

He didn't know what was going on, but he had never heard her sound the way she had. It was obvious something had tremendously upset her and all he wanted to do was get to her as quickly as possible.

He drove as fast as he could, given the other traffic on the road. What on earth had happened to her? He couldn't imagine and he refused to allow his imagination to roam free. He just needed to get to her as soon as possible and find out what was going on.

It didn't take him long to reach the swamp's entrance, where he jumped out of his car and headed in. He moved quickly along the paths that were now fairly familiar to him.

It seemed like it took him forever but he finally reached her bridge and raced across it to her front door. "Dominique, it's me," he called out.

He heard her unlock the door and then it opened and she half collapsed into his arms. Her sobs tore at his heart as he held her tight for several long moments. At least she didn't appear physically hurt.

He moved her farther inside and then closed the door behind them and led her to the sofa. She remained clinging to him as she continued to weep.

"Hey, hey," he said softly as he caressed her up and down her back in an effort to comfort her. He gazed around the room to see if anything looked amiss. But the room was as neat and tidy as it always was. "What's happened? Tell me what's going on, Dominique."

She finally released her hold on him and sank down on the sofa. He sat next to her as she drew several deep breaths in an obvious effort to get her tears under control.

"I—I was walking back here a-after work," she began. Although the sobs had finally stopped, tears still oozed from her eyes. "I wasn't paying a-attention. Th-that was my mistake because I never heard him come up behind me."

Her words instantly made all of Luke's muscles tense

and a chill walked up his spine. He reached for her hand and she grasped his tightly, as if it was a lifeline. She released a deep, shaky breath and stared down at the coffee table as she continued to speak.

"He came up behind me and pulled what felt and smelled like a burlap bag over my head. Oh Luke, I was so terrified. For a moment I just froze. As he tried to pull the big bag down farther on my body, I fumbled in my purse and managed to grab my knife. I started stabbing out all around. I guess he didn't expect me to have any kind of weapon."

The words now tumbled from her, nearly tripping over each other as she continued to relay what had happened to her. Her fingers squeezed together with his even tighter as tears once again filled her eyes.

"I... I think I managed to stab him somewhere because he let out a low grunt. I kicked and stabbed and tried desperately to get the bag off of me. I fought as hard as I could and then I heard him running away. I pulled the bag off my head and tried to get a look at who it was, but he was already gone."

She released his hand and instead swiped at her tears, then finally gazed at him. The fear was still in the depths of her eyes and her lips trembled slightly. "I don't know if he wanted to rape me, kill me or kidnap me."

He reached out and gently drew a thumb across her cheeks to wipe away the last of her tears. His heart still thundered in his chest with fear for her. "Thank God you managed to fight him off, Dominique," he said. "And now I need to call Daniel. We need to make an official police report of this."

She nodded and he pulled his phone from his pocket to make the call. Dominique looked so small, so fragile half curled up in the corner of the sofa. All he really wanted to do was hold her and comfort her until the residual fear was gone from her beautiful eyes.

Once he made the call to Daniel, he did just that. He reached out and pulled her into his embrace. She came willingly into his arms. They didn't speak. He just held her and occasionally he felt a small shiver go through her body.

She finally moved out of his arms and leaned back against the sofa. "I just can't believe this happened to me."

"Thank God you managed to get your knife out of your purse," he replied.

"If I hadn't, he would have had me." She wrapped her arms around herself, and once again looked small and vulnerable. She sat there for a long moment and then got up. "I'm going to go change out of my work clothes. I'll be right back."

As she left the living room and disappeared into her bedroom, Luke leaned back and released a deep sigh. Who had attacked her? It had to have been whoever had left her the note. Unfortunately, Clay had been unable to pull any prints from it.

You will belong to me.

The words now took on a far more ominous meaning. Whoever had written the note had been the man who had attacked her, Luke was sure of that. It had been a very bold move considering it had taken place in the middle of the afternoon and other people could have been around.

However, surely if anyone had seen her being attacked, the person would have come to help her. The fact that nobody had come to her aid let him know there were probably no witnesses to the assault.

She came back into the living room, now clad in a housedress that was dark with light blue flowers. It appeared there were snaps that ran from the neckline to the bottom of the garment. It skimmed her body and she looked beautiful and casual in it, except for her eyes. They remained dark and haunted with fear.

"Feel better?" he asked.

She nodded and returned to the sofa. At that moment there was a knock on the door. "I'll get it," Luke said and got up. He assumed it was Daniel and he was right. Clay was with him, along with Roger Teasdale, another day cop.

They all came inside where Daniel sat in the recliner facing Dominique on the sofa and the other two men stood on either side of him.

"Hi, Dominique," he greeted her softly. "Are you okay?"

"As okay as I can be," she replied.

"Luke told me a little bit of what was going on, but I want you to tell me exactly what happened," Daniel said as he pulled a notepad from his pocket.

As she once again relayed the afternoon event, Luke's muscles tensed up all over again. He wanted to find the man and beat the hell out of him for touching her...for frightening her so badly. He wanted the man in jail for what he'd done to her.

Once she was finished telling Daniel what had happened, Daniel began to ask her questions. "You didn't see him at all?"

She shook her head. "By the time I got free of the bag over my head, he was gone."

"Did you smell anything? Maybe cologne or something else?" Daniel asked. She paused for a long moment and then shook her head.

"All I smelled was the burlap of the bag," she replied.

"Well, it's obvious the note that was left for you is connected to this. I would guess he intended to kidnap you," Daniel said. His words shot a new fear for her through Luke.

Daniel continued to question her, including asking her where, in the swamp, this encounter had taken place. Once he had a good idea of that, he sent Clay and Roger out to see if they could find anything that might help them identify the perp. If they were lucky, he might have dropped something that would give them some clarity.

Once they left, Daniel continued questioning Dominique. "I want you to think of any man who has been giving you attention lately. Not only in your personal life, but in your work life as well."

"There's nobody in my personal life except Luke," she replied.

"What about at the café?"

She frowned. "I've got three regulars who instantly come to mind. They are flirty with me, but it's all in good fun. I can't imagine any of them being responsible for this."

"Names?" Daniel asked.

Another frown tugged across her forehead. "There's Burt Stanfield. Second is Austin Colbert and the third is Jacob Benoit. They're all regulars of mine and they all flirt with me, but it's nothing deep and I still just can't imagine one of them attacked me this afternoon."

Daniel wrote the names down. "The three of them are a good place to start my investigation. We'll check out their alibis for the afternoon and see what we come up with." He looked up at her at her once again. "What about old boyfriends? Who was the last person you dated?"

"Oliver LeBoeuf, but that was almost a year ago," she replied.

"Who broke up with whom?" Daniel asked.

"I broke things off with him, but we parted on a friendly

basis. I can't imagine him being behind all this, either," she protested. "This is all my fault," she added miserably, the words surprising Luke.

"How on earth could it have been your fault?" he asked incredulously.

"I should have been more aware. I should have heard him come up behind me long before he was close enough to put a burlap bag over my head. But I was into my own head and distracted. Had I been paying more attention this probably wouldn't have happened."

"That's not true," Luke said, jumping to her defense. "No way should you take on any responsibility for what happened to you."

"And I definitely agree with Luke," Daniel added. "Nobody is responsible for the attack on you except the perpetrator, and I promise you I'm going to do everything in my power to find out who that is as quickly as possible."

Dominique opened her mouth as if to say something, but then she grasped the locket that Luke now knew from one of their previous conversations held some of her mother's ashes, and bit her bottom lip.

Luke could guess what she wanted to say. Daniel had promised the very same thing concerning her mother's murder and here it was a little over two months later with nobody in jail for the crime.

At that moment, the door opened and Clay and Roger returned. Clay carried with him a large burlap bag. "We found it right in the area where Dominique told us she'd been attacked."

"Did you find anything else around that area?" Daniel asked.

"No, nothing more," Roger replied.

"And we checked the area very thoroughly," Clay added.

"Get the burlap sack into an evidence bag," Daniel said with a frown. "I don't know how well burlap retains fingerprints but hopefully you can go over it to see what you can find," he said to Clay.

"I doubt you'll find anything," Luke said. "We didn't find any prints on the note that was left so I would imagine the person wore gloves."

"You're probably right, but we'll check it out anyway," Daniel replied. "And the first person I intend to talk to is Jacob Benoit. Fishermen often use burlap bags to keep their fish in." He stood and Luke did the same while Dominique remained curled in the corner of the sofa.

"Dominique, I'm so sorry this happened to you," Daniel said sympathetically. "I'll be in touch, and if you think of anything that might help us identify who did this to you, then don't hesitate to tell Luke or call me."

"I will," she replied.

"I'll be in touch as soon as I have information or more questions for you," Daniel said.

Luke walked with him and the other officers to the front door. "I'll also be in touch," Luke replied. The men all said goodbye and then they left.

Luke relocked the door and then turned back to Dominique. At least some of the color had returned to her cheeks and she didn't look quite as frightened as she had when he'd first arrived.

He sank back down next to her and she moved closer to him. "How are you doing?" he asked gently.

"A little better now, although I still can't believe it all happened. He tried to kidnap me," she said softly. She gazed into his eyes. The gaze was so intense he felt as if she was looking into the very depths of his soul. "Luke, will you hold me again?" she asked.

"Of course," he replied. He pulled her back into his arms and she buried her face in his shoulder as her arms wrapped around his neck.

Her heart beat against his own and the scent of her eddied in his head. He was there to comfort her, but he couldn't help how the closeness to her half dizzied his senses.

They remained that way for several long moments and then she raised her head and once again gazed at him. Her eyes held a winsome plea. "Kiss me, Luke. Please, I want... I need you to kiss me."

He shouldn't. It wasn't right. The rational thoughts tried to find purchase in his brain, but it was impossible with the flames he saw in the very depths of her eyes. It was impossible with her luscious, full lips so close to his.

He knew her lips would be sinfully soft, and even knowing it was wrong, even knowing he would probably regret it later, he couldn't fight against his own desire to taste her lips.

She was a fever that burned hot, a rush inside his blood. He'd sworn he wasn't going to kiss her again, but here he was...about to kiss her once again.

Chapter Seven

Dominique's heart fluttered and a sweet desire filled her as Luke's mouth took hers. The kiss filled her with a warmth that sought out and banished all the cold places the attack had created inside her.

She opened her mouth to his and their tongues swirled together in a hot dance of desire. He smelled so good and his arms around her felt so familiar and so…safe.

However, it wasn't safety she was looking for from him at the moment. She tasted his passion for her and it made her feel wonderfully alive as it stirred a wealth of desire for him inside her.

She'd never loved kissing a man as much as she loved kissing Luke. His lips didn't pressure, rather they cajoled a response. And respond she did.

Her heart beat fast and furiously and she quickly became half breathless. She realized at that moment she wanted far more than a kiss from him. She wanted to explore completely the physical attraction that burned bright inside her.

She felt as if she'd desired him from the first moment he had shown up on her doorstep to act as her bodyguard. Now that desire was completely out of control and all she could think about was Luke and how much she wanted him.

The kiss finally ended. He was as breathless as she. She took his hand in hers and stood. "Luke, come to my bedroom and make love with me."

"That's probably not a good idea," he said, his voice deeper than usual.

"Why? Don't you want me?" She gazed into his beautiful eyes and was assured by the desire she saw lighting the green depths. He looked so handsome in his jeans and a mint-green button-up shirt, but she was eager to see him naked and she desperately wanted to have him in bed with her.

"That's not the point," he replied. "You've had a bad scare and—"

"And nothing," she said, interrupting him. "Luke, I wanted you last night and the night before that. This has nothing to do with the attack. This is just me wanting you. Come into my bedroom with me, Luke. Come and make love with me." She gave his hand a soft tug, thrilled when he finally stood.

She led him into her bedroom where she turned on the lantern next to the bed. As she turned to face him, he immediately drew her back into his arms for another kiss. She wrapped her arms around his neck and leaned into him as his arms tightened around her. She leaned close enough to him that she felt his arousal against her.

Raw, hot desire roared through her as his hands drew sensual circles on her back. All she could think about was Luke and how much she wanted him.

They kissed for only a moment and then she pulled her hands from around his neck and instead began to unbutton his shirt. He stood perfectly still, his eyes smoldering as she slowly worked the buttons.

As she unfastened each one, she kissed the warm, bare

skin that was exposed. As she worked down his chest, his breathing quickened and he released a low moan.

"Dominique, you're driving me absolutely crazy," he half growled.

She smiled up at him. "That's the whole point." She shoved his shirt off his shoulders and it fell to the floor behind them. Oh, he had a glorious chest, broad and firmly muscled.

He kicked off his loafers as she unbuttoned the fly on his jeans. "Take them off, Luke," she whispered urgently.

She didn't have to ask twice. As he unzipped them then pulled them and his socks off, she turned down the spread, exposing pale pink sheets.

When she gazed at him again, he was clad only in a pair of navy-blue boxers. Her breath caught in her throat at the sight of his beautiful body. Rather than being an overly muscular, bulked-up man, Luke had the kind of wiry build she'd always found attractive on a man.

As he stared at her, his eyes lit with green flames of want, she began to unsnap the housedress she'd thrown on earlier. With each snap she opened, the flames in his eyes grew more intense.

She wore no bra beneath, so once the housedress was open, she was clad only in a pair of wispy pink panties. She shrugged the dress off her shoulders and it joined his shirt and jeans on the floor.

"You are so beautiful," he half whispered.

"So are you," she replied. She slid beneath the sheet on the bed and beckoned him to join her there. He got in next to her and immediately sought her mouth again with his. As they kissed, their legs tangled together. She loved the feel of his strong, naked legs against hers.

For a few minutes their bodies remained close and the

tactile pleasure of his bare skin against hers felt wonderful. His chest was so broad against her own and she could feel their hearts beating together in unison.

He shifted positions so he had a free hand to stroke down her body. He caressed first one breast and then the other, toying with each of her hardened nipples. He then lowered his head and captured one of the nipples in his mouth.

"Oh yes," she said on a moan as the pleasure shot an electrical fire from her nipples to the very center of her. He teased and licked first one and then the other until she was half mad with want.

His hand began to move lower, slowly trailing fingers down her abdomen and to the waistband of her panties. He slid his fingers back and forth across the panties' band, tormenting her as her desire for him raged completely out of control.

She reached down and removed the only barrier other than his boxers keeping them apart. She threw the panties to the floor and then she was back in his arms. This time as he slid his hand back down, there was nothing to stop him from touching her moist center.

She moaned and raised her hips to meet his intimate touch. His fingers danced against her. Her muscles tightened as she began to climb up and up to a place of pleasure she'd never been before.

She clung to his shoulders as she moved her hips more frantically, rising to heights that had her gasping with need. And then she was there, spiraling down with the force of the orgasm that shuddered through her.

As soon as she was able, she reached out to him and caressed down his chest. But he stopped her. "I don't need any more foreplay," he said, his eyes glowing with his desire.

He reached down and took off his boxers, then rolled her onto her back and positioned himself between her thighs. He bent down and took her mouth in a gentle kiss as he slowly eased into her.

Powerful and intense, the sensations that rushed through her were beyond wonderful. He began to pump in and out of her and thought was impossible. There was only her and Luke and these breathtaking moments.

He moaned and she grabbed hold of his buttocks. "Faster, Luke. Faster," she said. He quickened his pace and before long they became frantic, panting as they moved together.

Once again, she felt the tension building inside her, taking her to an unsustainable high. She cried out his name as her climax crashed over her and a moment later, he stiffened against her and moaned with his own release. When it was over, he collapsed on his back next to her, both of them wordless as they fought to find a more normal breathing.

Finally, he raised himself up on one elbow and gazed at her with a soft smile. He moved a strand of her hair away from her face. "That was amazing," he said.

"It was beyond amazing," she replied. It had been intense and passionate and more incredible than she had ever imagined. "Can you stay the rest of the evening with me?"

"Of course," he replied. "I would have been here anyway, but I think for tonight we shouldn't go out to follow Pierre."

She released a tremulous sigh. "I agree. I just need some time to process and get over the attack."

He leaned down and kissed her gently on the forehead.

"I'm just so sorry that happened to you. Let's hope Daniel can get us some answers very soon."

"Enough about that."

He stared at her, this time his gaze obviously curious. "Dominique, what exactly are we doing?"

"Nothing serious, so don't get weird on me, Luke," she replied. "Now, you can use the bathroom first."

"Okay." He slid out of the bed and grabbed his clothes from the floor, then left the bedroom.

She looked over to the window where twilight displayed itself in shades of dark purples and grays. The day was nearly done. She had no desire to go out into the swamp tonight. She just wanted to spend more time with Luke.

"The bathroom is all yours," he said from the doorway. "I'll just meet you in the living room."

She got out of bed, grabbed her housedress and a clean pair of panties, and then headed into the bathroom. Once there she looked at herself in the mirror. She'd wanted to make love with Luke and now she had. She'd wondered what kind of a lover he'd be and now she knew.

At times he'd been gentle but he'd also been masterful and giving and the whole thing had been utterly magical. She'd assumed once her curiosity about him as a lover had been sated then that would be the end of it. But to her surprise, she wanted him again…and again. It had nothing to do with love, but everything to do with the crazy, wild desire she felt for him.

She turned away from the mirror, cleaned herself up and then redressed and left the bathroom. He was seated on the sofa and he smiled at her as she entered the room.

"I just thought of something," she said.

"What's that?" he asked curiously.

"You missed your six o'clock dinner. How about I fry up some bacon and make some eggs and toast?"

He grinned. "Even though I'm off my schedule, that sounds really good."

"Why don't you come into the kitchen and talk to me while I cook?"

"With pleasure." He got up from the sofa and followed her into the kitchen. She gestured for him to sit at the table. "I'll be right back," she said and then went out the back door to start her generator.

For just a moment she stood at the railing and stared into the dark water beneath her. The last gasp of twilight played in the water, reflecting the colors of a dying day.

Who had attacked her? A chill walked up her spine as she thought about the unexpected assault. She wondered why they had tried to kidnap her. And more importantly, would they try again?

THEY ATE EGGS and bacon and small-talked through the meal. Luke still couldn't believe what had happened between them. Making love with Dominique had been the most powerful experience he'd ever had. Even now, as he gazed at her across her small kitchen table, he wanted her again.

He'd loved the feel and taste of her soft skin. It could become an addiction if he allowed it. She'd been so passionate and the whole experience had been mind-blowing.

"Dominique, everything happened so fast between us, we didn't even use birth control," he said once they were finished eating and she was cleaning up the dishes.

She turned from the sink to look at him. "It's okay. I'm on birth control pills and I haven't been with anyone for a long time."

"Same for me," he said. "Except the birth control pills part. You do realize we shouldn't have fallen into bed together," he added.

"Why not? We're both consenting adults and we wanted each other. We certainly didn't hurt anyone by acting on our desire for each other."

"Yes, but I don't want things to get confusing for us. I don't want to complicate a relationship that I enjoy," he replied.

"Luke, you're taking things way too seriously," she said. She turned back around to the sink.

He supposed he was getting weird about it. He wished he could be as nonchalant as she was, but he took making love with a woman seriously. He sipped his coffee in silence while she finished up with the dishes. But he wasn't in love with her. He couldn't be.

They went back into the living room where she turned on lanterns and then sank down next to him on the sofa. "Do you work tomorrow?" he asked.

"I do. I'm on breakfast duty." Her beautiful chocolate eyes appeared to darken. "And there's always a possibility a few of my regulars might come in. Sometimes they're there for lunch and sometimes they come in for breakfast."

"Keep in mind, right now they're just men Daniel will investigate, but that doesn't mean any of them are guilty."

"Then who is?"

"I wish I could answer that for you," he replied intensely. "If I knew who it was, I'd beat the hell out of him for what he did to you."

She grinned at him. "You'd do that for me?"

"In a short minute," he replied.

She sighed. "I'll just be glad if Daniel gets whoever it is behind bars."

"He will," Luke replied, confident in his friend's skills as a lawman.

"He hasn't done so well in my mother's murder investigation," she replied.

"That's a different animal altogether. Knowing somebody is guilty and having the evidence to prove it are two different things. And it wasn't just Daniel investigating your mother's murder—it was me, too."

"Do you think it will ever be solved?" she asked. Her gaze held his intently.

"Oh, I think it's already solved," he replied.

"Okay, wrong question...do you think Pierre will ever be arrested?"

He grinned at her. "Well, if you have anything to do with it, definitely."

"Now, you're making fun of me," she said, and her lower lip jutted out in a mock pout.

He laughed. "No, I swear I'm not, but I still have little faith that at some point in time Pierre will dig up your mother's missing book and we'll catch him."

"It could happen."

He laughed again. "Yes, it could happen, and that's why I'm here with you."

"Speaking of being here for me. Want to spend the night? We could be snuggle buddies."

Although her tone was light, there was something in her gaze that told him she wasn't quite ready to be alone yet. "I love snuggling," he replied.

"Then you'll stay?" This time her tone was less casual.

"I'll stay." It would be another blunder in the long list of mistakes he'd already made today.

"Thank you," she replied, her gratitude rife in her tone.

"And speaking of bedtime, I should probably head to bed now since I have to get up so early in the morning."

"Yeah, I'm tired, too," he admitted. It had been a day of intense emotions, both good and bad.

She stood and he also got up. She doused all the lit lanterns in the room. The lantern in the bedroom made it easy for them to find their way. She grabbed a pink nightgown from one of her drawers and then disappeared once again into the bathroom.

Luke stripped down to his boxers and then got into bed. He was happy to snuggle with her if that's what she needed, but he had no intention of repeating what they had shared in bed earlier. That had definitely been a blunder.

She came back into the room, looking beautiful in the lantern's soft light. The pink color of the nightgown was perfect against her dark hair and skin tone. Her hair was loose and spilled down her back like a waterfall of shiny silk.

"I wasn't sure which side of the bed you wanted," he said. She slid in next to him.

"This is perfect." She was next to the nightstand where she placed his phone and hers. "I've got my alarm set for five. I hate to wake you up so early. If you can, feel free to stay here and sleep longer when I leave for work."

"Nah, I'll get up with you and follow you into work and then I'll force you to wait on me by sitting in your section. I'll complain about the food and service and then I'll leave you a five percent tip."

She laughed. "You won't do that," she replied.

"No, I won't complain no matter how bad the service is," he said, making her laugh once again.

"Are you ready for the light to go off?" she asked once the laughter had passed.

"Whenever you are," he said.

She reached out and turned off the lantern on the nightstand. He then pulled her into him, spooning around her back while she snuggled into him.

Torture. It was sheer torture to have her so close against him. Her scent filled his head as her bottom wiggled into him. He tightened his arm around her, wanting her to feel as safe as possible as she fell asleep.

Meanwhile, he prayed sleep would come quickly to him as he fought against another wave of desire. "Luke?"

"Yes?"

"Thank you," she said softly.

"No need to thank me," he replied. What she needed from him now was a sense of safety after the assault, and that thought doused his desire. "Good night, Dominique."

"Good night, Luke."

He knew the moment she fell asleep. Her body went completely limp against his and her breathing became slow and rhythmic. Unfortunately, sleep was elusive for him.

His mind whirled with everything that had happened from the moment he'd gotten the frantic phone call from her until now. It had been such a wild day.

He hoped that tomorrow she wouldn't regret sleeping with him, and he hoped that she wouldn't realize she'd made an impulsive jump into his arms because of the terrifying incident she'd suffered earlier.

It had been a very long time since he'd cuddled a woman in sleep. In his last relationship, the woman had hated being touched at night. She stayed on her side of the bed and he had stayed on his. That had been over a year ago and since that time he hadn't dated or tried to cuddle with anyone.

He must have fallen asleep as he awakened to the sound

of raucous loud music coming from Dominique's phone. To his surprise, they were still in the position they had been in when they'd fallen asleep.

She stirred and he removed his arm from around her and moved away from her as she reached out to grab her phone. The music stopped and she let out a small groan. "Is it time to get up already?"

"Your phone says it is," he replied.

She sat up and turned on the lantern against the darkness in the room. At five in the morning, there was no sign of the morning sun. "If you want to, go back to sleep," she said as she got out of bed.

"Now that I'm awake, I'll just get up and get dressed," he replied.

"Why don't you go ahead and get in the bathroom while I'm getting my clothes together," she replied. As she turned on another lantern on top of the dresser, he slid out of the bed, grabbed his clothes and then headed to the bathroom.

He should have time to get home, take a shower and then head to the café for breakfast. Hopefully all of Dominique's regulars would show up this morning and he could get a good look at them all.

You will belong to me. As he thought of the note she'd received along with the attack on her, his biggest fear right now was that another attack would come—only this time the perp would be successful.

HE AWAKENED EARLY, a wild disappointment still raging through him. He should have been able to take her yesterday. It had been so perfect. She'd been alone on the narrow path and hadn't heard him creeping up behind her.

When he'd managed to get the bag over her head, he'd been so sure of his success. He hadn't counted on her having a knife and he also hadn't counted on how hard she would fight against him. It had been like trying to contain a hellcat in a paper bag.

He sat at his kitchen table, the eggs he'd made himself for breakfast growing cold as he stared out the nearby window and thought about her.

Dominique Santori. Her very name sang in his heart. She was the woman of his dreams and all he could think about was getting her into his house where he could enjoy her company forever. She would fill up the dark, lonely hours that had become his life.

He gazed down at the nick in his skin. The little knife cut was now covered with a small bandage and would heal up fairly quickly. But it was a reminder of his failure.

He got up from the table and dumped his eggs in the trash and then went down the hallway to the door that led into the room he'd prepared especially for her.

The walls had been soundproofed and were painted an eggshell beige. The twin bed was covered in a pink, frilly bedspread that nearly hid the ropes that fell to the floor on either side. He'd have to tie her down until she became obedient and understood that she was where she belonged.

He could just imagine her sitting at the vanity table in front of the aluminum mirror and brushing her long, beautiful hair. Then he would take his turn and brush through the silky strands.

The room also had a small table with two chairs. They would eat their meals there until the time came when he could trust her outside of this room. There was also an en suite bathroom for her to use.

He believed he'd thought of everything. There was nothing sharp in the room that she could use as a weapon and he had everything he needed for her, everything that would keep her here forever.

Oh, it was going to be so wonderful. He closed the door and returned to sit at the kitchen table. His life wouldn't be complete until he had her in it.

And he would get her. She'd gotten away from him yesterday, but the next time he went after her, he would be better prepared. Oh yes…his excitement made him half dizzy. Sweet anticipation roared through him. Soon…very, very soon, she would be his.

Chapter Eight

Waking up in Luke's arms had been wonderful. As Dominique drove to the café the next morning, she still felt the warmth of his body close to hers and his arm wrapped around her waist. She'd felt so safe...so protected and warm.

The kidnapping attempt that had occurred the day before now seemed oddly distant, as if it had taken place days ago. She knew it was because of so many things that had happened after the attack.

Making love with Luke and having him next to her all night long had taken away the rough edges of fear that the assault had left behind.

However, Luke couldn't be there all the time. She had to be there for herself, and that meant staying vigilante. She had to watch her surroundings and couldn't allow any mind lapses to make her an easy target again in the future.

As she parked behind the café, a nervous energy fluttered through her as she thought about waiting on her regulars. Was one of them responsible for the kidnapping attempt? Beneath the flirty words and easy smiles, did one of them have some sort of a dangerous obsession for her?

You will belong to me.

The words now definitely had an ominous meaning. Was it possible that one of the men she served breakfast to had written it? For the first time she could ever remember, she was dreading going in to work.

However, it was time she get her butt inside. She looked all around the parking lot before getting out of her car, and then she hurried in through the back door.

Things were wonderfully normal as she walked into the warm kitchen that smelled of frying onions and eggs, of bacon and ham and other breakfast items. Annie greeted her, as did Ed Slavoie, Annie's right-hand man, and several other members of the staff.

She walked into the break room where Cindy Lawson and Glenda Wright, two other waitresses, were getting ready to clock in. Sunny wasn't working this morning, but Dominique was friendly with the other two waitresses. There were three more waitresses scheduled to work and they should be rolling in at any time.

Once again, she dreaded seeing her regulars today. How would they all react when Daniel spoke with them? Would they be angry with her for giving him their names? Appalled that she would believe any one of them could be behind the attack on her?

By seven o'clock, the café was filling up and Dominique and the others were busy taking orders and running food. By eight o'clock, Luke walked in, looking handsome as the devil in a pair of jeans and a blue polo shirt that emphasized his broad shoulders.

His presence immediately made her feel less jittery about seeing her regulars when they came in. Luke offered her a huge grin as he sat in one of the two-tops in her section.

She walked over to the table to take his order. "Oh, you

again," she said teasingly. "Could you please tip me more than your usual five percent today? My babies are hungry and they all need new shoes."

He laughed. "We'll see," he replied. "Of course, it will depend solely on the service I receive."

"Then I'll see if I can get it right today," she replied.

The twinkling in his eyes dimmed a bit. "Anyone interesting in here?"

"Not yet." She knew he was referring to the three men she'd told Daniel about. "They should show up any minute now."

"When they do, point them out to me and let me know who is who."

She nodded. "Okay, now what can I get you to eat?"

"I'll take a number four special," he replied.

She raised a brow. The number four was the largest breakfast on the menu. "A bit hungry this morning?"

Once again, the twinkle was back in his eyes. "Yeah, I worked up quite an appetite yesterday afternoon."

She laughed. "Okay, a number four it is. Coffee?"

"Definitely."

"I'll be right back with that." She left his table, her heart warmed by the brief interaction with him. She served his coffee and then a few minutes later returned with his large platter of food.

By that time Burt had come in and had taken a seat in her section. She walked back by Luke's table. "Burt Stanfield," she said softly and then headed toward him. She knew Luke probably knew Burt since he worked for the city.

"Good morning, doll," Burt said in greeting.

"How are you doing this morning?" she asked him with what she hoped looked like her usual, friendly smile.

"I'm doing just fine," he replied. "And speaking of fine...you look mighty fine this morning."

"Thank you, Burt. Now, what can I get you?"

"I'll take the number two special with coffee."

"I'll be right back with your coffee," she said.

She wondered if he'd picked up on the fact that she really didn't want their usual flirty banter this morning. She served his coffee and then a few minutes later returned with his food order.

"Everything okay this morning, Dominique?" he asked her. So, he had sensed the difference in her.

"Everything is just fine, Burt," she replied with what she hoped was a reassuring smile. "I've just been really busy this morning."

"Then don't let me hold you up," he replied.

"Thanks, Burt, I'll check in with you a little later," she said and then left his table.

About fifteen minutes later Austin came in and the scene repeated itself. She walked by Luke's table and let him know who Austin was and then went to wait on him.

Luke stayed until just after ten. The only regular who didn't come in was Jacob Benoit, who she usually saw in the afternoons. Once Luke left, she felt oddly bereft.

Thankfully, the café stayed busy until almost eleven and then there was a lull. The breakfast crowd had left and the lunch crowd hadn't come in yet.

Annie sent her on break and this time—rather than stepping outside—she sat in the break room and played on her phone and tried not to think about what was going on in her life.

Still, her thoughts couldn't help but go back to the kidnapping attempt. How close was danger now? Was the person right now someplace plotting and thinking about how to get her?

Given the note and the attack, she was sure the person wouldn't just give up and go away. So, from what direction would danger come at her again? She could only wait and hope that she would survive whatever might happen.

IT WAS JUST after noon when Luke pulled up behind the police station and parked. He was eager to check in with Daniel and let him know his impressions of the two men he'd seen at the café.

He found his boss in his office. "Hey," he said as he sank down in the chair opposite Daniel's desk. "I had breakfast this morning at the café and saw two of our suspects in Dominique's attack case there."

"Which two?" Daniel asked.

"Burt Stanfield and Austin Colbert," Luke replied.

"I know Burt because he works in maintenance for the city, but I don't know Austin. Tell me your impression of him."

"Austin is about six feet tall and rather thin. I would say that physically he doesn't look like he would have the strength to carry a woman off somewhere, but I could be wrong."

"So, Burt is a much better candidate. I know he's burly and strong and could easily carry a petite woman like Dominique through the swamp," Daniel said.

"Right," Luke replied.

"I also don't know the other two men Dominique mentioned." Daniel flipped through the small notebook on his desk. "Jacob Benoit and Oliver LeBoeuf." He looked back at Luke. "Do you know either of them?"

"No, but I'd definitely like to get a look at them."

"Dominique said they were both fishermen. In fact, I was just about to get Clay and head to the swamp to interview them both. Want to tag along?" Daniel asked.

"Absolutely," Luke replied. He wanted…he needed to know who all the players were in Dominique's life. Of course, it was possible that none of the men she'd named was the guilty party. But he thought it was highly likely that one of them was the person who had tried what they now were sure was a kidnapping attempt on the woman he cared about.

It wasn't like he was in love with Dominique, but he considered her a close friend and he definitely cared what happened to her.

Fifteen minutes later, Luke was in the back seat of Daniel's car while Clay rode shotgun as they headed toward the swamp. As Daniel and Clay small-talked in the front seat, Luke stared out the window and thought about the men they were about to interview.

He was particularly interested in meeting Oliver LeBoeuf, a man Dominique had dated. Even though, according to her, their relationship hadn't lasted long, he still wanted to see the type of man Dominique had chosen to go out with.

Then he wondered why he was interested. It wasn't like he and Dominique were dating. As far as their lovemaking, it had been based solely on the very hot physical attraction that had simmered between them almost from the very beginning of their friendship. *Don't get weird about it*, he reminded himself.

So, they were friends with benefits, but he was determined there would be no more benefits between them in the future. The last thing they needed was to complicate their friendship. All he wanted now was to keep her safe, both from her nightly sojourns following Pierre and now from this new dangerous threat.

As Daniel parked in front of the swamp entrance, a rush of adrenaline flowed through Luke's veins. "Do you know where these men live?" he asked.

"No, I figured we'd stop by George's place. He seems to know where everyone lives in the swamp," Daniel replied.

George was George Trahan, a gator-hunter. It had been his new girlfriend who had tried to kill Angelique. Angelique and George had briefly dated. After they stopped, George had fallen in love with a woman named Desiree Augustine. Desiree had hated Angelique and was filled with a deadly rage. She believed George wouldn't truly be hers unless Angelique was dead.

With that thought in mind, one night she had gone to Angelique's shanty, the place where Dominique now lived, and had nearly succeeded in stabbing Angelique to death. Thankfully, Daniel had shown up and had gotten Desiree under arrest before that could happen.

The three lawmen now got out of the car and headed into the swamp. It was odd that so many people lived here, yet rarely did you see another person on the paths.

Hopefully, by now if the two men were morning fishermen, they'd be back in their shanties. If they were night fishermen, then they probably hadn't left their shanties yet.

It didn't take them long to reach George's shanty. Daniel knocked on the door and George answered. He stared at all three of them and then focused on Daniel.

"Am I in trouble?" he asked. Since Desiree's arrest, George had lost weight and looked rather haggard. He'd had no idea what Desiree had been up to, but he'd felt terrible that she'd attacked Angelique.

"No, nothing like that," Daniel said hurriedly. "We were hoping you could help us with some directions."

"Sure. What kind of directions do you need?" George asked, visibly relaxing.

"We want to find Jacob Benoit's shanty and Oliver LeBoeuf's place," Daniel replied.

"Yeah, I can help you with that," George said and then proceeded to give them directions to both the shanties. "Are they in trouble?"

"No, we just have a few questions to ask them to clarify something we're working on," Daniel replied. "Thanks for your help, George. See you later."

George went back inside. "We'll head to LeBoeuf's place first. It's on the way to Benoit's shanty." Daniel led the way as they got back on the main trail.

It didn't take them too long to find LeBoeuf's shanty. It was a relatively small, but neat place. The front of the shanty had been cleared from the encroaching swamp vegetation. Daniel knocked on the door and it was answered by Oliver. He had long dark hair that was tied back with a piece of rawhide.

Luke had to admit Oliver was a handsome guy with well-defined features and an athletic build. So, this was the man Dominique had dated. A wave of jealousy swept through Luke, surprising him.

Why on earth would he feel jealous? It wasn't like he and Dominique were dating or anything like that. They were just friends and he was working as her bodyguard when she went out at night. So, jealousy had no place at all in his head.

"What can I do for you all?" he asked, concern causing deep furrows to dance across his forehead.

Daniel introduced himself and Luke and Clay. "Mind if we come in? We have a few questions we'd like to ask you."

Oliver frowned. "Questions about what? Is this about Mystique's murder? I had absolutely nothing whatsoever to do with that."

"No, this isn't about Mystique. We have some questions for you about another matter," Daniel replied.

Oliver hesitated a moment and then allowed them to come inside. The interior of the shanty was neat and clean, although it smelled faintly of fish.

He gestured them to sit on the brown sofa and he took a seat in a chair across from them. "Now, what's this all about?"

"Dominique Santori," Daniel said.

One of Oliver's dark brows rose up. "Dominique? What about her?"

"We understand that you had a relationship with her about a year ago," Daniel said. Luke watched the man's face closely, looking for any tells that might expose something.

"Yeah, we dated for a little while," Oliver replied easily.

"We understand she broke it off with you. Were you upset when that happened?" Daniel asked.

"Well, yeah, I was upset. I was crazy about her, but that was a long time ago," Oliver replied. "You know, you can't make a woman love you if she doesn't, but I've moved on from her. Why? Did something happen to her?"

"She was attacked by somebody we believe intended to kidnap her," Daniel replied.

Oliver's eyes widened slightly. "But, she's okay?"

Daniel nodded. "She managed to fight the assailant off."

"Thank God," Oliver replied.

Daniel began to question him on his whereabouts at the time of the attack.

"I was here...in my home," Oliver replied.

"Were you with somebody or alone?"

"I was alone, but I swear I had nothing to do with the attack on Dominique. I would never do something like that to her," he said fervently.

For the next fifteen minutes, Daniel continued to drill the man with questions. Oliver's replies were all the same, indicating that he was either telling the truth or was a very good liar.

"I have one last question for you and then we'll leave you to the rest of your day. I see you have a bandage on your finger. What happened?" Daniel asked.

Luke hadn't even noticed the small bandage. He mentally kicked himself for not noticing it before now.

"Oh, yesterday I caught a fishhook in my finger," Oliver replied. "It was my own damn carelessness."

"Mind if I take a look at the wound?" Daniel asked.

Oliver took the bandage off and held out his finger. Both Daniel and Luke got up to take a closer look. Although small, it was a nasty wound. With Oliver's consent, Daniel took a picture of it and then the three left.

It was only when they were some distance away from the shanty that they stopped to discuss the interview. "What do you think?" Daniel asked Luke while Clay remained silent.

Luke frowned thoughtfully. "I believed he was innocent until I saw the wound. Dominique said she might have managed to stab the man assaulting her."

"So, was that a fishhook wound or a small stab wound?" Clay asked. His question hung in the air as they continued on their way to Jacob Benoit's shanty.

Was it possible that Oliver had never gotten over Dominique, that since their breakup he'd become obsessed with having her once again? Or was it possible the man was innocent and had really gotten a fishhook caught in his finger?

A deep frustration welled up in Luke. He hoped they would gain more clarity with the other men they interviewed. They had to catch the person before he acted again because the next time something like this happened, Dominique might not be as lucky.

Chapter Nine

For the next week and a half, each night Luke came to her shanty and they stalked Pierre through the marsh. However, to Dominique's frustration, Pierre still hadn't dug up the book she was so sure he'd stolen.

Luke had started coming to her place extra early so they had plenty of time to talk, time she enjoyed tremendously. Not only did she learn something new about him each time they had a deep conversation, they also laughed a lot, too. Twice during the week, they had gone to lunch together at the café.

She found him to be thoughtful and kind and funny. She also knew that when she was in his presence, she was absolutely safe from harm. When she wasn't in his presence, she continued to keep her guard up.

There were no more times when she allowed her mind to wander when she was out in the swamp by herself. She stayed focused on her surroundings, kept her knife clutched tight in her hand, and thankfully there had been no more kidnapping attempts.

Today was her day off and she was headed into town to do a little shopping at All That Jazz. Tonight, she was cooking dinner for Luke. She had to make a stop at the grocery store as well to get a couple of pork chops to make for him. And, she intended dinner to be served promptly at six.

She was lucky to find a parking space right in front of All That Jazz. She parked and then went inside the store. "Hey, sis," Monique greeted her in surprise. At the moment they were the only two inside the place. "What are you doing here?"

"I could say I just stopped in to have a short visit with you, but the truth of the matter is I have a purse full of tip money and I'm in the mood to shop."

Monique grinned. "Well, then you've come to the right place. What are you looking for?"

"I don't know."

"That doesn't help me help you," Monique replied.

"How about I just browse for a few minutes," Dominique said.

"Browse away." Monique stepped back toward the register, and at that moment a couple of young girls came into the store.

While Dominique began flipping through the clothes on the sale rack, the girls went straight to the section of tops featuring tiny straps and cropped length. The style certainly wasn't for Dominique.

Monique helped them by telling them who would look good in what color. She had an eye for such things, which was why she was such a good salesperson.

Dominique moved from the sale rack to the loungewear, where she found a red two-piece outfit. The top was sleeveless and sleek and the pants were a bit wide and flowy. She loved it and it would be perfect for her to wear this evening before she changed into the boring dark clothes she wore to stalk Pierre.

She threw it over one arm and continued looking. By the

time she was finished, she had the red loungewear and a cute emerald-green blouse that matched Luke's eyes. The girls had left empty-handed amid much giggling.

"Good choices," Monique said as she rang up the items for Dominique.

"Thanks. Maybe some of your fashion flair is finally rubbing off on me," Dominique replied.

"Dom, you've always had good taste," Monique replied. Dominique paid and Monique placed the items into a sack. The two visited for a little while longer and then Dominique left to head to the grocery store.

It was another hot, humid day without a cloud in the sky. Thank goodness it was always cooler in the swamp. Dominique's shanty rarely got hot and there was often a slight breeze coming off the water.

It took her only minutes to arrive at Howard's Groceries. It was a relatively small place but it was the only food store in town and Howard stocked nearly everything a shopper would need.

She walked in and grabbed a basket and headed toward the meat section. As she looked at the pork selection, she couldn't help but notice Jacque LeBlanc standing nearby and looking over the steaks.

Jacque was something of a mystery. He was a tall, well-built, handsome man who lived deep in the swamp. He was a gator-hunter, but nobody knew much about him. Still, he supposedly knew a lot about what went on in the swamp.

Dominique made a mental note to herself. Maybe he was a man she should talk to concerning the attack on her. Maybe he knew something that would help them find the culprit.

Before she could approach him, he turned and wheeled his basket in the opposite direction. Maybe it was better that she and Luke talked to the man together. She made another mental note to herself to mention it to Luke when she saw him later that evening.

She found a package of three nice-looking pork chops and put it in her cart, then headed to the canned vegetable aisle where she grabbed a can of carrots. She then went to the produce aisle where she got a sack of potatoes.

The last thing she bought was a large block of ice. Since there were no refrigerators in the swamp, most people used a big cooler with the ice as a refrigerator of sorts. The ice would last about a week and then she would have to buy another block.

She checked out and then got back in her car and headed home. She was actually looking forward to cooking for Luke tonight. From what he'd told her in one of their many conversations, most nights he simply zapped dinners in the microwave. Tonight, he would eat far better and that made her happy.

Happy. It was funny that she would feel happy. She was stalking a man she believed murdered her mother, she had some obsessed person stalking her and yet spending time with Luke had given her a happiness she hadn't felt for a long while.

It was going to be difficult to tell him goodbye when this was all over. She would miss their conversations and their laughter. Her evenings would become boring and lonely once again and she would be no closer to finding the man of her dreams, the one who would give her a happily-ever-after.

The physical chemistry between her and Luke still burned hot and bright but they hadn't made love again—even though she would have liked to have him once again in her bed.

She pulled up and parked at the swamp's entrance. She'd have to juggle her bags or make two trips because she wanted one hand free to hold her knife as she walked home.

She got out of the car and pulled the bag with the ice over her left arm. She then grabbed the small shopping bag and her clothes bag and managed to get them over her left arm as well. Finally, she got her knife out of her purse and held it firmly in her right hand.

This was better than making two trips. She began the trek in, staying acutely aware of everything around her as she listened for any sounds of somebody approaching her.

Even though nothing had happened over the past week, she remained vigilant whenever she was outside by herself. She was determined she would not be a victim a second time.

As she reached the bottom of her bridge, she saw the piece of paper tapped to her door. Instantly, all her muscles tensed and her heart beat wildly as her gaze shot all around.

Seeing nobody lurking about, she hurried across the bridge and nearly screamed at the sight of a dead bird in front of her door. It looked as if its neck had been broken. The bird wouldn't have flown into her door and died accidentally. Its death looked deliberate. She grabbed the note from the door, stepped over the bird and went inside.

She immediately locked the door behind her, dropped all her packages on the floor and collapsed on the sofa, the note held in her trembling hand. The back of her throat closed up and she felt as if she couldn't draw a breath.

Who would be so cruel as to kill that poor bird? What kind of a monster would wring the neck of an innocent creature? After several moments she finally felt steady enough to read what was written on the paper.

STOP SEEING THE LAWMAN. YOU BELONG TO ME.

The words seemed to jump off the page and once again her heart began to beat frantically as she dropped the note down on the coffee table.

She remained sitting on the sofa for several long minutes as she tried to get her fear under control. She didn't intend to call Luke. There was nothing he could do. Besides, he'd be here later and hopefully he could take care of the dead bird.

Stop seeing the lawman.

There was no way that was going to happen. Nobody and nothing was going to make her stop seeing Luke. She definitely didn't intend to obey some creep who had killed a poor bird and left her the note. Still, a new fear rushed through her. Did this mean Luke might be in danger?

Apparently, the person had been watching them to know she and Luke were spending a lot of time together. Dammit, who was doing this to her? Luke had told her Daniel had interviewed all the men who she'd named. None of them had a real solid alibi for the time of the last attack on her so any one of them could be guilty or all of them could be innocent.

She finally got up from the sofa and grabbed her groceries. She needed to get the ice and pork chops into the cooler. Once she'd taken care of that, she carried her clothing bag into her bedroom.

It was time for her to get her clothes changed and start cooking. She pulled on the new loungewear and then brushed her hair and put on a little mascara and then went out the back door to start her generator.

She stood for a few minutes on her deck, trying not to think about the note and the poor dead bird. Somehow in her mind, since over a week had passed with nothing happening, she'd hoped the person who'd tried to kidnap her had given up.

However, now she knew he hadn't given up. He'd been watching her movements, and apparently, he felt threatened by Luke's presence in her life.

She'd been afraid before. Now she was even more frightened. There was no question somebody was still after her, now making demands and watching her and waiting... waiting for the perfect opportunity to make her his own.

AS LUKE DROVE toward the swamp's entrance, he felt great. Tonight, he'd decided to wear a pair of black dress slacks with a green-and-black short-sleeved dress shirt. He had his surveillance clothes in a bag to change into later.

He'd decided to dress up a little because tonight was a special occasion—Dominique was cooking for him and she was even feeding him on his time, at six o'clock. Oh, she'd cooked bacon and eggs for him, but this just felt special and so he'd decided to dress up a bit.

The past week and a half had flown by. They'd gone out every night to follow Pierre. Unfortunately, he still hadn't dug up the missing client book.

Equally frustrating was the fact that Daniel and his men hadn't been able to pin down the man who had left the note and tried to kidnap Dominique. Still, he was grateful that no other attempts had been made on her and in that it had been a fairly peaceful ten days.

After today, his vacation time was over. He'd spoken with Daniel earlier in the day and they had decided he'd come in to work at nine-thirty in the mornings and work until four-thirty.

It was going to be difficult to work and still be there for Dominique during the nights, but he was really hoping he could talk her into stopping the nightly trips through the swamp. They'd been surveilling for over two weeks now without any success.

He reached the swamp's entrance and parked. He had stopped by the café earlier and had picked up a peach pie for dessert. In one of their many conversations she had mentioned she loved peach pie.

He grabbed the pie from the passenger seat and then picked up the bag containing his black jeans and black T-shirt. He then headed in, a rich anticipation rushing through him.

He was now quite familiar with the paths that would take him to her shanty. He walked quickly and it didn't take him long to reach her place.

He stopped short at the sight of a dead bird in front of her door. What the hell? Had the poor thing flown into the door and broke its neck? He knew occasionally birds might fly into a window, but a door?

A sense of dread filled him as he stepped over the bird and knocked on the door. "Dominique, it's me," he called out.

The lock disengaged and she opened the door. She looked positively stunning in a red outfit. The top hugged her breasts and showed off her slender build while the pants swirled around her long, shapely legs. Her hair was loose, but the smile she offered him appeared a bit forced.

"You look absolutely beautiful," he said.

"Thanks, you clean up nicely yourself," she replied. She

opened the door wider to allow him entry and then closed and locked the door behind them.

"I come bearing a gift. It's a peach pie." He held it out to her.

"Thank you. This is very thoughtful of you." She took it from him and then led him to the kitchen, where she placed it in the center of the table.

"I couldn't help but notice the poor bird," he said as he sat in one of the chairs at the table.

"Yeah, I'm hoping maybe you could get rid of it for me, but we can talk about all that after dinner," she replied.

"Something sure smells good," he said. The air was redolent with the scent of cooking meat.

"That will be your dinner. We have smothered pork chops, crispy fried potatoes and honey-drizzled carrots. We also have corn bread with honey."

"Wow, that all sounds absolutely delicious," he replied. "Way better than a meal in a box that you zap in the microwave for five minutes."

She moved in front of a skillet on the electric burners. "It will be on the table at precisely six o'clock so you have about ten minutes to wait." She flashed a quick smile over her shoulder.

Despite the smile, he sensed a tension radiating from her, a tension he believed didn't have anything to do with her cooking dinner. Was it because of the dead bird? Or was he just imagining something that wasn't there?

The ten minutes passed fast as they small-talked about their days. She told him about shopping at All That Jazz and he talked about a book he'd been reading.

"If you'll hand me your plate, I'll fill it," she said.

He picked up the plate in front of him and gave it to her.

The table was already set with a platter of golden corn bread, butter and a bear-shaped bottle of honey.

She filled his plate with one of the chops, a healthy serving of the diced, crispy potatoes and the carrots. Once his plate was on the table, she filled her own and then sank down across from him.

"Dig in while it's hot," she said.

"It all looks delicious," he replied.

"Let's just hope it tastes delicious, too."

It took him only a couple of bites to assure her that everything was delectable. For a few minutes they ate in a comfortable silence. That was one of the things he liked about her—silence didn't intimidate or bother her.

When they were about halfway through the meal, they continued with their small talk. She offered him a second pork chop, but he was too stuffed to even consider it.

"I hope you saved room for a piece of your peach pie," she said when they finished eating.

"Maybe I'll have a piece a little later. Right now, I'm just too full," he replied. He still felt like something was slightly off with her this evening, but he figured if something was going on, she'd tell him in her own time.

Perhaps it was the dead bird. It had to have been shocking for her to discover it on her doorstep. Before he left here tonight, he would use a paper towel or something to move the bird from her door to someplace in the swamp.

"At least let me help with the cleanup," he said once they had finished eating.

"The best way you can help me is to stay out of my way. Just sit there and look pretty," she replied.

He laughed. "I'll sit here, but I don't know about the looking pretty part."

He watched as she efficiently cleared the table and then

washed the dishes using a large bottle of water and detergent. It always amazed him when he saw how the people who lived in the swamp had adapted to a life with little electricity and no running water.

"Have you ever thought about moving into town where you would have the convenience of a refrigerator and a dishwasher?" he asked.

"Sometimes it crosses my mind," she replied. She placed the last clean dish in the drainer and then they moved into the living room and sat on the sofa.

"I think more about it now, since Angelique has moved into town," she said, continuing the conversation. "She loves it, and I'm not sure if the appeal is because Daniel is there or that she can now take long, leisurely showers and use a dishwasher."

Luke laughed. "Maybe it's a combination of all of that. I will say it's nice to see Daniel so happy."

"Same with Angelique."

"I have a feeling Daniel is planning on proposing to her very soon, and I also have a feeling there will be a wedding before the end of the year," Luke said. "I'm curious," he continued. "When you get married, which sister will be your maid of honor?"

"Hopefully, by the time I get married Angelique is already married, then I'd have her stand with me as a matron of honor and Monique would be my maid of honor."

"Good decision," he replied. "Uh… I don't know if you realize it or not, but today is the last day of my vacation time."

She frowned. "Then you won't be available anymore to be my bodyguard during the nights."

"Daniel and I have worked my hours out so that I can still be here for you at night," he assured her. "Although I wish you'd stop the nightly stalking. Seriously, Dominique, tell me the truth. Aren't you growing tired of doing it?"

Her frown grew deeper, indicating a deep anguish. "But, my mother—"

"Wouldn't want you out doing this," he said, cutting her off.

She released a big sigh. "I'll admit I'm a bit tired of it, but if I don't do it, then how are you all going to prove Pierre is guilty?" Her doe-like eyes gazed at him intently.

God, he wished he had a good answer for her, but he didn't. "I don't know the answer to that right now," he admitted.

"I saw Jacque LeBlanc at the grocery store today, and I wondered if maybe it would be a good idea if we talked to him. Rumor has it he knows things about what goes on in the swamp. Maybe he knows something about the attacks on me."

"If he knows anything definitive, I believe he would have already come forward. Daniel and I spoke to him before about your mother's murder, but if you think it might be helpful, you and I could go to speak to him again about what's happening with you." He moved a little closer to her, wanting to be as supportive as possible.

She released a deep, heavy sigh. "Right now, I have more important things on my mind."

"Like what?" He reached out and took her hand in his. "Dominique, I've noticed you haven't quite been your sparkly self tonight."

Her fingers tightened around his for a long moment and then she pulled away and stood. "The dead bird wasn't the only thing left at my door this afternoon."

As she walked over to the bookcase, his heart thudded into the pit of his stomach. She grabbed a piece of paper just like the last note that had been left on her door and then rejoined him on the sofa and handed it to him.

STOP SEEING THE LAWMAN. YOU BELONG TO ME.

"Dammit, who is this bastard." He exploded with frustration.

"I don't know who he is, but he can't tell me what to do and I'm not about to stop seeing you whether we stop our nightly stalking or not." Her stubborn chin rose upward. "I'll see you as often as I want as long as you want to see me, too."

While that part of the note concerned him, far more concerning were the words *you belong to me*. It was a reminder that somebody out there wanted her and still posed a very real danger to her.

"Could this mean that you're in danger?" Once again, her gaze was intense as it held his.

"Don't you worry about me," he replied firmly. "I can take care of myself. I'll take the note with me when I leave and we'll check it for prints," he said.

"And you know there probably won't be any on it," she replied. "I'll go get a baggie." She got up and went into the kitchen and returned a moment later with the baggie in hand. He slipped the paper inside it and then set it back down.

"We'll check the alibis of all the men on our suspect list and see who has an alibi for this afternoon. Maybe that will help us shorten the list a bit."

She blew out another deep sigh. "I can't imagine what I've done to get the attention of this person. Have I been too flirtatious with the men in the café? I thought it was just all in good fun."

"Dominique, don't blame yourself for this, and I've

watched you and listened to you with your regular customers at the café and you don't do or say anything out of line with them," he replied firmly.

She once again reached out and took his hand in hers. "I swear, I don't know what I'd do without you right now, Luke."

He smiled. "I have a feeling you'd be just fine. You're not only a beautiful woman, Dominique, but you're also smart and incredibly strong."

A small laugh escaped her. "I'm not feeling so strong these days."

"You've been through a lot and here you are, still standing." He hoped she heard his admiration in his voice.

"I don't feel like standing right now. I think maybe I'll just stay in tonight and not torture you with a dark traipse through the marsh. In fact, even though it's relatively early, I think I'm ready to call it a day. Do you mind?"

"How can I mind? I got a great dinner and good conversation out of the evening." He stood and grabbed the note from the coffee table. "Are you sure you'll be all right?"

"I'll be fine. I'm on the breakfast shift in the morning so I'm just going to go to bed," she replied as she also got up from the sofa and walked with him to the front door.

He opened the door and then turned back to gaze at her. She looked tired. He raised a hand and cupped her cheek. She turned her head into the caress.

As the nights had passed, he'd tried not to touch her except for occasionally holding her hand as his desire to have her again still bubbled hot inside him, but he was determined not to make love with her again.

He finally removed his hand from her. "Since you're working the morning shift, I'll come in and eat breakfast. So, I'll just see you then," he said. He hated to leave her, but she hadn't asked him to stay and in any case, he shouldn't spend the night with her again. It would be far too big of a temptation to make another mistake. "Thanks for the delicious dinner."

"You're welcome. I wouldn't mind cooking for you again sometime soon, and now I'll just say good-night," she replied.

"Good night, Dominique." With that, he went out the door and nearly stepped on the dead bird. Dominique closed and locked the door behind him.

He'd grabbed a paper towel after dinner and he now pulled it from his pocket and bent down to pick up the dead bird. He gently scooped the poor thing up and carried it down the bridge.

He'd decided not to return the bird to the swamp. He would take it into the police station in the morning. It, along with the note, was evidence in Dominique's assault case. Pictures would be taken and then the bird would be disposed of.

When he reached his car, he placed the note and the bird on his passenger seat and then headed home. As he drove, his thoughts were scattered.

Stop seeing the lawman.

Was it possible the perp would come after him? Luke didn't think so. Whoever the man was, he was a damned coward, frightening a woman with notes and now the dead bird.

Was Dominique safe alone in her shanty? He knew the locks on her two doors were good and sturdy. They had both been changed after the attack on Angelique.

The windows would also be difficult to reach as most of them looked over the deck, which would be hard for anyone to access as the back door was the only way to get to the deck.

He believed she was as safe as she could be there, otherwise he would have been there for her full-time.

The events of the night played through him mind. She had looked so beautiful tonight in her red outfit. Still, he had hated the dark haunting that had been evident in the depths of her eyes.

He desperately wanted to fix things for her. He wanted Pierre under arrest for the murder of her mother. He needed to find the person who had attacked her with the intent to kidnap her. He wanted to fix her world so badly it ached inside his chest.

It was at that exact moment he realized he was deeply in love with Dominique Santori. He had no idea exactly when it had happened. He had believed he was keeping a healthy distance between them. But the truth of the matter was he had fallen hard for her.

His sudden awareness of his feelings for her shot a wave of warmth through him. The warmth only lasted a minute and then the reality of the situation washed a wave of cold despondency over him.

First of all, she hadn't indicated in any way that she was in love with him. Even if she was, it wouldn't matter. They weren't made for each other. He wasn't even sure he could live with her full-time.

He would be there for her if she wanted to continue with her nightly stalking of Pierre, and he would be there for her as she faced the threat of some creep who wanted her.

However, it was time he begin to emotionally distance himself from her. Already, he felt his heart breaking but the truth of the matter was he'd fallen in love with the wrong woman.

Chapter Ten

For the next three nights, Dominique stayed in and didn't go out to follow Pierre. That also meant she hadn't seen Luke for three nights. She had insisted he stay home and get some extra rest since he was now back on full duty with the police force.

The only place she was without her knife was when she was in the café working or when she was at home. She'd had several awkward conversations with her regulars, who had been questioned not only about the attack on her, but also about the day the note and dead bird had appeared at her door.

All of the men had claimed their innocence and they were appalled that she would even entertain the idea for one minute that they were guilty. Somebody was lying or the perp was somebody not even on her radar. And somehow, that was even more frightening.

Her days and nights were filled with a simmering fear, wondering when she might be attacked again. The only person she trusted completely was Luke, and tonight she was cooking for him once again.

She'd missed his company over the past three nights. She'd grown so accustomed to having him there to fill the hours of her evenings. She'd missed his laughter and the way he could make her laugh. She'd also missed their conversations about anything and everything.

She'd worked the morning shift and then stopped in the grocery store to pick up a few items. When she got back home, she was grateful there was no note on her door and nothing left on her doorstep. She'd packed her groceries away and then had taken a short—but nice—shower.

By the time she dressed in a pair of jeans and the new emerald green blouse she'd bought at All That Jazz, it was time to get into the kitchen and start preparing dinner.

On the menu tonight was fried fish, a broccoli rice, and a cucumber and tomato salad. She also intended to make skillet corn bread once again as Luke had loved it the last time she'd made it.

If she were honest with herself, she'd admit that she was hoping she could talk Luke into staying the night. As the days had passed, she'd yearned to be in his arms once again.

She wanted to feel his naked body against hers and make slow, sweet love with him. Then afterward she wanted to fall asleep in his arms as she knew that was the only place she truly felt safe and secure.

She knew Luke wanted her again, too. It was in his eyes when he gazed at her for any length of time. She felt it in his simplest of touches. The physical chemistry between them was still off-the-charts strong.

Eventually, it would all have to come to an end. If she decided to stop following Pierre, then there would be no more reason for Luke to come over each night. After the last three nights of not being out in the swamp, she was now reluctant to continue going out.

She'd come to the realization that catching Pierre digging up the missing book was a very long shot. As much as she wanted to see him behind bars for her mother's murder, she no longer believed she was the one who could get the evidence.

She wasn't a quitter, but she also wasn't ignorant. Besides, she was tired of spending hours of her nighttime, when she could be sleeping or reading a good book, watching a man who did nothing but fish and hunt gators.

In fact, tonight would be her goodbye to Luke. She knew he would continue to work on discovering who had tried to kidnap her, but he would no longer need to be her bodyguard at night.

He would probably be relieved. He would be able to go back to his regular hours and routine. The idea of no longer seeing him in the evenings broke her heart just a little bit, but releasing him from his bodyguard duties was the right thing to do.

She knew Luke wanted to find a special woman who would be his wife, but how could he find that woman with Dominique taking up all his nights? She realized now she'd been selfish. In her quest to catch her mother's killer, she hadn't thought about how much she had affected Luke's life.

She tried to push all her thoughts out of her head as she got busy preparing the evening meal. At ten to six, a knock fell on her door and she knew it was Luke.

He identified himself and then she unlocked and opened the door. As always, her heart fluttered a bit at the sight of him. He was clad in a pair of jeans and a dark green polo that emphasized his bright green eyes.

His slightly shaggy dark hair gleamed with rich highlights and she immediately wanted to dance her fingers through the silky strands. The scent of his delicious cologne radiated out from him and enveloped her with a sense of familiarity and comfort.

"I see you got the memo to wear green," she said as she led him to the kitchen.

"Great minds think alike," he replied with one of his gorgeous grins.

"Have a seat," she said. "Dinner will be ready in five minutes."

"Good thing I brought my appetite because everything smells really good." He sank into the chair he'd sat in the last time she'd made dinner for him. "So, how was your day?"

"Nothing exciting or troubling happened, so in that aspect it was a good day."

"That's what I like to hear," he replied.

"What about you?" She turned from the stovetop to look at him. "How was your day?"

"It was okay," he replied.

She turned back to the stove where everything was ready to serve. Instead of placing the plates on the table, she had them on the counter next to her.

The butter and honey and corn bread were already on the table, as was the cucumber and tomato salad. The fish was golden brown and she put several of the bigger pieces on his plate, along with a large serving of the broccoli rice.

"This all looks amazing," he said as she placed the plate in front of him.

She filled her own plate and then joined him at the table. "Eat up while it's warm," she said.

"You don't need to tell me twice," he replied and then used his fork to cut into a piece of the fish.

"Feel free to use your fingers. This is a manner-free zone."

He shot her another one of his dazzling grins, set down his fork and then picked up the fish by his fingers. Oh, she was going to miss that boyish grin of his.

The conversation was light and easy as they ate. He entertained her with more stories of when he had first become a police officer, making her laugh over and over again.

They finished the meal and she cleaned up the mess, then they moved into the living room where they both sat on the sofa. "So, are we going out into the swamp tonight?" he asked.

"No, and I'm ready to give up on spying on Pierre," she replied.

He sat up straighter and looked at her in surprise. "What made you decide to stop?"

"I just realized how futile it is. Like you told me before we even started following him. I could watch him for months and he might never dig up the book." She shifted her position, bringing her a bit closer to him. "I don't want to waste any more of my time, but I especially don't want to waste any more of yours. I've been quite selfish in using you as my bodyguard."

"There isn't a selfish bone in your body," he replied in protest. "You were just hurting and frustrated, but never selfish."

"I'm still hurting and frustrated, but I'm also tired of traipsing through the swamp on the off chance we'll get lucky."

He took her hand in his, his eyes glittering like bright emeralds. "I promise you we will get justice for your mother and that we'll find the creep who is after you."

She squeezed his hand and smiled. "You're a very nice man, Luke Madison."

"I try to be," he replied and then released her hand. He studied her for a long moment. "I guess this means I won't be seeing as much of you."

"You can now spend your evenings looking for that special woman you want in your life," she replied, surprised by a small pang of sadness that resonated inside her. She told herself it was just because he'd been such a big part of her world. Habit. He was a habit that it was time she break.

"Just because we aren't going into the swamp at night doesn't mean I can't occasionally invite you to lunch or dinner at the café," he replied.

"And I suppose I wouldn't mind occasionally cooking dinner for you," she added. There was no reason why she had to go completely cold turkey and never spend any time with him again.

He smiled at her. It was a soft smile that sparkled in the gold shards of his eyes and shot an unexpected warmth into her heart. "Then we'll still see each other," he said.

"Since this is kind of our last official night together, do you want to spend the night?" she asked. She stared at him intently, wanting this one last night with him.

He sat back on the sofa, a pained expression on his features. "Dominique, we both know that's not a good idea."

"It would just be a final, casual hookup," she replied, hoping to entice him into staying. "It doesn't have to mean anything."

"It's still not a good idea," he replied.

Disappointment rushed through her. She had so hoped to have one last time in his arms, but obviously he wasn't keen about it and she certainly wasn't going to beg.

"So, what does your work schedule look like for the rest of the week?" he asked.

They small-talked for another half an hour or so, but

things suddenly felt awkward between them. She felt as if they were two strangers making nice with each other instead of friends who had spent an inordinate amount of time together. It was almost a relief when he indicated it was time for him to leave.

She walked with him to the door, disappointment mingling with sadness inside her. "Luke, thank you. I've truly appreciated everything you've done for me," she said.

"No need to thank me. I've enjoyed my time with you," he replied. "If you ever think about going back out there to follow Pierre, I want you to call me and I'll come to be your bodyguard."

She forced a smile and then released a small laugh. "Why do I feel like I'll never see you again when we live in a little town and I'll probably see you tomorrow."

He grinned at her. It was that charming smile that she'd always loved. "You're right, you'll probably see me tomorrow. Now that I know you're working the mid-shift, I intend to eat my lunch in your section. I'll complain about the food and the service and I'll leave you a five percent tip," he said, repeating his fake threats.

She couldn't help but laugh. "You are such a goofball."

He reached up as if to cup her cheek, but dropped his hand back to his side and instead opened the door. "Good night, Dominique," he said as he turned back to her. "You know I'm here for you. As I've told you before, if something happens that frightens or concerns you, then call me."

"I will. Good night, Luke."

He disappeared out the door and she closed and locked it behind him. She went back to the sofa and collapsed into the corner.

The fact that he'd turned down the offer to stay the night

with her, to be intimate again with her made her realize that it was possible she really had only been a job to him.

Sure, they'd been intimate the one time, but maybe he'd only slept with her because he was curious and wanted to explore his physical desire for her. He'd satisfied his curiosity and now he was done with that aspect of their relationship.

A wave of unexpected sadness swept through her. She hadn't expected it would be so difficult to tell him goodbye. But now it was done and it was time she think about her future.

Maybe it was time she started dating. Maybe it was time for her to agree to go out with some of the men who had invited her out over the past few months. One of them could be the man of her dreams…the one who would give her children and a happily-ever-after.

If she was ever going to find a husband, the only way she could do it was to begin dating again. Would Luke start dating now that his evenings belonged to himself again?

She knew he wanted to find that special woman, the one who would fit into his life of routine and structure. She could only wish him well because more than anything she wanted to see Luke happy.

GUTTED, LUKE SAT in his car, not yet ready to drive home. He stared at the swamp entrance, now barely discernable with the darkness of night falling.

While he had wanted her to agree to stop going out in the swamp chasing after Pierre, he was now faced with the realization that he would no longer be spending his evenings with her. Even though he knew it was for the best, that didn't stop the heartache that rode with him as he finally started his car and began the drive home.

When she'd asked him to stay the night, he'd been so tempted to agree. He would have loved to hold her in his arms once again, to taste the sweet heat of her lips and to make love with her one last time.

It had been his overwhelming love for her that had stopped him. He'd recognized that he didn't want another memory of her to keep him mourning her and his ill-fated love. It had been that, plus the fact that she'd said it would just be casual. He couldn't do casual anymore with her.

He'd been a fool to let her get so far into his heart. He should have protected himself more. She'd never indicated to him that their relationship was anything other than casual for her.

It was time now that he move on with his life and somehow, someway get over loving Dominique. He had a feeling that was going to be a difficult thing to do.

By the time he got home, he was exhausted. It was a mental tiredness coupled with the heavy weight of his heart. He would miss their conversations and their shared laughter. He would miss the very scent of her and the way her facial features displayed her every emotion.

That night, it took him a very long time to fall asleep, and when he did sleep, he fell into dreams of dancing in the rain with her.

He awakened early and for the first time in a long time he was at the police station early. It was just after seven when he walked into the murder room where Clay and Daniel were already seated.

Both men looked at him in surprise. "Hey, Luke. You're here early this morning," Daniel said.

"Yeah, Dominique didn't go out in the swamp last night so I got home at a decent time." He sank down in the chair between the two men. "In fact, she's decided she's done stalking Pierre."

"Really? Well, that's really good news," Daniel replied. "If it's true. Are you sure she's really done?"

"Yeah, I'm sure," Luke said.

"Well, that's one less thing for us to worry about and I get back one of my best officers. A win-win situation as far as I'm concerned." Daniel took a sip from his coffee cup.

"We've got plenty of other things to worry about," Clay said. "Like finding the creep who's after her and getting some evidence so we can make an arrest in Mystique's murder."

"I still don't know how we're going to get any evidence to prove Pierre's guilt beyond a reasonable doubt." Daniel frowned.

"Somehow, someway, something is going to break in the case," Clay said optimistically. "Maybe Pierre will get drunk one night with his fishing buddies and he'll let something slip."

"We can only hope something like that happens," Daniel replied.

"Right now, I'm more concerned about Dominique's safety." Even saying her name aloud ached in Luke's heart.

"Too bad we haven't been able to pin down solid alibis with all the potential suspects she gave us," Daniel said, his frown cutting across his forehead. "It would be nice if we could at least rule out some of those men."

"What I worry about is that none of them are guilty and the perp is somebody not even on our radar," Luke replied.

"We just have to keep working the case and see what pops up," Daniel said.

"I don't want to wish anything bad on Dominique, but it would almost be helpful if the perp left another note or something for her," Clay said. "Maybe the next time he'll get sloppy and leave me some nice prints."

"As long as it's just a note or something like that. Of course, my biggest concern is that there will be another kidnapping attempt and this time he'll be successful." The very idea of that tightened all of Luke's stomach muscles and made him half sick. "So, what's on today's agenda?"

Daniel released a deep sigh. "We do our usual patrol. Keep your eyes and ears open for any information that might help in either of the cases. Then, why don't we plan to meet back here right before lunch time."

All three of them stood. While Daniel headed down the hallway toward his office, Luke and Clay headed out the back door.

"It's going to be nice to have you back here where you belong," Clay said.

"Thanks. I have to admit, I'm glad to be back in my regular routine," Luke replied. Routines he clung to…routines that assured he would never be the right man for Dominique.

In the mornings, Luke was usually on foot patrol. He headed down a very quiet Main Street. It was too early for the stores to be open and so the sidewalks were void of people.

The only place where there was any activity at all was the café, where already cars were parked as people went in to enjoy an early breakfast.

Dominique wouldn't be there yet. He knew from talking to her last night that she was working the mid-shift. Was his plan to eat lunch at the café today because he was hungry for the food? Or was he just hungry to see her again?

By nine o'clock, Main Street began to fill up as shoppers arrived and stores opened. Luke greeted the people he met as he walked. He stopped and went into the feed-store, where he visited for a few minutes with the owner, Ben Jackson.

He always tried to stop in some of the stores and speak with the owners or whoever was working. It was part of Daniel's plan to keep relations good between the police department and the business owners.

As he stepped out of the store, he ran into Nola Fontenot. "Good morning, Officer Madison," she greeted him cheerfully.

"Morning, Nola. How are you doing on this fine day?"

"Oh, I'm doing okay. Of course, I'm just waiting for you all to do your job and get that murderer Pierre Guidry under arrest."

"We're doing the best we can," Luke replied.

She cast him a sly smile. "I understand you've been spending a lot of time with Dominique."

Luke's heart squeezed tight. "Yeah, I was helping her out with an issue, but now that issue is resolved and so I won't be seeing that much of her."

"Oh, that's too bad, I know how much she was enjoying spending time with you," Nola replied. "You know, I've known the Santori women since they were babies. They are a fine bunch and now that Mystique is gone, I think of those girls as my very own."

"I know how close you were—are—to all of them," Luke said.

"Well, I'd better be on my way. I have a few errands to run and I always like to be back in my shanty during the heat of the day."

"I'll see you later, Nola." He watched as the plump woman headed on down the sidewalk. He was glad she'd moved on, for talking to her only reminded him of Dominique.

The morning passed uneventfully and at eleven thirty, he returned to the police station. It was difficult for him to think that tonight he wouldn't cross Dominique's bridge with the sweet anticipation of seeing her again.

He met Daniel and Clay in the break room. "How about we all head to the café for lunch?" Daniel suggested, as if reading Luke's mind.

"Sounds good to me," Clay said agreeably.

"Me too."

"So, did either of you encounter any trouble on your morning patrols?" Daniel asked once they were in his car and headed down the street to the café.

"I spoke to Nola, who once again berated us for not doing our job and getting Pierre under arrest," Luke said.

"And I wrote out a speeding ticket to Alex Whitmeyer. I clocked him going seventy miles an hour on Magnolia Drive, where the speed limit is fifty-five," Clay said. "The little snot told me his parents would speak to the prosecuting attorney and he wouldn't have to pay the fine and wouldn't be in any trouble."

Daniel snorted. "That kid thinks just because his parents have money, no rules apply to him."

"That's all I've got to report," Clay said.

"That's it for me, too," Luke added.

By that time, they'd reached the café. Luke saw her the moment they walked in. As always, she looked stunning in the pink T-shirt and jeans that was her uniform when at work. She was waiting on an older couple Luke didn't know.

Daniel chose a booth in her section and they all settled in. Luke didn't know why anxiety filled him at the prospect of just ordering his lunch from her. After all, he had just seen her the night before.

Then she was there, smiling at them all and his heart expanded with his love for her. "Hi, Luke," she said, her beautiful chocolate eyes lingering on him for a long moment.

"Hey, Dominique," he replied.

She took their orders and then left their booth. She returned with their drinks and then a few minutes later with their food.

As they ate, the discussion was about things going on in town. A fall festival was planned in another month. It was a day when the streets filled with people. Not only did the stores run sidewalk sales, but local artists and craftsmen would sell their wares as well.

While they talked and ate, Luke couldn't help but look at Dominique again and again. In spite of his personal feelings for her, she was a joy to watch as she smiled or laughed with the customers she served.

Was the person who had written her the notes and tried to kidnap her in the café right now? Luke's stomach muscles tightened as he did a slow glance around the room. There was only one of the regulars she'd named there.

Jacob Benoit sat alone at a two-top. The fisherman had been interviewed concerning his whereabouts on the dates in question. His alibi had been like the others. He'd been in his shanty alone at the times of the attack and when the notes had been left.

They finished eating and then headed back to the station. On the short drive back, Luke decided that was the last meal he'd eat in the café for a while. It was just too painful to see her and know she didn't love him.

He realized he wanted—he—needed to keep busy.

He desperately needed his mind focused on other things. Whenever there was a quiet moment, his head filled with thoughts of Dominique, and the heartbreak would come crashing down on his head all over again.

They had just gotten back and settled in the murder room when Gus called from the front desk. "I got a man here who wants to talk to the person in charge of the Santori murder."

The three men looked at each other. Was it possible that finally this was the break they'd been waiting for? Could the man tie Pierre to the murder scene? Had Pierre finally made a mistake and talked to somebody about the murder?

"Send him to my office," Daniel said as he stood. He hung up the phone. "You two come with me. Let's hear what this man has to tell us."

The three of them hurried up the hall to Daniel's office, where Daniel sat behind his desk. Luke and Clay stood against the wall, leaving the chair in front of the desk for the new visitor.

They all had just settled in place when a knock fell on the door. Clay opened it and a tall man Luke had never seen before entered.

Daniel stood and held out his hand. "I'm Chief of Police, Daniel LeCroix, and these are two of my officers, Luke Madison and Clay Caldwell."

The man grabbed hold of Daniel's hand and shook it. "Lucien Rousseau is my name and I'm a fisherman by trade."

"Please, have a seat, Mr. Rousseau." Daniel gestured to the chair before him.

Lucien Rousseau looked to be in his mid-forties. His long dark hair was tied back at the nape of his neck and his features were bold and well weathered. He was also missing one of his front teeth.

"I understand you might have some information that would help in solving the murder of Mystique Santori."

"I do."

"Is this something you heard or learned recently?"

"No, I've known about it for months," Lucien replied.

"Might I ask what took you so long to come in?" Daniel asked.

"A couple months ago I got a gig on an offshore fishing boat. The work was hard but the pay was good. I just got back to my shanty yesterday and got caught up with all the swamp gossip."

They spoke for a couple of minutes about the name of the offshore boat and exactly who had employed Lucien. Daniel asked him several questions concerning his employment.

"Enough about me." Lucien suddenly leaned forward in the chair. "I heard you're wanting to put Pierre Guidry away for killing Mystique."

"We definitely believe he's guilty of her murder," Daniel said.

"Well, you're wrong. You're all wrong. He didn't kill Mystique. He's not guilty," Lucien finished flatly. Luke felt as if the bottom of his stomach fell out at the man's words.

"H-how do you know he isn't guilty?" Daniel asked, obviously stunned by the man's words.

"Because on the night and time she was murdered, I saw him fishing in the honey hole he thinks is a big secret. He keeps a pirogue there hidden under some brush. Sometimes, when he goes out in the pirogue to hunt the big gator he wants to catch, I fish off the bank there."

"Are you sure you saw him on the right night?" Daniel asked.

"Positive, because when I woke the next morning, I heard the Voodoo Queen was dead and then I left to get on the fishing boat." Lucien flashed his dark eyes to each one of them. "I got no friendship with Guidry and no reason to come in here except I don't want to see an innocent man go to jail for a murder he didn't commit. Pierre isn't your man and that's all I got to say."

Abruptly he stood. "And now it's time for me to go. I got a wife who is mad I stayed out and away from home for so long and kids clamoring to spend some time with me. If you got more questions for me, you can find me at my shanty in the swamp."

On that note, he opened the door and stepped out and then closed the door behind him. For a long moment, a stunned silence reigned among the three of them.

"Did you believe him?" Luke finally broke the silence.

"I'm not sure," Daniel replied slowly.

"If he's right, then we're no closer to solving the murder than we were on the night it happened," Clay said dismally.

"Before we jump to any conclusions, we need to thoroughly check out Lucien's story," Daniel said. "Clay, why don't you look into the offshore fishing boat. See if you can find out when he was hired and when he left the boat."

"Got it," Clay said.

"And Luke, why don't you head into the swamp and see what you can find out about the relationship between Guidry and Lucien," Daniel continued. "Talk to George and any other men you come across. If it turns out that Lucien and Pierre are close, then I'll be less likely to believe this new alibi for Pierre."

"And if they aren't close?" Luke's question hung in the air.

Daniel released a deep sigh. "Then we'll have to face the fact that we might have been chasing the wrong man for the murder."

Luke felt as if the entire world was exploding apart. The murder they believed they had solved was no longer a sure thing, and he'd fallen deeply in love with a woman he knew he couldn't live with and who didn't love him back.

HE WAS READY. He was so ready to make her his own. Even though he had only communicated with her so far with the notes he'd left for her, she obviously cared about him, too. She'd stopped seeing the lawman, just like he'd told her to do. That proved to him that she wanted to please him.

Every time he saw her, she half stole his breath with her beauty. She was cheerful and lively and that's what he needed, that's what his house needed.

Once she was here where she belonged, there would be no more loneliness for him, no more grief to deal with. Her bright energy would fill up all the dark places in his house, and more importantly, all the dark places in his heart.

He needed her and he was ready to take her again. Only this time it wouldn't matter if she had a knife. Once he pierced her skin with the injection he had ready, there would be no fight. She would fall into his arms and he would bring her here, to be his forever more.

Now it was just a matter of waiting for the right time and place. He would find that right time very, very soon. And he couldn't wait. A sweet anticipation rushed through his body.

Soon, she would finally be his and his alone, and with enough time he would make her love him. Oh yes, all his dreams were about to come true. The beautiful Dominique would be his. She would fulfill the promises that had been broken by another. She would be his through eternity.

Chapter Eleven

Dominique sat with her two sisters on the sofa in her shanty, waiting for Daniel to arrive with an update on their mother's case.

It was the first time he'd called them all together and all three of them were hopeful that Daniel was bringing them good news. Of course, the best news of all would be that they had found the evidence they needed to get Pierre behind bars.

She was hungry for something good to happen. Since Luke had walked out of her house two nights before, she had been filled with a sadness she didn't understand and couldn't quite shake.

She missed Luke desperately. He'd taken a big piece of her heart with him and had left behind an aching emptiness she certainly hadn't expected.

Angelique now looked at Dominique. "You've certainly been quiet this evening."

"Yeah, you haven't been your normal bubbly self tonight," Monique added.

"I'm just tired. I didn't sleep well last night and then I worked the early shift this morning," Dominique replied.

"You haven't mentioned your nightly stalking of Pierre lately," Angelique observed.

"That's because I gave it up a few nights ago," she replied.

"Thank the lord," Monique replied and placed a soft hand on Dominique's. "I was so worried about you when you were doing that at night. Even taking Luke with you didn't make me feel much better about it."

"I felt completely safe with Luke by my side," she said. Again, a pang of sadness shot off in her. What was wrong with her? Why couldn't she straighten out her emotions? "Didn't Daniel give you an idea about why he wanted to meet with us?" she asked Angelique.

"No, he didn't. He just called me at the store and told me to meet him here," she replied. There it was…that love she had for her boyfriend so rich in her tone.

Dominique wanted that for herself, but she didn't feel like dating at the moment. Still, how was she ever going to find her person if she spent all her evenings alone in her shanty?

A knock fell on the door and Dominique hurried to answer it. Not only was it Daniel, but Luke and Clay were with him, as well.

Luke looked wonderfully handsome in his blue uniform, but she refused to let her gaze linger on him. She missed him so much. Her life just wasn't the same without him in it.

"Gentlemen, have a seat," she said. She gestured to the chair across from the sofa and then hurried into the kitchen to grab two more chairs.

Clay met her halfway and took the chairs from her and carried them into the living room. "My love, what's up?" Angelique asked once everyone was seated.

"We've had a new development in your mother's murder case," Daniel said.

"A new development?" Dominique leaned forward, eager to hear the news. She kept her gaze fixed on Daniel. Maybe this was what they'd all been waiting for. Maybe they'd finally arrested Pierre.

Daniel frowned. "Unfortunately, somebody has come forward to alibi Pierre for the night and time of the murder."

Dominique stared at him, as if he'd suddenly begun speaking a foreign language. She leaned back against the sofa, stunned by this unexpected news.

"What are you talking about?" Angelique asked.

"Who's come forward and why now after all this time?" Monique asked.

Dominique looked at Luke as the floor beneath her feet fell out from under her. How she wished she could be in his arms right now as the world tilted and half dizzied her.

"The man's name is Lucien Rousseau," Daniel said. "Do any of you know him?"

They all shook their heads and listened as Daniel told him about the man working on an offshore fishing boats since the day after the murder until yesterday when he'd come in to speak to them.

"I looked into his story about spending time on the offshore boat. I spoke to the captain of the boat, who confirmed Lucien's story," Clay said.

"And I checked out the relationship between Lucien and Pierre and from everything I heard, the two men didn't have much of a personal relationship," Luke added.

"Therefore, we have no reason not to believe Lucien's story that he saw Pierre out at his fishing hole on the date and time of your mother's murder," Daniel said.

"So that means you all are back to square one," Dominique said in deep frustration. How many hours of her life had been wasted foolishly shadowing an innocent man? Still, she couldn't regret that time, for it had given her Luke for a little while.

"Are there any new suspects in the case?" Monique asked.

"None, but we're going to get there. I swear to God I'll find the person responsible for Mystique's murder," Daniel said fervently.

Dominique knew he meant well, but now there was no real suspect in the case and justice for her mother might never come. Again, her grief welled up inside her.

What she wanted now was to collapse in Luke's strong arms. She wanted him to caress his hands up and down her back in an effort to soothe the disappointment inside her. But she couldn't ask him to do that, and in any case, it wasn't long after that the three men left, taking Angelique with them so she could go on home with Daniel.

"I guess we'll all just be in limbo longer," Monique said. She gave Dominique a quick hug. "I know how disappointed you must be. I know you truly believed Pierre was the killer."

"I am terribly disappointed. I was so certain he was guilty and I know you're disappointed as well," Dominique replied.

"I am, but they still have another suspect…remember there's Charles Lathrop," Monique said.

"I just don't believe Charles killed her in such a horrid way because he thought the love spell she cast for him didn't work." Dominique released a deep sigh.

"On another note, things seemed to feel a little tense

and strange between you and Luke tonight. What's going on with that?" Monique studied her.

"Nothing's going on. Since I decided not to follow Pierre anymore, there's really no reason for us to keep seeing each other."

Monique's gaze continued to hold Dominique's. "And you're good with that?"

"Of course. It's time he get back to his life and I get back to mine," she replied, even as she felt the hot burn of tears behind her eyes. What on earth was wrong with her? "I'm just sorry I wasted his time foolishly chasing after Pierre."

"You were doing what you believed was right," Monique replied. Monique stood. "Guess I'll just head on home."

Dominique got up and walked her sister to the door. "Are you going to be okay walking home?"

Monique released a small laugh. "I'll be just fine. I'm not afraid of the dark and I'm far stronger than you and Angelique give me credit for. Besides, I don't have a creep bothering me like you do. You stay safe and we'll talk tomorrow."

She opened the door and the two sisters said their goodbyes, then Monique disappeared into the darkness outside. Dominique closed and locked the door behind her.

She sank back down on the sofa and found herself once again fighting back tears. Why was she so emotional? It wasn't like she was pregnant. She didn't think she was having a mental breakdown, so what was bringing tears to her eyes so often?

Maybe it was just because there was so much going on in her life right now. She had just learned that the man she'd believed had killed her mother was probably innocent. She had a dangerous man trying to kidnap her and make her his own, and she still grieved for the mother she had lost. It was enough to make a grown woman emotional.

Even though she was working the dinner shift the next day and it was still early in the evening, she decided to go to bed. Only in sleep did she escape the tears that haunted her far too often lately.

She awoke early the next morning and turned on her generator so she could get some coffee brewing. Once the coffee was ready, she poured herself a cup and then sat on the deck to watch the sunrise.

It was always quite stunning at this time in the morning as the sun rose just enough to send golden rays across the landscape. The dark water beneath her lit up as if it had swallowed a lantern. Fish jumped, telling her good morning with their splashes.

Morning birds sang from the top of the tupelos and bald cypress trees. The waves lapped against the wooden stilts that held the shanty up, creating a pleasant, rhythmic sound that was as soothing as the squeak of a rocking chair.

She sipped her coffee, her mind filled with the beauty of the swamp and nothing more. The Spanish moss that draped from the trees sparkled in the soft glow from the sun.

This was what would be hard to leave behind if she ever decided to move into town. Granted, it would be far more convenient for her coming and going to work if she got an apartment in town. But it would be hard to leave the place that had cradled her since her birth.

She finished her coffee and then moved inside and got out the two-top cooking burners to make her breakfast. She had nothing on her agenda today until she had to go into work at two.

After she ate a breakfast of scrambled eggs and toast,

she cleaned up the kitchen and then took a shower. She dressed in one of her housedresses and then sank down on the sofa with a book she wanted to read.

She needed to keep her mind occupied and reading was the perfect way to do that. It wasn't long before she was captivated by the story unfolding in the book.

Time slipped by and before she knew it, it was time to get ready to go to work. As she dressed in her jeans and the official Dark Waters Café pink T-shirt, she congratulated herself on getting through the day without thoughts of Luke.

Surely it was just going to take some time, and then she'd eventually stop missing his presence in her life.

It had been a while since she'd worked an evening shift. When she'd been chasing after Pierre, she had requested to work only mornings and afternoons, but now she was back to her normal routine and that often had her working in the evenings.

She got to work and for the next six hours she put on a happy face and served her customers with care. None of her regulars were there, which made her time more pleasant.

There was still an awkwardness between her and the men she used to banter and tease with. She felt a wariness when she served them now, as she wondered who was tormenting her with scary notes and dead birds. Who had thrown a burlap bag over her head with the intention of kidnapping her?

By the time her shift ended, she was exhausted. The café seemed to have been particularly busy tonight. She stepped out of the back door to head to her car that was parked next to the large trash container in the corner of the lot.

It was just a little after eight when she got home. She

changed out of her work clothes and into one of the housedresses she favored when she was home alone.

Even though she was tired, she wasn't ready for bed yet. She picked up the book she'd been reading and curled up in the corner of the sofa.

She'd only been reading a few minutes when a knock sounded at her door. She frowned and her heart beat a little quicker as she stood. Who would be at her door at this time of night? Friend or foe?

She walked to the door. "Who is it?"

"Dominique, it's me... Luke."

Relief fluttered through her and she quickly unlocked the door and opened it. "Luke, what are you doing here?" she asked. He was clad in a pair of jeans and a red T-shirt and as he entered the shanty, he filled it with his familiar scent.

She closed the door after him. "I just wanted to check in with you," he replied.

She gestured toward the sofa. "Do you want something to drink?"

"No thanks, I'm good." He sank down on the sofa and she joined him there. "I wanted to see how you were doing since Pierre was alibied for your mother's murder?" His soft gaze held hers for a long moment.

She broke the connection and looked at a space just over his head. "At first, I was so shocked. You know how much I believed he was guilty." She looked back at him. "Now I'm just depressed that we have no idea who killed her."

"I just wanted to let you know that we're starting all over again and tearing our investigation apart to see if there's something we missed. We'll find the guilty party, I swear we will," he said fervently. "Your mother needs justice."

She smiled. "I hope eventually you'll get it for her. I had just hoped it would be sooner rather than later."

"I know, and I'm so sorry," he replied.

She leaned back from him. "So, have you started your hunt for that special woman you want in your life?" she asked lightly.

His gaze grew especially intense on her. He was silent for a long moment before finally speaking. "I don't need to hunt for her. I already found that special woman. I am in love with you, Dominique."

His words positively stunned her. She hadn't seen it coming. "Surely you're mistaking lust for love," she replied.

"That's not true. I know the difference between physical desire and love, and I am deeply, madly in love with you," he replied and leaned toward her, enveloping her in his achingly familiar scent.

"Oh Luke, it would never work between us," she said softly. Despite the warmth that had filled her heart at his words of love, she was a realist.

"I am not the special woman for you and you aren't the special man for me. I need a mate who is spontaneous and unstructured. And you need a woman who can live in the world of routines and structure. We'd be divorced before the writing on the marriage certificate dried."

He stared at her for a long moment and then slowly nodded his head. "Of course, you're right," he said, the brilliance of his eyes dimming a bit. He stood, obviously uncomfortable now that he'd spoken of his love for her. "Well, I guess I'll head on home."

She got up from the sofa and followed him to the front door. Her heart was unusually heavy. She couldn't be in love with him. Could she? Even if she was, it wouldn't change their situation.

He reached the door first, unlocked it and then opened it. He turned back to face her and his eyes still held a sadness that broke her heart.

"I'll be in touch concerning the two cases," he said.

"Thank you, I appreciate it."

"Dominique, if you get scared or something happens you aren't sure of, please don't hesitate to call me. Above all, I want you to be safe."

"I'll call if I need to," she replied.

"Good night, Dominique."

"Good night, Luke."

With that, he walked out of the door and into the darkness of the night.

She closed and locked the door behind him, her emotions a jumbled mess. She'd never meant for him to fall in love with her. Many times, they had talked about how different they were and how they had different needs in the person they would marry. She'd tried to keep things casual with him. Dammit, he wasn't supposed to fall in love with her.

She sank down on the sofa once again. She refused to consider her own emotions where he was concerned. It didn't matter how she felt about him. She knew they were not a match. She just didn't understand why she suddenly felt like crying.

GUTTED. LUKE WAS once again absolutely gutted as he left her shanty and headed back to his car. He hadn't meant to speak of his love for her, but he'd been unable to hold it inside him any longer.

She'd looked so pretty in the pink-and-yellow flowered

house dress, with her hair loose around her shoulders and down her back.

But it wasn't her physical beauty that had made him fall in love with her. It was her kindness and the way she cherished her family. He'd fallen in love with her sense of humor and her intelligence. There were so many things that had drawn him to her.

And now, more important than ever, he had to figure out how to stop loving her. In his heart of hearts, he knew she was right about them. They would never work. But that hadn't stopped him from falling deeply in love with her.

She would be a deep ache in his heart for a very long time to come. Besides, she hadn't told him she was in love with him. It was obvious that she wasn't by how easily she had dismissed the idea of a romance between them.

He finally got home and went directly to bed, hoping she wouldn't visit his dreams. He awoke early the next morning, eager to get into the station.

The least he could do for the woman he loved was find the person who had killed her mother. He needed to immerse himself in not only that case, but in the case that was even more important. He needed to figure out who wanted her so badly he'd attempted to kidnap her.

By seven he was back in the murder room with Daniel and Clay. A pall of disappointment draped over them like a heavy shroud. It had been like this since the moment Lucien Rousseau had come forward with his alibi for Pierre.

The setback in the case had made them all sick. They had been so sure that Pierre was their man, that he had been the one who'd murdered Mystique, but now they were back to square one.

"So, what's the general thought now about Charles Lathrop?" Daniel asked.

"I never really thought he was a good contender in the first place," Luke admitted. "He's definitely an arrogant creep, but I didn't believe he'd kill Mystique just because the love spell she cast for him didn't work."

"Maybe he figured out that his personality made the love spell not work," Clay added drily, causing both Daniel and Luke to laugh.

"Then where do we go from here?" Clay asked.

"Like I said yesterday, we start the investigation all over again. Hopefully we can look at things with fresh eyes. We all decided on Pierre's guilt early on and now that he's off our suspect list, we need to look hard at everyone else who was in Mystique's life at the time of the murder," Daniel said.

"And I don't believe some stranger wandered in and killed her," Clay said. "Her throat was sliced and that's a very personal way to kill someone. Somebody was filled with a tremendous rage when they killed Mystique Santori."

"Pierre was the perfect suspect for us to focus on, but with everything checking out with his alibi for that night, that leaves us needing to look elsewhere," Daniel said. "So, we start all over again…at the very beginning when we first arrived at the shanty because of the frantic phone call from Angelique."

Daniel began handing out assignments of people to begin reinterviewing. Luke hated to admit it, but they had all rushed to justice in staying focused on Pierre and they had really not thought about anyone else as a viable suspect.

He hated to think about all the time he and Dominique had wasted in following Pierre and often sitting in the swamp for hours upon end while the man had hunted his prize gator or fished.

Dominique...her very name was now a sad song in his heart, an unfulfilled dream that he'd entertained for just a short moment in time.

He couldn't regret those hours wasted, for it had been those nights that had brought her into his life even if only for a brief time. He would remember the laughter in her eyes and the softness of her skin. He would forever remember their deep conversations and the fire in her kisses.

He could never regret falling in love with her, he just wished she had felt the same about him. And then what, a small voice taunted him. What was it she'd said to him? *We'd be divorced before the writing on the marriage certificate dried.*

"Luke, you with me?" Daniel's voice sliced through Luke's thoughts.

"I'm sorry, I drifted off for a moment," Luke said with a touch of embarrassment.

"Okay then, Clay, you can go ahead and take off. Luke, I'd like to see you in my office," Daniel stood.

As Clay headed out the back door, Luke followed Daniel down the long hallway. Was Daniel angry with him? Never, in all the years they'd been working together, had the two ever had words.

But his boss had evidently seen Luke daydreaming instead of focusing on the job. Once inside Daniel's office, Daniel sat at his desk and Luke sank down in the chair before him.

"I'm sorry, boss," Luke said immediately. "I've been having a little trouble focusing lately."

"Yeah, what's up with you? You've seemed a bit off your game for the last few days," Daniel replied.

Luke released a deep sigh and stared at his friend. "I made a mistake... I got too close to her. I... I'm in love with her, Daniel."

Daniel's eyes widened slightly. "And what does she have to say about all this?" he asked.

"Not much," Luke replied with a wealth of sadness. "I want to believe she's in love with me, too. But we both know it wouldn't work between us. At our very core, we are two different people who have very different needs in a partner. So now, I'm just a damn fool nursing a very broken heart."

"I'm sorry, man," Daniel replied with sympathy. "I warned you not to get too close to her, but I could see this train wreck coming from a hundred miles away."

"I got embroiled in my own thoughts a few minutes ago, but I swear I won't let that happen again," Luke replied.

Daniel reared back in his chair, his gaze thoughtful. "Maybe I should pull you off this case and put you back on regular patrol."

"Please don't do that," Luke protested as he leaned forward. "I've already put in so many hours on Mystique's murder case. I know the details and the people better than any other patrolman you might use to replace me."

"I'm assuming nothing more has happened with Dominique and the man who is after her. Otherwise, I would have heard about it," Daniel said, an obvious change of subject.

"No, nothing more has happened. My fear is that this is somehow the calm before the storm," Luke replied, his worry rife in his tone.

Daniel leaned forward, his eyes burning with a sudden anger. "Two damn cases, and we can't get a break on either one of them. I know I have smart men working for me. I know for sure we're all fine lawmen, but I'm so frustrated right now with both these cases."

"That makes two of us," Luke replied.

"Actually, I can't afford to take you off these cases, Luke. You're right, you know the details and the people far better than anyone else on the force, and you're one of my best men."

"I swear I'll be at the top of my game, Daniel. I feel like I'm personally invested in both these crimes," Luke said.

Daniel offered him a sympathetic smile. "I'm sorry about your love life, Luke. I know how much you want to find a good woman to marry. It's unfortunate that the woman you fell in love with isn't a woman who would be good for you."

Luke desperately wanted to protest Daniel's words, but ultimately, he feared his friend was right. "Thanks, man. I'll get over it." He just didn't know when he would get over her. He suspected it was going to take a very long time.

Daniel tore a piece of paper out of his notebook and handed it to Luke. "This is a list of the people I want interviewed today. Get together with Clay and decide who is doing who, and then as usual we'll meet back here at noon."

Luke stood. "Thanks, Daniel," he said and then moments later he left Daniel's office.

A call to Clay settled who each of them were interviewing and then Luke set off to interview Nola again. After that he would speak to Corrine Fortier and Helene Benoit, Jacob Benoit's older sister. All three of the women lived in the swamp and were frequent visitors of Mystique.

Luke still had his doubts that a woman would be responsible for the heinous crime, but at this point nobody could be ruled out. These women went through fairly light interviews immediately following the murder. Luke intended to press them much harder now.

By noon he'd managed to speak to all of them. Corrine and Helene both had solid alibis for the time of Mystique's murder, but the alibis would be checked to make sure they held up under tough scrutiny. Nola didn't have a solid alibi. On the night of the murder, she had been in her shanty alone.

She would be the first on the new potential suspect list, although Luke couldn't imagine the older woman murdering her best friend.

He checked in at noon and had a half an hour for a lunch break. Was Dominique working the lunch shift? It didn't matter. He wasn't going to eat there so soon after professing his love to her.

He drove through the burger place for lunch and ate in his car, his thoughts drifting back and forth between the woman he loved and the murder case.

For the next few weeks, they would be retracing footsteps they'd already taken in order to find a killer he suspected was hiding in plain sight.

He'd told the truth to Daniel when he'd said he felt as if in Dominique's case this was the calm before the storm. He was sick at the very idea that the man who wanted to make her his own would succeed.

Stop seeing the lawman. You belong to me.

She'd stopped seeing him, although it wasn't because of the note, but the perpetrator wouldn't know that. He'd believe she had complied with his request. That thought definitely made Luke sick but there was nothing he could do about it.

All he could do was hope she remain vigilant when she was out and about. He knew she had her knife. He hoped she would use it if necessary to keep safe.

Chapter Twelve

It had been four long days since Luke had professed his love to her. Dominique felt as if she was just existing, but not enjoying life like she used to.

She went to work and then came home to the silence of her shanty…silence that had once been filled with Luke's presence. She missed him. She just hadn't expected to miss him so much.

So, she read each hour that she spent at home. She went to dinner with her sisters one night and even their chatter didn't help the wealth of loneliness that was inside of her.

She would have liked to invite Luke over and cook for him again. But knowing his feelings for her, it just wouldn't be right. A clean break was what they had needed and in the four days of working and eating out, she hadn't seen him at all.

Aside from her unsettled feelings about Luke was the ever-present fear that somebody was going to snatch her up and carry her away, and nobody would ever see or hear from her again.

She kept her knife at the ready anytime she was outside and alone. There was no way she could forget that somebody was after her. There hadn't been any more notes or anything to trouble her, but each day her fear grew more intense. Something was going to happen soon...something bad. The ominous feeling had grown inside her with each day that passed.

She now dressed for work. Tonight, she was on dinner duty. It would be a short night for her as she was only scheduled to work from four to eight.

Before she left her shanty, she grabbed her knife firmly in her hand and then set out walking. The skies overhead were as dark and dreary as her mood. The weather report was for storms moving into the area later this evening.

As she walked through the swamp, she thought about the last time it had rained. That was the night Luke had danced with her...the night he had kissed her with so much passion.

She snapped her thoughts away from the memory. *Stay focused*, she told herself. *Watch your surroundings and listen for anyone creeping close to you.*

She breathed a deep sigh of relief as she reached her car and slid in behind the wheel. She immediately pressed the button that would lock all her doors and then started up her engine.

It was only as she was driving toward the café that she allowed herself to relax a bit. And in that brief time of relaxation thoughts of Luke once again intruded into her mind.

She had a feeling she'd remember him long after she was married and had kids. She would remember the soft glow of his green eyes and the infectious nature of his grin.

She hoped to find a man who would make her laugh like Luke had, a man who would make her feel safe in his presence. Of course, he would have to be a man who could be relaxed and comfortable in her crazy schedule of no schedule.

She intended to live the lifestyle her mother had with no nod to conventional ways, and that was why Luke was definitely the wrong man for her.

Arriving at the café, she pulled into one of the few empty spaces in the lot. It looked like it was going to be a very busy dinner time. But that was good. She needed to stay busy.

Once again, she grabbed her knife as she exited the car and hurried toward the back door. She was a few minutes early for her shift, so she sank down at the table in the break room and just breathed.

It wasn't long before she was joined by a few more waitresses and then it was time to go to work. Thankfully, the dinner shift was much different than the morning and afternoon shifts since her regulars rarely showed up for dinner.

Knowing she wouldn't have to put up with the awkwardness that still marked her encounters with the three regulars caused her to relax and just enjoy doing her job.

Couples and families usually filled the café in the evenings. She always enjoyed interacting with the children who came with their parents. Their orders usually consisted of one of three things...grilled cheese, chicken nuggets or a hot dog with ice cream for dessert.

"Hi, sweetie." Nola greeted her from her seat at a four-top table. She was with two other women who smiled and nodded at her.

"How are you all doing this evening?" Dominique asked.

"We're all well, but what's wrong with you, honey?" Nola asked.

"What do you mean?" Dominique asked.

"The normal sparkle isn't in your eyes and that means something is troubling you." Nola looked at her intently. "Dominique, I've known you since you were a baby and I could always tell when something was wrong by looking at your eyes."

"Oh, it's nothing," Dominique replied with a small laugh.

"It's definitely something," Nola pressed.

"I'm just very disappointed by the murder investigation," she finally said.

"Who would have thought that Pierre was innocent," one of the other women said.

"I still don't know if I believe it or not," Nola said. "I never liked that man. He and your mom were so different and they should have never been together. All they ever did was fight with each other."

"So, what can I get for you ladies this evening?" Dominique asked, needing to get things moving so she could attend to her other tables.

They placed their orders and then Dominique left their table. That was what she and Luke would be like if they ever tried to be together, she told herself. The two of them were so different and they would probably fight all the time. It definitely wasn't a match made in Heaven.

She stayed busy for the rest of her shift and then at eight o'clock she went back into the break room to grab her purse and head home.

Once again, she pulled her knife from her purse as she stepped out of the back door of the café. The skies overhead were angry looking and there were no signs of the stars or the moon.

There was nobody around so she had nothing to worry

about. She'd had to park her car by the dumpster and she now hurried on her way to it.

She'd heard of people dumpster diving into the café's trash bin, but she'd never seen anyone actually doing that. She would like to think that in the small town of Dark Waters, nobody was hungry enough to have to seek their next meal out of the dumpster.

The only sound came from the voices that spilled out of the kitchen where the back door was open and an occasional rumble of thunder in the distance. She definitely wanted to get home before the storm was upon her.

She'd nearly reached the driver door when he appeared. Clad in dark clothes and wearing a ski mask and gloves, the man seemed to materialize out of the dark shadows.

He rushed toward her, barely giving her time to process what was happening. With her heart beating frantically, she tightened her grip on her knife.

She slashed out at him with the knife and at the same time, he lunged forward and hit her upper arm with a hypodermic needle. Whatever was in it burned as it entered her. She flailed her arm out once again as she tried to stab him, but he'd stepped back from her and was too far away for her to strike.

Danger! Danger! Get in your car and get away, a voice screamed inside her head. *Run back to the kitchen. For God's sake, do something and do it now.*

Her arms and legs felt strange, as if they were all wrapped up in cotton and wouldn't work. Her brain became too slow to process everything as she became disoriented. What was happening to her?

She knew she had to do something, but the knife slipped from her hand and clattered to the pavement. She tried to scream, but only a soft mewl escaped her.

Dizziness whirled in her head as the dark edges of unconsciousness reached out to take her. She fell into strong arms and had one last rational thought. She was in deep trouble. That was her final thought before the darkness took over and she knew no more.

LUKE ONCE AGAIN joined Daniel and Clay in the murder room as they shared and discussed what they had learned the day before with their interviews.

"I really don't believe that the women I interviewed had anything to do with the murder," Luke said. "The only connection Helene Benoit has is that Jacob Benoit is her brother, and that's connected to Dominique's case and not the murder."

"What about the men you interviewed in the afternoon?" Daniel asked.

"I spoke to all of Mystique's closest neighbors to find out if they saw or heard anything on the night of the murder. None of them did," Luke said with frustration. "Of course, Mystique's nearest neighbors aren't all that close to her shanty."

He sat back and listened as Clay gave his report. He had spoken to several of the fishermen in the swamp and he'd come up with nothing as well. Somewhere in their small town, a murderer was hiding and they were going to have to work hard to ferret him out.

There was also another man probably hiding in plain sight. He was a man besotted with Dominique and he wanted her badly. Two criminals and they couldn't find squat on either one of the cases. It was so damned frustrating.

"I hate to do this to you, but I want both of you to look at the crime scene photos again and see if you can find anything we missed." Daniel opened the file folder in front of him and began to pull out the crime scene photos.

The photos were gruesome and hard to look at, but it was part of Luke's job to thoroughly dissect them for any anomalies they might have missed. Thank God, Dominique hadn't seen any of them.

Dominique. It felt as if it had been forever since he'd seen her, although it had only been four days. It was certainly not long enough for his heartbreak to ease.

They spent the morning going over the various photos, but the pictures gave up no further information than they'd already gleaned from them.

It was just after one when they stopped working for their lunch break. Daniel went to Angelique's store where he was going to have lunch with her. Clay went home where his girlfriend had lunch ready for him.

Even though he knew it was probably a bad idea, Luke headed to the café. He didn't know if he hoped Dominique would be working or if he hoped she wasn't working the mid-shift. But it was silly to avoid the one decent place to eat in town just because he was a lovesick fool.

She was the first person he looked for when he walked through the café door. Apparently, she wasn't working this shift for he didn't see her anywhere.

He settled in at a two-top near the window and smiled at Glenda Wright as she appeared to take his order. "How are you this beautiful day, Officer Madison?"

"I'm doing just fine," he replied to the older woman. "What about you?"

"Oh, I can't complain. Now what can I get for you?"

He ordered a cheeseburger, fries and an iced tea and then stared out the window once Glenda left his table. Going over the crime scene photos that morning had reminded him of how heinous the crime against Mystique had been.

Had she been murdered by somebody who was afraid of the voodoo queen and wanted her dead? Or had it been one of the people who came to her for help?

There was no way Luke believed they had identified everyone who had visited Mystique. If they had her client book, then the investigation might have been much easier. However, without it they were just flailing in the wind.

Secrets... Mystique had dealt in secrets. She knew things about people that nobody else knew. Ultimately, was that what had gotten her killed? Had somebody been afraid that she would spill their secrets?

He continued to think about the murder as he ate his cheeseburger. Funny, it was easier to think about a crime rather than think about Dominique.

He finished eating, paid and then walked to his patrol car parked at the curb in front of the café. He was at his driver's side door when Sunny came running out of the building.

"Officer Madison," she called and ran toward him.

"Hey, Sunny." He looked at her curiously as she stopped short in front of him. "What's going on?"

"I was hoping you could tell me. Have you spoken to Dominique this morning?" she asked.

"No, I haven't. Why?" Luke's heartbeat began to race as a furrow of obvious concern fluttered across Sunny's forehead.

"She was supposed to be here today to work the mid-shift, but she didn't show up and she didn't call in, and that's not like her at all."

"Maybe she's sick? Or overslept?" Luke grasped for a logical explanation.

"To make matters even more confusing, her car is parked in the back lot."

Luke stared at her for a long moment as his stomach churned and his brain whirled with suppositions...all of them bad. "I'll check it out," he finally said.

As Sunny headed back into the café, Luke raced around the building to the parking lot. He checked out all the cars and finally spied Dominique's blue Honda parked by the dumpster.

He ran toward it, his heartbeat pounding in his head and a sense of doom crashing through him. When he reached it, he knew she'd been taken.

The air whooshed out of his lungs and he nearly fell to his knees as he saw the pink-handled knife she always carried for protection on the pavement next to the driver's side door.

He fumbled and pulled his cell phone out to call Daniel. "She's gone," he said. "Dominique has been kidnapped."

"Where are you?" Daniel asked.

"I'm next to her car in the back parking lot of the café," Luke replied as despair nearly choked him. "She's gone, Daniel. She's gone."

"Stay put. We'll be right there." Daniel hung up.

Luke hoped the whole police force showed up. They needed to find her. He didn't even know how long she'd been missing. With that thought in mind, he raced over to the café's back door. When he reached it, he asked to speak to Annie.

The older woman came to the door. "What can I do for you, Officer Madison?" She swiped a tendril of her gray hair back from her face.

"When was the last time Dominique was at work?" he asked.

"Last night. She left here a little after eight. But she didn't show up to work the mid-shift today. Is she in some kind of trouble?"

"Yes, she's in trouble," Luke replied, once again a wild despair spearing through him.

Annie frowned. "Then I hope you can get her out of trouble. She's family to us here. If I can help in any way, just let me know."

"Thanks, Annie. We may talk to you later."

Luke left the back door and returned to stand next to Dominique's car. As he stared at the knife on the pavement, tears blurred his vision.

He quickly tamped back his emotion. Crying wasn't going to get Dominique back. He needed to stay strong and focused. And where in the hell was Daniel?

Time was ticking by...precious moments they could be out there looking for her. She had to have been taken last night when she'd left the café. That meant she had already been missing for a full night and over half the day today.

He looked inside the car window but didn't see anything. He didn't want to open the vehicle or search it until Daniel showed up. He was afraid of disturbing any evidence that might be around.

Finally, he heard sirens in the distance. Within minutes, Daniel pulled in, followed by two more patrol cars. Daniel and Clay got out of Daniel's car while Officers Sam Summers, Roger Teasdale and Johnny White got out of the other cars.

Luke quickly relayed what he knew to Daniel. When he was finished, he grabbed hold of Daniel's forearm. "We have to find her, Daniel," he said desperately.

"We will, Luke. We'll find her," Daniel replied.

Luke released his hold on Daniel's arm. They had to

find her, but where did they begin to look? He watched as Daniel instructed Sam, Roger and Johnny to begin processing the car and surrounding area. Daniel then got on the phone and instructed two other officers to go to the swamp and check out Dominique's shanty.

"Clay and Luke, let's head into the station," Daniel then said.

Luke wanted to protest. He wanted to bang on doors. He wanted to tear apart every house in town and every shanty in the swamp to find her. Ultimately, he recognized they needed to go to the station and form a plan. That way they wouldn't waste more precious time.

Once again as Luke followed behind Daniel's car, his emotions roared to the forefront again. It didn't matter that she didn't love him. It didn't matter that they would never be together. All that mattered was finding her safe and sound.

Unfortunately, there was no way to know what the kidnapper was capable of. The strangled, dead bird indicated the person was capable of a brutal act. So, it was possible Dominique's very life was on the line.

Chapter Thirteen

Consciousness came slowly. The first thing she became aware of was a pounding headache. She winced and tried to climb out of the dense fog that seemed wrapped around her brain.

She attempted to open her eyes, but it was too much of an effort. What was wrong with her? She tried to gather her thoughts. She'd worked the late shift at the café. So, what had happened after that?

Suddenly, memories flooded through her brain. Walking out to her car…the masked man jumping out from behind the dumpster…the prick in her arm…and then nothing.

She gasped and sat straight up as her eyes flicked open. She released another gasp as she looked at her surroundings. She was in a bed, covered with a pink spread.

As she took in the room, her headache banged harder. It was only when she tried to raise a hand to her head that she realized her wrists were tied down.

A rope also surrounded her waist along with another rope around her ankles. She yanked on the ones holding her wrists down. Desperately, she jerked and pulled in an effort to get free, but there was no give at all in the ropes.

Who had brought her here? The door to the room was

closed and she didn't hear anything or anybody. Who had drugged her and put her in this bedroom?

She knew it was the person who had written her the notes...the man who had killed a poor bird and left it on her doorstep. Was it one of her regulars at the café, or was it somebody no one even considered?

Once again, she tugged at the ties that bound her as her veins iced with fear. Did anyone even know she'd been taken? Was anybody out looking for her? How on earth would they find her? She didn't even know where she was.

Deep sobs exploded from her as frightened tears raced down her cheeks. "Somebody help me!" She began to scream at the top of her voice. She screamed over and over again as she bucked and kicked in an effort to get free.

Finally, she collapsed back on the bed, her throat hurting and her sobs slowly halting. Surely, if anyone was nearby, they would have heard her screams.

She listened for a long moment. The room was obviously in a house, but she sensed she was all alone. She looked around again at her surroundings, hoping to see something that would give her an indication of where she was and who had taken her.

There was a small dinette table with two chairs, and a vanity with a plush bench seat. What she didn't see was anything personal and she also realized there was no window in the room.

A closet door was open and inside women's dresses hung from the hangers. Somehow the sight of the dresses terrified her almost more than anything. It was an indication that somebody had gone to a lot of trouble to make sure they could keep her here. There was another door that was closed and she assumed it might be a bathroom.

Whoever held her captive could feed her at the dinette

table. She would wear the dresses from the closet and there would never be a reason for her to leave this space.

With this thought in mind, she screamed again. She screamed as loud and as long as she could until she was finally out of breath.

Luke. Was he looking for her? Oh, how she wanted his strong arms around her now. She wanted to be enveloped by his familiar scent and feel his heart beating against her own.

If he knew she was missing, then he would be out pounding on doors and searching everywhere to find her. He would hunt for her with everything he had because he was in love with her.

She began to cry once again. She was afraid and alone and she didn't know what would happen to her. Who was going to walk through the door?

The only positive she could see in the situation was if he killed her, then she would be reunited with the mother she loved.

BY THE TIME they reached the station, Luke was beyond frantic. They went into the murder room where Daniel and Clay sat and Luke paced the floor. How could they sit when Dominique was missing? Kidnapped?

"Luke, I know this is difficult for you, but you need to keep yourself together," Daniel said.

"How are we going to find her? We have no idea where to look," Luke replied, his anguish deepening his voice. "I should have been shadowing her movements. Dammit, I should have been a real bodyguard keeping her safe."

"Right now, what we need is a game plan to find her. The first place we need to start is with the men who were her regulars at the café," Daniel said.

"Burt Stanfield, Austin Colbert and Jacob Benoit." The names tripped off Luke's tongue.

Daniel nodded. "Clay, why don't you and Roger go check out Austin Colbert. If he isn't at work at the library, go to his home." Daniel quickly looked up the address. "Call me as soon as you check him out."

"I'm off," Clay said. He stood and quickly left the room.

"Luke, you and I will see if Burt is at work today. We should be able to find him in his office. And if he isn't there, we go to his house and check it out."

This is what Luke wanted…action. "What about Jacob?"

Daniel stood and frowned. "I honestly don't think anyone who lives in the swamp has her. It would be very difficult to hold a woman there and keep it a secret."

Luke followed Daniel out of the room. Burt's office was in city hall and that building was close enough that they could walk. "I have all the men out looking for her," Daniel said as they hurried down the sidewalk.

God, they had to find her. They had no idea what the kidnapper might do to her. Hopefully, he wouldn't hurt her in any way. The thought of that happening shot a shaft of pain through Luke's heart.

They reached city hall and went inside. Daniel led him down a long hallway and then stopped and knocked on one of the closed doors.

"Enter," Burt's voice called out.

Daniel opened the door and as he and Luke walked into the office, Burt jumped up from behind his desk. "Chief LeCroix… Officer Madison," he said with surprise. "What can I do for you?"

"We have a few questions for you," Daniel replied.

"Questions about what?" Burt asked. He sank back

down behind his desk and gestured them to two chairs in front of it. But Luke and Daniel remained standing.

"Dominique Santori," Daniel said.

Burt once again looked surprised. "What about her?"

"When was the last time you saw her?"

Luke stared at the man, looking for any signs of deception.

"Uh... I guess it was the day before yesterday when I went in for a late breakfast. Why? Has something happened to her?"

"She's been kidnapped," Luke blurted out.

"What?" Burt stared at Luke and then back at Daniel. "Oh my God. What can I do to help?"

"Nothing at this point," Daniel replied. "What were you doing last night around eight?"

"I was at the office working overtime to get things ready for the upcoming fall festival," Burt replied.

"Did anyone see you there?" Daniel asked.

"I'm not sure but I think Margaret Delaney might have seen me. I think she was working late that night, too," Burt said.

Luke shifted from foot to foot as a deep anxiety filled him. It was time to get moving...but get moving where?

They finally left Burt's place and headed to the café. "We need to question all the people who were working in the kitchen last night," Daniel said. "Maybe one of them saw something that might help us in our search. Whoever took her had to have had a vehicle. Maybe somebody saw it."

By that time Clay called and told them that Austin was at work in the library. His alibi was that he had been at the Voodoo Lounge the night before and it had been two days since he'd seen Dominique. Clay was headed to the bar now to check out the alibi.

When they reached the café, several of the busboys who had been at work last night were there. Daniel interviewed them one at a time, but none of them had seen or heard anything from the parking lot the night before.

It was almost seven o'clock when they went back into the station. When they walked through the front door, Angelique and Monique were there, both frantic with fear for their sister.

"Any news?" Angelique asked, her light brown eyes simmering with emotion.

"Not yet," Daniel replied.

It would be dark soon and the darkness crept into Luke's very soul. If they didn't find her soon, then this would be the second night she'd be with her kidnapper.

The very idea tortured him. What was she going through? She had to be scared out of her mind. The thought of her frightened tore him up inside.

"Luke, I've changed my mind. I think we need to head into the swamp and check out Jacob Benoit and Oliver Le-Boeuf. No stone left unturned, right?"

"Right," Luke replied.

Daniel turned back to the two women. "Go home," he told them. "I promise I'll call you both with any news we get. There's nothing you can do here."

He reached out and touched Angelique's cheek. It was the same way Luke had touched Dominique and it brought the sting of tears to his eyes.

The four of them left the station together. Angelique and Monique headed to their homes and Luke and Daniel with three other patrolmen headed for the swamp.

Luke was grateful Daniel turned on his lights and siren,

indicating it was an emergency. It *was* an emergency. It didn't take long for them to reach the swamp entrance.

They all got out of their cars and pulled flashlights against the encroaching twilight shadows. Daniel led the way and the rest of the men followed him on the narrow path.

They had been to both men's shanties before. Both were small. All they'd have to do was open the front doors and it would instantly be known if Dominique was being held in one of them.

Let her be here, Luke prayed. *Let her be here so we can rescue her and take her home.* They would arrest the kidnapper and she'd never have to worry again. And let her be okay.

At the idea of the kidnapper harming her in any way, a rage momentarily stole the fear from Luke. Who was this creep who thought it was okay to take a woman from her life and those who loved her?

It didn't take long to learn that Dominique wasn't in either of the shanties. Neither man had a solid alibi for the night before, but it didn't matter. She wasn't there.

As they headed back to their cars, a new, deep despair took hold of Luke. They had checked all the men who had been on their suspect list and had come up with nothing.

Where did they go from here? How on earth were they going to find her? A dreadful thought shot through his head. What if they never found her?

IT FELT AS if she'd been alone and tied to the bed forever. Without a window in the room, it was impossible for her to see what time it might be. She didn't even know if it was day or night.

She continued to pull and tug at the restraints until her

wrists were raw and burned from her efforts and she became breathless and had to rest.

She didn't scream anymore. She'd realized there was no point in it. She'd screamed enough already and nobody had come to help her. Wherever she was, there apparently wasn't anyone else around.

What she did know was she wasn't in the swamp anymore. This room smelled faintly of sawdust and paint, not the sweet green and floral scents of her home.

When she was exhausted by her exertions, her thoughts ran free. She thought about her life. She thought about her mother's murder and the loss and grief she still felt. Finally, she thought about Luke.

She was in the midst of thoughts about him when she heard the sound of a door slamming shut. Heavy footsteps came closer and she tensed with terror. Who was going to come through the door? Who had done this to her and what did they want with her?

The steps came closer and closer and then a lock clicked and the door slowly crept open. He stepped into the room. "You," she gasped in stunned surprise.

He smiled at her. "Hi, Dominique. You really belong to me now." He pulled out one of the chairs at the table and sank down.

"Please, you need to let me go. This isn't the way to go about things," Dominique said feverishly. "Untie me and let me go and you won't be in any trouble."

"I'll untie you when you're truly ready to be my wife," he replied. He leaned forward. "Oh, Dominique, I've been so lonely. You know I'm crazy about you. Now, are you hungry? I have a nice steak for dinner for us this evening."

She stared at his familiar face. Had he lost his mind?

She was tied up in a bed after having been kidnapped and he was talking about steak for dinner?

"Actually, what I'd like is to use the restroom," she replied. He would have to untie her and maybe she would be able to get away.

"Of course." He jumped up out of the chair and moved to her side. She remained frozen in place as he untied first her wrists, then the rope around her waist and finally the one that had kept her legs from moving.

"You shouldn't have to be tied up after today," he said as she sat up and swung her legs over the side of the bed.

"That would be nice," she replied evenly. Maybe untied she could figure out a way out of this nightmare. He gestured toward the closed door. "The bathroom is right there."

She stood a bit unsteadily. She stayed in place until the pins and needles in her feet and legs stopped. After being in the same position all day, they all had gone numb.

"Feel free to use the shower in there whenever you want, and there is a large variety of dresses in the closet for you to wear." He beamed a smile at her. "I'm particularly partial to the yellow dress."

He stood. "Oh, Dominique, we're going to have a wonderful life together. Now, I'll be back with our dinner very soon." With that he walked to the door, stepped out and when he closed it behind him she heard a lock fall into place.

Slowly, she walked into the small bathroom. She needed to find a weapon…something she could use to disable him so she could escape.

In the bathroom there was a stool, a sink and a shower with a bar of soap on the floor. There was no mirror that could be broken and no window to crawl through.

She left the bathroom and began to explore the rest of the bedroom. The vanity held nothing but a plastic bristle brush. There was absolutely nothing in the room that could be used as a weapon.

She sank down on the bed. *Oh, Dominique, we're going to have a wonderful life together.* His words played and replayed in her head. The man was obviously delusional.

Maybe she could rush him at the door when he came back in. He would probably be carrying a couple of plates of food. It might be her only chance to escape.

With this thought in mind, she moved to position herself just inside the door. He was bigger than her, but she would have the element of surprise on her side.

She gathered every inch of strength she had inside her. She would fight like a wildcat to get away. This had to work...it just had to!

She remained in position as minutes ticked by. She didn't know how long she waited before she heard his footsteps coming back. She tensed, adrenaline rushing through her veins.

She heard the click of the door being unlocked and when he came through, she screamed and pushed to get past him. The plates he was carrying fell to the floor as he grabbed her by the shoulders and shoved her back into the room.

She punched and kicked, still trying desperately to get through the door. He reared his arm back and hit her on her chin, the blow careening her backward as a horrendous pain stabbed through her jaw. She stumbled and fell to the floor on her hands and knees, panting from the exertion of her unsuccessful efforts.

"I don't tolerate disobedience," he said angrily. "Now, your dinner is all over the floor and that's where you can eat it." He stepped out of the doorway, slammed the door and then locked it once again.

Dominique slowly pulled herself up off the floor, silently weeping with pain and frustration. She sank down on the side of the bed as an icy chill walked up her spine. She now knew the man was not only delusional, but dangerous as well.

Chapter Fourteen

The nighttime hours passed in agonizing increments as Luke remained at the police station. He and Daniel had interviewed everyone who might be guilty and they'd come up empty-handed.

It was just after two in the morning, and Luke paced back and forth in the break room, his heart absolutely bleeding with the need to find her. Daniel was in his office, working to figure out where they went next. He had all the night force driving the streets and keeping an eye out for the missing woman.

However, Luke knew they had no place to go next. Luke now believed somebody who had not been on their suspect list was responsible. Hell, that could be almost any male in town.

It had been around ten when Adam Kincaid, one of the night cops, had driven through to get burgers for everyone. Luke's burger remained untouched on the table. How could he eat when Dominique was missing? He had no appetite, except for his intense hunger to find Dominique.

Daniel had tried to get him to go home and get some sleep, but Luke refused to leave. He needed to be here in case something happened.

The last thing he wanted was for any of the night crew to find her on the street because that would mean they had found her body. Once again, he prayed that the person who had taken her didn't hurt her.

He threw himself into a chair at the table and stared unseeing at the wall. Instead, he saw Dominique's beautiful face and her gorgeous smile. Visions of her laughing and dancing in the rain, of her eyes sparkling so bright, rushed through his head.

He must have nodded off for he jerked awake as some of the day cops entered the break room. Morning. And still she was gone.

For the next two days they interviewed more people who had been in the café on the night she was taken. They spoke to more of the swamp people, but nobody had any news for them. It was as if a UFO had beamed her up without a trace.

During those two days, Luke ate only what he needed to keep going. He dozed in the murder room, what little sleep he got troubled and full of nightmares. He went to his home twice, just long enough to shower and change clothes.

Finally, desperate for answers, at nine in the morning he drove to the swamp wanting to touch base with Jacque LeBlanc. Jacque himself was shrouded in mystery. Nobody knew where he'd come from or anything personal about him. Luke didn't care about any of that. What he did care about was the man was rumored to know what was going on in the swamp.

Jacque's shanty was secluded but Luke had been there before when he and Daniel had first spoken to the man about Mystique's murder.

This time, Luke was by himself as he made his way

through the swamp. It was difficult for him to focus on anything but Dominique. He just wanted her to be found. He couldn't imagine going on for the rest of his life not knowing what had happened to her.

Jacque's shanty came into view and Luke hurried his footsteps to the front door. "Jacque, it's Officer Madison," he shouted as he knocked on the door.

The dark-haired, well-built man opened the door. "Officer Madison. How can I help you?"

"I'd like to ask you a few questions. Can I come in?"

The gator-hunter opened his door wider to allow Luke entry. The shanty was spotlessly clean with a dark gray sofa and chair and a large bookcase filled with books on all types of subjects. Definitely unusual in the world of gator-hunters.

"Please, have a seat." Jacque gestured to the sofa. Luke nodded and sat. "Now, questions about what?"

"I don't know if you've heard or not, but Dominique Santori was kidnapped three nights ago," Luke said.

"Oh, I've heard. The swamp has been buzzing with the news. Dominique and her sisters are well-liked here," Jacque replied.

Luke leaned forward. "Have you heard anything that might help us find her?"

"I'm afraid not. But I can tell you that I don't believe she is being held here in the swamp. All the fishermen and gator-hunters are genuinely worried about her and secrets are hard to keep here," Jacque said.

"I'm worried sick about her," Luke replied, his desperation ringing in his voice.

Jacque gazed at him sharply. "It's like that?"

Luke offered the man a weak smile. "It's like that," he replied.

"I really wish I could help you, but I haven't heard anything."

"I knew it was a long shot," Luke replied and stood. "Thanks for your time."

"No problem." Jacque walked with him to the door. "I hope you find her safe and sound." For a moment Jacque's green eyes darkened. "Because there's nothing worse than losing somebody you love."

"Thanks again." Luke walked slowly away from the shanty, despair once again filling his heart…his very soul. It had been so long now, too long. Three nights she'd been with her kidnapper unless he'd already… He snapped his thoughts away from that torturous thought. It couldn't be too late to save her. It just couldn't be.

It was just about ten o'clock when he arrived back at the station. In the murder room, half a dozen officers were gathered along with Daniel and Clay.

"Luke," Daniel greeted him. "We've decided to start a grid search of the town. I want officers knocking on doors and asking questions," he said. "What I need you to do is go to the café. Annie called a few minutes ago and said she'd put together a platter of sweet rolls and pastries for the officers. We'll put it in the break room where they can grab one and go. So, if you want to head over there now, I'd appreciate it."

"I'll go right now."

He left the murder room and headed back to his patrol car. It took him only minutes to arrive and park in the café's lot where Dominique's car was still parked by the dumpster. The sight of it wrenched his heart.

This was the crime scene, but it had yielded no answers. They had used a locksmith to get into the car, but nothing of value had been found inside. The entire area had been meticulously searched and the officers had found nothing useful.

He was slowly losing hope and that frightened him. He headed around the building to the front door. He stopped just inside the entrance and gazed around, somehow seeking her where he knew she wouldn't be. He didn't know how long he'd been standing there when Sunny approached him.

"Officer Madison, can I help you?" she asked softly.

"Yeah, I was sent to pick up a platter that Annie prepared for the men at the station," he replied.

"Oh yes, it's in the break room. She has it all ready to go. Just follow me."

He walked behind Sunny and she led him to the small break room. Lockers lined one wall. There was a round table and in the center of it was a large platter of breakfast sweets wrapped in plastic.

"No news yet?" Sunny asked.

"None," Luke replied grimly.

Sunny lightly touched Luke's shoulder. "I know you miss her...we all do. All her regulars ask about her every day—well, all of them but Burt."

"He doesn't ask about her?" Luke asked in surprise.

"He hasn't been in for breakfast since she disappeared." She leaned over the table and grabbed the large platter. "Here you are," she said as she handed it to him. "I hope all the officers enjoy it."

"Thanks, and please tell Annie thank you. It was very thoughtful of her to do this," he replied.

"I'll tell her." She walked with him back to the front door. "You have to find her, Luke." Sunny's blue eyes filled with tears.

"We're doing everything possible," he replied, emotion

rising up inside him. "I'll see you later." He hurried out the front door before he embarrassed himself by blubbering in front of Sunny.

Dominique was missing and he was picking up pastries from the café. He had a feeling Daniel was just trying to keep him busy, but he didn't want to be the errand guy, he needed to be involved in the search.

As he pulled out of the café parking lot to head back to the station, something niggled in the back of his brain, but he didn't know what it was.

He arrived back and carried the platter inside to the break room, where he placed it in the center of the table. Nobody was in there at the moment and there was nobody in the murder room. Apparently, all the officers had left to begin the grid search.

He found Daniel in his office and sank down in the chair across from him. "The platter is here. Now you need to tell me where to go to help in the search."

"Luke, you're exhausted. You haven't really slept or eaten in days. You need to go home and get some rest and leave the search to the other men."

"You know I can't do that," Luke replied. "I need to be here in case something breaks." He frowned, the niggling feeling back inside his head. Somehow, he was missing something…something that could be important. The thought suddenly unfolded in his brain.

"Burt," he said, his heart beat beginning to race.

"What about him?" Daniel looked at him curiously.

"I spoke briefly to Sunny when I was at the café. She told me Burt hadn't been in since Dominique went missing. Why isn't he going in to eat his breakfast as usual?"

"He had an alibi for the night in question," Daniel protested.

"An alibi we didn't check," Luke said. He realized in the thick of things, they hadn't followed up on Burt's alibi. "We checked his alibi but we didn't follow up on it and we didn't check out his house." Luke leaned forward, a new burst of adrenaline rushing through him. "Daniel, we need to get inside his house."

"We'll head to his office and get him to come with us and let us in to look around. I'll contact Judge Blakely and see if he'll sign off on a search warrant for Burt's place."

"We need to go there as soon as possible," Luke replied, his stomach churning. "Can't we just go there and break down the door?"

"Luke, the last thing we want to do is jeopardize the case. We do things by the book. Give me five minutes to cross my t's and dot my i's so we don't make any mistakes. Wait for me in the lobby and when I'm done here, we'll go talk to Burt."

Luke walked out to the lobby, where Gus sat behind the desk. "How are you doing, Luke?" the older man asked.

"I'm okay," Luke replied. But of course, he wasn't okay. He began to pace, his thoughts on the possibility that Burt might be their kidnapper.

Was this just another wild-goose chase? Was he taking a casual statement from a waitress and making too big a deal out of it? He didn't know. All he did know for sure was that they needed to check this out.

Daniel joined him and together the two men swiftly walked to city hall. "I got hold of Judge Blakely but he wouldn't sign off on a search warrant. We don't have enough evidence for one. We'll just have to hope Burt lets us in without needing the warrant."

"All I know is I want to get into his house as quickly as

possible," Luke replied. "If she's not there, then at least it's one place we cleared."

They reached city hall and headed down the hallway to Burt's office. When they reached it, Daniel knocked firmly on the door. There was no response. Daniel knocked again, this time louder. "Burt, it's Chief LeCroix," he called.

The door to the office next to Burt's opened up. "He's not there," Margaret Delaney, the city clerk, said.

"Do you know where he's at?" Luke asked.

"I'm assuming he's at home. He called in sick this morning," she replied.

The tension in Luke's body tightened. Was he right about this? It felt right. *Please let it be right*. He turned and practically ran out of the building with Daniel hot on his heels.

When they reached the police station they got into Daniel's car to head to Burt's place. As they drove, Daniel called in several more officers to meet them there.

Luke's heart beat so hard it felt as if it might explode out of his chest. Hope surged up inside him, a hope he prayed wouldn't be dashed by the end of this search.

By the time they reached Burt's house, a rich adrenaline flooded Luke's veins. Burt's house was a ranch located at the back of a dead end. On one side some distance away was a house that was obviously abandoned and on the other side was another ranch house, also some distance away. There was a red pickup truck in the driveway, indicating that Burt was home.

Before he could get out of the car, Daniel grabbed his arm to hold him in place. "We go in slow, Luke. If she's in there, the last thing we want is for any sort of a hostage situation to unfold."

Luke nodded. Even though he was ready to storm the

door, he knew Daniel was right. They didn't know if Burt would be armed and they didn't know where, exactly, in the house Dominique might be located. The best they could do was get Burt out of the house before they went in to search.

The last thing he wanted was to do anything that might put Dominique at more risk if she was inside the house. They sat and waited until two more patrol cars pulled up. Together, they all got out of their cars.

Daniel instructed two of the officers to wait near the front door and he told Clay to head around the back of the house and guard the door there.

With everything in place, Daniel and Luke approached the front door. Daniel knocked and Luke held his breath. Please let her be inside, he inwardly prayed.

Daniel knocked again. "Burt, it's Chief LeCroix."

After several moments, the lock on the front door sounded and then Burt opened the door. "Chief... Officer Madison, what's going on?" He appeared confused as he gazed at them.

"We have a few more questions to ask you," Daniel said. "Can we come in?"

"Uh...it's really not a good time right now." He offered them an easy smile. "I've been doing a little cleaning and, in the process, I've made quite a mess in my living room. But I'll be glad to answer any questions you might have." He stepped out on the porch and closed the door behind him. "Now, what can I help you with?"

"Burt, we'd really like to come in and search your place," Daniel said. "We're checking all the homes of people Dominique was close to."

"Well you aren't checking mine without a search warrant," Burt replied.

"Chief, I think I heard somebody cry for help inside," Johnny said. "I think we need to go in."

"That's a damn lie," Burt exclaimed. "You can't hear anything."

"I'm telling you, I hear a woman crying for help," Johnny said.

"I heard it, too," Roger said.

Daniel motioned the two officers, Roger and Johnny, forward. "Burt, you need to turn around. Roger is going to cuff you. You aren't under arrest, but you are detained while we do a complete search of your house."

"A search of my house?" Burt jerked against Roger, who successfully got him in handcuffs. "What on earth is wrong with you people? What right do you have to do this to me? You need a damned search warrant."

"Not if we think somebody is in imminent danger," Daniel replied.

Luke shoved Burt out of the way, opened the door and walked in. Rather than things being a mess, the living room was neat and tidy. He heard nothing to indicate that there was a woman being held prisoner inside, but that didn't mean she wasn't here. He was grateful that Johnny and Roger had given them a reason come on inside.

Daniel entered the house as well, but Luke was three steps ahead of him as he ran down the hallway. The house appeared to have three bedrooms and all the doors to those rooms were closed.

Luke ripped open the door to the first one. Masculine furniture and a brown plaid spread on the king-size bed let him know this was probably Burt's bedroom.

As he stepped out of the bedroom, he saw it. On the door on the left end of the hallway was a lock. It was a simple hasp lock. Why would somebody put that on the outside of a bedroom door—unless they wanted to keep somebody inside?

He gasped and raced to the door. He disengaged the hasp lock and then opened it. His heart nearly wept with relief. Thank God, she was there. She was tied to the bed.

"Luke!" she cried out at the sight of him.

He rushed to her side, along with Daniel. "It's okay, Dominique. We're here now and you're safe," Luke said as he began to work the ropes to untie her. She was clad in an ill-fitting red dress and her hair was a tangle around her head. She began to cry and tears of relief burned at his eyes.

Together, he and Daniel finally got her untied. She jumped out of the bed and fell into Luke's arms. He closed his eyes and held her tight, breathing in the very scent of her as he reveled in the fact that she was alive.

She continued to weep until Daniel interrupted. "I've got an ambulance on the way," he said.

"I... I just want to go home," she said.

Luke looked her over. When he saw the bruise on her jaw, a rage nearly overwhelmed him. She'd been hit. And she'd been hit hard.

"Dominique, you need to go to the hospital and get checked out," he said softly.

She gazed at him and then nodded. At that moment, a siren screamed in the air. "That will be the ambulance," Daniel said.

Together, the three of them walked outside with Dominique clinging to Luke's arm. "Dominique, I did this because I love you," Burt yelled out.

Without warning, Luke stepped up to the man and hit him hard in his jaw. Burt's head snapped back with the blow and he gasped with obvious pain.

"Did you all see that? It was police brutality. I'll sue you all for that," he yelled.

"What I saw was a kidnapper trying to escape," Johnny replied easily.

"Yeah, that's what I saw, too," Roger added.

"Liars!" Burt exclaimed, his face reddened with anger. "You're all a bunch of liars."

"Good luck proving that in a court of law," Johnny said.

"Don't try to escape again. I'll just have to subdue you with another punch to your face," Luke warned, his anger as he stared at the man nearly out of control.

"Take him to jail," Daniel said.

"With pleasure," Roger said.

"And then come back here to help process the scene," Daniel added.

Luke led Dominique to the awaiting ambulance, where the two EMT's attended to her. Once she was loaded up, the ambulance pulled away. Luke stared after the vehicle.

Intense relief nearly cast him to the ground. Hopefully, she had no other physical injuries than the bruised jaw, which was bad enough. But it would heal and eventually she would be fine.

"Go," Daniel said from behind him. Luke turned to look at his friend. "I know you want to go with her. We can handle things here." He tossed his car keys to Luke. "I can catch a ride back to the station later. And in the meantime, I'll give her sisters a call. I'm sure they'll meet you there."

"Thanks," Luke replied and then raced for Daniel's car. Once in it, he turned on the siren and then hurried to catch up with the ambulance.

They arrived at the hospital at the same time. Dominique was taken to the emergency room bay and Luke parked and then ran for the hospital's front door.

Once inside, he checked in with the receptionist and told her he wanted to speak with Dominique's doctor when he finished checking her out.

He then sank down in one of the plastic chairs in the waiting room. For the first time in what felt like forever, he was able to breathe.

He leaned his head back against the wall as a deep wave of exhaustion struck him. She was safe. Finally, she'd been found. It was as if he'd been missing a large chunk of his heart but now that chunk had been restored.

Love for her flooded through his veins, warming the icy chill that had been inside him since the moment they had discovered her gone.

He wasn't alone in the waiting room for long. Angelique and Monique joined him there. "Thank God, you found her," Angelique said, her eyes misty with tears as she hugged Luke.

"We've been so afraid," Monique added, tears of relief also shimmering in her eyes.

They sank down in the chairs next to him. "Have you heard anything yet?" Angelique asked.

"No, nothing," he replied.

"Daniel told me she has a large bruise on her jaw. He also told me you gave Burt a bruised jaw," Angelique said.

"I hope I broke his damned jaw," he confessed.

"So do we," Monique said with a small smile. She sobered. "I can't believe it was Burt, a well-respected man who works for the city."

"I'm just glad she's safe now." Once again, love for her filled his heart.

The three of them sat in the waiting room for about an hour and finally Dr. Gregory Harmon stepped in. They all stood at the sight of the older doctor.

"How is she?" Angelique asked before Luke could.

"She has a bruised jaw, but thankfully nothing was broken. She is dehydrated and exhausted. I'm keeping her overnight so she can rest and we can get some fluids in her."

"Can we see her?" Luke asked.

"I've given her a mild sedative and she's already sleeping. I would prefer she not be awakened. I imagine she'll just be here for one night. As long as there are no complications, she'll be released tomorrow. You can all see her then."

A swift disappointment swept through Luke. He'd just wanted to see her...maybe hold her hand and assure himself that she was truly okay. But, if she was resting peacefully, he also didn't want to disturb her.

The three of them walked out of the hospital together. They said their goodbyes and then Luke got into his car. He dropped his forehead on the steering wheel and the tears he'd fought back for the past three days began to fall.

Each tear washed away the terror he'd had since the moment she'd been kidnapped. The tears were thanks to the vast relief that she'd been found alive.

He finally pulled himself together and called Daniel. He updated Daniel on Monique's condition and told him that both her sisters had come to the hospital and had gone home. "I'm just now leaving the hospital and can be back at Burt's house in about fifteen minutes."

"You are not to come here," Daniel said firmly. "I don't need you here. I have plenty of officers to process the scene. I want you to go home, Luke. Get something to eat and get some sleep."

"I have to admit, that sounds like a great idea. Then, I'll be in as usual in the morning," he replied.

The two men hung up and Luke pulled out of the hospital parking lot. Night had fallen as it was almost nine o'clock. Tonight, the darkness of night was soothing, unlike the last three when the darkness had been torturous knowing that Dominique was out there somewhere all alone with a kidnapper.

He drove through and got himself a burger and fries and then headed home. Suddenly, he was ravenous and the added bonus was that he knew tonight he would sleep peacefully, knowing Dominique was safe and sound.

Chapter Fifteen

Dominique awakened to the scents of bacon and eggs and fresh coffee. She raised the head of the hospital bed, hoping that meant she was going to get some breakfast soon. She was definitely hungry. She really hadn't eaten anything while she'd been held.

Burt Stanfield. She still found it hard to believe that the man who had joked with her, the man who had appeared to be hardworking and kind, had kidnapped her.

It was only a few minutes later that Daniel and Luke walked into her room. Luke looked so achingly handsome in his uniform and her heart squeezed tight in her chest at the sight of him.

"Dominique, how are you feeling?" Daniel asked.

"Amazingly well...except for the pain in my jaw," she replied and then smiled at Luke. "And thank you for giving Burt a pain in his jaw."

"I would have liked to give him more," Luke replied with the boyish grin that always made her heart beat a little faster.

"If you're up to it, we need to get an official statement from you detailing everything that happened from the moment you were taken."

"I'm up to it," she replied.

Daniel pulled a mini recorder from his pocket and she started talking. She began from the moment Burt had attacked her in the café parking lot.

"He talked about his dead wife and how the silence in his house since then was driving him crazy," she said. "I was a replacement for her. He believed she'd broken her promise to be with him forever by dying. He had all her clothes for me to wear."

She told them about trying to escape and Burt hitting her. "I knew then that he could get violent so I tried to be as quiet and compliant as possible when he was in the bedroom. But when he wasn't in the room, I continued to look for a way to escape or some sort of weapon I could use against him. Unfortunately, I was unsuccessful on both counts."

She offered a bright smile to both men. "But all's well that ends well, right?"

"Right," Daniel replied. "But I have one last, very personal question for you."

She tensed. "Okay, what is it?"

"Did Burt hurt you in any other way, assault you physically, sexually?" he asked.

"No, thank God he didn't," she replied. "But I'm sure that was in his plans. Only in his head it wouldn't be an assault. He'd believe it would be a mutual decision no matter how much I kicked and screamed. He was definitely delusional in his thinking."

"Thanks, Dominique. I think I got enough from you. Burt is going to go away for a very long time," Daniel assured her.

"That's good news for me," she replied. She kept her gaze focused on Daniel. For some reason, looking at Luke hurt.

At that time an older woman Dominique didn't know pushed in a cart with her breakfast. "Bacon and eggs, toast and orange juice for our patient," she said as she placed the plate on a table she pulled out over Dominique's lap.

"I hope there's also some coffee," Dominique said.

The woman grinned at her. "Definitely I have coffee for you."

"We'll just go now and let you eat your breakfast in peace," Daniel said. "I know you'll be available if I have further questions."

"Of course," she replied and then she looked at Luke. His gaze was soft and full of love. And then the two men left.

As she ate, a sadness filled her. It was the same sadness that had been with her since the moment Luke had spoken of his love for her.

She had spent a lot of time while she'd been held captive thinking about him and thinking about her mother. By the time she finished eating, Dr. Harmon came in.

"How's my patient today?" he asked with a kindly smile.

"I'm good and ready to get home," she replied.

"I don't see a reason to keep you any longer, so I'll have my nurse prepare your discharge paperwork and then you're free to go."

"Thank you, Dr. Harmon," she replied.

When he left the room, she used the hospital telephone on the nightstand to call Monique. Her sister not only agreed to come and get her, but also agreed to bring her some clothes. When Dominique had been rescued, she'd been wearing one of the dresses from the closet.

An hour later, she walked out of the hospital with both her sisters at her side. They fawned over her until she assured them both she was just fine.

Within minutes, they were at the swamp's entrance. "Do you want us to walk you in?" Angelique asked as Monique parked.

"No, I'll be fine, and I know you both need to get back to work," she replied.

"We're just so grateful to have you back with us," Angelique said.

The three of them hugged and said their goodbyes and then Dominique began the trek home.

It was wonderful to be able to walk through the swamp without a knife clutched in her hand and without fear in her heart. This, more than anything, made her realize her ordeal was truly over.

By all accounts, Pierre was innocent in her mother's murder and the person who had been after Dominique was under arrest. She no longer needed Luke as her bodyguard. She probably wouldn't see him much anymore. Once again, a wave of sadness filled her heart.

She reached her shanty. Since she didn't have her purse, she had no key, but thankfully she had one hidden under a rock at the foot of her bridge. She retrieved it and then used it to go inside where she sank down in the corner of the sofa.

She didn't have her cell phone. Eventually, she'd have to buy a new one. She'd also need to get a driver's license and other things that had been in her wallet. She needed to check in at the café and get back on the schedule to work. And she'd have to make arrangements for one of her sisters to take her to get her car which was in the police station parking lot. It had been towed there for further processing following her disappearance. But not today.

Today, she just wanted to rest and revel in the fact that she was free and didn't need to be afraid anymore. There would be no more troubling notes or anything else left at her shanty door. And no more Luke.

Unable to sit still for long, she passed the afternoon by cleaning. She wiped down the cabinets in the kitchen area and then mopped the floors. After that, she changed the sheets on her bed.

By that time, she was hungry and so she started the generator and hunted in the cooler for something she could cook. The ice inside was nearly gone. She'd have to throw most of the food away and go shopping.

She made herself a grilled cheese and ate it with some chips and a soda. She had just finished eating when there was a knock on her door.

It was Luke. At the sight of him, her heart expanded. "Luke," she greeted him in surprise.

"Hi, Dominique," he replied.

"Come in." She opened the door enough so he could walk in. It was only then that she saw her purse in his hand.

"We found this at Burt's place. It looks like everything is still inside it. Your phone and driver's license are inside and I knew you'd need them back as soon as possible." He held the purse out to her.

"Thank you," she replied. "Can you sit for a few minutes?" she asked.

"Okay." He walked over to the sofa as she dug into the purse to retrieve her phone.

"Let me just plug this in to charge and I'll be right back." She hurried into the kitchen to take care of the phone, then returned to the living room and sank down next to him. Instantly, she was surrounded by his familiar scent...the one that had always made her feel safe and protected.

"How are you doing?" he asked. His eyes filled with a wealth of concern. "Does your jaw hurt badly?"

"Not too badly," she replied. She looked away from him and instead gazed across the room. "Luke, I did a lot of thinking in the three days I was gone. I thought a lot about my mother and I realized something really important." She gazed back at him. "In my grief, I've been trying to live the wild and free life she always had. I guess I felt that if I was just like her, then she wouldn't really be dead."

"Oh, Dominique," he said softly.

She heard it. When he said her name, she heard the love. When she gazed in his eyes, she saw his love. And in her time alone, she had realized the depths of her love for him. Her love for him was what had caused the sadness inside her, but she wasn't sad anymore.

She held his gaze for a long moment. "If I'm not working the late shift at the café, I could have your dinner on the table at six every night," she blurted.

He looked at her in surprise and then that wonderful smile curved his lips. "I don't have to eat at six o'clock every night. I could eat earlier or later, depending on your schedule. I could definitely cook for you, too."

Hope lit up the gold flecks in his beautiful green eyes. Hope filled her heart, her very soul.

"Luke, we've been a couple of fools," she said. "I know we can make it work between us. If we both give a little, I think we could be very happy together forever."

He grabbed her hand, stood and pulled her up and into his arms. "Are you trying to tell me you love me?" he asked, his hope shimmering in his eyes.

"Oh Luke, I am wildly, madly in love with you." She barely got the words out before his mouth took hers in a long, slow kiss that spoke of a happy future together.

When the kiss ended, she remained in his arms, reluctant to move away. He gazed deeply into her eyes. "There was a time I didn't think I could live with you, but now I know I can't live without you," he said.

Her heart swelled with her love for this man who had been her bodyguard, her friend and her lover. "I will do what I can to adhere to your schedules," she said.

"And I will dance in the rain with you and be ready for your spontaneity any time of the day or night," he replied. His gaze grew more serious. "I also intend to work hard to solve your mother's murder. I promise you, Dominique. I won't stop until we get justice for her."

She placed a hand on his lower jaw. "I know that. Somehow, I wonder if it was her magic that brought us together. I mean, without me believing Pierre was guilty and running with my scheme to bring him down, you and I probably wouldn't have ever spent any time together."

"Thank God for Mystique's magic," he replied, his gaze once again soft and loving on her.

She ran a finger over his lower lip. "Want to see what kind of magic we could make in my bedroom?" she asked, wanting nothing more than to truly make love with the man of her heart.

"There's that spontaneity in you again," he said teasingly. "I'll definitely roll with this one." He took her hand and pulled her toward her bedroom.

There would be things they'd need to figure out later, like where they were going to live and other logistics, but for now, that was the last thing on her mind, as she knew they'd conquer anything as long as they were together.

Epilogue

Monique sat on her small deck and watched the sunrise awaken the swamp. She sipped her cup of coffee as brilliant rays of gold and pink and orange lit up the eastern sky.

The colors reflected on the water as morning birds began to sing from the trees. Nocturnal creatures would be going to bed while others would be waking up for another day.

She should be at complete peace in this moment of solitude. Dominique had been rescued safe and sound and that's what she had prayed for.

However, she wasn't at peace. It had been three months now since her mother had been viciously murdered and there was no suspect in sight.

She loved her work at All That Jazz and she loved her life in her quiet, peaceful shanty. But she desperately needed closure in her mother's murder. She needed justice to be done in order to make her feel whole.

Right now, there were ragged holes in her heart and she knew they wouldn't heal until her mother's murderer was arrested and put behind bars.

Angelique had tried to solve the crime by questioning potential suspects. Dominique, certain that Pierre was guilty, had put herself at risk by shadowing the gator-hunter.

Maybe it was time Monique formulated a plan to find the person who had killed her mother by slashing her throat. Obviously, the police had no clues to follow.

She took the last drink of her coffee. The sun was up and a plan had begun to brew in her head. It would be dangerous, but something had to be done and maybe it was up to her to help the police.

All she knew for sure was the anxiety that fluttered through her most of the time and the missing piece of her heart was due to the fact that nobody had been arrested for the crime.

The only way to fix both those things was for her to do what she could to finally solve the case once and for all. She got up from her chair, set her cup to the side and started up her generator.

Nervous energy filled her, along with a simmering sense of anticipation. It was time for her to begin her day, but tonight when she got off of work, she would set her plan into motion.

* * * * *

PROTECTIVE REFUGE

JANIE CROUCH

To Denise... I couldn't tie my own shoe without you.
Thank you for making this series happen.

Chapter One

"Get down!" Xavier Michaels roared to the rest of his team, gesturing for them to get behind the bullet-riddled truck that served as their only cover. The sound of gunshots filled the air, and his team—what remained of them, anyway—dove behind the truck after Xavier.

Xavier pressed his back to the vehicle, breath tearing from his lungs, and glanced over to Max, his younger brother, hunkered down behind the blown-out front wheel of the truck. He had that look on his face, the look that Xavier knew meant bad news.

Max rolled out from behind the truck and fired off a few shots, until his gun clicked uselessly—empty. No more ammunition around them. A couple of the other members of the group were scrambling to try to find cover, to no avail. Most of them were hit, carrying injuries, their blood mingling with the dust on the ground.

"Max!" Xavier called to his brother, and Max flashed him a grin. Xavier could hear the steady pulse of automatic weapons beyond them, and his own blood rushing in his ears. He didn't know what to do, but he had to keep his brother close.

Keeping his head down, Xavier crawled over to his

brother, pulling him back behind the truck. He felt the tension in his brother's body as he tried to keep him out of the line of fire, but Max was already squirming away from him, ready to get out of there.

"Listen to me," Xavier ordered his brother, and Max finally turned to look at him, remembering that Xavier was technically the one in charge here. They both ducked as a bullet bounced with a metallic clang off the hood of the truck, sending shrapnel spraying into the ground around them.

"I have a few bullets left," he explained urgently, his voice low. "And I'm going to use them to cover you. That building, right there? You make a run for it and take cover inside. I'll be out to meet you in no time, okay?"

"And then what?" Max shot back. "We're outnumbered. And you know backup isn't going to make it in time."

Xavier's mind raced. He wanted to be able to argue with his brother, but he knew he was right.

He could feel the situation quickly spinning out of his control. He couldn't put his baby brother in harm's way. He had promised their mother when they had both left for the army that he would never do that. But the way Max was staring out across the dusty ground before them, spattered with bullets and blood, Xavier knew there wasn't a chance he could stop his brother from what he was about to do.

Max flashed him another grin. That devil-may-care look that told Xavier he was ready to do whatever it took to make it out. He had survived so much, and it had made him cocky. There were only so many chances he had before his luck ran out.

"If this is how I have to go," he remarked, tightening his grip on his vest, "so be it. I had a good run."

"Max, you can't—"

But before Xavier could finish what he had to say, another spray of bullets rattled the truck. Xavier ducked, turning his back, and they skipped past him onto the ground below.

But when he turned back to his brother, he saw that he hadn't been so lucky.

A bloom of blood started to form around Max's throat, a wet darkness spreading out across his camouflage uniform. His eyes were hazy and distant, and Xavier's stomach dropped as he lurched toward him.

"Max!" he yelled. His hands reached out for his brother, but he couldn't get hold of him. He watched as his brother slipped away right before him, and he tried to scream his name again, but it did no good...

"Max!"

XAVIER CAME TO with a start, the sound of his own voice pulling him out of his nightmare. It took him a good thirty seconds to remind himself where he was. The memories were so vivid, the smell of blood and the sound of bullets so fresh in his mind, he couldn't seem to shake them.

But after a minute or so, he sank back into the bed and closed his eyes once more. He was in his room in the lodge at the Warrior Peak Sanctuary. It was the middle of the night, and silence filled the air around him. He wasn't at war; he wasn't fighting anyone. He was safe.

And yet the memory of that dream pressed heavily on his mind as he tried to come back down to earth. His body was still racked with tension, and his insides felt as though they had been shredded as he was forced to relive the worst moment of his life for the hundredth time in the last few months.

When was it going to end? If it ever ended. Before the

fire, the dreams had at least been a little more manageable, but since the fire on the property outside the main lodge nearly three months before, it felt as though he had been tortured nonstop by these memories.

If there was one thing that always served to bring him back to real life, it was a freezing-cold shower—a tip he learned in basic training as a way to wake himself up for any particularly early morning missions. He didn't want to wake anyone up, wandering around the lodge at this hour, but he needed something to blast the memories of what had happened out of his mind, at least for a little longer.

Until he fell asleep again, of course.

He grabbed a change of clothes and made his way down to the showers. The whole place was quiet and peaceful. Normally, he would have enjoyed a little piece of silence, but right now, he could have used the company. Not that he would have made a point to talk about what was going on in his mind. No, running this place, people expected him to be strong.

People came here because they relied on him to handle himself and what he had been through. If they knew how tortured he really was, how much the guilt played on his mind and how much he had let his own brother down, they would never be able to trust him the same way.

He blasted the water on as cold as he could take it and stuck his hand beneath the shower head to try to ground himself. After stripping off his clothes, he stepped into the shower. His teeth started to chatter immediately as the cold seeped into his system.

He closed his eyes, but even with the cold water pounding on his back, he found his mind returning to the night of the fire. The way those flames had licked at the sky, the way it had felt like everything they had worked for was being ripped right out from underneath them. Sometimes, he wondered how they had made it through without any major injuries. Things had looked so bleak at the time; he had accepted in the back of his mind the possibility that the main lodge might go up in smoke with the paddock and surrounding grounds.

But Lawson would never have let that happen. They had both worked too hard to get to this point, to create a sanctuary for people like them who needed a chance to get their feet back under them. They weren't going to let something like a fire change that.

Plenty of people didn't like what they were doing here, but that wasn't his problem. No, he just had to focus on keeping the place open and doing everything he could to protect those who trusted him enough to stay here.

He wasn't sure how long he stayed in that shower. But by the time he stepped out, the cold had soaked all the way through to his bones and his mind felt a little bit clearer. He knew there were probably better, more comfortable ways of dealing with these dreams than ice-cold showers, but the showers worked just fine for him in a pinch.

Maybe it would be smart to utilize some of the therapy they offered to their guests, but he had too much to do to spend his time talking about his feelings. Plus, again, what would everyone think of him? The lodge still needed some fixing up, even though it had been months since the fire, and he felt like it would be a long time before it was truly back to the way he wanted it.

Making his way back up the corridor toward his room, he found himself slowing, not wanting to be alone in there again. Instead of a place to rest and rejuvenate, his bedroom had become a place of torment these last few months with the nightmares that filled his head whenever he closed his eyes.

Even though it had been years since he lost his brother, the memories of that day still bled into his mind all the time. That last look Max had given him, the way he had told him that he was happy going out this way... Had he meant it?

Xavier had to believe he did. Because the alternative was too horrible to imagine.

He reached his bedroom door once more and was immediately struck by how cold it was. Not just the cold he was carrying in from the shower but something else—something that jumped out to him at once. He tensed, looking around, his instincts telling him something was wrong.

Inside the room, he took in anything that had changed since he was last there.

The curtains had been pulled back. The window had been thrown open, letting in a rush of the freezing mountain air. No way would Xavier have left it that way himself. He never slept with the curtains or the window open. It was way too dangerous to open yourself up to an enemy like that, especially when you were in such a vulnerable state as sleeping.

But he flicked on the light and saw more out of place.

The dresser drawers had all been pulled open, and it looked as though his clothes had been rummaged through. He widened his eyes, making his way toward the piece of furniture cautiously, as though it might have been rigged with something. He rooted through his belongings, trying to see if there was anything missing, but nothing jumped out at him.

He had left the door unlocked when he went for his shower. A mistake on his part—but he had no reason to think he couldn't trust everyone in this lodge. Unless there was someone here who meant trouble, someone they hadn't done enough research into, someone who was going to cause problems down the line.

Whoever had been in here, they hadn't just been going through his stuff for no reason. No, the way the room had been turned over, they had been looking for something. Searching for something specific. But what?

He couldn't see anything missing, and it wasn't as though he kept anything of importance in his room anyway. Unless they counted the small handful of family memorabilia he kept on his bedside table, pictures of him and Max and their parents.

But just because he didn't think there was anything worth taking in here didn't mean everyone else agreed. Someone had to have been keeping a close eye on the place to know when he had left his room, and they had pounced on the opportunity to get in there and search through all of his stuff.

He closed his dresser drawers, then pushed the window back into place and locked it. Then, he scanned the dark grounds outside, checking to see if there was anything that looked suspicious before pulling the curtains shut again. Not that he thought whoever did this would hang around long enough to be seen.

There was nothing but the sound of crickets in the air, and stillness that suddenly seemed eerie knowing there was trouble afoot.

Whatever it was, he would get to the bottom of it, Xavier promised himself. He always did.

And this time would be no exception.

Chapter Two

Hannah Davies wandered away from the lodge, the scent of maple syrup still fresh in her senses after cleaning up from the breakfast crowd in the cafeteria. Part of her morning routine after eating her first meal of the day was to go out for a walk around the property. She used it as time to clear her head and ready herself for her daily duties and to see how the seasons were changing at the place she had come to call home.

It was a cold, crisp February morning as she made her way down the path toward the cabins in the forested area. Along the edge of the path were the flowerbeds she had planted before the first frost back in the fall. It was going to be a few more months before she saw them come to fruition, but she could hardly wait for the explosion of color and scent her tulips and peonies were going to bring. Lawson, her brother, had tried to tell her there was no point putting so much energy into the flowers here, but she knew he was going to see why she had done it when they all started to bloom. This place could use a little color after the fire, and she was glad to be the one to make that happen.

She could still hear the buzz of activity inside the lodge as everyone went about getting settled into their daily routine. Hannah would be at the front desk for the rest of the day, which was why she was so intent on stretching her legs and clearing her mind for a while. If there was one thing she had learned in her time here, it was that it didn't suit her to be cooped up all day. With the beautiful scenery just a few feet from the door, she had no excuse not to get out into nature for at least a few minutes every day.

Tipping her head back, she paused as she reached the small cluster of cabins at the end of the path. Inhaling a deep lungful of air, she let the chill rush through her. Nothing cleared her head like the cold. She loved the summer, of course she did, with all the brightness of life around her, but there was no doubt she was going to miss these cold mornings when they passed.

Suddenly, a noise caught her attention—a laugh. She glanced around and quickly located the source coming from the newest cabin that had been built over the last few months. Through the large front window, she saw Bailey laughing as Aaron playfully chased her.

Hannah smiled. She was so happy for the two of them and that they had found each other once more. Every time she saw them together, it was clear they had been made for one another. Anyone could tell how much they loved each other. It was obvious in their actions and written all over their faces whenever they were together.

A little pang of jealousy twisted in her chest, but she tried her best to ignore it. She wasn't going to let her own lack of luck in love stop her from being happy for her friends. That was what this place was for, right? A chance for people to make a new start and discover their own calling in life. And for these two, that calling was with one another, taking care of each other and supporting each other through whatever life threw at them. And life had thrown a lot at them over the past several months.

Turning her back to give them some privacy, Hannah was about to head back up to the lodge when she caught sight of someone else making their way up the path toward the cabins. A familiar figure, hands stuffed in his pockets, eyes downcast, about thirty feet away.

She bit her lip and smiled, then lifted her hand to greet him. "Hey, Xavier!"

He didn't seem to notice her.

She frowned. It wasn't windy or raining. There was no reason he wouldn't have heard her. She called to him again, but he still didn't seem to hear. Finally, when she got closer and lifted her voice a little, his head snapped up, and he seemed almost startled to see her.

"Oh hey, Hannah," he greeted as he closed the distance between them.

She frowned again. What was wrong? Something was clearly bothering him. He always paid attention to his surroundings and wasn't usually quite so somber.

"You okay?" she asked.

He ran a hand over his short cropped dark hair, his hazel eyes darkening slightly as he frowned. But then he nodded firmly, clearly deciding against telling her what he was so deep in thought about. "Yeah, I'm fine."

She could tell he was lying. Maybe if she gave him a little encouragement, he would be more willing to share. "Didn't see you at breakfast," she remarked, trying to keep her voice casual. "You don't normally miss pancakes."

"Guess I must have overslept," he replied with a shrug.

"That's not like you," she pointed out. "Military man, you always keep good time, right?"

He managed a smile. His eyes creased as he looked

down at her, and she felt an all-too-familiar flip in her chest. God, she needed to do something about that. She should have known better by now than to let the chemistry between them mess with her head. One kiss all those months ago should have been enough to get it out of her system, and yet, here she was, just as fluttery as she had always been about her brother's best friend.

"I try," he replied, and he glanced around. "What are you doing out here this morning anyway? It's freezing."

"I like the cold," she told him. "Helps clear my head."

"I get that," he said.

They were dancing around the real point here. She could feel that in her bones. But she didn't know how to nudge him along to what was really on his mind. There were dark circles beneath his eyes—it was obvious he hadn't been sleeping much. But what had been keeping him up?

Maybe she was overthinking it. Ever since the night of the fire, she had been more nervous than ever before, worried that something might disrupt the comfortable peace she had found at the lodge.

She shifted a little closer to him, looking up into his eyes. For a split second, she felt it, the same draw that had led to their impromptu kiss last year. She had done everything she could to keep that out of her mind, to force herself to forget about how good his lips had felt on hers, but it wasn't that easy. No matter how much she tried to shut it off, the long-standing crush she had on him just wouldn't go away. Even knowing her brother hated the thought of his baby sister and his best friend together.

He was just protective of both of them.

"Is something going on?" she pressed.

He paused for a second, as though he was really considering telling her the truth. But then, he withdrew once more. Shaking his head, he glanced back toward the main building. "Nothing," he said at last. "I should get to work for the day. See you around, Hannah."

And with that he was gone.

She watched as he went and thought about calling after him once more. Begging him to tell her what was troubling him. She parted her lips, about to call his name, then stopped herself. His business and troubles were his own, even if she wished for something different. He had made it clear where he stood after their kiss all those months ago, and the last thing she needed was to make things more complicated than she already had.

Her shoulders slumped as she stood there, trying to calm the pounding of her heart. How was it that he could still have this effect on her even after all this time? She had felt it the moment she met him so many years ago when he served in the military with her brother. What had started as a simple crush had developed into something way more prominent.

He never seemed to return the feelings, always keeping her at a distance. And then after the moment they'd shared, she was more confused than ever. Even though she had started it, when their lips touched, he immediately took over—like he'd been waiting for the chance—and all but devoured her. But then suddenly it was over, and it felt like there was more distance between them than ever.

Even though she had tried to forget, she found herself thinking about it all the time. What it would be like to be with him and kiss him anytime she wanted, not having to worry about what someone else thought, especially her brother?

She could still remember the way Lawson had flipped his lid about it, as though he hadn't noticed the tension between them. Maybe he really hadn't, and all of this had come as a complete shock to him. But everyone else seemed to be able to tell how much chemistry she and Xavier had. Was her brother really that clueless?

It didn't matter. He had made himself clear. He didn't want anything happening between his best friend and his sister, and she supposed she couldn't blame him. What guy would be all right with his business partner and closest friend making a move on his little sister?

Lawson had always been way more protective of Hannah than he needed to be. No matter how much she tried to convince him that she was perfectly capable of taking care of herself, he would brush her off and act like she needed someone looking out for her. It was frustrating sometimes, but hey, he was her big brother. It wasn't as though she could expect anything else—it had been that way her entire life.

She watched from a distance and waited for Xavier to make it back to the lodge before she started walking again. She didn't want him to feel like she was following him or chasing him around. God knew she had done enough of that as it was.

Sometimes, she wished she could just ask him where his feelings for her stood. Surely, her brother's attitude hadn't been enough to shut down everything Xavier felt for her. Would it? She didn't know. And with no way to ask him without giving away her own lingering emotions, she had decided it was best to just keep it all to herself.

Another explosion of laughter burst from the cabin closest to her, and this time the sound of River and Cade's flirtation echoed down the pathway. Hannah knew she wasn't going to get far being envious of the other women around here, but damn, sometimes she wondered when it was going to be her turn to fall for someone and have them want her back.

She couldn't fault either couple for their happiness, either. All four of her friends had been through some hard times and she was grateful they'd all made it beyond their troubles to find contentment together at Warrior Peak.

She remembered back when Cade first showed up with his own healing to do and had River in tow. He'd spotted her hitchhiking at night in the rain and brought her up to the lodge unaware of the trouble following her. Then Aaron had shown up fighting his own demons and took the job as the sanctuary's handyman. He kept to himself until Bailey showed up looking for him with bad people on her trail.

Yeah, they'd all been through some trouble, but had fought their battles hard and won, and even come out the other side stronger together.

That was what she wanted. Not the battles and dangers, per se, but the deep connection, the strength and unity. Being together with that one person who wanted you back with the same fierceness.

Her time would come. She had to tell herself that. She had done her best to stay optimistic, but sometimes, it felt like none of this was really fair. She didn't know how much longer she would have to wait—and if the man she was meant to be with was already right there in front of her.

But Xavier was her brother's best friend and had been part of their lives forever. She knew it would make everything crazy-complicated if the two of them got involved. Plus, they worked together, too. Wasn't that a cardinal sin, dating someone you worked with? God, it was all so complicated, Hannah didn't know where to start.

Maybe a little more time out here in the cold would do her good. She decided to head a little farther into the forest, hoping the canopy of trees around her would give her some space to think.

The look on Xavier's face told her there was more going on with him than she knew about. And she wasn't sure exactly what to think about that. After the fire, she was uneasy in a way she hadn't been before, and any little thing that seemed off was enough to get her mind spinning.

Especially when it came from the man she couldn't get out of her head.

Chapter Three

Xavier stepped back inside the lodge, rubbing his hands together as the warmth of the crackling fire in the reception area rushed through his body. It had been Hannah's idea to put it in, to create a warmer and cozier ambience for those first arriving at the lodge, and it had been a great addition. Every time he saw it, he felt a little more relaxed. God only knew how much he needed that right now.

His stomach grumbled as he headed down to the kitchen. He had skipped out on breakfast, oversleeping after he had been up in the middle of the night. Even when he fell back into a fitful sleep after his cold shower, the dreams had plagued him enough that he hadn't been able to get any real rest, no matter how hard he tried. Now, he could feel the weight of that lack of sleep pressing down on his shoulders. He hoped it wasn't too obvious.

Though, judging by the way Hannah had looked at him when he ran into her outside, he wasn't doing a good job keeping it to himself. He didn't want to worry anyone, but at the same time, there was only so long he could wait this out before he had to admit defeat and get help.

Arriving at the kitchen, he found Sarah Peterson, Warrior Peak's counselor, finishing up with the dishes.

She flashed him a grin. "All the pancakes are gone," she told him. "But there's some bacon and eggs left on the stove if you want something."

"Thanks, Sarah," he replied, and he went to help himself to a hearty breakfast, even if he really didn't feel much like it. His stomach twisted into knots as he thought about what he had come back to the night before. He still had no explanation for what had happened to his room, and that bothered him. He liked everything in his world to be in order, everything in its place. That was how he handled the stress of everything he had been through, how he survived in the mess of the life he'd led so far. But someone tossing his room was something he hadn't been ready for, and he didn't like the way it made him feel.

"You need a hand with those?" he asked Sarah, nodding to the dishes she was working through.

She waved a hand. "I'm fine," she replied. "Hannah already brought everything in from the dining area, and I'm just finishing up. You have something to eat."

He nodded at her gratefully and went to take a seat in the empty dining hall. The smell of pancakes and maple syrup lingered in the air, a reminder of what he had missed. Even if he had been awake, he doubted he would have bothered coming down here to join everyone. He wouldn't have been in the mood to put himself in a roomful of people who might guess something was up.

He didn't want questions, he didn't want interrogation, and he didn't want anyone to know what was really going on inside his head. He'd needed the cool morning walk and space to clear his head a little more and think. Someone there at the lodge, after all, had likely been the one to go through his room in the middle of the night. If that was the case, he didn't want to give them any indication that he was on to them.

He knew from his CIA days that playing it cool was the best way to get a rat out of hiding, and he intended to smoke out this person one way or another.

Just as Xavier was finishing his food, Lawson appeared in the doorway. Xavier caught his friend's eye, and as soon as he did, his stomach dropped. Lawson's mouth was set into a hard line, and judging by the look on his face, Xavier could tell he wanted to have a serious conversation.

Xavier sighed and set aside his plate as Lawson came to join him, sliding in to the long wooden bench that ran along the other side of the communal table.

"Didn't see you at breakfast today," Lawson stated.

Xavier had hoped his absence wouldn't be that obvious, but looked like he hadn't gotten so lucky. He shrugged and tried to keep his voice steady. "Overslept."

Lawson paused, giving Xavier a chance to share more, but when he didn't, he sighed and cocked his head at him. "I know something's going on with you," he said bluntly.

Leave it to Lawson to jump right to the heart of the matter. His friend had never been one to mince his words, but Xavier's back was instantly up. Did he know something about the room invasion last night? "What are you talking about?" Xavier fired back. He knew Lawson was on his side, but there was a part of him that didn't like letting anyone in. After everything he'd been through in his life, he felt like he needed to be on his guard at all times, even around his best friend.

"The nightmares are back, aren't they?" Lawson pressed.

Xavier looked down at the table. He didn't need to reply. Lawson had been there with him when Xavier was first navigating the nightmare of surviving his brother's loss.

Lawson had seen how much it tore Xavier apart. Xavier wished he had some way to deny it, but there would have been no point. Lawson knew him better than anyone else in the world.

"You've been off ever since the fire," Lawson continued, raising his eyebrows pointedly. "You don't need to hide it from me, man. I remember—"

"It's fine," Xavier cut him off before he could go any further. He didn't want to get into it, not now. There were other, more important things to think about. He wasn't going to dwell on the memories that he had worked so hard to leave in the past. Even if his brain didn't agree while he was sleeping.

Lawson grimaced. "Healing isn't linear," he reminded him. "God knows you've learned that just like I have, seeing what people go through here. There's no shame in needing help. That's what we have Sarah for—"

Xavier shook his head again. He knew Lawson was just trying to help, but that was the last thing on earth he needed right now. His best friend was trying to look out for him, but the thought of dredging up all those old memories once more made his chest hurt. He wasn't going to put himself through that. Not a chance in hell. "I'm fine," Xavier insisted, brushing him off.

"I saw how bad it got last time," Lawson reminded him, dropping his voice slightly.

Xavier straightened up, rolling his shoulders back and trying to figure out the best way to get his friend off his case. "Someone was in my room last night."

Lawson stared at him for a moment, frowning at the sudden change of subject. Then he blinked and blinked again like he was trying to process the information. "What are you talking about?"

"I went down to the showers in the middle of the night," Xavier explained, skipping the part where he'd been woken up by a nightmare. "When I got back, the window to my room was open, and someone had been through all my drawers."

Lawson's eyebrows rose. "Was anything missing?"

"Not that I could see," Xavier replied. "I'll have another look today, now that I'm all the way awake, but it didn't seem like anything had been taken."

"Damn," Lawson muttered, shaking his head. "Who do you think it was? Got any ideas?"

"None," Xavier admitted. "I don't know anyone here who would want to go through my stuff like that."

"You have any idea what they were looking for?"

"Not like I've got anything worth taking," Xavier pointed out with a shrug. "But if I figure it out, I'll let you know."

"Who could have got in like that?" Lawson wondered out loud. His voice turned hard and tense, the prior conversation forgotten.

Much to Xavier's relief. "I don't know. If I'm being generous, I might have said it was just someone sleepwalking, but..."

He trailed off. There was nothing else they needed to say, not really. After the fire, everyone at Warrior Peak had been unsettled. They couldn't let their guard down, and they had to assume everything was a threat after what had happened. The attack on the sanctuary grounds had underlined just how vulnerable this place was. With the doors open to anyone who needed it, it was difficult to track who might have been here for reasons other than the right ones.

"You keep your doors locked and your head up," Lawson told him. "I'll have a look through the security footage around the area. I know we don't have any cameras in the rooms or inner hallways specifically, but we might be able to catch someone sneaking around in the outer hallways and doors and the common areas. Maybe they didn't realize they were being recorded."

"Thanks," Xavier replied. "Let me take a look at it, too. I want to know who was poking around in my room."

Lawson nodded, then stood like the conversation was over.

Xavier got to his feet as well, grabbing his dishes to take them back to the kitchen. He was glad he had managed to deflect the more serious conversation before they got too deep into it. He didn't want to have to flesh out the details of his bad dreams to Lawson. They were just dreams, after all. Of course they sucked, but other than messing with his sleep, which made him tired the next day, they didn't have an impact on his real life. No matter how real they seemed in the moment.

"You better wash that up or the women will have your head," Lawson joked, walking toward the kitchen.

Xavier grinned and headed over to the sink to start taking care of his dishes. He knew Lawson was right. Sarah and Hannah were sticklers for cleanliness, always making sure the kitchen, dining hall, and other common areas were as clean as possible with so many different people always around. He wasn't going to be the idiot who left a dirty plate out under their watchful eyes.

He turned on the water and let it run until it was warm. Though most of the lodge building had been refitted, the pipes still took time to get going once the water was turned on, especially in the colder weather, rattling and groaning in the walls. And even more so with multiple people in the showers at the same time. It turned into a clinking and clanking symphony of sounds.

But that was why he liked this place so much. Even after all these years and all these changes, it still held some memories of what it had been in the first place, a rustic retreat built for a family to escape to. They had managed to build on that legacy, turning it into a new safe space for all the people who needed one.

He didn't even know the extent of everything the guests here had been through, but he didn't have to. He could see it written all over their faces, the tension and drawn expressions when they first arrived, and then the slow unfurling of their true personalities and potential the longer they stayed and the more they healed. It was an honor to bear witness to the healing and growth that happened at Warrior Peak.

Maybe he was a hypocrite for not doing the same, but he couldn't find it in him to want to heal right now.

Lawson leaned in the doorway, and Xavier could feel his eyes on him. Xavier glanced over at him, raising his eyebrows as though nudging him to say whatever was on his mind.

"Just think about it, man," Lawson told Xavier, coming over to slap him on the shoulder. "Sarah's here to help people. What you're going through, it's exactly her realm of expertise. You should consider it, at least."

Xavier sighed. He knew Lawson wasn't going to let this go until he had at least agreed to that. He nodded. "Sure, I'll consider it."

"Good," Lawson replied and headed for the door.

As he left, Xavier realized that he had let the water run until it was far too hot, and his hand was nearly scalding beneath the flow. He drew it back quickly, sucking in a sharp breath, and put on the cold tap to try to even it out.

Staring down at the dishes before him, his mind drifted back to his room, ransacked and rummaged through. That was the most important thing to get to the bottom of right now, not his nightmares and why they were so frequent again after the fire. There was someone, maybe even someone staying at the lodge, who was causing trouble, and he wasn't going to let them get away with it.

This place was his home, and these people were his family. He was going to protect them at all costs.

Chapter Four

Hannah wrapped her hands around her hot chocolate, the last of which was swirling in the bottom of her mug, as she glanced out into the darkness and tried to muster the courage to go outside and head back to her cabin.

"I don't think I'll ever get used to this kind of cold," Bailey complained as the two women sat in the small common room toward the back of the lodge.

Hannah chuckled. "Oh trust me, you're not going to have much of a choice," she teased.

Bailey rolled her eyes. "I have no idea how I'm going to survive," she announced, laying the back of her hand on her forehead in a dramatic swoon.

"At least you have Aaron to keep you warm," Hannah pointed out without thinking.

Bailey cocked an eyebrow. "You think it'd be easier for you if you had a guy waiting back at your cabin for you?"

Hannah shrugged, feeling her cheeks start to get a little warm. "I don't know," she muttered. She didn't want to admit how lonely she'd been feeling these last few months. More than ever she found herself wishing for companionship like River and Bailey had with their men.

Both women had fought hard for their relationships,

and deserve every moment of happiness they had. Bailey against the crooked cops she and Aaron had to expose to find their second chance and River and Cade dealing with River's past, including an obsessed cult leader. They'd all faced devastating odds and had come out the other side stronger and more settled as couples in loving relationships. Hannah longed to have what her friends had.

Someone to stay in and cuddle with on the dark, freezing winter nights. Someone to share the day's troubles and setbacks. Sometimes, she would lie in bed and stare out into the cold night beyond, wondering how she was supposed to get through another year without someone by her side.

It felt like everyone around her was settling down and getting comfortable in a life with someone else, but she was still in her cabin alone. She didn't want to go back to it, not quite yet, not when this hot chocolate and company was so cozy.

"Well, I guess I should get back to my cabin. Aaron will be wondering what happened to me," Bailey announced, getting to her feet and stretching. "You ready to brave the cold with me, Hannah?"

"Guess I could give it a shot," Hannah agreed, standing.

But before they could make it anywhere, the lights cut out.

"Oh no," Bailey muttered in the sudden darkness. "What's going on?"

Hannah pulled her phone out and switched on the flashlight so the two of them could avoid bumping into furniture while the back-up generators kicked into action. It wasn't entirely unusual for things to go wrong around here, especially in the winter. The cold weather sometimes froze the pipes and made it difficult for repairmen to get out as quickly as they might have normally.

But as they stood there, nothing happened. The beam of Hannah's phone light cut through the darkness, but no other lights were clicking back on.

"Shouldn't the backup generators have kicked in by now?" Hannah asked, a little nervous. She suddenly felt like the darkness was consuming them. Her mind couldn't help flashing back to the fire a few months earlier, like it did every time lately when something went wrong. Something like this was enough to make her palms sweat and her heart beat out of her chest.

"I think so," Bailey muttered. "Come on, let's get out to the front. The fireplace will give us some light, at least."

Hannah let Bailey lead the way but kept her phone flashlight trained in front of them as the two women made their way to the reception area of the lodge. The fire crackled cozily when they got there, but the usual comforting aura of the flames in the hearth didn't do much to settle Hannah's nerves.

"I swear," a voice cut through the darkness, two sets of footsteps coming toward them, "if the power in this place has gone down after I paid all that money to set up new generators, I'm going to kick some serious a—"

"It's going to be okay," Xavier soothed Lawson, and Hannah felt calm wash over her as soon as she heard his voice. Even after everything that had happened between them, she found his presence enormously comforting. As long as he was around, she knew they would figure out what was going on somehow.

"You know what's happening?" Bailey asked Lawson and Xavier as they reached the women.

Lawson shook his head, lit by the glow of a flashlight

in his hand. "No idea. I just got those generators for the winter, so they should have kicked on by now. Xavier and I are going to go out and check what's going on."

"I'll come with you," Hannah replied at once, without thinking. Her brother pulled a face, clearly trying to think of some way he could talk her out of it, but Xavier nodded in agreement.

"We could use as many eyes on it as possible," Xavier agreed. "Bailey, you want to come, too?"

"I think I could brave the cold," Bailey replied. "Plus, I really don't want to stay in here alone." She put on the coat she'd been carrying. Hannah did the same, and they followed the guys out to the generators at the far side of the lodge.

It was bitingly cold outside, and the freezing air nipped at Hannah's skin. She moved to zip her coat up, but with her phone in one hand she couldn't get a proper grip on the zipper. She turned off her phone's flashlight, intent on putting it in her pocket, but with the light off, it was too dark to see the ground in front of her. Suddenly, her shoe snagged in a crack in the sidewalk, and she tripped.

"Ahh!" she yelled and fell to her knees.

Everyone spun around to make sure she was all right, but she had already hit the ground with a painful thump, scratching up her knees in the process.

"Hannah, are you okay?" Xavier asked as he rushed over. Crouching down, he put his arm around her, and the feel of his warm touch on her made her head spin.

"Uh, I'm fine," she managed, glad he couldn't see the flush to her cheeks or just how much she enjoyed having him so close to her. He helped her up, and she leaned on him a little longer than necessary.

Lawson chose that moment to sweep his flashlight over

her, to make sure she was okay, and Hannah had to lower her gaze to the ground to avoid being blinded by the light in her eyes. She hoped he hadn't noticed the dreamy look on her face while she leaned into Xavier, enjoying his comfort and warmth.

"Someone must have cut the power on purpose," Xavier growled, his arm still around Hannah holding her to his side. It didn't strictly need to be there, but there was no way she was going to be the one to pull back.

Bailey shot her a pointed look in the flashlight's glow, as though she could sense the tension between them too, and Hannah bit into her lip and quickly lowered her gaze again. She hoped the other woman wouldn't say anything in front of Lawson. As far as her brother knew, there was nothing left between her and Xavier at all. The last thing she needed at a time like this was Lawson getting mad. They had other things to focus on.

"And it's getting people hurt," Xavier added, squeezing Hannah's shoulder slightly.

Hannah's pulse fluttered, hearing the protectiveness in his voice, as if he wanted to do everything he could to look out for her.

"I just scuffed up my knees, that's all. I'm okay, really," Hannah replied. "Let's go out to the generators and see if there's anything we can find."

Xavier finally let go of Hannah, and she immediately missed his warmth.

The group continued along the path to the generators without any further injuries. When they got there, sure enough, lengths of wire had been yanked out of the control panels and snipped. It looked neat and precise, as though someone had come with the tools to make it happen and knew what they were doing.

Lawson grabbed the wires, inspecting them closely. "Who the hell would have done this?" he demanded to nobody in particular, turning back around to face the group.

"The Haynes brothers, I bet," Bailey cut in.

Hannah turned to Bailey with a groan. "The guys who live at the ranch just over the mountain?"

"Yeah, them," Bailey replied. "They'd be my first suspects anyway."

"But why would they have done this?" Hannah asked, confused. She didn't exactly have many good things to say about the brothers, but she doubted they would have gotten involved in something like this.

"I don't know," Bailey replied. "To cause trouble."

Lawson and Xavier exchanged a look.

All of a sudden, Hannah felt a familiar feeling deep down in her stomach—a feeling she had promised herself she would never ignore again. It was the same feeling she'd had on the night of the fire, just before she had smelled the smoke filling the air and been faced with the cruel reality of what was happening.

She wrapped her arms around herself. "I want to go back inside."

Bailey nodded. "Come on, let's go," she agreed, taking Hannah's arm and steering her back down the walkway toward the main doors. "I'll take a look at those knees for you."

Hannah was more careful about where she stepped this time. Sneaking a look at Bailey out of the corner of her eye, she tried to ask her next question as carefully as she could. Bailey was a police officer down in Blue Ridge and she didn't want to cause problems or get the other woman in trouble by asking too many questions. "Why do you think the Haynes brothers might have had something to do with this?" she asked. "They've pestered us on and off in the past but it's never been anything that's caused real damage. Is there something official going on with them in town?"

"Because they live nearby and like to cause trouble, and I've seen plenty of reports at the police station coming in about them over the last few months." Bailey sighed. "Nothing too serious, mostly just intimidation around town, but they've clearly gotten it into their heads that they have some kind of ownership of the lodge. They've been heard mouthing off to whoever will listen when they've been drinking. I don't know how far that might go."

Hannah shivered. Her only encounter with the Haynes brothers had been when the younger one, Ron, had catcalled her in town. And then he had followed her almost halfway back up the mountain to Warrior Peak before he gave up. It had spooked her, sure, but she had just chalked it up to a bad experience and figured they would leave it there.

"That definitely is unsettling. But I still don't understand why they would want to cause trouble here? I mean, are they targeting this place or Lawson and Xavier specifically?" Hannah wondered aloud as they entered the lodge once more. The two women paused in front of the fire, turning their hands back and forth in front of the flames to warm themselves through.

"Honestly, I don't know," Bailey admitted. "They were just my first thought with all the other complaints about disturbances by them in the area.

"Do you think they know about Lawson's and Xavier's backgrounds?" Hannah asked. "I mean, it seems kind of crazy to start something with both being former military and CIA."

"Yeah, but the Haynes brothers have never struck me

much as guys with any smarts," Bailey pointed out. "There might be a reason they're doing all this now. Maybe I'll go around to their ranch with Sheriff Willis tomorrow, see if I can figure out what they're doing."

"You don't think that might aggravate them?" Hannah asked nervously. She didn't like the thought of Bailey getting into trouble, though she knew Bailey could handle it a million times better than she would ever have been able to.

"It might," Bailey admitted. "But I can't just stand aside and let them do whatever they want to this place. Warrior Peak is sacred ground as far as I'm concerned."

Hannah smiled. She was right about that. The lodge and the core staff here were a safe place for Hannah, had been for years now. She loved it up here, even if it was cut off from the rest of the world. She had everything she needed, and she wouldn't ask for a thing more than that.

Apart from the Haynes brothers, if they really were behind this, to leave them the hell alone, of course.

The sound of a car drew their attention, and both women lifted their heads. A pair of taillights were vanishing out of sight, and Hannah knew from a glance who they belonged to.

Uh-oh. Looked like Xavier was going to confront the Haynes brothers all on his own.

Hannah didn't envy them one bit.

Chapter Five

Xavier drummed his fingers on the wheel, his teeth gritted as Lawson stared out the passenger window.

"They can't keep getting away with this," Lawson stated suddenly. "All the problems they've been causing around town have gone on for way too long. It has got to stop."

Lawson had agreed with Xavier the moment he suggested they go to the Haynes' ranch and talk to them face-to-face. Might not have been a good idea, since they didn't exactly have hard proof that the brothers had been the ones to vandalize the generators at the lodge, but they had been causing enough trouble these last few months to at least warrant a visit.

The Haynes brothers, Ron and Dave, were making waves in the small town of Blue Ridge, North Carolina, every time Xavier turned around—or at least, that was what it felt like. Whether it was squaring up to someone at the local bar, getting drunk and causing a commotion, minor vandalism, or attempting to expand the edges of their property right on to Warrior Peak Sanctuary land, it was enough that someone should step up and show them they weren't going to get away with it for another moment.

Xavier narrowed his eyes as he stared out on to the dark

road ahead of him. The main thing on his mind right now was Hannah. He had heard the fear in her voice when she said she wanted to go back inside the building, and he knew it wasn't just from the fall she'd taken.

It made him so angry to hear her like that—not angry at her, and not because she didn't have any reason to be afraid, but because he hadn't made this place safe enough for her to feel comfortable. She had been there on the night of the fire, and he could tell she still carried the psychological scars, just like he did. The dirty cops who had set fire to the lodge property months before had been dealt with, but everyone there was still dealing with the emotional fallout in their own ways. This incident had stirred all those feelings back up. So, it needed to be dealt with. Tonight.

"We're going to have to move everyone down to that crappy hotel in town if we can't get the heat back up and running by tomorrow morning," Lawson added. "This is a bad situation, Xavier. We need to make this quick. Everyone at the lodge will be feeling the cold soon. We need to find a fix fast."

"I know," Xavier muttered. The sanctuary grounds were supposed to be a safe place, a place where their guests could come to heal, where they could rely on Xavier and Lawson to provide them everything they needed. At this time of year, heat was the bare minimum. They would already be waking up to the freezing cold, and Xavier hated the thought of it.

All the more reason to go and confront the Haynes brothers and make sure they understood exactly how seriously Lawson and Xavier took the current situation. Even if they hadn't made the attack outright, they probably knew who did. Something told Xavier they had connections to every shady corner of this community. And Xavier had seen that there were far darker edges to this town than he would have liked to imagine.

They pulled the SUV up at the Haynes ranch. The small ranch house at the center of the property was lit up. Lawson and Xavier exchanged a look, and both of them climbed out of the vehicle. As they headed up to the building, the older brother, Dave, came stumbling out on to the porch. The air stank of booze and weed, the thick smell coming off the man in waves.

"What the hell are you doing here?" Dave called to them, clearly unable to tell who it was.

Xavier slowed his pace slightly. "We're here to talk," he replied. It was true, though he doubted that would be the only thing they did if they found out that either of the Haynes brothers had been involved in cutting off the power.

"It's too damn late for a social call," Dave protested, spitting off the porch just as Xavier reached the bottom step. He was stumbling drunk and had to grab on to the rickety porch railing to keep upright.

"Looks like you're still up," Lawson pointed out. "Just about."

Dave grinned, a crooked smile that didn't reach his eyes.

Xavier felt a wave of anger rush through him. These guys had been trouble for years, ever since he and Max were kids. Even back then, he hadn't liked either one of them, but if they were thinking of causing serious trouble at Warrior Peak, they had another think coming.

"Soooo what do you want to talk about at this time of night?" Dave slurred, his eyes darting between the two men. They settled on Xavier for a moment, and he laughed and shook his head. "Haven't seen you around here since your little brother was throwing stink bombs on to my father's property," he sneered, still clearly holding a grudge against him for it. "What ever happened to Max anyway?"

Lawson sucked in a sharp breath, and Xavier took a step forward. Lawson grabbed his friend's arm to halt his progress.

Dave knew damn well what had happened to Max, and he was trying to get a rise out of Xavier by bringing him up. It was working. The animosity between them was heavy on the air but they didn't have time to get in a skirmish. They needed to ask their questions and be on their way. They still had the generators to worry about. Lawson let go of Xavier's arm and turned to Dave. "Look, we didn't come here for a fight. We just need to know if either of you were up at the lodge tonight?"

Confusion crossed Dave's face. "The lodge?" he asked, shaking his head. "What the hell would I want with that place?"

But before he could say another word, the door next to him opened, and Ron came out, holding a shotgun. It was aimed squarely at Xavier, though his grip was clearly shaky from all the partying they'd been doing.

"Get off our property," he snarled at Xavier, but Xavier wasn't going to take orders from someone like Ron. He grabbed the gun, twisting it out of Ron's hand with an almost comical ease. He checked the chamber—empty.

"Maybe try putting some bullets in next time, dumbass," Xavier told him, as he tossed the gun back to Ron. He caught it awkwardly, and Xavier took a step toward him.

"What about you?" he asked. "Were you up at the lodge tonight?"

"I don't know what the hell you're talking about." Ron was clearly delighted to frustrate Xavier.

"We've been here all night," Dave started waving his

arm back and forth between himself and Ron. "Had a little party with some friends."

Xavier and Lawson shared a glance then Lawson stepped to the side to look through the open door. Sure enough, there were beer cans scattered around and what looked like a poker table set up inside. Lawson caught Xavier's eye and shook his head. It looked like they'd been set up here for a while playing cards. Plus, they looked too wasted to be behind a wheel. They could barely stand up without help.

"Any of your friends been there, that you know of? Or have you heard of anyone wanting to mess with us?" Xavier asked, watching them both for signs of nervousness or deceit.

Ron shook his head then walked toward the door, gesturing inside. "Look, man. Like my brother said, we've been here. We don't know anything about trouble. See for yourself." He motioned for the two men to step inside.

Xavier stepped forward and peeked inside, confirming what Lawson had seen. Poker table, chairs, snacks, and empty beer cans littered the area.

Lawson gestured to Xavier and turned toward the vehicle. Xavier followed his retreat, stopping at the bottom of the steps to leave the brothers with a warning.

"You guys stay away from the sanctuary property," Xavier told them both.

Ron rolled his eyes in exasperation. "Sure thing, captain!" He gave Xavier a mock salute. Dave snickered at his brother's antics.

Xavier shook his head in frustration as he settled behind the wheel.

"Make sure we don't see you there," Lawson warned them one more time, before climbing in the passenger seat.

Xavier felt the anger buzzing through his system, but now, it had nowhere to go. He doubted the brothers had anything to do with what had happened over at the lodge that night, given the state they were in. But even though they most likely didn't personally mess with the generators earlier didn't mean they were completely innocent.

They were known for causing all sorts of mischief, but it really didn't seem logical that they'd cause that kind of disruption in the middle of winter when they knew that the power was more important than ever at the lodge with guests inside.

"What do you think?" Lawson asked.

"I don't know," Xavier replied tersely.

It seemed unlikely the brothers would have managed to pull off something that focused and specific, even at the best of times. They weren't known for having a brain cell between them. Doing something like that would take actual coordination, and they didn't seem to have the capability to do that. They were more likely to use intimidation or petty destruction than they were to come to the sanctuary in freezing weather to cut the power. It seemed too specific, too direct.

Which meant someone else must have done it. But who? And did they have anything to do with the way Xavier's room had been rummaged through the other night? He doubted that had been the Haynes brothers. They would have been out of place and someone would have noticed. Whoever had done it clearly knew how to pull it off without leaving a trace of their identity. He was sure the clumsiness of the Haynes brothers would have left some sign of them behind.

"Me, neither," Lawson admitted with a sigh. "But we can keep an eye on them these next few days. They might not have done it themselves, but it seems like the kind of thing they might have paid or blackmailed someone to do."

"Could be," Xavier replied. He didn't bring up his room again—he was sure he didn't need to. Lawson would already have that on his mind right now, and Xavier didn't need to push it to the front of the conversation again.

"Anyway, we should get back to the lodge," Lawson added. "We're going to need the whole night to get the generators working again. And I don't want anyone to wake up tomorrow with no heat and nothing to eat."

Xavier could already feel his heart sinking at the prospect, but Lawson was right. As the guys who ran the place, they had a duty of care to everyone who stayed there, everyone who relied on them.

His mind drifted to Hannah before he could stop it. How quickly he reacted when he saw her hit the ground. It hadn't been intentional, but he knew Lawson would have noticed.

He had done everything he could to try to keep the truth of his feelings for her under wraps, but at times like this, they came out before he could stop them from showing. He just wanted her to be okay. The same thing had happened on the night of the fire. As soon as he had seen the flames licking the horizon, the first thing on his mind was what he could do to keep her safe.

He started the drive back to the sanctuary, lost in his thoughts, trying to nod in the right places as Lawson talked to him, discussing what they were going to do when they got back to the lodge.

Lawson frowned at him as Xavier pulled the SUV to a halt outside the lodge, looking over at him with an inquisitive expression again. "What's on your mind?" he asked.

Xavier tried to keep his face neutral. "Nothing. Just trying to figure out how we're going to fix the generators."

That was only half of the truth—and far removed from anything Lawson wouldn't have been able to take, especially with everything else they had to deal with right then. If Lawson had any idea Xavier was stuck thinking about his little sister, he would have freaked out.

It was safer for everyone if Xavier kept his mouth shut and focused on the task at hand. Even if the only thing on his mind right now was Hannah.

Chapter Six

"I'm so sorry about last night," Hannah apologized again.

From the other side of the desk, Marnie grinned at her. "I was cozy in my bed," she replied. "I didn't even notice a thing, honestly. You've got nothing to be sorry for."

Hannah found that hard to believe. The power had been out almost all night before Xavier and Lawson managed to get it back on, and the lodge had been freezing. She was sure Marnie was just being polite so she could get on her way without making waves and start her new life.

It was hard to believe she'd already been there for three months; Hannah could still remember the day the middle-aged woman had arrived, fidgety and freaked out, a bruise over her left eye from the abusive ex she had just fled. Hannah had tried to calm her down that night, but she had been so terrified she was hardly able to take in a word Hannah said to her. But now? She looked like a whole different person. She was glowing, her bruises healed, and her face lit up with a bright, easy smile that came from a joy deep inside of her.

It hadn't been easy for her; Hannah knew that much. She had seen the work Marnie had done to keep on top of her scattered mental state and had seen her coming out of therapy appointments in tears more than once. But slowly, she had started to get her feet back under her again, settling in to her treatment plan at the sanctuary and making herself useful.

By the time February came around, she was already planning what she was going to do once she left, and she had organized a trip with her brother to move out to her new place across the state. A fresh start. With a restraining order in place against her ex, hopefully she would never have to worry about him again.

"I can't believe you're going," Hannah told her as she tucked away the keys to Marnie's room. It was a bittersweet moment, for sure. Of course, she was beyond happy that Marnie was able to get back on her feet and start over, but Hannah was going to miss her. It was always the same, when someone who had been there for a while moved on—difficult for Hannah not to let her emotions get the better of her.

"Oh me, neither," Marnie replied with a sigh. "I can still remember when I first got here. I never thought I would get to the point I am now. But…" She grinned, biting her lip. "Here we are."

"You've earned it," Hannah told her. "You put in so much hard work, Marnie. We're all so proud of you."

"Stop, you're going to make me cry," Marnie protested, fanning her hand in front of her face and laughing. "I don't want to look a mess when my brother gets here."

"Sorry, sorry," Hannah apologized, and she darted around the reception desk to give her a huge hug.

Marnie squeezed her back, as though she wasn't quite ready to let go yet. "Thank you, Hannah," she murmured to her. "For everything you've done."

Hannah didn't feel like she had done enough to earn that

kind of comment, but it still meant the world to her. Being able to make a difference like this, really help people in a practical way, it was everything she had always wanted. Working at Warrior Peak Sanctuary wasn't how she had expected to do it, but she was so happy with where she was and grateful for the opportunity to help people every day.

Hannah looked past Marnie to see a car pulling up outside the lodge doors in the parking lot. "Is that your brother?" she asked, nodding outside, and Marnie turned around.

"Yeah, that's him," she replied, quickly wiping away the tears that had slipped down her cheeks. "I should get going, I guess."

"You should," Hannah agreed, giving her hand a squeeze. "You keep in touch, okay? Let us know how things go at your new home."

"I will," Marnie replied, and she lingered for one more moment before she headed for the door. She embraced her brother as he climbed out of the car.

Hannah watched them happily before she made her way back behind the desk. She was just arranging a few intake papers for later in the month when a voice caught her attention.

"Uh, hello."

Her head snapped up, and she found herself staring at a man she had never seen before. She smiled quickly, trying to look as welcoming as possible. She was the first point of contact most people had with the sanctuary, and she wanted to make sure they felt safe from the moment they stepped through the door. "Hi," she greeted him. "Can I help you with anything?"

The man looked a little disheveled, with a beat-up backpack over one shoulder and scruffy stubble just shy of a beard that told Hannah it had been a while since he'd actually had a decent place to stay. He looked tired, with dark rings underneath his eyes, and his clothes were scuffed and smudged with various stains.

Racking her brain, she tried to remember if any new arrivals were scheduled to come in today. She couldn't remember anything, but maybe there had been a last-minute change of plans she hadn't been made aware of.

"Yeah," the man replied, rubbing the back of his neck worriedly.

Hannah looked him up and down; if ever there was a poster boy for ex-military, this guy would be it. He wore combat boots, an old army jacket and a pair of sweatpants that looked as though they had seen some action. The way he carried himself, too, told her that he had at least been through basic training. She ran into plenty of military guys working here, and she'd developed a sense for them.

"You here to visit someone?" she asked. Maybe he was just stopping by to catch up with an old friend.

He shook his head. "I came here because...because I want to check on your availability." He dropped his chin to his chest as he said it.

Hannah stared at him for a moment, surprised. It wasn't often they got walk-ins like this, but when they did, it was usually because the person was in need of some serious help. She quickly clicked through a program on her computer to see if there were any rooms free. She probably should have consulted with Xavier or her brother first, of course, but she knew they wouldn't want her turning away someone who was so clearly in need of help.

"We don't have any rooms in the lodge right now, but we try to keep a few cabins available for overflow guests. We have one you can use, if that's okay with you. It's only a short walk, and you'll still have access to everything here in the lodge," she said.

"No problem." She could hear the relief in his voice.

Where had this guy come from? Her mind was racing with questions, but she knew it wasn't her place to interrogate him just now. She wasn't even sure how he'd gotten up here. She hadn't seen a vehicle coming up the drive or heard one in the parking lot. She knew she would have noticed it, especially with Marnie's brother stopping by.

"Okay, sir, let me get a file started for you and then I'll go over a few other things with you." Hannah told the man, as she opened the computer program to log new arrivals.

"May I get your name and how long you'd like to stay?" She asked moving her hands to the keyboard.

The man hesitated and look around again before replying. "Jed. Jed Black. And I'm not sure yet, maybe a week or two."

"Nice to meet you, Mr. Black."

Hannah asked him a few basic questions, starting an intake file for him. She wasn't sure what to make of him, but he seemed fidgety and nervous, as though he was worried about something—or someone. But she was used to this, given the people she'd dealt with over the years. She knew better than to judge. He could have been through anything before he arrived here, and this might be his last resort. The last thing he needed was her judgment.

"Okay, so here's a key to cabin G3," she explained, pushing it over the counter toward him. "You can get settled and stay there tonight, and then you'll have a meeting with our resident psychiatrist, Dr. Sarah Peterson, at 9:00 a.m. tomorrow. She has an office just down that corridor, you can't miss it. Just take a left, and you'll see her name on the door. All our guests see her first for an assessment, then we'll make a treatment schedule for you to follow while you stay with us."

Jed paused for a moment, as though he wasn't sure he wanted to agree to the appointment.

"I know it seems intimidating," Hannah assured him. "But this is the best way we can evaluate your needs while you're staying with us. There's nothing to be worried about, she's a total professional, and she's not going to force you to talk about anything you don't want to in any great detail."

He breathed a sigh of relief. "Okay," he muttered, and he grabbed the key from the counter and tucked it into his pocket quickly. His eyes darted left and right, like he was waiting for someone to jump out at him at any moment. "I'll be there," he replied. "Wherever there is."

"I'll walk you to your cabin," Hannah offered. "And then I could come by first thing in the morning and walk you to Dr. Peterson's office, if you'd like."

"Sure. I really would," he agreed, and suddenly, he flashed her a smile.

She wasn't sure what it was about that smile, but it caught her off guard. He had been so reserved and so nervous up until now, and yet all of that seemed to fall away for a moment. Like it had just been an act he was putting on.

"Would you like to grab some coffee or a bite to eat from the cafeteria before we head out to your cabin?" Hannah offered.

Jed shook his head. "No, thanks. I'd like to get settled in and cleaned up first, if you don't mind."

"Okay, let me grab my coat," she told him, and she made her way around the counter to get her jacket. It was still bitingly cold out there, and she could have sworn that the shower didn't feel as hot as it normally did when she had used in that morning. Might have just been her imagination, given that the generators had been out, but she was still chilly.

"I heard really good things about this place," Jed remarked.

She smiled and nodded. "Well deserved, trust me," she replied, zipping up her jacket and stuffing her hands into the pockets. "Do you need a hand with your bag?"

"I'm fine," he promised her. "Thanks for all your help, by the way. You're the best. Miss…?"

"Just call me Hannah," she replied.

"Hannah," he repeated, nodding. There was that smile again, broad, handsome, slightly disarming. She would bet he'd used that smile to get anything he wanted in the past, though clearly it hadn't worked out for him if he had wound up at the sanctuary.

"Well, let's get you settled. Shall we?" Hannah opened the door and motioned for Jed to precede her. He fell into step beside her as they walked down the path to his cabin.

Chapter Seven

As the sound of chatter and plates clattering filled the communal dining hall, Xavier couldn't let himself relax. He knew this should be a chance for him to switch off after everything that had happened. After the stress of the generators going out last night, and then his encounter with the Haynes brothers and Dave mentioning Max, Xavier had ended up having nightmares when he finally made it to bed. He'd been up all night tossing and turning, trying to clear his mind so he could get a few hours of sleep.

He would much rather go to his room and eat there to avoid the noise and chaos, but he was sure his absence would be noted. He also didn't want to give whomever had sneaked into his room the heads-up that he was on to them.

Lawson was next to him, chatting away to Sarah, and Xavier knew his best friend would notice if he tried to slip away. He didn't want to deal with another interrogation about his well-being, but he was sure it was only a matter of time before Lawson brought up how Xavier should talk with Sarah to get passed the nightmares. He knew it was just Lawson trying to help, but the thought of dredging up his past like that seemed counterintuitive to him. He had always dealt with things on his own.

And this was no different.

Nor was the mission he was currently dedicated to—finding out who had broken into his room the other night while he had been down in the shower. He scanned the tables, trying to catch someone watching him. Something, anything he could draw from to figure out who it had been.

But everyone seemed caught up in their own conversation, not paying any attention to him.

Which was a good sign, really. Sarah had recently put forth the idea of bringing more of the guests into the day-to-day cooking and food preparation at the lodge. She thought it would be a good way to coax some of the more isolated members into a better, healthier headspace and more ordinary routine. So many of their guests had a habit of hiding out in their rooms and cutting themselves off from everyone else, but it wasn't going to do them any good in the long-term. Convincing them to help out with the cooking and cleaning might lead them to socialize more, giving them a sense of purpose that really helped with their recovery.

At least, that was what Sarah had said.

And, judging by the way everyone seemed to be chatting to each other right now, what she had suggested was making a difference. Xavier was always pleased to see people getting along, people coming out of their shell. He had struggled with socializing himself for a long time after he got back from overseas…and losing his brother. If he hadn't had the planning and setup of Warrior Peak Sanctuary to focus on, he didn't know what he would have done.

All the more reason to be protective of what they'd built here. And precisely why he was smoking out the rat in their midst. Nobody seemed to be acting suspiciously, at least from what he could tell, and he usually had a pretty good eye for this stuff. His gaze was drawn to the far end of his table, where Hannah sat with a new arrival. Xavier hadn't had a chance to read his intake file yet, but it looked like he was settling in.

It was impossible not to feel at home around Hannah. Her beautiful honey-brown eyes sparkled when she smiled, and she had this way about her that was impossible to deny. A bright, bouncy energy that seemed to fill every room she stepped into.

Xavier glanced around the rest of the room, taking note of all the guests he'd interacted with and those who were new. Nothing seemed off with anyone. No odd looks, no one acting strange. His gaze tracked back to Hannah and the new guy. He had a strange feeling he'd seen him before. He'd have to think on it, maybe it would come to him later.

As though sensing his eyes on her, she glanced across the table at him, and he nodded in silent greeting. She flashed him a dazzling smile in return.

He tried to focus on the task at hand, sipping his water and keeping his eyes open for suspicious behavior. He didn't know what he was looking for, exactly, but he would know when he found it. He always did.

When everyone was finished, Hannah shooed the rest of them away. "Xavier and I will clean up," she announced.

Xavier rolled his eyes playfully. "Do I have to?" he asked like a whiny kid being forced to do chores.

Lawson laughed and slapped a hand on to his shoulder. "You can't keep getting away with doing nothing," he teased.

Xavier shook his head. "Wasn't fixing the generators last night enough?"

"Everyone has to pull their weight around here," Hannah told him cheerfully as she began gathering up the plates.

"And you've got a lot of weight to pull. Come on, give me a hand. Let's start clearing the tables."

In truth, Xavier didn't mind at all having the opportunity to spend a little more time with Hannah alone. Even though he had sworn up and down to Lawson that nothing was going on between them, he still had feelings for her. How could he not? Her warm, bright kindness was impossibly attractive after he'd spent a lifetime working with people who shut that side of themselves off. And the way her freckles wrinkled when she smiled... Yeah, he still had it bad for her. He hoped it would pass eventually. It had to in order for him to maintain his friendship with Lawson.

The two of them started carting plates to the kitchen. As Xavier set about washing while Hannah dried, she glanced over at him. "What happened with the Haynes brothers last night?" she asked.

"Nothing," he admitted. "They were just drunk and talking crap like they always do. I don't think they actually had anything to do with the generators."

"You guys just took off last night," she remarked. "I had no idea what you were doing."

"Yeah, sorry," he apologized. He knew he owed her more of an explanation. It wasn't just that they worked together, he had been friends with her for a long time, too. She had been there since day one of the sanctuary opening, and she'd always been a huge part of why people felt as safe and comfortable as they did here. If it hadn't been for her, it would have just been his grumpy ass at the reception desk, and he knew that wouldn't have been very welcoming for new arrivals.

"There's just been a lot on my mind," he admitted before he could stop himself. It was always like this with her—he could never stop himself from telling her the truth. He didn't want to worry her, but she was so easy to talk to that he couldn't help but share what was on his mind.

"Lodge stuff?" she asked. "Or...?" She lifted her finger to her temple and tapped the side of her head.

He shrugged. "Both, I guess," he replied quietly, handing her another plate.

Their fingers touched for the barest moment, and he had to draw his hand back quickly, hoping she hadn't felt the spark rushing between them. The two of them hadn't talked about their attraction or the kiss they shared since Lawson had blown up at them both about it, but he could tell it was still on her mind, too.

"You should talk to Sarah," she suggested.

"Yeah, that's what Lawson said, too."

She raised her eyebrows at him. "Well, you know how much I hate agreeing with my brother," she joked. "But maybe you should actually listen to him."

Xavier chuckled. "Yeah, maybe," he replied. "You know I'm not good at taking advice."

She smiled wryly. "Yeah, if you were, I might tell you that you're doing a crappy job with these dishes," she teased, flipping one over in her hand demonstratively. "See? This one still has food on it."

"Hey, that's just an old stain," he protested, as he took the plate back from her.

She laughed. "Mmm, not sure I believe that. Here, why don't we swap? You probably can't screw up the drying part."

"I'm not screwing up the washing part, either," he replied, but he was laughing. Her attitude was infectious, even when he had so much on his mind. Sometimes, he felt like she was the only person who could force him out of his own head for a while and into the moment.

They scuffled for a moment over the dishes, and she dipped her hand into the water and pulled out a handful of fluffy suds, tossing them at him. "Here, soap," she teased. "It's that thing you're supposed to use to wash dishes, remember?"

"Oh, you mean this?" He grabbed a handful himself and launched it at her.

She shrieked and jumped out of the way, nearly knocking down a stack of plates piled up behind her on the counter. He reached past her to catch them.

She narrowed her eyes at him. "Oh, you are so going to pay for that," she warned him, and she grabbed some more suds, hurling them in his direction.

He dodged out of the way, ducking just in time, and the dishwater landed on the plates behind him. "You're going to clean those up," he shot back.

"Not a chance," she replied. "You were the one on washing duty, remember?"

But before she could say another word, Aaron appeared in the kitchen doorway and cleared his throat.

Both Hannah and Xavier spun around as soon as they heard him.

"You guys okay in here?" Aaron asked.

Xavier nodded, wiping off his hands. "Yeah, we're fine."

"Okay, good." Aaron cocked an eyebrow as he looked between them. "Because some of the guests are just settling down for the night, and they heard a ruckus and were worried that there was something going on down here."

Hannah and Xavier exchanged a glance, grinning like a pair of schoolkids who had been caught skipping classes.

"Sorry," Hannah apologized. "We'll keep it down."

"Thanks," Aaron replied, and he paused for another moment, looking between them. There was clearly some other comment he wanted to make, but he thought better of it, much to Xavier's relief. Last thing he needed was to have someone else speculating on what was going on between him and Hannah. It would drive Lawson insane if he found out that they were still flirting with each other, even after he had made it clear what he thought of that. Lawson had warned him off his sister because he didn't think Xavier was stable enough to be in a relationship and he didn't want Hannah to suffer because of it.

Aaron left, and Hannah pulled a face at Xavier.

"Guess we should get back to work," she told him. "Without scaring the guests."

"Guess so," Xavier agreed. "You want to wash this time?"

"I think I'll just supervise," she replied. "I don't trust myself with those slippery plates, I can already see myself breaking one."

"Okay, back to drying duty then," Xavier told her, nodding to the spot beside him.

She took her place and stole a glance at him out of the corner of her eye.

"What is it?" he asked her quietly. He wasn't sure what he wanted her to say, but he knew he had to find out what she was thinking.

She paused for a moment, biting her lip, like her mind was wandering to a million different places at once. "Nothing," she said finally, shaking her head. "I just… You know you can always talk to me, right? If something's bothering you?"

"I know," he replied softly. He had no intention of burdening her with the information of the break-in; she didn't need to worry about him any more than she already did. But there was some relief in knowing that she was willing to listen to him. Sometimes, he felt like he was dealing with so much alone, so many of the memories in his mind still so fresh thanks to the nightmares he was being tortured with every night.

"Good," she replied, and she bumped her hip against his. The small touch alone was enough to make him smile, her closeness always welcome for him. "Back to work then, soldier."

They went back to washing and drying the dishes in companionable silence, but Xavier's mind was still wandering. Wandering back to all those nights he had woken up in his bed alone, and wondering if his nightmares might have eased up a little if he had been sleeping next to her instead.

Chapter Eight

Hannah stared out the big window in the lodge's reception area, scanning the quiet grounds. She was so warm and comfy in the lodge, and she dreaded the thought of having to venture back out into the frosty morning.

She had come out early to help get breakfast made, and now she was going to walk Jed to his first meeting with Sarah so he'd know where her office was for future appointments. Letting out a big sigh, she wrapped her arms around herself in a futile attempt to ward off the cold, opened the door and made her way toward his cabin.

Shoving her hands deep in her pockets as she trudged down the misty path, she couldn't stop from wondering how much longer spring was going to take to show up.

Chatting with Jed last night, she had gotten a strange vibe from him. She couldn't quite put her finger on what it was, and she had dismissed it out of hand, convincing herself that it was nothing more than his trauma or stress making him act a little off. Once he got a little more settled here, she was sure she would feel more comfortable around him.

Reaching his cabin, she was just lifting her hand to knock on the door when it opened in front of her. She offered him a smile in greeting.

"Good morning," he announced, stepping out from the cabin quickly and closing it up tight behind him, like there was something in there he didn't want her to see.

"Hey," she greeted him. "You sleep okay?"

"Great, thanks," he replied, though the dark rings around his eyes told her differently.

She decided not to press the issue, and gestured back toward the lodge. "You ready for your meeting with Sarah?"

"Sure," he replied. "Lead on."

He kept pace with her as they made their way back to the main building. Something seemed to have shifted in him since the night before, and he was spilling his story to her before she had a chance to respond.

"I've heard so many good things about this place," he remarked brightly. "I wanted to come here for a long time. Got so much to work through, you know?"

She nodded, remembering him saying something similar the day before. "Lots of the guests here do," she replied. She wasn't going to delve any deeper, but there was something about the way he spoke that told her he wished she would.

"Yeah, wartime really does a number on you," he remarked. "I saw some pretty messed-up stuff out there."

He paused expectantly, but Hannah didn't take the bait. She didn't want to hear those stories. She knew he must have been through hell to end up here, but that didn't mean she had to go into the details first thing in the morning. "That's what Sarah's here for," she told him with a smile. "She's amazing at helping people work through their trauma. I bet you'll find her really helpful."

He paused as they stepped inside the lodge together and rolled his shoulders back. A hint of defensiveness came off of him, and Hannah held his gaze steadily. She was better at managing grocery lists and intake forms than listening to people's deepest, darkest secrets, and she wanted to keep it that way.

But the way he was looking at her, it was clear he felt she'd said the wrong thing. Did he expect her to sympathize, tell him how sorry she was? Maybe she had been too blunt. Just as she parted her lips to apologize, footsteps caught her attention, and she turned to see Xavier approaching the two of them.

"Oh, Xavier," she greeted him, glad for the distraction. "This is Jed, one of our new arrivals."

Xavier extended his hand to Jed, and it seemed as though his presence instantly shifted something in Jed's mood. Jed cast aside the grim expression on his face and put on a smile instead, shaking Xavier's hand enthusiastically.

"Good to meet you," he remarked jovially. "You're one of the owners, right?"

"Yeah, I am," Xavier replied.

Hannah's ears perked up. Wait, how did Jed know that? He must have really been doing his research on Warrior Peak before he got here.

"Well, I think I can take it from here," Jed told Hannah. "You said the therapy office was down there, right?" He pointed down the corridor.

Hannah nodded.

"Thanks for your help," he told her, and then he took off down the hallway.

Hannah watched him as he went, and so did Xavier. Xavier had always had a good eye for people, and she was sure he could tell as much as she could that something was off here. "What's up with him?" she wondered quietly.

"I don't know," he admitted. "But he reminds me of someone."

Hannah looked to him in surprise. "Reminds you of someone? Who?"

"Not sure, there's just something familiar feeling." Xavier shrugged and turned his attention to Hannah. "I need to head into town to see Sheriff Willis, want to come along?"

She felt a smile spread over her face before she could stop it. Time alone with him? Yes, please. "Sure," she agreed.

They headed out to his SUV, where Hannah cranked up the heat. She was still freezing from her trek to get Jed earlier, and the way his tone had shifted when Xavier walked up had sent a shiver down her spine in a way she couldn't quite understand.

"So what do you need to see the sheriff about?" she asked.

Xavier paused before he responded, his eyes fixed on the road in front of him, as though he was considering exactly what he was going to tell her.

God, he looks so handsome in this light, the way it picks up the sharpness of his jawline...

"There was a break-in at the lodge earlier this week," he explained. "One of the rooms. Mine, to be precise."

"Oh no way," she gasped, panic gripping her chest. "Did they take anything?"

"Can't seem to find anything missing," he replied, shaking his head. "So probably not, but I wanted to check in with Sheriff Willis anyway. Especially after the generators were taken out the other night."

"You think there's a connection?" she wondered aloud.

"Could be," he replied. "Better to be safe than sorry."

"Does anything ever go smoothly at Warrior Peak?" she remarked, only mostly joking.

Xavier turned one of the heating vents toward her, apparently noticing she still felt chilled. "It will," he assured her.

She couldn't help but notice how tense he was right now, the way the tendons in his arm flexed when he palmed the wheel. He was clearly anxious, and she wondered how much was going on that she had no idea about. She got it, she really did. Hannah wasn't involved in the big decisions of the day-to-day running of the sanctuary, and she didn't need to know every little detail. After the fire, though, she felt as if she should have been kept a little more in the loop with whatever went on around the place. She did live there, too, after all.

But she knew it went deeper than that for Xavier. Of course it did. She knew what he had lost when he was in the army. His little brother had followed him into active service and had died out there—right in front of Xavier, from what Lawson had told her. She couldn't even imagine what that must have been like.

And that would have been bad enough, but when he came home, his parents blamed him for the loss. The funeral had been a mess—his mother jumping on the coffin while Xavier tried to hold her back, only for her to turn around and blame him publicly for Max's death. Hannah hadn't been there, but she'd heard about that from Lawson, too, and it made her chest ache to think of what that must have done to him.

Xavier had been grieving, too. She didn't know why his family had a hard time seeing that. She understood that it was normal for grieving people to look for someone to blame, but he had needed their support instead of their guilt and accusations. He was the one who had to watch Max die, after all.

The family went to pieces after that.

His parents passed away one after another—first his father, then his mother. She was hardly speaking to Xavier, even when she was on her deathbed, and Xavier had been left alone to bear the brunt of everything that had happened, all the pain and suffering that his family had struggled through.

Hannah had no idea how he even kept his head up sometimes. She couldn't imagine carrying on in the face of losing so many people close to her, let alone knowing that most of them blamed her for kicking off the chain of events that led them down that path. All of it just felt utterly sick and twisted, but here he was, still standing.

Even if sometimes it looked as though he wanted to fall apart entirely.

But he didn't. He held himself together, and Hannah knew a big part of that was because he felt so much responsibility to the people at Warrior Peak Sanctuary. He had worked hard to make it as safe a space as he could for those who were going through so much of the same trauma as he had.

If it hadn't been for his dedication, she was certain there were those who wouldn't have made it through at all. The struggle they faced was so unique, sometimes they needed people around them who really got it, rather than some expert who only had a distant understanding of what it must have been like.

But Hannah wondered why he couldn't extend the same kindness to himself. He must have needed the support, especially after what he had been through, but he always seemed to reject it. Maybe he didn't feel as though he was worthy of it, given the way his parents had turned on him when he lost his brother. It wouldn't have surprised her.

He must have taken some of their blame to heart, even if it was wildly misplaced. She had heard a little about his brother from Lawson, and she knew that Xavier would have done anything to look out for him. Like he did now for the guests of Warrior Peak.

As they wound their way down the mountain into Blue Ridge, Hannah watched Xavier out of the corner of her eye. She had tried to talk to him about getting help before, when they were doing the dishes, but he seemed to just brush her off without really taking any of their conversation to heart.

And she understood that. It had to be painful to bring all those memories back to the surface again. But he couldn't keep living like this—torturing himself, treating himself like the perpetrator when she was sure he did everything he could to protect Max. Hannah knew Xavier would have given his own life in Max's place if he could have.

Though, if what he was saying about the break-in was true, she understood why he felt like he had more important things than his mental health to focus on. There could be someone targeting the lodge again.

The thought of that happening, their safe space being violated again, spooked the hell out of her. She knew it worried Xavier and Lawson, too.

She focused her gaze on the road ahead of her as they pulled into town and Xavier took a turn to head to the police station. She silently promised herself she was going to do everything she could to help keep the sanctuary—and the people who relied on it—safe.

Chapter Nine

"Be sure to reach out if there's any other disturbance," Sheriff Willis told Xavier as he walked him to the door of the police station.

Xavier nodded. "Anyone looks at me funny, you'll be the first to hear about it," he assured him.

Willis nodded and reached out his hand to shake Xavier's. "Thanks for coming in," he told him. "We'll file those reports today, make sure there's a paper trail if anything else happens."

Xavier shook his hand in appreciation. Having the local cops on their side, at least, was something. Willis was a good guy, and they'd had a positive relationship with the local police with him as sheriff. Warrior Peak had done a lot of work with former police as well as former military, and Willis appreciated the work they did to get them back on their feet.

"You think it's going to help?" Hannah asked Xavier as they stepped back out on to the street.

"I don't know," Xavier admitted. "But at least we have a case open if something else does happen."

"Yeah, I guess that has to count for something," she agreed, but she sounded pretty doubtful.

Xavier felt a twinge of guilt for telling her about the break-in, but he knew there would be no point in hiding it from her. She could always guess when something was going on inside his head, and he was done pretending otherwise.

He felt a little better now that he had told Willis about what happened. Xavier had filled him in on everything, from the break-in in his room to the generators going out and their trip to the Haynes' brothers' ranch—though Xavier had added that he and Lawson were pretty sure the brothers had nothing to do with what had gone down.

"You want to get something to eat while we're here?" Xavier suggested. He knew he and Hannah should probably be getting back to the lodge, but it wasn't often he got to spend time alone with her, and he didn't want to waste it. Yes, he knew he shouldn't be doing anything to encourage his feelings for her, but they were friends, right? And friends sometimes got lunch together. It didn't have to mean anything.

"That sounds great," she agreed. "I'm starving. I hardly got breakfast this morning before I had to go meet Jed."

Jed. There was another nudge at the back of Xavier's mind, though he was sure he had no reason to be suspicious of the new arrival. He had only just gotten to Warrior Peak, so the chance of him being involved with everything that had been going on was next to zero.

They drove to the closest café down the street. Mary Cinder, who owned the fabric store next door, was just gathering herself from the last table by the window to go back to work.

"Oh, you two take this table," she told them. "I should be getting back to the store anyway."

"Thanks, Mary," Hannah replied with a smile, taking a seat at the vacated table.

Xavier ordered for the two of them at the counter before he came back to join her. He knew what she liked—he always paid attention to what she chose at mealtimes, taking in all those little details about her that he doubted she even paid much mind to herself.

Returning to the table, he noticed a line of lingering frost around the edge of the window. Hannah had noticed it, too, and she sighed.

"I can't wait for spring," she remarked to him. "Winter lasts way too long here. I do enjoy my cool morning walks, but I feel like I'm going to freeze to death before I see the flowers bloom."

"Yeah, agreed," he replied.

Back when he had been growing up, winter had been his favorite time of the year. He had counted down the days until the first snow, when he and Max could go out and have a snowball fight and sled down the large hill behind their house. Their hands would burn with the frozen cold when they came in, and their mom would always have a hot cocoa ready and waiting for them on the stove when they got back. He could still remember that sweet aroma, the way it smelled like home to him.

He suddenly realized Hannah was staring at him, a small smile on her face, while he'd been lost in his head. "What is it?" he asked, shifting slightly in his seat.

"Nothing," she replied, shaking her head. "You just looked…content there for a moment. I don't see that a lot in you."

He grimaced. Yeah, she had a point there. Especially these last few months, as much as he had tried to pretend otherwise. He had been on edge, tormented by the memories of losing his brother, and he knew he hadn't been doing a good job of hiding it.

"Winters have always been long here," he remarked, changing the subject. "Ever since I was a kid. My brother and I—" The words were out before he could stop them, but he clammed up the moment they were out of his mouth.

Hannah must have been able to tell how much his memories got to him. "I like hearing about the sanctuary when it was your family home," she told him, offering him a smile. "And about your brother. Max, right?"

Hearing her say his name like that made him tense. He flinched, and she must have noticed. She reached across the table and placed her hand on top of his. Her touch took him back to a better place—a place where he had never lost his brother, where the pain of what he had been through didn't weigh so heavily on him. Warm, full of love and light, where he didn't carry the shame of what he had done.

Or what he had failed to do.

"Yeah, Max," he replied, reaching his thumb up to brush against her skin. This was dangerous, too dangerous. He should have stopped it before it went any further, but how the hell could he, when having her this close felt so right? He felt the electricity racing from her skin to his.

"You should talk to Sarah," she suggested again, and he drew his hand back at once. He could feel that defensiveness rising inside of him, that urge to push back against what she was suggesting and tell her to back off. "I don't want to go through all that again," he muttered.

"You don't have to talk about the bad stuff right away," she suggested. "You could start with the good memories. The stuff you want to remember."

He drew his gaze away from her and shook his head. "It's not a good idea."

"I'm worried about you, Xavier," she told him, a sadness to her voice. "I know... I can see how much you've been struggling. I just want the best for you."

He didn't know what to say. Thankfully, he didn't have to come up with anything, because the cheery waitress arrived with their food a moment later, placing it in front of them as she chattered away about the weather.

Hannah sighed, clearly seeing that the moment was lost, and tucked in to her meal.

Afterward, when they stepped outside, she seemed subdued. Xavier could tell she was still bothered by the conversation they'd had before lunch. It would have been easy for him to just leave it there and hope she didn't bring it up again, but something in him was urging him to tell her more. No matter how much it hurt, no matter how much it dredged up for him. She was trying to reach out, trying to make a difference, and she deserved more than to just be brushed off.

He didn't look at her as he spoke. "I'm sorry for shutting you out."

She glanced up at him in surprise. "What do you mean?"

He still didn't meet her gaze. "I know you're trying to help," he explained. "With the...the stuff with Sarah, I mean. But I just can't go back there and pull all those memories up again. They're bad enough as it is, with the dreams and everything..."

"The dreams?" she asked softly.

"I—I used to have these dreams all the time, about what happened to my brother," he continued, stilted. He wasn't used to being this honest with anyone, let alone her, and making himself so vulnerable felt like a mistake. He had held it all in for so long, so how could telling the truth fix any of this? "And I thought they were done a long time ago," he went on. "Actually, they were. Up until the night of the fire. Ever since then, I've been...dealing with them again. I don't think I've made it through a whole night without having them at some point."

"But the fire was nearly three months ago," she whispered.

He grimaced. "Yeah. I know."

She fell silent for a moment and followed behind him as they made their way back to his vehicle. It was obvious she still had a lot of questions, but he wasn't sure he had it in him to keep answering. Even sharing that much hurt. It brought to mind all the memories of Max that Xavier had been torturing himself with for so long now.

He wished he could just focus on the good times, but every time his beloved baby brother came into his mind, it was with the harsh reminder of how he had been lost. How Xavier had been there, right there next to him, and unable to stop it. Maybe his mom had been right when she blamed him for his brother's death.

How could he have let it happen?

Whenever he closed his eyes, that was all he could see. Fire, blood, the sudden blank look in Max's eyes, the blooming red stain on his neck running down his camouflage uniform as he fell to the ground. Nothing could have saved him, but that didn't mean that Xavier didn't wish he had tried. He had been so frozen in shock and horror, he had taken vital seconds to snap back into reality, and if he had acted sooner...

He climbed into the SUV, and Hannah scrambled in the other side, not taking her eyes off of him. Gripping the wheel, he kept staring straight ahead. Had he said too much? Maybe now she thought he was weak, pathetic for being so consumed by the memory of what had happened.

But if she wanted to know, he would do his best to be open with her. She was about the only person in his life he felt like he could be honest with about this, even if he didn't know why.

No, that wasn't true. He knew exactly why. As much as he might have tried to deny it, it was the same reason he had been so shaken after the fire. He had seen far worse, far more violence than that, but it was the first time in a long time that he felt like he had a life worth protecting.

Like he had someone in his life he wanted to protect.

Instead of sitting in the passenger seat like he expected, Hannah got to her knees on the seat, not taking her eyes off of him. He turned to her, confused, and before he could say anything, she launched herself into his arms, wrapping herself around him, one hand at the back of his neck and the other slowly rubbing against his shoulder.

He thought about pushing her away, setting her back in her own seat, he really did. Maybe a stronger man would have, but he knew that he couldn't. It felt too good to have her that close. As soon as she touched him, he felt everything else just fall away, all the fight he'd had to keep his distance vanishing.

"It's going to be okay, Xavier," she murmured to him.

He couldn't think of anything to say back, but he didn't need to. Instead, he slipped his arms around her waist and pulled her in even closer to him. The scent of her shampoo and perfume filled the air around him, creating this little protective bubble that seemed to keep them safe from the rest of the world. He didn't care what anyone else thought in that moment. The only thing that mattered to him was the feel of her small, strong body pressed against his and her promise that everything was going to be okay.

Because, when she said it, he could almost believe her.

Chapter Ten

The embrace caught her off guard, but it felt so deliciously good, Hannah couldn't find it in herself to pull back. The pressure of his strong hands around her waist, pulling her in close; the feel of his breath on her neck... All those touches that she had craved for so long but denied herself for fear that it would just drive a deeper wedge between her and her brother.

But now, here, in the quiet of the vehicle, there was no way either of them could deny it, this sweetness between them, this need. She pressed her head into his shoulder, inhaling the scent of him, and wondering how she had lasted so long without this.

When she pulled back slightly and looked into his eyes, she had no idea how he would react. Would he push her off, tell her they couldn't do this? Or would he give her what she had needed for so long?

Her heart slammed up against her ribs as he slowly lifted his hand to her face and cupped her cheek. His thumb rubbed against her skin in slow, soft motions.

And then, at last, he dipped in close and kissed her.

It wasn't a peck—it was a real kiss, a kiss that tingled from the top of her scalp to the very bottom of her toes.

She smiled against his mouth and pressed herself into him, arching her back so she could show him just how much she wanted him. Nothing else made sense to her right now but the feeling of his mouth against hers, his tongue caressing the inside of her lip, a soft, delicious tease that made her whole body light up.

When he drew away from the kiss, he was breathing hard, but there was a smile on his face. She gazed at him, a little more nervous than she would care to admit. But God, that smile—it was everything to her. When she saw him smile, she knew there was no denying it. She was in love with him. She had been for years now, for so long she had lost track of it, but that didn't matter.

The way he kissed her, she knew he loved her, too.

"We should get back to the sanctuary," she murmured reluctantly. "Someone'll notice we're both gone."

"Yeah, someone like your brother." He sighed.

She pulled a face. "Oh don't bring him up. Let me pretend we can get away with this a little longer, huh?"

He chuckled and lifted his hand to her cheek again, gazing at her as though he could hardly believe she was right there in front of him.

She tilted her face into his palm, enjoying the feel of his calloused hands against her skin. She wasn't sure she would ever get tired of it—there was something addictive about the way he touched her, even when her good sense told her she should be holding back.

She leaned in and kissed him softly once more before pulling away and resituating herself on her own side of the SUV. She immediately missed his warmth.

"You think he's going to be angry again if he finds out?" Xavier asked as he took the wheel once more.

She shrugged. "Maybe," she admitted. "But we've done

a lot of talking since that first kiss all those months ago, you know. By now, Lawson's got to see that he was acting like an idiot. Big brother or not, he has no right to tell me, or you, how to live our lives. If we like each other..." She trailed off.

Like was far too weak of a word for everything she felt for Xavier right now, but she didn't want to jinx what had just happened by overstating it.

"He'll just have to get used to it," he finished up for her.

"My thoughts exactly. But we should still get back to the sanctuary—catch everyone up on what happened with the sheriff."

"Agreed," he replied, and he turned the key in the ignition and pulled away from the café.

She couldn't stop staring at him, now that she knew he felt at least some of what she did for him. For so long, she had denied herself this—this closeness, these sweet moments where they could just be together. She hoped this would be the start of him opening himself up a little, too. Maybe to her, maybe to Sarah; it didn't matter as long as he got some of the weight off his mind.

As they drove, heading up the mountain road that led through the dense forest and back to Warrior Peak, he glanced out the window at the passing scenery.

"Remind you of growing up here?" she asked.

He nodded. "Yeah, my brother and I used to play in these woods a lot when we were young," he remarked, smiling slightly. "I think it drove my mom insane. Max was always getting into trouble, falling out of trees, stuff like that. I can't count the number of times I would get yelled at when we came home and he had another scrape on his elbow."

"So he was kind of a daredevil then?" she prompted.

She liked hearing these stories about his youth. It felt as though she was seeing some hidden side of him, something he did his best to keep from everyone else. It might do him good to reflect on some of the happier memories he had of his childhood. No matter how dark things had gotten, it didn't mean he had to leave behind everything good that had ever happened.

"I think he liked everyone to think he was," he replied, amused. "But you should have seen him when he was younger. He would come to my room at least twice a week, asking me to check under his bed for monsters. Or to sleep on the floor to keep him safe."

"And did you?"

"Of course I did." He laughed. "I couldn't turn him down, and he knew it. Anything he wanted from me, he got."

"Damn, I didn't realize you could have that kind of power over your big brother," she joked. "I should have tried to get more out of Lawson growing up."

"He didn't do all of that for you?"

"He did some of it," she replied. "But grudgingly. Don't know why he's got such a stick up his butt about protecting me now."

"Maybe because he's seen a bit more of the world," Xavier suggested. "He knows what can be out there if you're not careful. He just doesn't want you to have to deal with any of that."

"Yeah, I guess," she agreed.

She tried not to get upset with her brother, knowing that he was just looking out for her. But she didn't understand how he could feel like her being with Xavier was anything other than a good thing. If there was anyone in the world he trusted, it should be his best friend, right?

Well, they would figure that out when it came up again. For now, what mattered was the relaxed smile on Xavier's face as they drove. He reached out to give her leg a squeeze, his touch casual and easy, just as she had always wanted it to be.

"I love spending this time with you," she blurted out before she could stop herself. "I know I tried to keep my distance after what happened with my brother, but…" She trailed off with a shrug.

"Me, too," Xavier assured her, grinning.

She wished she could take a snapshot of his face like that and commit it to memory. She never wanted to forget the way he looked at her, the way it made her feel like she could take on the world and win.

"So you guys played a lot out here in the winter, too?" she asked, turning her attention back to the forest outside. "You must have been freezing."

"Yeah, but we always had a warm home to go back to," he replied. "We never wandered too far. Mom was always waiting, ready with a hot drink and a bandage for any bruises Max got along the way."

"Oh don't act like you didn't get a few, too," she teased.

He chuckled. "Yeah, okay, maybe I did sometimes, too," he admitted. "I wasn't always the sensible older brother."

She could hardly imagine him like that, relaxed and fooling around. All the time she had known him, he had seemed to be this solid, strong guy who took everything seriously—well, everything outside of her, of course. She always tried to bring out a lighter side of him, never wanting him to feel like he had to put up that front when he was with her. She wanted to see the man underneath, the man who had grown up from that little boy who had played in the snow with his baby brother.

"But in my defense, I..." Xavier began, but then, he sharply cut himself off, his words faltering as he looked in the rearview mirror.

Hannah craned her head around to see what he was looking at, and her stomach lurched. A big truck was racing up on them from behind.

The two-lane road was winding with a ravine on one side and a fast-flowing river on the other; the entire length of it was a no-pass zone. If another driver happened to be coming down the mountain, it would be bad for them all. As the truck sped toward them faster than anyone needed to on an icy road, she couldn't help but feel a familiar terror curling inside her stomach.

"Who the hell is that?" he muttered. "And why are they coming at us so fast? It's icy as hell out there."

"Maybe they're just trying to pass?" she offered optimistically, but she knew that wasn't the case. Nobody would dare speed around these mountain roads in this weather unless they were stupid. Or trying to intimidate someone.

Or drive them off the road.

"No, that's not it," he replied, his voice dropping to a growl. "You're buckled in, right?"

"Yeah," she squeaked, hoping he couldn't hear the fear in her voice. She could hear the other vehicle's engine on the road now, drawing ever closer, and it took everything she had not to let the panic get the better of her. Her eyes slid to the sides of the road—noting how close their SUV was to the edge. She shivered at the thought of how frigid that water must be.

"It's okay," Xavier murmured to her, sensing her tension.

She clasped her trembling hands in her lap. She wanted

to believe him, God, she wanted to believe him, but she was struggling to contain her panic. After the fire, she hadn't been able to assume anything was innocent. Any danger in her vicinity, she was hyperaware of it.

Then the big truck was beside them on a curve. With the vehicles almost pressed up against each other, Hannah tried to look around Xavier to see the driver of the truck, but in her panicked state, she couldn't get a good look through the darkened windows.

Suddenly, the driver twisted the wheel and slammed their truck into Xavier's SUV.

"Hold on!" Xavier yelled, but his voice sounded far away.

Hannah's head spun, and everything slowed as the vehicle flipped off the road. The sickening crunch of metal and the sound of tearing filled the air, and she felt her scream stick in her throat. She wanted to yell out for help, but she knew it was no use.

But as their SUV spun through the air and down toward the water below, she finally let it out. A scream that bounced around the interior of the vehicle, her hands scrambling for purchase on something, anything.

But it wasn't enough to brace for the final impact as the SUV landed with a crash in the cold, murky river.

Chapter Eleven

Xavier sucked in a long breath, trying to ground himself as the SUV finally came to a halt in the river several feet from shore. It was upside-down in the water, the sunroof smashed, and the freezing, dark liquid was starting to inch in through the gap between the doors and the roof.

"Xavier…" Hannah whimpered, and he reached over to squeeze her hand.

"It's going to be okay," he told her, as calmly as he could. "Just unbuckle your belt. We can get out of here."

She reached down to hit the button to release her seat belt, but it didn't budge. She stabbed at it a few more times, growing increasingly desperate, and then turned to him, eyes wide. "It's stuck," she told him.

Xavier grimaced and reached for the glove box where he kept a small blade. It would be enough to free her if he could get to it. But he couldn't reach the compartment from his side, restricted by his own belt. In order to help Hannah, he had no choice but to unclip it and let himself fall into the rapidly rising water below.

"Just hold on, I'm going to get you out," he promised her, and he unclipped his belt. Thankfully his wasn't stuck, and he landed with a grunt on the roof of the SUV. No matter what it took, he was going to get them both out before the vehicle completely filled with water.

The ends of Hannah's dark brown hair were already dangling into the freezing water, making them look more black than brown. In a few minutes, it would reach her face as the SUV continued to slide deeper into the river as more water rushed inside.

He grabbed the door handle and heaved himself up toward the dashboard, pressing the button to release the small compartment where he kept his knife. It didn't budge. Damn. Was anything still working in this thing?

"What are you doing?" Hannah asked. He could hear the terror in her voice, and he wished he could stop to comfort her, but he knew he needed to keep focused on the task at hand before it was too late.

"I'm getting a knife to cut you free," he told her through chattering teeth. He could feel the chill of the water starting to set into his bones, and he knew they wouldn't last long out here without some help—but he could deal with that when the time came. What mattered now was getting that blade, cutting Hannah out of her seat belt and getting them out of this vehicle before it filled up or moved farther into the river.

He slammed his fist into the glove box a couple of times, until he felt the spring lock break, and it fell open. A bunch of stuff dumped out—maps, pens, a notepad, a granola bar—and he managed to catch the small knife before it dropped into the water below. Wrapping his hand around the handle, he turned to Hannah. "Can you pull the belt taut?"

The water was inching higher now, reaching her hairline, but she nodded, shivering. Taking the belt in her hand, she pulled it hard to create an easy surface for him to cut into.

"P-p-lea-se hurry," she begged him through her own chattering teeth, as though he would have done anything else.

He brought the blade to the thick fabric of the belt and started to saw at it, all too aware of how quickly the water was inching up her face. "It's going to be okay."

She let out another whimper as the water reached her eyes. She squeezed them shut, and her grip tightened on the belt. The fabric was starting to fray now, and he knew it was only going to be a few more seconds until it—

It snapped. Xavier dropped the blade and reached out to catch her before she fell into the roof of the vehicle, pulling her into his arms.

She gasped, wiping the water from her eyes, clinging on to him for dear life.

"You okay?" he asked her, and she managed to nod, though he could tell she was having a hard time pulling herself together. She gripped him tightly.

"We need to get out of here," she told him, voice shaking. "Are the doors stuck?"

He tried the handle on her side, but it wouldn't move. The SUV had sunk too far, and the water pressure on the doors was too great.

"Looks like it," he replied. "Here, go over toward the driver side—get back as far as you can."

He set her down next to the driver seat, and she wrapped her arms around the back of it for purchase as he pulled back to slam his foot into the opposite door. It didn't budge, but he could hear the metal groaning underneath the pressure. Going again, he mustered up all the force he had in him—not that there was much of it left. He was running on pure adrenaline now, doing his best to ignore the shock of the accident and the cold water. But it was just a matter of time before his body shut down.

He kicked again, and again.

Thankfully, on the fourth kick, the door finally came loose, leaving a gap large enough for him to get his hands in between the door and the frame.

Unfortunately, the opening also gave enough room for the frigid river to come rushing in as well. The SUV started filling faster, the water no longer held at bay. Reaching back for Hannah's hand, Xavier continued to push against the force of the icy river, using his shoulder and dragging Hannah out behind him.

The water they were in was only about chest deep for him, a little more for Hannah, but they struggled to trudge back to dry land through the freezing, mucky water.

"Thank God," Hannah breathed as soon as they were out of the water. They collapsed on the riverbank, and Xavier shot a look up to the road to make sure the person who had done this to them wasn't still there.

But it was totally quiet.

Whoever had taken them out had made a run for it already. A good thing, because even though Xavier was exhausted and fighting off hypothermia, he thought he probably could have mustered the strength to kill them with his bare hands for almost ending Hannah's life.

Did they think they had finished her and Xavier off? Or was this just meant to be a warning, a sign for them to keep their heads down and out of whatever trouble these people didn't want them knowing about?

He didn't know, but he was definitely going to get to the bottom of it.

Xavier wrapped a protective arm around Hannah,

squeezing her in close. He could feel her shivering from the icy water as well as the cooler temperature, and he wished there was something he could do to make it better. He was wearing a jacket, but it wouldn't provide her any warmth because it was soaking wet. Their best bet was to get back to Warrior Peak Sanctuary as soon as possible and into dry clothes.

"How f-f-far are we from the lodge?" Hannah asked, and he looked over at her. There was a bloody mark on her head, just below her hairline.

"You're bleeding," he murmured.

She reached up to touch her head and pulled her hand away with a smear of blood on her fingers. Her eyes widened.

"Do you feel dizzy?" Xavier asked. "Nauseous?"

She shook her head. "N-no, nothing l-l-like that," she stuttered, but she winced. "I do have a bit of a headache, though."

"Okay, we need to get you checked out," he replied, and he steered her up toward the road. "Once we get back to the lodge, we'll get you looked over."

"And how a-are we going to g-get back there?" she asked, her voice laced with panic. "I mean, it's too far to walk, and it's too cold this time of the year, plus we're soaking wet, and we'll probably freeze to death..."

"I'll flag down a car," he replied before she spiraled any further. He was doing his best to keep her calm, though he could tell that she was on the brink of losing it completely. He smoothed a hand over her back, trying to soothe her. "You stay here," he told her. "I'll find someone. I promise."

She parted her lips to protest, but the fight seemed to leave her just as soon as she had thought of it.

He knew as well as she did that there weren't many cars

that came around this way at this time of year, and they would have to get seriously lucky to run into one. But he had to believe they would. The thought of being trapped out here, in the cold, with her bleeding head wound... No, he couldn't even consider it. He had to get them out of there as quickly as possible.

He could feel the chill start to settle in his bones and slow down his movements, but he tried to ignore it. He had dealt with worse.

He looked up and down the road, trying to make out any oncoming headlights that might indicate someone coming to help them, but there was nothing. What if the people who had driven them off the road came back to finish the job? He would fight with everything he had if he needed to, but he wasn't sure how much of a chance he stood against them, especially if they were armed.

Silence filled the air around him, and fear started to tug at the corners of his mind. He couldn't let anything happen to Hannah. He had lost too much already, and he wasn't going to lose her. He would do anything in his power to protect her.

Glancing back down the bank to check on her, he could see her eyes starting to droop as the shock and adrenaline wore off. He was about to run down to keep her awake when the sound of an engine drew his attention.

He spun around to see a car coming up the road toward them. He stepped out on to the pavement, lifting his hands above his head to flag it down. There was no way the driver would be able to ignore him, standing right in the middle of the road.

The car screeched to a halt in front of him, sliding slightly on the icy road. When an older man stepped out, Xavier lifted his hand to shield his eyes from the glare of the headlights and recognized Mr. Barkley, one of the local farmers he occasionally saw at a bar in Blue Ridge when he went to grab a drink. Mr. Barkley s walked to the front of the car, and stopped a few feet in front of Xavier and frowned when he realized who was standing in the road.

"Thank God," Xavier breathed. "We need your help. I'll be right back."

"Xavier?" the farmer asked his retreating form. "What are you…?"

But Xavier rushed down the bank, pulled Hannah into his arms and carried her up to the car. She might have been able to walk, but he didn't want her wasting any more of her energy.

"We need a lift," he told Mr. Barkley quickly. "Do you have any blankets in there? She's frozen."

The man nodded, and he pulled a couple of scratchy woolen blankets from the trunk of the car while Xavier helped Hannah into the back seat. Xavier shook the second blanket out before sliding in behind her, then pulled her close and wrapped it around them both.

Hannah's grip on him was firm, as though she didn't want to let go, and he shifted more into the seat to pull her tighter against him.

"What happened?" Mr. Barkley asked, clearly confused as he climbed into the driver seat once more.

Xavier guided Hannah's head to rest on his shoulder, not caring about her damp hair. He just wanted her close, where he could keep an eye on her. "We had an accident," he lied swiftly. He had no reason to think the farmer was in on anything, but there wasn't a chance in hell he was going to risk it.

"You want me to take you to the police station?" Mr. Barkley asked, putting the car in Drive.

Xavier shook his head. "Up to Warrior Peak Sanctuary, please," he told him, and the old man started driving up the mountain.

Xavier carefully stroked Hannah's hair and checked her wound again. It didn't look too bad from where he was sitting, but it was still bleeding some. He wanted to get her back and looked at by a medical professional. If anything had happened to her, if she had really gotten hurt while she had been with him…

He would never forgive himself.

More to the point, he would never forgive the people who had done this to her.

He was going to make them pay in any way he could.

Chapter Twelve

"Here, have another blanket," River told Hannah, draping yet another heavy blanket around her shoulders as she shivered in front of the fire.

"I'm o-kay," Hannah tried to protest, but her teeth were chattering so much she could hardly get the words out. She clutched the cup of hot cocoa River had made for her and exchanged a glance with Xavier.

They had made it back to the lodge... That was something. The way Xavier was looking at her, though, she could tell it was far from over. Anger was written all over his face, his shoulders hunched up, his fists clenched on his lap. His hair was damp from the warm shower he'd just taken, and he was waiting for Aaron and Bailey to come down to reception so he could fill them in on everything that had happened.

Hannah was still trying to wrap her head around it herself. All of it was such a blur of terror and pain—she wasn't entirely sure how they had made it out, but she knew she had Xavier to thank for it. His calm tone as he had talked her through what he was going to do had been the only thing keeping her grounded. If it hadn't been for him, she was sure she would have drowned in the water that was filling the SUV.

She shivered at the thought. She still didn't know why someone had driven them off the road, but whoever it was had clearly meant them some serious harm. She kept replaying the moment Xavier's vehicle spun off the road, the way time seemed to slow down as it hung in the air, before the sickening thud of it landing in the river below.

Who would have done that to them? And why?

As soon as Xavier and Hannah had stumbled through the lodge doors, everyone in the place sprang into action to take care of them. Lawson had rushed off to find River so she could check them over, and Aaron had gone to get Bailey. She worked for the local police department in Blue Ridge and could take an informal statement to give to Sheriff Willis in the morning.

"Can I have a look at your head now?" River asked gently as she crouched down in front of Hannah.

Hannah nodded, a little worried. She didn't feel too bad, but what if she had a concussion or something?

River ran through a few simple tests, getting Hannah to follow her finger with her eyes, checking out the depth and severity of the wound. Finally she leaned back and nodded. "It doesn't look like it's a concussion," River told her. "Just a cut. I'm going to clean it up and bandage it, okay?"

"Sure," Hannah replied, trying to keep her voice steady. She didn't want anyone to see how shaken she really was, even though she was sure it was obvious.

Xavier reached over to rub her shoulder gently, and she managed to smile at him—God, she was so grateful for everything he had done for her. If it hadn't been for him...

Hannah winced as River cleaned off the cut, then gently placed a bandage over it to keep it from getting infected. She smiled and gave Hannah's hand a squeeze when she was done. "There you go, all finished," she assured her.

Hannah looked toward the front doors as Bailey burst into the reception area, followed closely by Aaron. Lawson and Cade behind them.

"Oh my God," Bailey gasped when she saw Hannah and Xavier. "What happened? Are you okay? Aaron filled me in on some of it, but—"

Xavier gestured for her to take a seat and caught her up on a little of what had happened. He seemed to be able to remember so much more than Hannah did. Her memories were frayed around the edges, and she couldn't piece together everything that had gone down.

Hannah clutched her mug, trying to ignore her brother's heavy gaze, and listened to Xavier speak, trying to let herself be soothed by the sound of his voice. He had made it out okay. They had both made it out okay. That was what mattered right then.

"Do you remember anything specific about the vehicle that hit you?" Bailey asked, pulling out a notebook.

Xavier grimaced. "A little," he admitted. "It was a black truck, looked like a Ford, maybe early 1980s. Custom fog lights and grills."

"Good, good," Bailey muttered, scribbling away in her notebook.

Hannah raised her eyebrows. And that was him only remembering some of it? Damn, he was doing a lot better than her. Thank God he had been there. She wouldn't have been able to give Bailey much more than the color and how terrified she had felt when it was closing in on them.

Aaron shook his head. "I've got a bad feeling about this," he muttered. "Who do you think it was?"

"The Haynes brothers, maybe?" Bailey suggested. "You and Lawson went to their ranch to confront them about the generators. This could have been their way of getting back at you for accusing them."

"I don't think the Haynes family would do something like this," Xavier replied. "They're jerks, sure, but this would have taken some planning—to figure out when we were going to be on the road, finding a place to push us off where nobody else would see. I don't think they've got that in them."

"I agree." Lawson chimed in. "This is not their style."

"Yeah, they've caused a bar fight here and there," Aaron added. "But they've never deliberately endangered lives. This feels more—"

"Personal," Hannah whispered, finishing his sentence for him. The thought of this being a specific, targeted attack scared the hell out of her, more than she could put into words.

"You think it's connected to what happened with the generators?" Bailey asked, continuing to write in her notebook.

"It could be," Xavier agreed, then he hesitated, glancing over at Lawson.

"Tell her," Lawson prompted, realizing what he was about to say.

"Someone broke in to my room a few days ago. I don't think they took anything, but I do think it might be related."

"What?" Bailey replied, looking confused. "I didn't hear about that."

"I hoped there was nothing to it," Xavier admitted. "I just told the sheriff today. That's where we were coming back from when the wreck happened. I should have said something sooner, but I guess I was in denial. This, though…" He shook his head. "Everyone needs to keep their wits about them," he warned the small group. "There's trouble brewing around here. We have to look out for each other."

Silence weighed heavily over everyone for a moment. Hannah knew what was going through their minds—the same thing going through hers. They had been so sure their troubles were over, and now this. A new reason to be scared and watching their backs at all times.

Just when she thought the worst was behind them, something like this sneaked up on them again. The reality of it hurt to think about. This place was supposed to be a safe haven, but instead, someone was intent on tearing it apart and hurting the people who lived and worked there.

"That's enough for now. I'm going to write this all up and you two need to get some rest," Bailey told Xavier, rising to her feet. "And I'll take it to Willis in the morning. He can add it to the file he's building. I don't know what's going on here, but we're going to figure it out, okay?"

Xavier nodded.

Aaron clapped Xavier on the back and followed Bailey back out the door to their cabin.

Silence settled over the remaining group. Hannah could feel Lawson's eyes on her again. She could feel the worry and frustration pouring off him. He'd have questions about her being with Xavier, but she didn't want to address him now.

Hannah was starting to warm up a little, though the cold that gripped her heart was still sending shivers down her spine.

"You should go to your cabin, too, and get some rest," River told her gently. She took the empty cup from Hannah's hands. "I'll take this back to the kitchen."

"Glad you two are okay." Cade nodded toward them both and followed River down the hallway.

Hannah bit her lip and sighed. She knew River was right, but the thought of trying to sleep after what just happened seemed damn near impossible. How was she supposed to get any rest with everything going on right now…all the possible danger coming their way? Every time she closed her eyes, she had flashbacks of Xavier's SUV flipping off the road into the freezing cold river and being trapped upside down in the rising water. She wasn't sure she would be able to get any rest at all.

Xavier seemed to notice how scared she was, and he reached out for her hand. For a brief moment, the warmth of his skin against hers was enough to ground her, and she looked up at him again.

"You're okay," he promised her. "We're okay. Right?"

"I don't know," she admitted. If there was anyone who could convince her that everything would turn out all right in the end, it was Xavier. He had rescued her from the crash and gotten her out of the water in one piece. He'd carried her up the bank and to the car he had flagged down for them, helped her back to the sanctuary and made sure she was safe and warm.

She felt guilty, almost ungrateful, for feeling as afraid as she did right now, but she couldn't help it. How would she ever be able to rest easy again after what had happened? She felt like it could happen again the next time she got into a vehicle.

"I get that," Xavier assured her. "I know how it feels, when something like this happens. How you can't shut your mind off and stop thinking through the what-ifs."

She chewed her lip. "Does it get better?" she asked

softly. She needed to hear it from him. He had always been honest with her, and she knew he would tell her the truth.

He nodded at once. "It does," he promised her. "It really does. You just need to get some rest. I promise it'll start feeling better in the morning, once you've had a good night's sleep."

"I don't know how I'm going to be able to sleep," she admitted as she got to her feet, casting off the blankets River had piled around her. "I feel like I might never sleep again."

"That's the adrenaline," Xavier told her, walking over to her and holding out his hand. Before she could reach for it, her brother appeared at her side.

"Hey, sis. How are you feeling?" Lawson's eyes roamed over her before gently wrapping her in a hug.

Hannah pulled back and gave him a wobbly smile. "I'm tired and achy, worried. But, I'm here. Xavier made sure of that."

Lawson nodded and turned to look between his sister and his best friend.

"So, what were you doing down in town together? I wasn't aware you were leaving the lodge." Lawson inquired, eyebrow raised.

She heard Xavier suck in a breath and her eyes darted quickly to him before back to her brother.

"I ran into Xavier when he was leaving and asked if I could go with him. I just thought the drive would be a nice break. We had lunch after he saw Sheriff Willis, then we came back."

"I see. I thought we talked about this? We discussed—"

"Lawson, can we not do this right now?" Hannah interrupted, wrapping her arms around herself. "Please. It's been a long day and I just want to rest and not think about anything right now."

"Hannah." Lawson sighed and locked his eyes on Xavier for a long moment before turning back to her. "Fine, we'll talk later. I'm glad you're both okay." He shook his head, then turned around and headed across the lobby.

She wasn't ready to leave the warm comfort of the lodge, but she also didn't want to stay and argue with her brother. Her best option right now was her own space. She offered Xavier a small smile and held out her hand. He interlocked their fingers and led her outside.

They walked hand in hand to her cabin, her fingers squeezing his tighter the closer they got. She wasn't ready to be alone yet.

Xavier seemed to since her anxiety.

He brought her hand to his lips and brushed his mouth against it in a soft kiss. "You want me to stay with you tonight?" he murmured.

Relief flooded through her, and she nodded quickly. "Yes," she blurted. "Yes, please. I don't want to be alone."

As he reached for her cabin door, some of the tension she had been carrying was starting to lift slightly. It wasn't much, but it was enough for her to settle her racing heart and take a breath. Maybe she would be able to rest after all.

The adrenaline was starting to fade now, and she could feel the tiredness sweeping through her body. Letting out a yawn, she leaned in to him as he took the key from her, slipping it into the lock.

Xavier pushed the door open and let her inside. "Come on, let's get you settled."

"You want some tea?"

"I'll make it," he replied, guiding her to the small couch in her living room. "You sit down."

She sank into the seat and stole a glance toward the window opposite her. Outside, it seemed as though everything was quiet and still, but she wasn't sure she could believe that. After the fire and then being run off the road, she wasn't sure if she would ever feel safe and secure at Warrior Peak again.

The nagging unease tugged at her stomach, and she tried to ignore it, focusing on the sound of Xavier in the kitchen behind her. As long as he was there with her, everything was going to be all right.

She was sure of it. Right?

Chapter Thirteen

"Here you go." Xavier handed Hannah a cup of hot chamomile tea as he took a seat next to her on the couch. He took a moment to look her over again, battling both fear and anger at her being caught up in whatever this mess was with him.

It was bad enough that it had started at the lodge, threatening their peace and safety. But then to drag Hannah into it as well, and try to kill them both… He still didn't know if it was coincidence that she happened to be with him when they were run off the road, or if whoever had done this had specifically targeted them both.

She looked a little better since her shower and fresh clothes but fatigue was pulling at her hard, and he could still see the anxiety lurking behind her gaze and the dark circles under her eyes. He was so thankful that they had made it out mostly unscathed. But his eyes caught on the bandage on her forehead and grimaced.

"Does it hurt?" he asked, raising his hand to brush back the hair from her face.

She shook her head. "Not really."

He frowned. She was likely just saying that to keep him from worrying about her. It looked as though it must hurt like hell.

"It's not your fault, Xavier," she reminded him, clearly noticing whatever look was on his face.

He knew she was right, of course, but that didn't stop him from feeling guilty about it. He should have done more to protect her. The fact that she was injured because he hadn't been able to keep her safe didn't sit well with him.

Xavier couldn't help but worry what would happen next. What else would these people try? The thought of it worried him more than he could express.

He was more determined than ever to find out what was going on. He was going to track down whoever was responsible for these things and make them pay. No one messed with Hannah or the lodge on his watch without serious consequences.

"Who do you think it was?" she asked, stealing a glance at him out of the corner of her eye. "I know you told Bailey you weren't sure, but…"

"I have no idea," he admitted with a sigh. "I have to think it has something to do with whoever broke into my room the other night, but that's about as far as I've gotten. I'm not sure what the motive would be for that or for running us off the road."

"Do you have any enemies?" she wondered aloud. "I mean, from your time in the military? Or the CIA?"

"None that I'm aware of," he replied with a shrug. "But they might just have been keeping their heads down until they were able to make their move. I really don't have a clue."

She chewed her lip. That answer didn't seem to be the one she wanted, judging by the troubled look on her face. He guessed she was hoping for something a little more direct, something she could actually work with, but he didn't have anything more for her.

"You know I would tell you if I did, right?" he questioned with one brow raised.

She locked eyes with him and nodded. "I know you would," she agreed, managing a small smile.

She was still seriously shaken, there was no doubt about that, but it meant the world to Xavier that she trusted him and knew that he trusted her as well. He would always be honest with her.

She paused for a moment, blowing on her tea thoughtfully. "Do you think they might have mistaken us for someone else?" she asked hopefully. "Thought someone else was in the vehicle, and that's why they did what they did?"

"It's possible," he replied. Though he didn't think that was very likely. It would have been a relief if this was a case of mistaken identity, but it would still leave unanswered the questions of the damaged generators and who had been rummaging through his stuff.

"But you don't think so?" she prompted him, able to read his face just like always.

He sighed. "I don't think so," he admitted. "I don't think someone who came after us with that much anger would mistake us for anyone else. I think it was about…about me."

His voice cracked. He wished he didn't have to come to terms with that part. He didn't want to acknowledge that he had been the one to pull her into this, to put her in danger. He was the reason she was sitting there with a bandage on her head, in pain and afraid to be alone.

She widened her eyes, and they started to gloss with tears. From fear? For him or for her or maybe for both?

Xavier would never forgive himself if something happened to Warrior Peak or any of its employees or guests because of some vendetta a person he didn't even know had against him. Let alone if something happened to Hannah as a result.

"What happens if they come after you again?" she asked, her voice taking on an edge of panic. "They're going to escalate, right?"

"They might," he agreed. Truthfully, he didn't even want to think about how far they would take it. Not because he was worried about himself—he knew how to handle anything the world threw at him. He had learned that from his time in the military and the CIA. Nobody would outsmart him. Nobody who didn't have those skills themselves, at least.

"What's going to happen to you?" she whispered, as though she hardly dared to consider the possibility of it.

"Nothing will," he promised. "You don't have to worry about me. Whoever is doing these things, they don't know who they're dealing with. I'll figure this out, and I'll handle it." He reached over and gave her hand a squeeze. "But I... I'm not sure if you should be around me right now, Hannah."

She stared at him, and for a moment, she looked so small and vulnerable, it made his chest hurt.

He wanted to be close to her, of course he did. He wanted to keep her by his side to protect her, but after what had happened today, he was worried what that closeness might cost her. He was already beating himself up about her being with him on the road and the attack. His gut tightened at the thought of anything worse happening as a result of her being with him.

"What do you mean?" she asked, her voice quivering.

"I don't know who's after me," he confessed. "But after today, I know they're willing to go pretty damn far to try to hurt me or get my attention. And if they know how much I care about you, it could put you in danger, too."

She sat there for a moment, taking in what he had just. A tear rolled down her cheek, but she wiped it away quickly and lifted the tea to her lips to take a sip. "I don't care about that," she said at last.

"Hannah, you can't say that—"

"Yes, I can," she replied firmly, shaking her head. "Listen to me, Xavier. I know you're trying to protect me, I get that, and I appreciate it. But… I care about you. I have for a long time now."

He gave her a small smile at her confession. There was really no reason for either of them to deny their feelings at this point. It was written all over their faces when they were around each other anyway.

"I'm not going to let these people scare me away from what I want. What I need," she continued, reaching out for his hand, her small fingers wrapping around his. "I can't lose you. I've waited too long for this. The way you kissed me in town today, I… It was everything I've been waiting for. Everything I've been too scared to hope for. I'm not letting it slip through my fingers again, not a chance in hell."

He couldn't speak, just rubbing his thumb along her knuckles as he listened to her. He should have cut her off before this went any further, but he just didn't have it in him to stop this, not when her words were everything he had been craving, too.

"I want…us. Together. I want you, Xavier," she confessed. "The waiting and hoping and holding back and pretending I don't feel the way I do… It's been killing me. I don't care what I have to deal with to be with you. I want you. I want us. And if you can't handle that, I need you to tell me now." Her voice was taut, but her words were firm.

His eyes searched hers, doubtful. He wanted her, more than anything. The thought of more harm coming to her, especially because of him, was almost more than he could bear. "You could get hurt again," he warned her with narrowed eyes.

She smiled. "I could get hurt again," she repeated. "But if you break this off now, I *am* going to get hurt. No doubt about it. And I can handle it, if that's what you really want. But I... I think you want this as much as I do."

His head warred with his heart as he took in her words. Of course he wanted to be with her. He had dreamed of being with her for so long, it was almost too much to hope for. He craved that more than anything in the world, even more than finding out who had done all these things to Warrior Peak. He needed her. There'd always been a place deep down inside of him that called out for her.

He reached out to caress her face, and she closed her eyes and rested her head in his hand. Even a simple touch like this told him what he wanted. No matter what the risk was, he had to have her. There had always been something in their way, something pushing the two of them apart, but he was well and truly done with it now. Whether it was her brother, his PTSD, or whatever outside threat was bearing down on them, he was finished with it. He couldn't let it stop him from being with the woman he loved.

He leaned in and planted a kiss against her lips, his voice fierce when he spoke again.

"That kiss today was the best thing that's happened to me in a long time," he murmured to her. "I want you, Hannah. I want us to be together."

She smiled, looping her arms around his shoulders.

As he gazed into her eyes, he was struck by her strength and determination, yet at the same time her fragility underneath it all. How much of his own pain and suffering would bleed on to her if he didn't do something to deal with his past? He had avoided getting help for his PTSD and nightmares for so damn long, but maybe this was the push he needed to finally deal with them—to finally start addressing all that pain he had hoped would just fade on its own.

He swore to himself, in that moment, that he would do whatever it took to keep her safe. Not just from whoever was targeting them but from himself, too. He wasn't going to let her suffer from the trauma that he still carried with him. The first chance he got, he was going to go to Sarah and tell her that he needed her help. God only knew how true that was, no matter how much he had tried to deny it. He was ready to move forward.

Hannah kissed him again, this time, a little more intention behind her touch. She knew as well as he did that they couldn't deny what they felt for each other any longer. Regardless of her brother or whoever else might stand in their way, they were meant to be together. Maybe life would have been simpler if they could resist, but now there was nothing left to do but give in to the feelings they'd denied for so long.

He didn't need to say the words, but he was sure she felt them, too, as their kiss deepened. He drew her into his lap, needing her closer. He wasn't sure if he would ever get close enough to her, if the need that had throbbed inside of him for so long would ever be sated.

He could no longer deny his true feelings or his desire to be with her.

He was in this. They were in this.

Whatever happened going forward, they would be together.

Chapter Fourteen

Hannah slowly came to, and the sensation of a weight in bed next to her drew her attention. Her head hurt, but she could hardly pay attention to it as she glanced over at the other side of the bed. Then she buried her face into the pillow to hide her grin.

Xavier. He was right there next to her. Last night had been amazing. It was the first time they had truly come together in the way she had fantasized about for so long, and it had been *good*. Way better than even her wildest fantasies were able to prepare her for. His touch was so strong, so effortless—the way he kissed her, the way he held her, the way he looked at her—it made her head spin with the most delicious pleasure she had ever experienced.

And now, here he was, sleeping next to her. He was lying on his side facing her so, she reached her arm out over his chest tentatively, not wanting to wake him up. She was sure he needed his sleep as much as she did right now, and she didn't intend to disturb him. She lightly brushed her hand along his strong chest, marveling at how good it felt, and an excited little giggle bubbled up in her throat. After all this time, all this waiting, it felt wonderful to finally have him there with her.

Snuggling against him, she flipped over so that her back was pressed against his chest. He wrapped his arm around her waist almost on instinct and pulled her closer.

Hannah closed her eyes, savoring the feeling and wanting nothing more than to doze off again. She was sure there were plenty of tasks she needed to do today, but the only thing she cared about right then was resting up and feeling the warm comfort of him close to her.

She was just starting to fall asleep once more, feeling the faint sensation of his heartbeat against her back, when suddenly, something shifted.

His arm constricted around her all of a sudden, gripping on to her like he didn't want to let go. His breath was coming harder and faster, but not like it had when they were intimate the night before. This felt like something else entirely.

Hannah wiggled to get a little more room between them, then she drew herself back and slowly turned to face him.

His eyes were open but unfocused. He was looking at her but not seeing her. His body was stiff and twitching slightly, as though he was in the middle of some deadly battle right there in his mind.

"Xavier?" she whispered to him nervously, but it didn't draw a response. He was dreaming. This must be one of the nightmares he'd told her about. Seeing him in the midst of it, and not knowing how to help him, hurt her heart. This was far different than what she'd thought it would be like.

His hands bunched up the covers, and his body jerked sharply, then contorted like he was in pain, before straightening out again.

She lifted her hand and waved it a couple of times in front of his face, but there was no response. She had never seen anyone in this state of distress before, and she wasn't sure of what to do. Her heart clenched at the thought of him reliving this terrible pain. She felt all but helpless.

His lips parted, and he croaked out a word. Over and over again, his voice so low and muffled she could hardly make it out.

She shifted a little closer to him, making sure not to touch him, trying to understand what he was saying.

Max.

He was saying his brother's name. Chanting it almost as though it was some kind of spell that would bring him back to life.

Tears sprang to her eyes at the thought of what he must be seeing in his dream. Was this what it was like every night for him? Remembering that one battle that took his brother's life over and over again? Hannah wished she knew what was going on inside his head, but the best she could do was try to pull him out of the memory as safely as possible.

Sarah had talked her through it before, the basics of how to pull someone out of a flashback like this. She had suggested it would be a good idea with the guests they catered to, just in case Hannah was around when someone had an episode and needed assistance. It would save time rather than trying to find another person to help.

Hannah wasn't sure if the same thing would apply for a dream, but it was all she knew to try. She didn't want to call someone else, knowing that Xavier wouldn't want anyone seeing him in this vulnerable state.

She sat up and moved back some to give him a little more space, suddenly distinctly aware of just how powerful Xavier was—how strong and lethal he could be. Not that he would ever have used that against her willingly, when he was awake and conscious of his actions. But right now, he was definitely *not* awake, so she needed to be damn careful about how she approached this.

"Xavier," she spoke his name quietly, not wanting to suddenly shock him into wakefulness.

He was still mumbling rapidly under his breath, his eyes sliding sightlessly back and forth as he witnessed who knew what horrors inside his head.

She knew she couldn't stop them entirely, but she could at least try to pull him out of this and bring him back to the real world, remind him that he was safe, with her in her cabin, in her bed. She didn't want his first night staying with her to be marred with these memories.

She took a calming breath before speaking to him again. "Xavier, can you hear me?" she asked gently but firmly. She wanted to reach out and touch him, but she knew it might trigger a more violent response. In his addled state, he might think someone was attacking him and lash out. She wished she could just take his hand and give it a tight squeeze or give him a big hug and make all of this go away, but she had to be smart and help him the right way.

She had to show him that she was capable of handling whatever came with being with him—even when it was scary or tough.

"Xavier, I don't know what's going through your head right now," she continued softly. "But I need you to know that you're safe. Okay? You're in my cabin. You're in my bed. This is Hannah, and I'm here to help you through this."

For a moment, his mumbling stopped, like he could actually hear her. She continued talking, repeating what she had just said again. She spoke slowly and clearly, even though inside, her heart was breaking at the sight of him like this. Realizing that he'd been struggling with these nightmares all this time, she just couldn't wrap her head around it. To think he was doing this all alone, with no one there to pull him back. It wasn't right.

She was never going to let him deal with them alone again.

The third time she repeated herself, something seemed to shift in him. His breathing began to slow and level out, and his eyes drifted shut once more. The grip he'd had on the covers loosened slightly, and he let out a long, shaky breath.

"Xavier?" Hannah murmured, still a little wary. Had she done the right thing? Perhaps she should have gone up to the lodge and got proper help for him. Wake up Sarah, or even her brother. Lawson would have some words about Xavier being in her bed, but she knew he'd help his best friend. Either one of them would be more equipped to deal with this situation.

But then, Xavier's eyes opened once more. They flitted around the room before settling on Hannah. He wiped away the sheen of sweat on his forehead and then reached out to take her hand. "Hannah?" he muttered. His voice was hoarse and quiet, but he was here—he was back with her, not lost to that nightmare that had just consumed him.

She breathed a sigh of relief. "Yeah, it's me," she told him, squeezing his hand. "Are you…are you okay?"

He paused before he replied, and she knew the answer before he spoke it out loud. Of course he wasn't okay. How the hell could he be? Whatever he had just been through, it had been really bad. Even last night, faced with the car crash and having to find a way out of the sinking SUV, he hadn't looked as shaken as he was right now.

She hated seeing him like this, but the fact that he didn't

feel the need to hide it from her felt like a big shift. A huge relief.

"No, not really," he replied. "I'm sorry. Did I wake you?"

She shook her head. "I was already up," she assured him. "I saw there was something wrong. Do you...do you have nightmares like this a lot?"

"Usually worse," he admitted.

Her eyes widened. Worse? How could they be worse than that?

"I'm sorry," he murmured again.

She gripped his hand a little tighter. "You have nothing to be sorry for," she promised him. "I—I knew things were bad, but I didn't realize just how bad they were for you. This has been happening for a while now?"

"Since the fire," he replied with a sigh, propping himself up. He still seemed a little off, as though he was still shaking off the remnants of the nightmare.

She thought, for a moment, about asking him what he had dreamed about but quickly decided against it. As curious as she was, she didn't want to ask him to go through those memories again, especially when they were still so fresh in his mind. The best thing she could do was show him support, let him know she was there for him and encourage him to get proper help.

"I'm sorry you're having to deal with that. I do hope you'll reconsider talking to Sarah about them," she added gently. He had seemed resistant to it before, but a lot had changed since then. Between them, especially. She hoped it would be enough for him to stop denying himself the help he so clearly needed.

"Yeah, I am," he replied. "I don't even know where to start, though."

"You don't need to know where to start," she reminded

him. "That's what she's there for. She'll know how to sort through all of this way better than either of us could."

He nodded but then offered her a smile. "I think you did a pretty damn good job there," he remarked.

She glanced away from him, shaking her head. "Oh, I just did what anyone would do."

"You did amazing," he replied firmly. "I don't know many people who could pull someone out of a flashback like that, especially without some form of training."

"Sarah offered to guide me through the basics a while back. Thought it would be good to know working here. Never thought I'd have to try it out."

"You handled it just fine. You didn't panic or get frustrated or overreact," he pointed out. "You shouldn't downplay it, Hannah. You should be proud of yourself. I sure am. I would be doing a lot worse right now if it wasn't for you. I'm usually a whole lot more stressed and anxious when I come out of a nightmare."

He pulled her to him, and she snuggled against his chest, grateful for their closeness once more. His presence next to her was everything she needed right now, even if she could still feel some of the tension in his body from that nightmare he'd just had.

And she knew it wouldn't be the last time she would have to talk him down from one of those flashbacks. It didn't work that way. No matter how much better things seemed to be between them now, how much closer they'd become after sharing their feelings for each other.

Healing wouldn't happen immediately; it would take time and proper therapy for him. At least he was willing and ready to try, and she'd be there for him in whatever capacity she could be to help him through it.

She wanted Xavier no matter what he was dealing with;

wanted to be with him fully and completely. She wanted to be with him as he healed, to see him grow and change into the man he wanted and deserved to be. The man who was free from the pain and guilt he had carried around for so long. She didn't want him to live in the past and suffer over and over again, reliving his brother's death.

Hannah closed her eyes and nestled against him, breathing in his scent. She was so thankful that they had finally been open and honest about their feelings. And that they were together. Despite the stress of the nightmare, she was content and happy.

He pushed a hand through her hair and kissed her temple, and she smiled against his chest. Yeah, she might just stay in bed a little longer yet.

Chapter Fifteen

Xavier shifted in the chair. He wasn't sure why, but he didn't like the feel of it. It was comfortable, almost too comfortable, like it would have been all too easy to just sink in to the soft fabric and never get out. He had already pulled off all the pillows and piled them on the floor in front of him when Sarah had told him to arrange the room however he felt most at ease, and he was sure she already thought he was crazy for that.

She offered him a smile from the large, heavy chair she sat in opposite him.

He never imagined that he would find himself here, of all places. He never thought he would be in therapy talking about his feelings and sharing his innermost thoughts. When they hired Sarah, it had been for her to take care of the guests at the lodge, not one of the owners. But he knew, clearer than ever, how much he needed this help, even if he was having a hard time figuring out how to start the conversation.

Seeing the look on Hannah's face when he woke up from that flashback had been enough to make him certain he needed to be here. He couldn't keep putting her through having to help him out of his nightmares or possibly even put her in danger from them. It wasn't fair to her or their newfound relationship. He felt bad enough that she'd witnessed the one she did.

She'd handled the situation well and had done a good job of bringing him back to the present, but he didn't want to be a burden on her or their relationship in that way. He wanted to be her partner, not have her see him as someone broken and reliant on her for help every time he had a nightmare. If they were going to be together, he needed to embrace these head-on and get the help he'd needed for a while now.

And Sarah was offering him a chance to do that. Beside her, on the desk, a small diffuser puffed out scented steam. It smelled like the vapor rub his mother used to put on his chest when he had a cold—menthol and medicinal. Sarah had a notepad sitting just next to her and a pen ready to jot down any observations she might make on what he had to say.

For some reason, this made him uncomfortable—talking about it was one thing, but having it written down and made permanent? That was something else entirely. It made him feel more vulnerable. Exposed in a way he didn't like at all.

"So," Sarah began as the silence hung heavy in the room between them, "I'm really glad you came to speak to me today, Xavier."

He grunted his acknowledgment and shifted in his chair. He was uncomfortable with the thought of spilling his guts to this woman. He'd never told anyone the specifics of the nightmares he'd been dealing with. Not even his best friend and business partner, Lawson, knew the full extent—just what little he'd shared after Max's death since Lawson had been there at that time to offer his support. And Hannah only knew what little she'd witnessed.

He never liked burdening people with what he was going through, but right now, he didn't have a choice. He knew he just had to push himself to get started, but he couldn't find the right words to say what he wanted to.

"You mentioned to me before that you'd received a diagnosis of PTSD from a previous physician, is that right?" Sarah asked.

"I had to see someone before I started working for the CIA," he explained. "That's what he told me it was. Never put much stock in it, until…" He trailed off, tripping over his words again. He wasn't used to talking about any of this, and his instincts were screaming for him to stop. He'd dealt with his nightmares on his own for so long, it seemed unnatural to share his troubles with someone else.

"Until?" she prompted him.

He shook his head.

"It's okay," she assured him. "You don't have to talk about anything you're not ready to. I just want to get a general idea of how you're doing and where you're at with your mental health. Do you mind if I ask a few questions?"

He gestured for her to keep talking, wishing he could pull himself together. It felt like he was stepping in the silt of his memories, all those parts of himself that he had tried to leave behind pressing up against him once more. How could he just talk about it? Say it out loud, when he still felt so much guilt and shame for what he had done?

Or, more accurate, what he had failed to do?

"We didn't talk much about your diagnosis before," she continued, jotting something down on her notepad. "But I've heard from Lawson that you've been struggling with nightmares recently."

Lawson. Of course he had talked to her about it. Xavier shook his head slightly. "He's been talking to you about it?"

"Nothing specific, but yes, he has," she replied. "Your friends are concerned about you, Xavier. They want the best for you."

He sighed. "I'm concerned, too," he admitted finally, picking at a loose thread on the chair beneath him. "I… I thought these nightmares were over, you know? I had them a lot right after I got back from overseas, but they started to fade after a while. I would still have these memories, but when I would wake up, I knew it was a dream, and I could bring myself back to reality pretty easily."

"And you've been having more trouble with that recently?" Sarah asked.

He nodded again. "Yeah, it feels like I'm right back there, all over again," he continued, his voice lowering. He was going to need to get used to talking to her like this; hopefully, it would get easier over time. "Like I'm watching my brother die all over again," he added.

He hated saying those words out loud. Acknowledging that Max was gone hurt in a way nothing else did—a permanent wound that would never heal, a reminder of how much he had failed his little brother. He had promised his mother he would do everything he could to keep him safe, but when it came down to it, he had failed. He knew he was never going to be able to forgive himself for that.

Sarah frowned, nodding kindly.

He averted his eyes to stare at the floor. What must she think of him, a man who failed to keep his own brother safe? He didn't even want to know. Logically, of course he understood that she had heard far worse things in her time here at Warrior Peak. He still felt like she would never look at him the same way again.

"It's really common to face a setback in your recovery after a traumatic event," she explained.

Xavier shook his head. "I haven't had a traumatic event." Not by his standards, anyway. Yeah, the fire wasn't exactly pleasant, but he had seen far worse in his time. He felt like he would have sounded crazy to compare that to what he'd endured in the service.

"The fire?" Sarah prompted him. "Isn't that when these dreams really started to cause you problems again?"

He nodded.

"I understand that you may not have felt traumatized by the fire, but chances are that it triggered your fight-or-flight response," she explained. "It's a method the nervous system uses to handle particularly threatening or dangerous situations, whether they're actually bad news or just perceived by your brain as such. Does that make sense?"

He shrugged. "Yeah, I guess." He didn't feel like he had any right to make the attack on the sanctuary about him. Everyone had felt the danger and struggled that night.

"And it seems like your brain has interpreted that as being back in the midst of the event that caused you the most trauma," she continued. "That's why the dreams have been coming up again. Your brain is trying to warn and protect you, even though there's nothing like that going on right now."

Like that. She was careful to phrase it that way. She knew there was something going on around here, just like Xavier did. Could he really put this work into recovery, when he was sure there were people after him right now? He shifted in his seat again, not speaking.

"And what I want to do with these sessions is teach your

brain that those memories are in the past, they're not happening now, and that you're safe," she continued. "I understand how hard that must seem to you, but it is possible. Lots of people suffer trauma as a result of being involved in combat, and it's really common to deal with PTSD and nightmares in the aftermath. But it doesn't have to stay that way, okay? You don't have to deal with this alone."

He could feel a well of emotion rising up in him, and he tried to push it down.

"Your friends here really care about you," Sarah went on. "I do, too. I've seen all the great work you've done here, all the ways you've created a safe space for the people who've been through what you have, and you deserve to give that kindness to yourself, too. Do you think you can do that?"

"I don't know," he admitted. Faced with the choice, there was a part of him that wanted to push back and deny himself what he knew he needed. But then, he closed his eyes, and he thought of Hannah. He thought of her lying beside him in bed, her eyes wide as she tried to pull him from the horrors in his head.

And he knew he had to try. He couldn't keep pretending this wasn't happening. He had tried that already, and he was pretty damn clear on the fact that it hadn't worked. His eyes were fixed on the diffuser beside her, and he tried to time his breath to the sound of its low hum. Anything to ground himself, to pull him into this moment instead of dealing with the usual fight that boiled in his system when he was faced with telling the truth about how he felt and what he had been through.

"Yes, I do," he corrected himself finally. "I... I want to try. I don't know how, but I want to try."

A warm, genuine smile lit up Sarah's entire face. "I'm

so glad to hear that," she gushed, and she reached over to pull her notepad into her lap. "And you don't need to know how—that's what I'm here for."

He nodded. He had to let her take the lead. It was fine for him not to know what he was doing here. That was why he had come in the first place.

"So, let's start by going through the content of these dreams," she prompted him. "Do you think you can manage that?"

He gritted his teeth, fighting the usual urge to just close off as soon as anyone asked him about that time in his life. But finally, he spoke. "They all start the same way. My brother and I are under fire…"

Chapter Sixteen

"Uh, do you have the manual there?" Hannah called to River, as she carried over an armful of lightbulbs, stakes and a couple boxes of screws.

"I think Bailey has it on her phone," River called back, pulling a face as she reached Hannah. "It's one of those downloadable ones."

"Oh, they're the worst." Hannah sighed. "Why can't they put a paper manual in the box?"

"My thoughts exactly," Bailey cut in as she followed River out of the main entrance to the lodge.

"I printed it out. Here, let's see where we need to get started." Bailey appeared from behind them.

Hannah grinned as the women joined her along the edge of the path they were working on today. Together, they were setting up some solar-powered lights that would lead the way through the darkness if there were any issues with the generators again. It had been River's idea, and Hannah had agreed to help her at once. After the tumble she'd taken, even though it just scraped up her knees, she didn't want anyone else to possibly come to harm if the power went out again.

None of them really knew what they were doing, but

between the three of them, she knew they'd figure it all out and get them working in no time. She had been working and living alongside River and Bailey for months now, and having the women around felt like second nature to her. They had become close in their time together, and though Hannah knew eventually they would likely move on to other things, she was glad for their company.

Especially now. It had been nearly a week since she and Xavier had been driven off the road, and she was still trying to wrap her head around it. They were no closer to finding out who might have done it or why. And it had left Hannah feeling spooked and worried. She was looking over her shoulder all the time now, waiting for something else to happen, worried she wouldn't be able to stop it if it did.

Putting in the solar lights was as much an attempt to get her mind on to something more useful as it was to make a difference around the lodge, and River seemed to know that Hannah needed something to distract her.

As they laid out their tools and started to read through the instructions, River glanced over at Hannah, a concerned expression on her face. "You all right?" she murmured quietly.

Hannah sighed. River was perceptive when it came to people's emotions, and it was clear she had good reason to be concerned about Hannah.

Hannah shook her head. "Not really," she admitted. "I… These last few days have just been a lot, that's all."

"I can imagine," River agreed as Bailey dropped the instructions and joined the conversation.

"We're doing everything we can to get to the bottom of it," Bailey assured her.

Hannah managed to smile at her. "Yeah, I know," she

replied. "And I appreciate it, I really do. It's just that... Well, it's not just me I'm worried about."

"Oh?" River prompted her, curious.

"No. Xavier, too," Hannah admitted. "He's been having these...nightmares. I think what happened to us out on the road is really getting to him. I just wish there was more that I could do to help."

River and Bailey exchanged a glance, and Bailey cocked an eyebrow. "Nightmares?"

"Yeah, there's just been a lot going on lately. Between the recent fire, the generators and then the crash..." Hannah trailed off, trying to answer without divulging details. She knew that the others there at the sanctuary knew Xavier had troubles in his past, but it wasn't her story to share. If he wanted everyone to know the particulars, that was his choice. She wasn't going to break his trust in her. "He just feels responsible for everyone here, you know?"

"Understandable. So, that's why he's been seeing Sarah?" River asked.

"River!" Bailey protested her nosiness. "That's not our business."

"No, that's okay," Hannah tried to ease the rising tension. "It's just not for me to discuss. I've been trying to help, but I can only do so much."

"That explains the nightly visits, then." Bailey waggled her eyebrows at Hannah.

"Bailey!" River scolded her in return. "That's not the issue here."

Hannah snort-laughed at them both under her breath. She reminded herself that they wouldn't be so nosy if they didn't care about her and Xavier.

"Hey, I'm just saying, I've seen Xavier come out of your cabin every day this week," Bailey replied, holding her hands up. "I wondered if that meant the two of you had finally done something about...well, the obvious."

"What's obvious?" Hannah asked, but she couldn't help but crack a smile.

"How much the two of you like each other," Bailey explained. "I mean, it's written all over your faces whenever the two of you are together."

"Is it?" Hannah replied, laughing.

"Yeah, come on, even Lawson can tell," River pointed out.

Hannah glanced back toward the lodge building. Yeah, she had to assume that her brother had figured out what was going on between Xavier and her.

After the crash, Lawson had tried to talk to her, but she'd shut him down and then left with Xavier. So, even if he didn't know specifics, he had to suspect. But, surprisingly, he hadn't confronted her yet. She hoped to keep it that way for a bit longer, they all had enough to worry about right now.

"I think we're giving it a real shot this time," Hannah confessed.

River reached out to give her arm an excited squeeze. "Oh, I'm so happy for you guys," she gushed.

Bailey chuckled. "Plus, I think that means I've won the betting pool," she added.

Hannah's eyebrows shot up. "The betting pool? On when we were going to get together? Don't tell me that was a real thing!"

"It isn't," River assured her. "We're just happy for you, that's all. The two of you deserve it."

"Thanks," Hannah replied. She felt her cheeks get warm from all this attention, but honestly, it felt good to share how thrilled she was about what they had going on. It had been crazy, these last few months, but if there was one thing she was sure of among all of the madness, it was him.

It had always been him.

"Anyway, we need to get these lights set up," Bailey announced, crouching down on her haunches and grabbing a screwdriver. "River, can you hold this in place while I screw it in?"

"Oh, why don't you get Hannah to do that?" River joked. "She's the expert after all."

"Huh—hey!" Hannah's cheeks warmed as she protested, and all three women burst out laughing.

Hannah could already feel herself starting to relax, starting to believe that everything was actually going to be okay. No matter what the outside world threw at them, Warrior Peak had a solid base of people who pulled together when they needed each other most, and she was beyond grateful that she was a part of it. They set to work putting together the lights. It was a pleasant day, one of the first of the year, with the sun attempting to peep out from behind some clouds.

It took a few attempts to get the lights right. Hannah managed to put the first one in back to front, and they had to take it apart and start all over again, but soon, they got into a pace and had almost filled one side of the path with new lighting. As Hannah straightened up to catch her breath, she noticed someone wandering out of the main entrance. And as soon as she saw who it was, she felt herself tense.

Jed. She'd almost forgotten about him in the midst of everything else. She wasn't sure what it was about him, but there was a part of her that really didn't like the way he strolled about this place. She had tried to brush it off as best she could, not wanting to assume anything about a man she hardly knew, but it was getting harder and harder to ignore. Most of the people here kept their heads down and focused on themselves when they first arrived, but he seemed intent on garnering the attention of anyone he was able to.

He made his way over to the women and greeted Hannah with a nod. "How's your head?" he asked, smirking as he gestured toward the bandage still covering the wound from the accident.

She reached up to touch it—she had almost forgotten it was there. "It's getting better, thanks," she replied. "How are you doing?"

"Good," he responded, that too-easy smile covering his face again as he looked between the three women. "It's starting to feel like home here. Fresh air, good food. And when you've got a therapist who looks like *that*, how can you complain, right?"

He laughed, but none of the women did.

Hannah stared at him, a sinking feeling in the pit of her stomach. How could he talk about Sarah like that? She was amazing at her job. And yeah, she was beautiful, but it had nothing to do with the relationship she had with her clients. Hearing him speak about her in that way…it didn't sit right with her.

"Anyway, I'll leave you ladies to it," he remarked, and he headed down toward the cabin he was staying in.

Hannah waited until he was out of earshot. "Well, that was gross and uncalled for."

"Wasn't it?" Bailey agreed. "Why is he talking about Sarah like that? And to us."

"He gives me the creeps," River added. "I don't like him. I haven't liked him since he got here. It seems as if he's just lurking around sometimes. Watching."

"Really?" Hannah replied, relieved. So, it wasn't just her who had noticed how off he seemed. It wasn't that he acted less nervous or insecure than most of the other guests. While he did seem cockier and more self-assured, that didn't necessarily bother her. It probably wouldn't have even stood out to her at all if it were anyone else.

"Yeah, I noticed him standing off path the other day, kind of back in the trees. Like he was watching something, or waiting. When he saw me, he turned around pretty quickly and walked off. It was weird."

Hannah and Bailey exchanged a worried look at River's words.

"Cade thought something seemed off about him, too," River added. "The more I see of him, the more I think he was right to have his doubts about him. I definitely don't want to be alone with him."

"I haven't seen a whole lot of him," Bailey interjected. "But if you guys think there might be a problem there, I'll speak to Aaron about it and see if there's anything he can do to keep a closer eye on him."

Hannah felt a little guilty for even considering speaking to Xavier about this, but at the same time, she didn't want to ignore what might end up being a problem. If she had learned anything these last few months, it was not to brush aside the emotions that she didn't want to deal with. Good or bad, she needed to deal with them and share her thoughts when something was bothering her.

There was no harm in the three of them being cautious and watching their step around the guy, right? If there was truly nothing going on, then there was no harm in just asking the guys to keep an eye on him for a while.

"I'll speak to Xavier about him, too," Hannah added, deciding that she needed to say something.

She didn't want to divide Xavier's focus any further right now or give him more to be concerned about, but at the same time, if there was something worrisome going on around the sanctuary, he would want to know about it. He was part owner, after all, and he and Lawson worked hard to keep out trouble and give their guests a safe place to recover. He wouldn't want anybody there feeling uncomfortable or threatened in any way by another guest.

Jed was probably less careful about what he said to the women, and he might put up a front when it came to the guys so they didn't get suspicious or look any further into his reasons for being there.

"Guess we should get back to work," Bailey remarked, gesturing to all the lights that still needed to be put into place.

Hannah nodded in agreement and tried to push the comment Jed had made about Sarah to the back of her mind. But it troubled her. There was something off about that guy. And she needed to find out what it was before anything came of it.

Chapter Seventeen

As Xavier tightened the last screw into place, he took a step back to admire his handiwork on the latest addition to the lodge building.

"Pretty impressive, if I do say so myself," Aaron remarked, grinning. "Though I still don't know why anyone would want to jump into freezing cold water first thing in the morning."

"Hey, if it helps them, that's what matters," Xavier pointed out. He dusted off his hands and reached for the half-full cup of coffee he'd been sipping on to help motivate him through the construction.

The cold plunge tub had been Lawson's idea, after he heard about it helping athletes in their recovery. He'd done a little research into it and found that it had some decent therapeutic value for people dealing with trauma, the shock of the cold sometimes enough to pull them out of a flashback. He wouldn't say anything to the others about it, but he could attest to the accuracy from his icy showers when he needed the extra help coming back to reality.

And besides, there was still plenty of work to do before it was ready to go. Aaron had offered to give him a hand putting it together, and they were making good progress.

Plus, it was a distraction from Xavier's meeting with Sarah in a bit, though he realized that he didn't feel the usual dread when he thought about seeing her. He was starting to get used to their meetings, even if he still came out of them feeling drained.

Slowly, he could feel himself starting to open up. Beyond just the question-and-answer sessions they had with her pulling information out of him, he was freely volunteering stuff to her now, glad to get it off his chest after so long holding it back. There were still so many painful memories to go through. He hadn't even really talked much to her about how his family had reacted after he had returned from service without his brother in tow, but he was getting somewhere.

The nightmares had still been pretty bad, but he figured that was a given, at least for the time being, as he brought up all these painful memories again. He was actually beginning to think they'd get easier, lessen in time. Sarah had already given him a few skills to help manage the immediate aftermath of his dreams when he woke up—grounding techniques to keep him from spinning out of control and to remind him where he was and that he was safe here.

And more than anything, he could tell how happy it made Hannah, which was reason enough to keep going. When Xavier struggled with motivation, he would just look at her and remind himself why he was doing this in the first place: to become the kind of man she deserved—without worry, without doubt, without second-guessing herself for being with him.

It wasn't her job to put those pieces of him back together and he didn't want to become a burden or a regret for her. It was his responsibility to fix himself, to do the work and put in the time to be whole again. He had to want to be whole again. And thanks to Hannah, he did.

Just as Xavier was about to put down his now empty coffee mug and get back to the cold plunge tub, Aaron brought up something that made him stop in his tracks.

"You know what Bailey said to me yesterday?" he asked.

Xavier raised his eyebrows at him. "No idea."

"She told me to keep an eye on that Jed guy," he replied, frowning.

Xavier paused. He'd had a similar conversation with Hannah the night before, too. She had tried to make it sound as casual as possible, but he could tell from her expressions and body language just how much it bothered her. Jed had said some stuff to the women, she'd told him, that had given them reason to wonder if his motivations for being at the sanctuary were entirely pure. She wouldn't go into the details, but she just asked Xavier to look out for Jed to see if there was anything strange that he noticed about him, too.

"What did she say?" Xavier asked. Had the women been talking about him among themselves or had they all just overheard him make a few off comments and wanted to do something about it? Either way, his ears perked up. He knew how guys could be when they thought there was nobody important listening. Unfortunately, for some men, *nobody important* included women.

"Apparently, she was helping Hannah and River put up lights outside and he approached them and made a comment about Sarah. It had them wondering why he was really here," Aaron explained. "Bailey hadn't really had contact with Jed before that, but she said Hannah and River were uncomfortable around him."

"Hannah mentioned something similar to me. She

doesn't really think he fits here, like he's putting up a fake front for some reason. What do you think of him?" Xavier asked, his eyebrows drawing together.

"I haven't spent much time with the guy either," he admitted. "I've seen him standing around some outside, not talking to anyone, just looking around. But nothing to make me think something was going on." Aaron shrugged. "However, River and Hannah are around the guests more than we are, so if they feel something's not quite right, I'm inclined to believe them. What about you?"

Xavier sighed. "I don't know, I haven't really been around him either. I met him when he arrived and he recognized me as an owner, which I have to admit was odd. That's not something we advertise outright," he answered thoughtfully.

"If the women are worried enough to bring it to our attention, we need to mention it to Cade and Lawson."

"River told Hannah that Cade's already aware. I'll bring it up to Lawson when I see him later."

Aaron nodded. "Sounds good. We all need to be alert."

"When I first saw him, I thought maybe I knew him from somewhere. He had a familiar 'feel' to him. He kind of reminded me of my brother."

Aaron cocked his head. "Your brother?"

"Max," Xavier replied. It felt strange to say his name out loud after holding it in for so long. "The look in his eyes, the way he carried himself."

Aaron nodded again, waiting for Xavier to continue.

Xavier could tell that Aaron knew how big of a deal it was for him to bring up his brother like that out of nowhere. It wouldn't have surprised Xavier if Lawson had mentioned Max to Aaron and filled him in on everything that had happened to allow Xavier's family ranch to fall into their hands, leading them to create Warrior Peak Sanctuary in the first place.

It used to hurt to even think of him. And there was still a deep, raw sadness when Xavier considered the fact his brother was gone—really, truly gone. But he couldn't keep hiding from it for the rest of his life, no matter how tempting it might have been. He was ready to face it. To talk about him, to remember more than just the last few brutal moments of his existence. Max had been so much more than his death, and Xavier was making a point to try to put that first in his mind.

He had been talking to Hannah a lot about him, which had helped. Just simple stories about the two of them growing up, nothing serious, but she listened intently like he was reading from the next great American novel. She peppered him with questions, encouraging him to keep going, and Xavier found himself chuckling fondly at some of the memories he hadn't touched in years.

"Nothing out of place turned up on the initial check run on him when he arrived or else it would have been brought to our attention immediately, and he wouldn't still be here. If he uses a different name than Jed Black, though, then we have no way of knowing."

"Since he seems legit on paper, what do you think we should do?" Aaron asked.

"I guess we keep an eye on him," he replied. "Make sure he's not up to something that we've been missing."

Xavier and Aaron turned their attention back to the tub and worked for the better part of another hour before Xavier checked his watch.

"I should go get cleaned up before my meeting with Sarah," he remarked. "Can I leave the rest with you for now?"

"Sure, I'll take it from here," Aaron agreed. "But if this ends up a hot tub by accident, then it's on you."

Xavier grinned. "I have faith in you," he assured him.

Aaron paused for a moment, as if considering his next words. "Everything going okay with Sarah?" he asked.

Xavier shrugged. "Guess so."

"You seem better," Aaron replied.

Xavier was surprised to hear that. He didn't think it would show that quickly, at least not to anyone outside of Hannah. "I do feel better," he admitted. Damn, he meant it, too—that was a new one for him. He had been doing such a good job covering up his real emotions for so long, he had almost forgotten what it felt like to be honest about them. He should have started working with Sarah a long time ago, but at least he was doing it now.

"And how are things going with Hannah?" Aaron asked.

Xavier chuckled. "Hey, at least let me keep some things to myself," he protested, holding his hands up.

"We've all seen you coming out of her cabin every day this week," Aaron pointed out. "If you want to keep it a secret, you're not doing a very good job at it."

"Point taken," Xavier replied with a grin. With that, he said his farewells to Aaron and headed back up to his room.

He supposed he would have to talk to Lawson about what was going on between him and Hannah. He'd been putting off the conversation because of how angry Lawson had gotten when he learned about Xavier kissing his sister last year. But knowing Hannah left the lodge with him the night of the crash, Lawson had to know they were together.

He wasn't exactly sure what he would call their relationship, being so new, but he loved it. He loved coming back to her cabin every single night, spending an evening with her talking and laughing and…well, the rest of it, too.

He had waited so long to be with her, and now that he was finally getting to enjoy that closeness, he would do anything he could to preserve it. Including taking her seriously with what she had said about Jed, even if he wasn't sure he saw much of it himself.

But he knew Hannah wasn't the kind of person to just start pointing fingers for no reason. She had worked with plenty of people like Jed over the time she had been at the sanctuary. So if she had doubts about his true intentions, he believed that they came from a place of real discomfort. He would need to talk to her a little more about it this evening, reassure her that he and the other guys were looking into the situation.

It was a warm day, now that spring was starting to come around, and he'd ended up pretty sweaty after all the work he'd been doing. He didn't want to subject Sarah to that and he had some time before his appointment, so he headed up to his room to grab a change of clothes to wear after he showered.

But when he reached his door—the door he knew he had locked, just like he always did—he found it pushed open a few inches. Again.

Chapter Eighteen

"Do I really have to spend the whole afternoon in the office?" Lawson complained as he pulled the door shut behind him. "When we're just getting the first sunshine of the season."

"Yes, you do." Hannah laughed at her brother, pointing firmly to his chair behind the desk. "Go on. Sit down. I want to talk about the finances."

"Good news, right?" he asked her a bit nervously.

"Yeah, great news actually," she assured him with a nod. She had been taking care of the finances at Warrior Peak Sanctuary since they opened. She had never imagined she would be any good at it, but there was something oddly satisfying to her about crunching the numbers, seeing how everything came together and what all was impacted with the changes they implemented. Watching as the sanctuary started to really thrive.

She was sure they would need to hire a full-time accountant eventually, the bigger they got and more money they brought in, but for now, she seemed to be doing a decent job keeping on top of it all. The bills were getting paid and employees got their salaries and their guests were being taken care of in a way that helped them recover and reacclimate to their lives in positive ways. Those were the most important things right now.

"Good," he replied, sitting down in his desk chair and grinning. "Thank God I have you around. I don't know what I would do if you weren't here to keep on top of the practical stuff."

"Yeah, you're lucky," she teased and pulled out the papers she had been working on earlier in the day. She had just finished looking at the intakes and outgoings for the previous year, and it seemed like they were doing exceptionally well.

Along with the funds they received from grants, they worked with several non-profits to raise funds for the upkeep of Warrior Peak. Since the place was originally Xavier's family home, he'd used the family money he'd inherited along with money he and Lawson had scraped together to get them started. Over the past few years, they'd continued to grow from word of mouth and additional donations from previous clients after their time at the lodge.

Lawson and Xavier had also agreed to rent out spaces in the paddocks at some clients' requests, so those who had horses of their own could bring them and tend to them while they stayed at the sanctuary. It became an additional layer of therapy to some, to bring something familiar that they loved and cared for to help ground them. Even Sarah thought it was a great idea, and it had worked out well so far.

"This is the first year we've had enough left over to start thinking about building another expansion," Hannah explained, placing the papers on the desk in front of her brother and running her finger along the numbers to show him just how well they were doing. "I was thinking maybe a separate office for Sarah next to the main lodge here, so she and her clients would have more privacy."

Hannah paused and searched Lawson's face for his immediate reaction to her idea. She didn't usually give specific input to new additions; that was his and Xavier's territory. But she just knew this was a good idea. It would be good for all the people who made appointments with Sarah, especially if they were reluctant to do so, wondering what others thought seeing them visiting her office space at the lodge.

"I've been doing some research and thought the empty section of land right next to the lodge would be perfect. It would be more secluded and quieter for her patients than having to deal with all the extra noises in the hallway and at the front desk when new people arrive. They'd have more privacy to focus on their needs and recovery. We could even add a connecting hallway between the spaces so clients didn't have to go outside in bad weather."

"I think that sounds like a great idea, Hannah," Lawson agreed, peering down at the numbers and squinting slightly. "How much do you think it'll cost?"

"We'd need to reach out to local contractors and get some estimates to get a better idea of that," she explained. "But I think we could easily cover it with the amount of profit that's come in these last few months especially. And maybe even see what additional funds would be necessary if we wanted to do a whole therapy space down the road, hire more therapists."

Lawson leaned back in his seat, nodding as he listened to her. For some reason, she always found herself a little nervous when she came to her brother with ideas like this. She figured it was a result of him being the older one in the family, the one she turned to for guidance. He had always been around to make the big decisions and put plans in motion.

"You want me to start sending out some feelers?" he asked.

"If you've got the time, that'd be great. If not, if you'll write me out a list of specifics I should inquire about, I don't mind doing it," she offered.

Ever since she and Xavier had started seeing each other properly, she had felt beyond nervous about how her brother was going to react. She was sure he knew about it by now, given that the others seemed to have figured it out, but that didn't mean she wasn't still worried about what he was going to say. In fact, she had called him in to talk finances in the hopes she could get him alone long enough to speak about what was going on with Xavier.

"You trying to get on my good side?" he asked bluntly, always able to see right through her.

She sat back in her chair and clasped her hands in front of her, feeling a buzz of anxiousness in her chest. "Uh, there was something else I wanted to talk to you about," she admitted.

He grinned. That annoying, knowing, brotherly grin that told her he had already guessed where she was going to take this conversation. "Let me take a wild guess," he remarked. "You want to talk about Xavier?"

There it was. She nodded, trying to keep her gaze steady. He didn't seem as angry as he had before, but did he know the extent of their involvement? Was he trying to look the other way? How would he respond when he found out that they had basically been living together since the accident the week before last? "Yes, it's about Xavier," she confessed, her voice wavering slightly as she spoke.

She could still remember the look of thunderous anger

on Lawson's face when he had found out last time about them kissing. As upset as he was then, it was hard to believe he would just suddenly let it go. Of course, she hoped his feelings had changed and things were different this time, but she wouldn't know for sure until she brought it up.

However, no matter what he said, it wasn't going to change her mind about pursuing a relationship with Xavier now. She wasn't going to let her brother dictate how she lived her life, no matter how angry he was about what she was doing. She was falling for Xavier, hard and fast, and she wasn't going to let a damn thing get in the way of that.

"I know that my interest in Xavier has caused issues in the past," she explained, not taking her eyes from his face as she spoke, watching every little reaction, every shift in his expression. "And I know that you're just being protective of me. But I… The two of us are together now. Really together. We've had feelings for each other for a long time, and I'm not willing to ignore them anymore, and neither is he. And neither of us want this to get in the way of our relationships with you. I want your blessing for this, as my brother. If you'll give it to me."

He paused for an excruciating second before he responded. A smile spread wide across his face. "Of course you have my blessing, Hannah."

Her eyes widened. "But I thought… I mean, the way you reacted before—"

"I wasn't thinking straight back then, and I'm sorry about that," he admitted. "We should have spoken about this way before now," Lawson rose from behind the desk and rounded it to stand in front of his sister. He folded his arms across his chest and leaned back against the desk. "I saw how much Xavier was struggling after he'd lost his brother, and all I could think about was you being the front line to have to deal with that. You're my baby sister, and I was concerned about what might happen, how it would affect you."

Hannah reached out and squeezed his forearm.

"I care about you both so much, and I want you both to be happy, but I just couldn't see how he could be with anyone without pulling them into all his struggles. I didn't think witnessing all that would be good for you." Lawson swallowed heavily, and she could tell how hard it was for him to even talk about his best friend like that.

But Lawson had been there with Xavier from the start. From the moment he had arrived home, when he had been forced to deal with the loss of his brother while also dealing with his parents blaming him and, as a result, having no one to stand by his side and help him through his grief.

Hannah knew Lawson had done his best to be there for Xavier, but what Xavier had really needed was the support and care of his family since they were all dealing with the same grief and loss. Her brother had seen how much he struggled, and it was no wonder he had been so protective about letting his little sister get too close.

"He's been working with Sarah, and he's doing so much better now," she assured him. "It's amazing how far he's come. He's actually started talking about Max to me for the first time."

Lawson's face lit up. "Really?" he replied in amazement. "Damn, I never thought we'd get to that point. That's wonderful."

"I know," she murmured, and she felt a swell of pride when she thought of how well Xavier was doing. And he was only just getting started, there was still so much room for him to grow. Hannah wanted nothing more than to see him come out the other side of it a better, stronger man. A man who didn't blame himself for what had happened, finally free of the guilt he had carried for so long.

"I've been trying to convince him to talk to Sarah about all of this for so long," Lawson remarked, shaking his head. "I didn't think he was ever going to actually do it, but you must have changed his mind. You must have given him a reason."

She lowered her gaze, smiling at the thought. The fact Xavier was willing to put himself through something as tough and demanding as therapy now that they were together meant the world to her. It felt like an investment in their future as a couple, his intentions clear—he wanted to make sure she got the best version of him, and he was putting in the effort to bring that version to life.

"So, you're really okay with us?" she asked her brother, shifting in her seat.

"Hannah, I just want you to be safe and happy. If being with Xavier is what you really want and you have no doubts about being with him while he deals with his trauma, then I will not stand in your way," he replied sincerely. "Hey, it's going to keep my Christmas card list short, right?"

She couldn't help but burst out laughing at that part. That was so typical of Lawson to turn all of this tension and stress that had hung in the air between them into a joke. "Yeah, guess so," she agreed, and she stood up to give him a hug. "It really means a lot to me, you know that, right? I wouldn't want to be with him if I thought it was going to be a problem for you."

"I know," he replied and pulled her close. "And I appreciate that. I'm sorry for trying to get in the way of it before, but I've learned my lesson. I can see how good the two of you are together. I'm not going to cause any trouble, I promise."

"Thank you," she murmured into his shoulder. "And please don't start pulling out my baby photos and telling him embarrassing childhood stories about me, okay?"

"Hey, it's my job!" he protested and pulled back with a laugh. "I'm your big brother. If I don't embarrass you in front of your new boyfriend, who will?"

She giggled, but at the back of her mind, she felt a warmth tingling through her at the sound of that word. *Boyfriend.* She and Xavier hadn't put a label on their relationship yet, but she liked the way it sounded, liked the way it felt. She could definitely get used to that label.

For so long, she had been alone. She had watched the women around her get close to men, fall in love, develop partnerships that would last a lifetime. She was happy for her friends but terribly envious at the same time. She never thought she'd have that kind of happiness for herself. Now, she got to include Xavier and herself into that equation.

"I should get going," she told her brother, stepping toward the office door. "Can you talk to Xavier about this, too? Make sure he knows you're okay with it?"

He nodded. "Of course I will." Then, as she opened the door and walked into the hall, he called after her, "And I'll make sure to tell him what a brat you are!"

"Don't you dare!" she yelled back over her shoulder, but she was already laughing. This was the last detail she needed to fall into place to feel totally confident about moving forward with Xavier.

She felt like a huge weight had been lifted. They didn't have to worry about hiding anything from anyone. They were free to be open about their relationship to everyone and finally be happy together.

Her feet felt as though they barely touched the floor as she skipped off down the corridor, a grin so wide on her face it felt as though it might burst. She knew Lawson was going to speak to Xavier, but she couldn't wait to celebrate the good news. He was already taking steps to heal himself, working on his mental health and coming to terms with his past. This would be another good step forward.

Chapter Nineteen

Xavier cautiously pushed his bedroom door open and stepped inside, looking for anything that seemed out of place. And damn, there was a whole lot in here that didn't look right.

His eyes widened as he took it all in. The covers had been tossed back off his bed, the pillows slashed—even the mattress had been pulled up at the sides, as though someone had been searching underneath it. The dresser drawers had been opened and rummaged through, some of them having fallen out in the search. The window was pushed open, and the screen had been knocked out.

His shower and his appointment with Sarah were forgotten; he needed to find out who had done this and just what they had been looking for.

A sudden thought occurred... Were they still here?

He couldn't sense anyone in the room with him, but they might be hiding. He opened the closet cautiously and then checked under the bed, but it seemed like it was just him.

His mind raced. What did they want? Did they find whatever it was? He couldn't see anything that had been taken, at least not right away, but his room was such a mess that it was impossible to tell. He would need to sift through the piles of his stuff before he would know for sure.

Xavier knew he needed to think clearly and not let panic get the better of him. He drew in a few long breaths, trying to remember all the tools Sarah had given him to navigate his emotions, but it wasn't working. He started to shut down; his mind felt far away from his body.

What could they have possibly been looking for? As he stood there, rolling the question around in his head, something finally struck him.

If he was right about this...then he was in bigger trouble than he thought. He needed a weapon, fast.

The safe in the back of his closet had a gun. He'd stored one there months ago but hoped he would never have to use. Now he was glad it was there because he needed it for whatever came next. He had to be armed if he was going to take on whoever had come in here. This was the second time his room had been searched and from the destruction this time, they were escalating.

He dropped to his knees in his closet, shifting stuff around and reaching toward the back for the gun safe when he felt a crack on the back of his skull.

He pitched forward with a groan.

Damn! Whoever had come to his room wasn't done with him yet. He should have called for backup as soon as he noticed his door ajar instead of trying to do it alone, but he didn't feel as though he had a choice. He had to move fast.

He tried to push himself up and turn to face his attacker, but before he was able, he felt the pressure of a cord around his neck. Someone jerked him backward out of the closet and into his room. He started to panic, but then his instincts and training kicked in.

He pushed a hand between his neck and the cord around

his throat, creating just enough leverage for him to move his head forward and keep the cord from doing its job.

Whoever was behind him moved in closer to try to get better leverage on his neck. As soon as he was sure they were in range, Xavier slammed his head back, landing a blow against their nose that made a sickening crunch.

The cord loosened for a moment, and Xavier ducked out of it, sliding to one side and panting for breath. His adrenaline was pumping, bringing him back to all the worst times of his life, but he couldn't let those memories get to him now. Whoever was attacking him was out for blood—he was going to have to fight them in order to stay alive.

He managed to spin around, but his eyes were still blurry from the blow he'd just taken. Still, he could make out a man standing above him. The mask he was wearing hid the man's identity, but he was tall, muscular, and had hatred burning in his eyes. The man muttered a curse, wiping his nose as blood dripped down the mask and into his mouth. His hand was left with a dark red streak from where he had swiped it across his face smearing the blood. He flashed Xavier an eerie smile.

And something about that smile made Xavier's blood run cold. He knew that kind of smile. It was the smile of a sadistic person who would kill or seriously injure someone without a second thought.

The man lifted the baton he was holding above his head and brought it down, the sound of it cutting through the air.

Xavier managed to roll out of the way just in time, and it slammed into the wall next to him. He was breathing hard, trying to pull himself together. He thought about calling out for help, but this part of the building would be deserted by now. Nobody would hear him, and he would have lost vital time trying to get aid when he knew he had to do this himself.

"Come on, Dutch," the man taunted.

Dutch? Xavier stilled, muscles going taut as his vision began to clear. That name. He hadn't heard that name in years.

The man standing above him suddenly took a step back and ripped off the mask.

Jed. All the pieces suddenly clicked into place: Hannah and Aaron's concerns, the feeling like he'd seen the man somewhere before, the car crash and generators...

There was only one person who had ever called Xavier by that name.

"How do you know that name?" Xavier asked as he tried to pull himself to his feet. His head was killing him. He reached around to touch the spot where the baton had hit him, and he felt the hot rush of blood beneath his fingers. Looked like he wasn't the only one who had managed to get in a good blow.

"Learned it from a colleague of mine. Does the name Sampson ring any bells? From what he told me, I thought you'd put up more of a fight." A smile tugged at the corners of Jed's bloodied mouth.

Xavier clenched his fists at his sides, trying to get his anger under control. It had been so many years since he'd heard Sampson's name, and he couldn't believe he was hearing it now. The one man he had hoped he would never run into again. "Just go," Xavier told him, voice low. "Nobody has to know you were ever here or that you're working with Sampson. Just get out of here. You hear me?"

Jed chuckled, twirling the baton in his hand as he took a step closer.

Xavier's eyes darted to the door, hoping no one else was

going to walk in and get hurt. What if Sarah showed up looking for him, or worse yet, Hannah?

No, he had to stop this now. It was up to him to get Jed out of here before something worse happened. Even though his vision was blurry and his skull felt like it would split open at any moment, he had to fight back.

Jed had infiltrated the sanctuary with one purpose—to find out about Xavier. His weaknesses and vulnerabilities. This man had known just where to strike him to make his mark, too. His experience was evident. He knew what he was doing.

And Xavier was a little out of practice. Not the best time to realize it, but he still had some fight in him. Especially when it came to protecting this place and his friends.

"All you have to do is tell me where it is," Jed growled, his voice low and threatening. "And then, I'll walk away from here. You'll never have to deal with me or Sampson ever again. Isn't that what you want?"

Xavier wished he could believe him. Hell, if he thought it would work like that, he would have handed it over a long time ago, but he knew it didn't. He knew Sampson would never stop. He would never back off, never stop coming after him. He wouldn't quit until he had what he wanted—and until he made Xavier pay for keeping it from him, too.

"I don't know what you're talking about," Xavier spat back at him.

A lie, and they both knew it. All the questions Xavier had asked himself about what was going on here and why it was happening were becoming clear. He was a target again, because of his past. Because of something he thought was over long ago.

But he should have known by now that his nightmares didn't have a habit of going down without a fight. He had to take them on himself—and if that meant fighting back again, he would do it.

Jed shook his head, letting out a long, demonstrative sigh. "I was hoping you would play along," he remarked.

Xavier leaned heavily against the dresser trying to steady himself. His head was spinning, and he was having a hard time keeping himself upright. The blow Jed had landed at the back of his head had been carefully crafted to render him helpless, a practiced move to immediately weaken his opponent. It was working, too. Xavier felt almost as weak as a newborn kitten. The other man had the perfect opportunity to take him out in his current state.

Jed quickly lifted the baton again and bought it down with a sharp strike on to Xavier's shoulder. Xavier let out a gritted cry of pain, trying to swerve out of the way of the next one, but the other man was too quick—or Xavier was too slow—following with another strike to his other arm.

Excruciating pain radiated through Xavier's entire system; he wasn't used to taking this type of beating anymore. It had been so long since he had been in the midst of an active fight, and he was rusty.

Jed swept his legs out from under him, and Xavier managed to catch himself before he landed face-first on the floor. This man knew exactly how to disable someone and make it impossible for them to fight back. More than that, he realized, Jed had been shown the exact moves Xavier had been taught in his own training.

He wasn't sure why he was just now realizing that fact, but Jed must have been trained by the CIA, just like he was. He knew the tricks of the trade, just like Xavier. How to expose and exploit weaknesses and then go in for the kill.

And he was willing to do whatever it took to get what

he wanted from Xavier, use any opportunity to his advantage to win. He took a step forward, crushing one of Xavier's hands under his leather boot.

Xavier groaned in agony, ripping his hand back before his fingers snapped beneath the pressure. His whole body was consumed with fiery pain all at once, and he tried to pull himself upright again, but it was too late. Xavier had nothing left.

Jed stood above him, baton in one hand, bloodstained smile painted on his face. As he lifted the baton above his head once more, Xavier closed his eyes and braced himself for the next blow.

Chapter Twenty

Feeling as though she could walk on air, Hannah made her way down to Sarah's office with a grin. She was planning to talk to Sarah about the new addition they wanted to add to the lodge to be able to provide more people with the therapy they needed. If there was anyone who would have some good ideas for how to best expand their therapy department, it would her.

And maybe Hannah wanted to share a little of her excitement with Sarah, too. She was so pleased that her brother had finally given his blessing for her to pursue a relationship with Xavier like she had wanted to for years.

Now that she'd spoken with her brother, his previous reactions made sense to her. Of course he was worried about her getting involved with Xavier; he was Xavier's best friend and knew that he was dealing with so much. Because he was also Hannah's brother, he wanted to keep her safe and didn't want her to be dragged into Xavier's issues. Anyone would have been protective in a situation like that.

But now, after their chat and knowing the hard work Xavier was putting into therapy to face his nightmares and heal from his trauma, there was no reason for Lawson to try to stop them from being together. He could see how good they were together, how happy they made each other.

Hannah couldn't wait to prove to her brother and everyone else, including herself, that the wait had been worth it now that they were finally together.

She had checked Sarah's therapy schedule, and she didn't have any appointments booked until Xavier's, which wasn't for another forty-five minutes, so she would likely be in her office writing up patient notes or sending emails. She didn't want to interrupt Sarah's quiet work time, but she knew that her friend would want to know the good news since she had suspected that something was going on between Hannah and Xavier for a long time.

Hardly able to contain her excitement, Hannah lifted her hand and rapped on the door. She listened for a moment, but there was no reply. She frowned and knocked again, but there was still nothing. Maybe she'd had a last-minute request for an emergency appointment. Sometimes, with the problems they were dealing with, the guests in residence needed access to immediate care. Sarah always obliged, as long as it didn't interfere with another patient who needed her.

Hannah was about to chalk it up to that and try back later when a thought struck her. Normally, if she was with a patient, Sarah would have just called through the door to tell her that she'd be out in an hour or so. The silence wasn't like her.

Hannah turned back to the door again, staring at it, suddenly feeling uneasiness rising up in her chest. She knocked again, a little louder this time, just in case Sarah was listening to music through headphones or something, but there was still no reply. Pressing her ear to the door, she couldn't hear anything. She was pretty sure the office was empty. Which meant it wouldn't be a big deal at all if she just pushed the door open and checked to make sure everything was okay.

She should just leave it alone, but her instincts were telling her that something was wrong and she needed to check it out. She tried the handle, and it was unlocked. When she pushed the door open and stepped through, she gasped at what she saw.

The office was completely and utterly trashed. Paintings hung askew on the walls, one of the chairs had been ripped open, and white stuffing overflowed like a twisted version of a snowscape. Pens were scattered all over the floor, and papers had been knocked to the ground. The desk drawers were torn open where someone had clearly been searching through them and the computer that usually sat on the desk was upside down next to it.

"Oh my God," Hannah gasped out loud, a cold grip of terror taking hold of her. Her eyes darted around the room as she tried to make sense of what she was seeing. Who would have done this? One of the clients could have just freaked out and gone on a destruction spree, but that didn't sound or feel right. This seemed deliberate, like a weird sort of organized chaos.

Someone was looking for something. But what? And why here in Sarah's office? And where was Sarah?

Hannah was just about to turn around and go in search of Xavier or Lawson for help, when she heard a noise.

"Hannah?" a tiny voice squeaked from underneath the desk.

Hannah dropped to her knees to look underneath it.

Sarah looked back at her, wide-eyed, trembling and clutching her knees to her chest.

"Sarah, what happened?" Hannah gaped at her. "Are you okay?"

"I'm... I'm okay," Sarah replied, her voice shaky.

Hannah rushed around the desk and offered her a hand to help her to her feet.

Sarah took it gratefully, grabbing on to the side of the desk for support as she tried to gather herself.

"You need something to drink? Do you need me to call River to check you over?" Hannah fussed over her urgently.

Sarah shook her head. "No, nothing like that," she replied. "I—I'm okay. Physically, I mean. I just..." She cast her gaze around the office, taking in the extent of the damage for what seemed to be the first time. She pressed her lips together, the distress written all over her face. "I..." she began, but then, the tears fell down her cheeks, the shock clearly getting to her.

Hannah had never seen her so shaken up before and instantly pulled Sarah into a protective hug, hating that she had been through something so scary.

Once Sarah managed to catch her breath again, Hannah pulled back slightly and raised her eyebrows. "What happened here?" she asked gently. She knew it was going to be hard for Sarah to talk about, but if the person who had done this was still loose in the building or on the property, it was important they figured it out before something else happened.

"Jed," Sarah finally breathed.

Hannah's heart dropped slightly. She knew there was something off with that guy. "What did he do?" she asked.

Sarah shook her head, clearly having a hard time going through the details again, even in her head. "He...he came in here for an appointment," she explained. "And I thought everything was normal. But he walked in, and as soon as the door was shut, he locked it, and he just started trashing my office. Started going through my files, going through the desk, the computer, everything. He told me that if Xavier didn't have it, then it had to be in here."

"It?" Hannah replied.

"Your guess is as good as mine," Sarah admitted with a shrug. "I have no idea what he meant. There's nothing in here worth taking." She trembled hard as she looked back up at Hannah. "I think Xavier might be in danger."

Now the break-in to Xavier's room made sense. Jed was searching for whatever he thought Xavier had in his room. Was that why Hannah had gotten such weird vibes from him right from the beginning? Why others had seen him lurking around? Had he just turned up here because he thought Xavier had something he wanted?

Hannah tried to remember what Xavier was supposed to be doing right then. He had been with Aaron, right? And then he was supposed to have an appointment with Sarah. She needed to go find him. Now. Tell him she was right about Jed and he was the one who had been in his room and about him trashing Sarah's office because he was searching for something he thought Xavier had.

None of this made sense to her, but hopefully Xavier would be able to make sense of it all. First, she had to find him.

"You call Lawson," Hannah instructed Sarah, pulling herself together. "Tell him what Jed did and that he's looking for something but we don't know what. And then call Bailey and tell her what happened. She'll send people up or she'll come herself. I've got to find Xavier and tell him what's going on."

"You sure?" Sarah asked. "Jed could be somewhere

close watching and waiting to see what we'll do. He could even be listening in right now."

"After this," Hannah replied, looking around the room at all the destruction. "I doubt he's still around since he didn't find what he was looking for. Plus, he's got to know that you'll report him. But we can't wait around either way. The guys need to know what's going on and everyone needs to be on the lookout now."

"How can we be sure that it's just him?" Sarah replied nervously.

Hannah frowned. "Did he say anything that might make you think otherwise?" she asked, her heart sinking. How many of them were there around here? How many of these guys had managed to infiltrate the sanctuary? She mentally flicked through all the people she had registered at the lodge in the last few weeks, trying to remember if any of them had given her a strange feeling the same way Jed had, but she couldn't think of anyone else. She would need to go through the files, see if there was anything suspicious in there.

But right now, there was a more pressing matter on her mind. She needed to get to Xavier and tell him Jed was searching for him and whatever he thought Xavier had. She wasn't going to stand by and let the man she loved get hurt or walk into a trap unawares.

Sarah wrapped her arms around her wait. "No, he didn't mention anyone else. That doesn't mean someone else isn't around watching or waiting. Just be careful, Hannah."

Hannah nodded and threw open the office door before she lost her nerve. Before she could race off down the corridor, a man stepped in front of her, leveling a gun at her head.

Her feet froze to the spot. She had never been on the

other end of a gun and had no idea how to react. It was like her breath had seized in her chest, and she couldn't find her voice. She wanted to cry out, but all she could do was stare down the dark, dangerous barrel of the weapon pointed in her face.

And at the man on the other side of it.

Jed.

His nose was bloody and swollen, and his lips were stained with the same redness. But there was a maniacal grin on his face, as though he didn't even notice his injury. The look in his eyes scared her almost as much as the gun he had pointed at her.

He slowly turned the gun to Sarah. "Put that phone down," he ordered.

Hannah's head was spinning. What the hell was going on? Why was Jed back, here of all places? Why didn't he leave when he couldn't find whatever he was searching for?

Hannah turned to Sarah, nodding at her to do as he said. They could work this out, as long as neither of them ended up with a bullet in their brain. Sarah slowly placed the phone back down on the desk, her hand visibly shaking, her face white. Hannah wished she could comfort her, but right now, she had to focus on getting them out of there alive. She couldn't let her panic get the better of her, no matter how terrifying the situation was.

"Good girl," Jed sneered, patronizing as always.

Hannah felt a flare of anger at his remark. But how he spoke to them was the least of her concerns right now. She needed to make sure she got both of them out of this mess without getting hurt. She would never be able to forgive herself if Sarah got injured because of her rashness.

"You, come with me," Jed ordered Hannah, jerking the gun toward her.

Hannah stood her ground. "Where are you taking me?"

"That is no concern of yours," he replied, flashing her a grin. "You just shut that pretty face and do as I say, you understand? Or someone's going to get hurt."

Fear rippled through Hannah at his demand. She wished she had a way to get by him without getting shot and find help. Even if she could get out in the hallway and yell at the top of her lungs it would be better than doing nothing. There were always people around this side of the lodge; someone would hear. But then they'd be put in harm's way because of her, and Hannah couldn't have that on her conscience.

She couldn't believe this was happening again. More danger to the lodge and its guests. First the fire several months ago, and now this. This was supposed to be a safe place, where people could forget their worries and concentrate on healing and bettering themselves. Instead, it seemed to have turned into a place where danger followed and threatened their family and friends. Hannah wanted to jump on Jed and claw his eyes out for the evil and terror he'd brought to their peaceful doorstep.

But she pushed down her violent urge with a calming breath. "Fine. I'll go with you," she murmured. "Just leave Sarah and the others alone."

"You don't have a choice, bitch." He laughed and pushed the tip of the gun right up to her forehead."

Hannah's lungs seized, and she started shaking. She couldn't help it. She didn't want to die here, not like this.

"Hannah—" Sarah attempted, but Jed turned the gun on her again, silencing her once more.

"I'm not letting a pair of bitches stand in the way of millions of dollars," he told them. "Move, Hannah. Now." He reached out and yanked her forward so fast she crashed into his chest.

She pushed back and tried to move away, but Jed pulled her back to him as he stalked out the door with her in tow.

As soon as they cleared the doorway, he grabbed her shoulder and shoved the gun in the small of her back, pushing her down the corridor. He was moving her at a rate faster than her feet could keep up, and she stumbled several times. As soon as she'd right herself, Jed would jam the gun in her spine again and keep shoving her forward.

She knew she needed to fight back, do something to try to get away, but with him constantly forcing the gun to her back, she couldn't think straight. She wasn't sure what she could do without getting her brains blown out.

Closing her eyes, she kept walking, counting her footsteps and praying that Xavier would somehow know where to find her. She wasn't sure exactly how that was going to happen, but she had faith in him.

And faith in him seemed like the only thing she could hold on to right now without losing her mind entirely.

Chapter Twenty-One

"Xavier, can you hear me?"

Xavier's eyes flickered open. What? Where was he again? He couldn't even remember. All he could think about was the pulsing, throbbing pain at the back of his head and the blurriness of his vision. He felt hands on his shoulders, someone trying to shake him awake, and he managed to focus his gaze on the person in front of him.

"Aaron?" he mumbled. "Don't do that, man." The shaking was making him nauseous.

"Yeah, it's me, Aaron," the man replied, sounding relieved. "Can you see me okay? Can you hear me?"

"You're a little fuzzy, but yeah, I think so," Xavier replied, trying to sit up. He winced as a jolt of pain rushed through his system again. He sank back down, letting out a groan as the memories began to surface.

"Do you know where you're bleeding from?" Aaron asked.

"My head," Xavier mumbled. "The back of my head, I think." He tried to reach up to touch it, but Aaron caught his hand.

"Let's not do that, all right? We'll get it looked over," Aaron promised. "Come on, let's see if we can get you up."

He managed to lift Xavier off the ground and get him planted on the edge of his bed, the mattress barely still on the frame. Everything was spinning.

Aaron sat beside him to get a look at his wound just as Lawson appeared in the doorway to his room.

"What the hell is going on?" Lawson demanded.

"Your guess is as good as mine," Aaron replied. "I heard a commotion in here, and when I came in, Xavier was down for the count but no one else was around. That's when I called you."

"Damn," Lawson muttered, shooting a look of concern at Xavier. But more than anything, Xavier could see the anger in his eyes. He knew that was how Lawson dealt with shock, but right now, he needed his best friend on his side.

"Do you know who attacked you?" Lawson demanded.

"Jed," Xavier replied, wincing as Aaron poked around at the back of his skull.

"Jed?" Lawson sounded surprised. "What happened?"

"I came to grab a change of clothes for the shower and the door was open again. I noticed the room trashed and was going to grab my gun and he nailed me from behind. We fought some and he got in a final hit and took off."

Lawson frowned in confusion. "Why would he attack you and trash your room? That doesn't make sense."

Xavier closed his eyes, trying to fight the nausea rolling up his throat. "Jed's looking for something he thought I had." He paused and sighed. "It's complicated." He chanced a quick look at Aaron, then locked his eyes on Lawson.

"He's not working alone," Xavier replied, starting to shake his head, then thought better of it. The movement was making his eyesight worse. "He called me something—a name I haven't heard since my CIA days. I'm certain he's working with someone I used to know. Someone called... Sampson."

Saying the name out loud seemed like a bad omen. But he knew he had to. He had tried to leave that part of his life behind, but clearly, he wasn't going to be able to get away quite so easily.

"Sampson?" Lawson asked, frowning. "You never mentioned anything about a Sampson before. And I don't remember meeting anyone by that name at the agency."

"He was another operative I worked with when we were on separate squads at the agency," Xavier explained. "The two of us had a few difficult missions together. I always got a strange vibe from him, but he never really did anything that gave me a concrete reason for that. It was just more of an unease of how he carried himself and certain things he said, so I just pushed it to the back of my mind and kept doing my job. Figured that was the best thing for me to do. Not make extra waves and complicate things further."

"But?" Lawson prompted him.

"The last mission we were on, it went sideways," Xavier explained with a sigh. He hadn't thought about this in so long. He had hoped he wouldn't have to deal with it ever again. He'd tried so hard to leave it in the past.

"In what way?" Aaron asked him.

Xavier reached to the back of his head, brushing his fingers against the bloody gash in his skull. He winced. He was going to need to be stitched up and checked for a concussion sooner or later, but right now, they had to deal with the issue at hand. "We were assigned to this case, tracking a lost arms shipment that we had reason to believe was going to fall into the wrong hands," he explained. "But the more time I spent on the case, the more obvious it became to me that Sampson *was* the wrong hands. He dropped a few hints about the two of us working together, coming up with a cover story so we could sell them ourselves."

"So what exactly are they looking for here?" Lawson asked. "What do they think you have?"

"A USB drive." Xavier sighed. "It was the one with all the information about the shipment, all the tracking details we had on it. I was supposed to pass it on to Sampson so we could find the container, but I destroyed it before he could get his hands on it. I knew I couldn't risk firepower like that ending up in rotation with the wrong kind of people. It was a tough choice, but I know it was the right one."

"But he doesn't know you've destroyed it," Aaron surmised. "And he sent someone to infiltrate the lodge to try to find out where you were keeping it."

"That's what I think," Xavier agreed.

"You think he would kill to get his hands on it?" Lawson's voice hardened.

"Definitely. He's killed before," Xavier replied, with a grimace. "When we were working together, he was always trigger-happy. Most of the time, they were the kind of people who would have ended up dead one way or another because of their line of work. Sampson just took great pleasure in being the one who pulled the trigger."

"Why do you think he's come after you now?" Aaron wondered out loud.

Xavier sighed again. "I don't know," he admitted. "I guess because he finally tracked me down and found a way to get closer to me without arousing any suspicion. Sending Jed in first... I don't know what he's promised that guy, but I think he'll just take him out the first chance he gets. He uses people to get what he wants. And he's going to use whatever means he can to get his hands on that USB drive."

"That doesn't even exist anymore," Lawson finished up for him. "Do you think he's going to believe it when you try to tell him that?"

"No," Xavier replied. "From what I know about this guy, he's going to put up as much of a fight as he can. That's definitely what Jed was looking for in here."

"And where did he go?" Lawson asked urgently. "Do you have any idea where he is now?"

Xavier slowly shook his head. "I wish I did, but he knocked me out and then took off. Next thing I knew, Aaron was waking me up here."

"Hell," Lawson muttered and began pacing back and forth.

Xavier could practically see his mind racing. His own was going a hundred miles an hour, despite the aching pain at the back of his head. He couldn't think straight. Was Sampson here on the grounds? Had he been watching from afar, making sure that his plan came together? Though he might have been a psycho, he wasn't stupid—he wouldn't have made it that far in the CIA if he was. Jed had to be in contact with him somehow to get his orders. Now they just needed to find Jed.

Hannah. Xavier felt a flood of terror grip him when he thought of her. She was out there, and she didn't know what had just happened. Yes, she had her doubts about Jed, but she wasn't aware of just how serious things had gotten. Hopefully, if she saw him, she would know to steer clear of him, but Xavier needed to get to her and catch her up on everything that had gone down. He would never forgive himself if something happened to her and he hadn't been there to stop it.

"I'll call Bailey, tell her to come up here and get a statement from you and process the crime scene," Aaron offered. "And I'll ask her to bring River along to look at that wound on your head and check for a concussion." He stepped out into the hallway, phone in hand.

"I need to get to Hannah," Xavier growled, trying to get to his feet.

Lawson put a hand on his shoulder and pushed him back down again. "You need to sit your ass right there and wait to get checked over," he replied firmly.

Xavier knew there would be no arguing with him.

"You can't walk into a fight with a wound like that on your head. You're going to be more of a liability than anything else," Lawson pointed out in his infuriatingly calm and logical way. "Now, tell me everything you remember about Sampson. He might have other people here he's been using to watch you. We've had an influx of new guests this week alone."

Xavier tried to catch Lawson up on every detail he remembered, but they were hazy. Their time at the CIA was long behind them—or so he'd thought. It had been the incident with Sampson that had driven him to leave in the first place, because he knew he couldn't handle winding up on a mission with someone else like him again.

He needed to get out and do things on his own terms, and he couldn't rely on the CIA to do the right thing. There were plenty of agents who had to be aware of what Sampson was up to, but they were willing to look the other way, either because they were scared of him or they were on his side.

And Xavier had no idea if that made him the enemy here. What if Sampson had the full force of the CIA behind him? Xavier would bet money that Jed had been an operative before Sampson pulled him into this, hell, maybe he still was. He seemed to have a certain comfort with putting on an act the way he had since he arrived here, as though it wasn't the first time he had gone undercover.

After Aaron had called Bailey, he stepped back into the room, eyes darting between him and Lawson, his face pale.

Xavier's stomach turned, and his nausea came on full force. He knew before Aaron even opened his mouth something terrible was wrong. There was only one reason he would have that look on his face. Xavier swallowed heavily, trying to prepare himself for the worst.

Lawson sensing the same, clenched his fists at his sides. "What is it? What's wrong?"

"Bailey just got off the phone with Sarah. There'd been an incident in her office, so Bailey's on the way. But..." His gaze shifted between the two men again. "It's Hannah. They've taken her."

"Jed." Xavier all but growled. He closed his eyes and took several deep breaths trying to control the immediate range that flooded his system. Tuning out Lawson's forceful steps pacing the room and his muttered curses.

That was the one thing he didn't want to hear above everything else—the one person he couldn't lose. Not now. Not after they'd just come clean about their feelings for each other and were finally together in the way he'd always hoped for. Hannah had always been special to him, but now she was his to protect. He wouldn't let her slip through his fingers. He wouldn't let some ghost from his past snatch her away.

He didn't care what it took. He was going to get her back. Sampson and Jed didn't know what kind of storm they had coming their way.

Chapter Twenty-Two

In, out, in, out, in, out. Hannah tried to count each breath as it came, doing everything she could to keep the panic from getting the better of her.

But as she sat in the back seat of the black Ford she had been bundled into, her hands bound behind her, she didn't know how much longer she could hold out.

Jed had forced her out the back door of the lodge and into his truck—the same one that had driven them off the road that night, she was sure of it. Wrapping her wrists in a plastic cuff, he had shoved her in the back and told her to keep her mouth shut.

She had done as she was told. She knew better than to fight him on this, when she was so clearly at a disadvantage. She didn't know where he'd taken her, some secluded wooded area, but she knew she just needed to stay alive, and then…

And then what? Then hopefully Lawson and Xavier would find her. She didn't know how, though. They might not even know she was gone yet. Shoving down her panic once more, she peered out through the windshield of the truck where Jed was talking with another man.

Suddenly, Jed stalked over to the vehicle and threw the

door opposite her open, grabbed her arm and yanked her out. "You're coming with me," he snarled.

She stumbled, trying to catch herself as he pulled her toward the side door of a white van sitting just a few feet off the road. She glanced around as she was pulled along but didn't recognize the area. He had taken a road away from the sanctuary she hadn't noticed before. They were parked close to the tree line where they couldn't be immediately seen. She could only guess this other man was his partner in some way.

If that was true, then Xavier was in even more danger since she had only mentioned her concerns to him about Jed. He wasn't aware anyone else was involved and she had no way to warn him.

She took a chance and glanced at the other man as Jed dragged her along.

He didn't even pay attention to her, his eyes only glanced up briefly from the phone he held in front of him, but the sight of him sent a shiver down her spine nonetheless. His hair was shaved close to his head, his eyes dark, almost black. Even from the brief moment he looked at her, she could tell they seemed blank, like those of a shark cutting through the water toward their prey. He wore large combat boots and a flak jacket—dressed, she noted to herself, like someone who was going to complete a messy job.

Was she that job?

Hannah hardly had time to think about it before Jed thrust her into the open door of the van, standing guard just next to her so she didn't think about trying to escape.

That wouldn't stop her though. She had to think of something.

She eyed the gun on his belt, wondering if he would turn it back on her soon. Her eyes darted to the window on the other side of the vehicle, noticing how close the van was to the tree line, but she knew she wouldn't be able to make a run for it with her hands behind her back and Jed standing right there. He'd snatch her back or shoot her before she took a step. No, she realized there was nothing she could do. She just had to sit tight, and...and hope for the best. Even if it killed her to be so passive right now.

She peered out of the van as the other man made a call. He lifted the phone to his ear, a grin spreading over his face but not reaching his eyes.

"Dutch," the man greeted whoever was on the other end of the line. "Long time, no talk. How's your head?"

Hannah strained to try to hear more, but he'd turned his back to the van and he was too far away. She tucked her legs up underneath her, scooting across the floor to lean against the wall of the van. Jed shot her a look, as though warning her not to push her luck, and she met his gaze with a defiance she mustered up from somewhere inside of her.

"Watch it," he hissed at her.

She glowered back at him. From somewhere, she could smell the metallic scent of blood—not hers. She glanced around the van and noticed a large box in the back. Unease rolled through her at the sight of it. She prayed that didn't have something to do with her. Hannah was about to ask what it was when the mystery man turned back around facing her and started talking again. She tuned in to the conversation once more.

"You bring me that drive, or we kill the girl, it's that simple," he explained. "And come alone, Dutch. I don't want to see any of your lodge friends with you. Just you and me, like the old days, right?"

Dutch? Who was Dutch? Hannah racked her brain, trying to remember if she had ever run into someone by that name or anything close to it at Warrior Peak, but she couldn't come up with anything. But she knew one thing for sure—she was *the girl* he was threatening.

She started to feel lightheaded, the shock of all of this settling in. They were threatening to kill her if this Dutch person—whoever they were—didn't give them what they wanted. She was completely and utterly helpless, at the mercy of these evil men, and it scared the hell out of her.

She wasn't used to things being out of her control like this. She was the one who was supposed to decide how her life turned out. But not this time. She was relying on someone she had never even heard of before to give these men what they wanted.

Why would this Dutch person care whether they killed her or not? What if they killed her anyway? From the lengths they'd already gone to in order to find this drive, who was to say they wouldn't destroy the entire lodge and all the guests to not have witnesses when they got what they wanted.

Oh God...

Spots started to dance in front of her eyes. She was starting to let the panic consume her, and she was hyperventilating. *Deep breaths. Slow and easy breaths.* She couldn't pass out, not now. But she needed to get farther away, put more space between her and the open door. Make it harder for Jed to get his hands on her again, should he try to yank her out.

The box...

As quietly as possible, Hannah shifted herself around and slowly inched her way to the back of the van where the box sat, taunting her. She needed to know what was in there. Maybe there was something she could use to help her escape. She kept shooting glances at Jed's back to make sure he wasn't aware of her movements. He truly scared her, and she didn't want his full wrath turned against her. The look of hatred in his eyes…cold, hard, soulless. She didn't want to give him a reason to act on that.

But, as soon as she made it to the box, she wished she hadn't. She wished she had stayed where she was. Hannah drew in a sharp, shocked breath, and wished he hadn't. The smell coming from the box had bile rushing up her throat. Her face paled at what she saw.

There, inside the box, was the crumpled body of a deer. Beneath it, a pool of dried, congealed blood had formed, and its eyes, once alive with energy and life, were glassy and empty.

She let out a groan of disgust and started gagging, wondering how long it had been in there. By the looks of it, it was starting to decay already.

"Get back here," Jed warned her, reaching in to the van and grabbing her ankle roughly, yanking her back toward the door.

She put her head down between her legs, feeling the bile twisting and burning in her throat.

Why did they have that here? Were they going to do the same to her? She couldn't believe this was happening. She had ignored her instincts about Jed too long. She would never let that happen again, not as long as she lived. *If* she lived. If there was someone who came into the lodge in the future who gave off a weird vibe, she would pay attention and tell one of the others immediately.

She hated how easy it had been for him to get close to her, to the other women, and it made her sick to think of how much danger they had been in without even knowing it. At least she had been the one he'd chosen. If it had been River, Hannah wasn't sure she would have been able to handle it, after everything else she had been through.

But could Hannah handle it? She had no idea. There was a part of her that wanted to take a chance and try to run to the woods and disappear. She wanted as far away from these vile men as she could get. But she knew she wouldn't get far, if any length at all, with her hands still bound and with the gun Jed now had pressed against her hip.

Her brain told her to wait it out, bide her time and see how things went down. It was really the only smart option in her current situation.

The man finished up his call, and then turned back to Jed. "Dutch'll be here soon. Get ready."

"Who's Dutch?" Hannah blurted before she could stop herself.

Finally, the other man turned in her direction, locking eyes with hers. The feel of his weighted gaze made her insides twist with dread, and she wished that she had kept her mouth shut.

The man reached out for her, and she tried to shrink away at once, but he grabbed her chin, forcing her to turn and face him. "He's the man you can blame for you being here in the first place," he replied. "He's the one who put you in this position. Wrong place, wrong time… Just bad luck, sweetheart."

"Don't call me that," she retorted defiantly.

But the man just smiled. "Oh, a bit of attitude, huh? I can see why Dutchy likes you. But it's not going to be enough to save you."

"Don't worry, not long now until you and Xavier will be together again," Jed told her, his voice mocking.

Xavier? That was who they were waiting for? Dutch was Xavier? Hannah was totally confused. She bit the inside of her cheek to keep from asking any more questions. She didn't want this man's attention on her any longer than necessary.

"You'll be all cozy like that deer in the back of the van," the other man added, stroking a hand down her hair. "Wrapped up in a tarp together. How about we bury you with one another? You'd like that, huh?"

Hannah's eyes shifted around to the box again and noticed a heavy blue tarp rolled up behind it against the back doors of the van. Her vision turned hazy, and she felt like she couldn't get enough oxygen. Xavier was walking into this thinking he was going to save her, but these evil men had always planned to kill them both no matter what. The nausea was starting to rise again. No…she couldn't lose him…

She was torn. She wanted him here with her, wanted him to be the last person she saw before she died, but not at the expense of himself. Not after he'd been working so hard to reclaim his life and his happiness. He didn't deserve that.

But at the same time, she wondered if he knew he was walking in to a trap. He'd have to know, though, right? The man was using her as bait to draw Xavier here, and he had to know that. She also knew that'd he'd come anyway; he'd try his damnedest to rescue her from these men. To end this nightmare for them once and for all. He'd do whatever it took to keep her safe.

Regret rolled through Hannah at the thought of losing Xavier before she'd had a chance to tell him how she felt. That she loved him. A sudden image popped into her head of Xavier in the same position as the deer, eyes glassy and blank and still as a board. She couldn't stop the bile from rising up her throat again.

She leaned over the edge of the van and threw up between her feet.

Jed jumped back in disgust, muttering a curse at her.

Her whole body shook violently and she was covered in sweat, but she was still frozen to the core at the thought of what these men were planning to do to them. It felt like such a sick, cruel joke. The two of them had come so far and finally had a chance at true happiness. For it to suddenly end like this, it just wasn't fair.

"Disgusting," the man tsked. "Keep an eye on her. I'm going to watch the road for Dutch."

Jed shot her a foul look. "You better not cause any more trouble, or I'll end you now," he snarled at her.

There was such hatred in his voice, she wondered for a moment how he could have hidden it behind a friendly façade for so many days. He was obviously a great actor to have been able to trick them all. Even if something felt off about him to the women, he hadn't raised any red flags around the men. It was clear from the way he looked at her that he had nothing but total and utter contempt for her.

Her mind was racing with questions—there were so many things she wanted to ask. But she knew to keep her mouth shut. She'd have a better chance of surviving this if she sat quietly and stayed alert to anything that might give her an advantage to escape.

Xavier was coming for her. She knew that now. He would never leave her out here alone with no help. Probably her brother, too. Lawson had always been overprotective of his baby sister, probably even more so now if she survived this. And he ran that tactical team out of the lodge, so the rest of the guys would be with them, too. These two men would be outnumbered and outmatched. They'd all show up to take them down.

As hard as it was for Hannah, she just had to be patient and wait. They'd already be on the way to find her. According to the other man, Xavier was en route. She just prayed they'd be safe, that no harm would come to any of her friends coming to rescue her. She couldn't bear the thought of them getting hurt because of her or having to face her girlfriends knowing she was the cause of their men being injured. She didn't want another mark of guilt on her conscience. It would take a while for the one for Jed to go away. If she'd just mentioned him earlier to Xavier or her brother...

She closed her eyes, drawing her knees up to her chest protectively. She didn't have any answers, only more questions that made her heart hurt. She supposed she was going to find out the answers soon enough, when Xavier and the others arrived.

They'd have a plan. They'd rescue her and take out the bad guys and everything would be good again. She couldn't let her mind go to darker places; she had to stay positive. They'd all make it out in one piece.

But as she sat there in the van in the middle of nowhere, she really didn't know for sure. And that scared her more than anything in the world.

Chapter Twenty-Three

Xavier palmed the wheel, his phone propped up on the dashboard. Lawson's voice came through the speaker. Aside from feeling guilty about not listening to Hannah when she'd shared her concerns about Jed, Xavier also felt bad because he'd never shared any details with Lawson about Sampson before.

Lawson had cut him off when Xavier had tried to apologize and explain separately in a little more detail. He'd immediately said he understood. There had been a few times when Xavier and Lawson were at the agency that they had separate assignments with other agents. They both knew the rules: you didn't share details if it wasn't an operation you were directly involved with or had permission from the higher-ups to do so.

Xavier was positive that Lawson had several things he hadn't been able to share with him during their time at the agency and since. Even though neither of them was active any longer, they both knew to keep their mouths shut about assignments from their time there.

However, Xavier still felt terrible about it because his secret had brought dangerous men to their door and put Lawson's sister directly in harm's way. Xavier wasn't sure he'd be as forgiving if it had been the other way around. He knew he'd never get over it if something happened to Hannah because of him.

"How far away are you?" Lawson demanded, bringing Xavier's thoughts back to their present situation.

"A few minutes," Xavier replied, trying to keep his voice steady, though all he wanted was to slam his foot down on the pedal and race to Hannah as quickly as he could.

It was hard to believe she had been taken, but Sampson was smart. He knew exactly what he needed to do to get Xavier to come to him. Thanks to Jed and his time at the lodge, Sampson knew Hannah was the one weakness he could use against Xavier to guarantee he'd come running. She was the one person he would protect at all costs, no questions asked.

Lawson let out a growl on the other end of the line. Xavier knew he was going through similar fear with Hannah being his baby sister. They both had everything to lose if this went sideways.

Xavier frowned. "You're sticking with our plan, right?" They were following behind, at a distance, in case Sampson and Jed had split up and one of them was watching the lodge. They'd wait a short time, then follow Xavier's general direction, but coming up on the other side through the forest instead of the road.

"Of course I am," Lawson muttered. "Wait until you get there, and then we'll all close in and cut them off so there's nowhere for them to go."

"Right," Xavier confirmed.

When Xavier had heard that Hannah had been taken, his first reaction was panic. He wanted to charge out to the location where Sampson was holding her and take them down in a fiery blaze, but Lawson had convinced him to wait. Make a plan and keep a level head.

He knew Lawson understood his urge to act. Of course he did, Hannah was his sister and he wanted her safe.

But Xavier knew Sampson too well to think he wouldn't follow through on his promise to kill her if they didn't play by his rules. If Lawson arrived before Xavier did, there would be hell to pay. Sampson would take her out before Xavier had a chance to do anything.

That thought had a sick feeling coursing through his stomach and made his headache pound more against his skull.

After he'd calmed down from the shock of Hannah being taken, Lawson had sent Xavier to his office to wait for River to come check him over. He'd grumbled slightly because they'd be wasting time but knew it was for the best. He wouldn't be any good to Hannah or himself if he couldn't even stand up straight.

Turned out Jed's beating had given him a slight concussion, several bruises and cuts over the top half of his body from that damn baton and had required sixteen stitches on the back of his head to close the wound. Xavier was achy and sore, and it felt like his brain was going to beat out of his skull, but he could see straight again.

While River was patching Xavier up, Lawson had called Cade to fill him in on everything and then gone to check on Sarah. Xavier felt horrible that her office had been trashed, too, and, more than anything, that she'd been traumatized. He was just glad she wasn't physically hurt. He would have never survived the guilt of that. Looked like he had a lot more therapy coming his way to get rid of all these new demons that had arisen.

Aaron had gone with Bailey, after she arrived with a

team, to process the two destroyed rooms and get statements. She had left not long before they did to head back down to Blue Ridge to fill in Sheriff Willis and put out an APB on Jed and Sampson. Xavier was reluctant to let her do that, but if they happened to get away, hopefully they'd be caught by being flagged in the law enforcement system.

He still couldn't believe this had all happened. He should have done more to keep Hannah safe. He wished he would have locked down the whole damn place, if that would have protected her from these psychopaths. He should have dug deeper into Jed and asked him to leave the moment Hannah expressed any kind of doubt about him. But he hadn't. And now, his worst enemy had gotten his hands on her, and Xavier was all too aware of what Sampson would do to get what he wanted.

There was no USB drive anymore, but that didn't matter. Sampson was clearly crazed by the obsession of finding it. God only knew why he had chosen to come back now, but it didn't matter, Xavier would take him on. He was going to get Hannah away from him and make him pay for what he'd done—to her and to their home.

He was going to end this for good.

He pulled the car to a halt at the edge of a forestry road that led into the woods. It had been unused for years, but there was dirt kicked up around the edges like someone had been there recently. Sampson? Jed? He had to assume it was one of them. Climbing out of the car, he glanced around, making sure he wasn't being watched, but there was no one around him—no one he could see anyway. Good.

Above him, the nearly full moon hung in the sky, casting a bright light down through the trees. There was a stalled feeling in the air, like the forest was holding its breath waiting to see what would happen next. Xavier felt a bead of sweat running down his spine and the cold press of the gun tucked into his pants.

It had been a long time since he had carried a weapon, not since his days at the agency. It felt like a bad sign, like each step he took was carrying him closer and closer back to the life he left behind, full of secrets and lies and death and destruction. Goose bumps formed on his flesh at the thought of becoming what he'd been all those years ago.

But if that was what it took to get Hannah to safety—if he had to walk through hell to make sure she came out the other side of this—then he would do it. He had lost Max, and he refused to lose the person who had finally brought him out of the dark place he'd been trapped in for such a long time.

Lawson would never forgive Xavier if something happened to her, and he knew he would never be able to forgive himself, either. He wouldn't deserve forgiveness if something happened to her.

Leaves crunched beneath his feet, an eerie quiet filling the woods around him. His eyes scanned his surroundings as he tried to figure out where he was headed. Sampson had given him general directions but had kept it vague enough that they would have the jump on him if they wanted. He was going to do his best not to let that happen.

Suddenly, the sound of muffled voices caught his attention from deeper in the woods. He followed them, and a few moments later, he came to a clearing.

There, sitting in front of him, was the lifted Ford that had forced him and Hannah off the road. He stepped around it, and then, with a flood of relief, he saw Hannah.

She gasped as soon as she laid eyes on him from where she sat in the open side of a van.

The moment the sound left her mouth, Sampson and Jed spun around to see exactly where he was. Jed grinned and grabbed Hannah, pulling her against him roughly. Even from where he was standing, Xavier could tell how terrified she was. Her face was drawn and pale and her whole body was stiff as Jed dragged her from the van and to her feet. She stumbled slightly at the jerking motion and her wide, scared eyes locked on Xavier's.

"It's going to be okay," Xavier told her, ignoring the other two as he lifted his hands up to show that he was unarmed. Well, as far as they knew anyway.

Sampson walked over and took Hannah by the collar of her shirt and yanked her forward. She stumbled behind him.

Xavier felt a flood of anger hit him, seeing them treat her like that. She was so sweet and sensitive in ways they would never be able to understand, and he loathed the way they dragged her about like she was nothing.

But he also knew she was fierce and brave and he was counting on that to keep her from panicking while he did what he needed to do. He didn't take his eyes off of her, silently pleading with her to believe him when he told her it was going to be all right, even though things seemed to have gone so wrong.

"Tell me where the drive is, Dutch," Sampson ordered, grinning at Xavier with a mad look in his eyes.

Xavier didn't know if he was stable enough to hear the truth of what he'd done all that time ago. Even though it had been so many years since he'd last seen the drive, Sampson still seemed to believe that Xavier was hiding it from him. He supposed Sampson was going to find out the truth sooner or later, whether he was ready or not.

Xavier took a breath, praying that what he said next didn't set Sampson off. "I don't have it."

A flash of anger crossed Sampson's face. "I know you do," he growled, jerking Hannah to a stop. "You were the last person who had it. Now, tell me where it is or—"

"I destroyed it," Xavier told him, keeping his voice as calm as he could. Lawson and the others would be on the way by now, and hopefully, they would catch up in time to help him. He just needed to keep Sampson talking long enough for them to get here.

Hannah bit down nervously on her lip, her eyes wide and laced with panic.

"You did what?" Sampson demanded. "You—"

"I destroyed it when we were on that last mission together," Xavier explained. "I was sure you were a rogue agent, and I couldn't trust you with it, so I made the executive decision to get rid of it. And it seems like I was right to do that, because look at you now."

The anger grew in Sampson's eyes. He shook his head like he couldn't believe what he was hearing. But on some level, he had to know it was true. Jed had turned Xavier's room upside down looking for the drive and hadn't been able to locate it.

"You were always too righteous for your own good," Sampson sneered. "If you don't have it, then you at least know where it is. Tell me."

"I just did," Xavier replied more forcefully. "I destroyed it. I don't have it. Nobody does. It doesn't exist anymore. I smashed it to pieces and then threw those pieces away years ago. It's probably scattered in some landfill somewhere now. You wouldn't be able to find it if you spent the rest of your life looking."

"That's too bad," Sampson replied, his voice taking on

an almost unnerving tone of calm. He reached behind his back and pulled out a gun, training it on Xavier.

"No!" Hannah screamed, her voice cutting through the quiet woods around them.

Xavier stared down the barrel, not moving. If Sampson was going to shoot him, so be it. As long as the weapon wasn't pointed at Hannah, he could handle whatever came next.

But then, like he was reading Xavier's thoughts, Sampson turned to aim the gun at Hannah instead, taking his eyes off Xavier for a moment.

Big mistake. A flash of rage took over Xavier, and he grabbed his gun and pulled it out. By the time Jed had opened his mouth to warn Sampson what was happening, Xavier had managed to get off a shot. The bullet whizzed by Sampson's head and hit the van behind him.

Startled by the shot Xavier fired at him, Sampson dropped his gun and raced for cover behind the van.

Hannah rushed over to where Sampson's gun fell and kicked it farther away.

Jed took that moment to race behind the van for cover with Sampson, yelling obscenities at Xavier, leaving Hannah standing there alone. She was free.

Hannah. She was the only thing on Xavier's mind. Eyes fixed on her, he rushed toward her, the adrenaline pumping in his system, his heart slamming against his chest.

"Xavier!" she called out to him, her voice sounding strangely distant.

But then, all at once, he reached her and pulled her into his arms. And for a moment, everything fell into place.

Chapter Twenty-Four

When Xavier pulled Hannah to him, she felt an instant wave of relief. She tried her hardest to keep the tears at bay, but they ran down her cheeks in waves. All she wanted to do was press further into Xavier's embrace and let everything else fade away. She knew they were still in danger but she couldn't seem to make herself move.

"Xavier. I was so scared." Her lips trembled as she mumbled into his shirt.

Xavier tightened his arms around her briefly, before setting her away from him. "I know and I'm sorry," he replied as he wiped the wetness from her face with his thumbs and looked around, noticed movement, and realized that Jed was making his way around to the other side of the van. He was going for Sampson. He and Hannah had to take cover now.

"We're not out of the woods yet, though. Come on."

Hannah looked around and realized Xavier was leading her to the other side of the truck for cover. She tripped, slightly off-center with her hands still bound.

"Quickly. Turn." He cut off her bindings so she'd be able to use her hands. She'd need them for balance and to help defend herself, if necessary.

As soon as her arms were loose, Hannah rubbed her wrists and shook out her hands to help regain feeling. Then she turned her wide eyes on him, seeking reassurance and direction for what to do next. "Xavier," she breathed in relief. "What do—"

Before she could finish the sentence, he was pulling her farther behind the truck as Jed and Sampson ducked into the van across from them and started firing off rounds.

"Get down!" Xavier yelled out.

Hannah followed his order almost on autopilot. She was still trying to process everything that had just happened and that Xavier was actually here. He'd come for her and pulled her to relative safety. Seeing that gun pointed at him had sent a shock wave through her that she hadn't been ready for, pure horror at the thought of losing him.

"Make sure to stay behind this truck," Xavier instructed her as he pulled his gun out again, his back pressed against the door of the truck. "And stay down."

Hannah nodded. The way he was carrying himself and giving orders right now, she knew this was the former military version of him that had existed out in the field—back when he had lost his brother.

Lost his brother. When she realized that, how close this must feel to that fateful day, her eyes widened, and she wrapped her arms around her waist, hugging herself like she was trying to hold herself together. She hated that he had to relive a version of that again.

Bullets pinged off the front of the truck, making her jump, and she hugged herself tighter. She glanced over at Xavier as he peered out around the bumper and fired off a few shots in the direction of Sampson and Jed. The man she knew seemed to have vanished for a moment, replaced by this soldier, an agent who would do anything it took to bring his enemies down.

And it scared her. More than she thought it would.

She wasn't afraid of him. What frightened her was knowing he was back there again, in his darkest hours, even if they didn't have a choice. If they made it out of this alive, how would it affect him this time? Would he be able to recover from this or would it break him for good?

He ducked back behind the truck, catching his breath and reloading his gun with a clip from his pocket. He moved with a practiced swiftness that spoke of years of training and experience. If she hadn't been so scared, she would have been impressed at how well he was carrying himself, at how easy it seemed for him to slip back into this role once more.

But all she could see was the man she loved being stolen from her by a dark part of himself he had done his best to leave behind. She wondered if he even realized it in the moment.

A bullet ricocheted off the hood, and she jumped again and let out a small squeak.

"Stay down!" Xavier ordered her once more, his voice sounding hard and tinged with worry, not like his normal voice at all.

She squeezed her eyes shut, and he reached over to grab her arm.

"You need to stay alert," he told her. "Eyes open. Stay with me, Max."

Max? His brother's name. Her heart sank when she realized she'd lost him to his past. His mind was reliving that tragic day, pulling him out of their reality and thrusting him back to the day of his brother's death. Whatever was going on in his head right now, he wasn't seeing her or living in their current situation.

She wanted to call out to him, to try to pull him back to the present with her, but she wasn't sure how to do that or if she even had the time right now. They were in a precarious situation with bullets flying around them and two men who wanted them dead. Now didn't seem like the time for a distraction that could possibly get them killed.

All she knew for sure in this moment was that Xavier needed her here with him now. She wasn't going to let him down. She'd do whatever she could to help them both survive.

"You're only delaying the inevitable here. Just come out," Jed's mocking voice came from behind the van.

His words hardly seemed to register with Xavier as he turned to duck out from behind cover once more, lifting his gun and firing off a few more well-placed rounds.

Hannah clamped her hands over her ears, the loud noise hurting her. She'd never seen Xavier fire a weapon before. He seemed so disconnected...so focused and formidable. Not like the man she knew and loved, but more like who she assumed he used to be.

The change in him was worrisome, and she hoped with all her heart she'd be able to pull him back when it was all over.

Suddenly, Hannah heard voices closing in and saw lights cutting through the trees. Flashlights! Her heart skipped a beat. Others were here! Of course, he wouldn't have come all this way without backup.

"Hey!" Hannah yelled out. "Hey, we're here! And we need help!"

She continued to call out to whoever was coming, hardly even caring who it was or if Jed and Sampson heard her.

She needed someone else here, someone who could be on their side.

All at once, Aaron, Cade, and Lawson emerged in the clearing, guns drawn.

Hannah wanted to sob in relief. Lawson immediately locked eyes with her, and Hannah could tell from a single look just how relieved he was to see her. But then, his eyes slid to Xavier, and something in his face shifted. Obviously, he could see that something was seriously wrong with Xavier...something dangerous. He instantly became more tense, more focused, as if aware of the potential threat next to her.

The Xavier both of them knew and cared for so deeply had vanished, taken over by the man who'd been consumed by the darkness of his life before.

"Xavier!" Hannah called to him. "Help is here!"

He didn't seem to notice or care. He slipped out from behind the Ford once more, firing off a couple more shots toward Sampson and Jed where they were still shielded by the van.

She tried to reach for him, but when she touched his shoulder, he shrugged her off like it was nothing. He wasn't the man she knew right now, and she didn't know how to reach him. Several rapid-fire shots hit the front of the truck as Sampson and Jed returned fire.

Lawson and the others darted back to the edge of the trees for cover.

"Stay down," Xavier growled at her. He was still firing off orders like he was in the middle of a war zone. Lost to the past and the last battle where his brother had lost his life.

"Xavier, stand down!" Cade yelled to him.

For the first time, Xavier seemed to notice that there

were other people here. He turned to face them, and Hannah saw in his cold, hard eyes that he perceived them as a new threat. He didn't recognize them. To his broken mind, they must look like enemies.

Hannah realized if she didn't think fast, he was going to do something awful and hurt someone he cared about. No amount of therapy would be able to bring him back from that.

Her mind raced with possibilities as to how she could help the man she loved right now. Shouting and gunfire were still all around them, and she knew that their friends would handle Sampson and Jed. Her primary concern needed to be Xavier, so she let everything else fade away.

She knew in that moment it wasn't just about them surviving these men, it was about getting Xavier back here in the present with her and their friends and realizing that they weren't the enemy.

While she was lost in thought trying to come up with a plan, she noticed that her brother had moved and was making his way toward them from the side.

"Xavier!" Lawson called to him.

Xavier immediately lifted his gun and aimed it at Hannah's brother.

Lawson stopped dead in his tracks, and Hannah's heart dropped.

"No! Xavier, he's not the enemy!" Her voice was filled with panic.

"What the hell are you doing?" Lawson asked Xavier, but Xavier didn't budge. He kept the gunned trained at Lawson's chest.

Hannah stood off to his side, but she felt as though she was a hundred miles away. She had to try something right now or she'd lose one or both of the men she loved more than anything. She took a deep breath and stepped closer to Xavier's side. With tears streaming down her face, she reached out and placed her hand on his chest right over his heart. She immediately felt his body go taut underneath her palm.

"Xavier," she spoke quietly in his ear. "Xavier, it's me, Hannah. I need you to come back to me."

He didn't acknowledge her, but she could feel a slight shift in him, his hand trembling on the gun aimed at her brother.

"Hannah, you need to step away. He can't hear you," Lawson told her, his voice rough with tension.

"Yes, he can. I know it," she breathed softly. With her hand over Xavier's heart, she could feel some of the tension easing in his muscles. She chanced a quick look up at his face and noticed some of the darkness leaving his gaze. He was coming back to her.

She stepped even closer, basically plastered to his side and tried again. "Please, please, come back to me. You're with me and our friends. You don't want to hurt anyone. Please."

"Hannah…" Lawson trailed off when she shook her head. Understanding she wasn't to be deterred, he heaved a large sigh and stood quietly, waiting.

Gunfire and yelling still surrounding them, she stepped directly in front of Xavier, took a deep breath, closed her eyes and planted her lips against his.

Chapter Twenty-Five

Xavier knew it; backup wasn't going to make it in time. These enemies surrounding them, they were more than he and his brother could handle. His heart slammed against his ribs while his mind raced. He could feel the bite of the air against his skin, the sound of yelling around him, but it all felt louder than ever. The screaming in his ears was more than he could take.

If he hadn't come here, if he hadn't brought his brother here, they would both be safe. His blood rushed in his ears as he heard Max calling to him, telling him he was slow and needed to hurry his ass up. Even despite his words, Xavier could tell his brother was scared, trying to overcompensate with his cocky attitude.

If something went wrong, then it would all be his fault. There would be no way to take it back, it would be too late. He had to protect his little brother. He tightened his grip on his gun, ready to pull the trigger...

AND THEN HE felt it. The press of her lips against his. The taste of her salty tears on her skin.

For a moment, he had no idea what was happening, and his whole body started shaking as he came back to reality.

"Xavier," she begged him. "Please, Xavier. Tell me you're here with me. Tell me you're here."

Xavier blinked, and blinked again, trying to recall where he was. First, he registered Hannah's face. Beyond her was Lawson, fists and jaw clenched tight, staring at him with stormy eyes. Xavier looked down and realized he was holding a gun and pointing it at his best friend. Eyes wide, he clicked the safety and shoved the weapon back in his waistband.

Next, were all the noises, guns, shouting, fighting. Too much for his brain to process all at once. So he focused on the woman in front of him, letting everything else fade away. *Hannah.*

"It's okay, Hannah," he murmured to her. "I'm here. I'm back." He wrapped his arms around her and buried his face in her hair, inhaling her scent to ground him further.

"Oh thank God," she breathed as she caught his face in her hands. "I thought... I thought I had lost you." Tears streamed down her cheeks unchecked.

Xavier felt her shaking against him, but she was smiling. This wasn't like the day he had lost his brother; this was different. Backup had made it in time, and they were going to be okay.

He'd never had a flashback that intense while he'd been awake. Hannah's kidnapping and the gunfight must have triggered his mind in a way that forced him back to relive that horrible day when he lost Max. If it hadn't been for Hannah, something similar probably would have happened here. He might have killed his best friend.

He wrapped his arms around Hannah once more and kissed her forehead. "Thank you. You saved me."

Her face broke out in a grin, and she kissed his chin.

"And you saved me. I'm just glad you're back with us. With me."

"You okay?" Lawson asked him gruffly, clapping him on the shoulder as Xavier pulled back from Hannah.

"I'm sorry," he told his best friend. "I didn't see you..."

"I know," Lawson replied quickly. "But we need you to be here right now. With us. We're still fighting."

Xavier nodded again and reached for his gun. He handed it to Hannah. "Hold this," he told her. "I don't trust myself with it right now."

"Xavier, they can handle it—"

Xavier shook his head, cutting off her reply. She didn't understand. He had a job to finish. He could have hurt the woman he loved and had almost killed his best friend, her brother. This had to end, and he needed to be the one to do it. This was personal to him.

The first thing Xavier noticed as he rounded the hood of the truck was the quiet, no gunfire. The second was that Cade and Aaron had managed to sneak up on both Jed and Sampson, probably while they had been firing at Xavier. From what Xavier could see, Aaron had Jed handled. He was on the ground, face down, Aaron half-sitting, half-leaning on his back. Aaron had Jed's arms pulled back and was securing zip-ties around his wrists. Sampson, on the other hand, had managed to shove Cade to the side and was trying to make a run for it toward the woods.

Xavier quickly ran around the opposite side of the van to cut Sampson off, slamming into him and knocking him off his feet.

Sampson hit the ground on his back and rammed his knee up into Xavier's stomach as he came down over him.

"You really think you can stop me?" Sampson laughed in his face as he knocked Xavier to the side.

Xavier pushed back to his feet and rounded on Sampson has he pulled himself off the ground. "Just give it up," Xavier told him. "You're done. There's no drive, there's no *nothing*. You wasted your time on this for no reason, and now you're going to prison for it."

Sampson's eyes narrowed with anger, his face tight as he glowered at Xavier. He must have known Xavier was right. He could have gotten away with everything else he'd done if he had just forgotten about the drive. He was just too damn greedy.

And it was going to cost him everything.

Sampson launched himself at Xavier again, knocking him off his feet, and Xavier lifted his fist to drive it up into Sampson's jaw. Sampson's head snapped back, and blood dripped from his split lip as he turned back to Xavier. He swiped at the blood with his sleeve and charged again, diving for Xavier's legs.

As soon as Xavier's back hit the forest floor, he pushed off with his legs, flipping them over, with Sampson flat on the ground. They both pushed to their feet and charged, both swinging at the same time. Xavier's fist slammed in to Sampson's chin, drawing more blood, at the same time Sampson's arm went wide, hitting Xavier in the shoulder.

Both sprang back, circling each other and breathing hard. Xavier heard footsteps behind him, and Cade and Aaron appeared ready to take over.

"Xavier, let us—" Cade started.

Sampson took advantage of the distraction and charged Xavier again. He dodged out of the way just in time, leaving Sampson punching at air.

"I've got this!" Xavier yelled back at the two men, stopping them in their tracks. He had to be the one to bring an end to this, no matter what.

A few years ago, he might have been tempted to just let it go. But now, things were different. *He* was different. He had a woman he loved and who loved him back, and a life he wasn't going to give up without a fight.

Xavier flew at Sampson again, both landing hard on the dirt. Grappling around, Xavier finally got the upper hand and rolled on top of Sampson, grabbing Sampson's head with his hands and slamming it down into the hard earth.

Sampson let out a long groan and tried to scramble out from underneath Xavier, but Xavier had Sampson right where he wanted him.

He landed hit after hit, until there was no more fight left in him. Sampson lay there on the ground, blood leaking from his mouth and nose, eyes hazy with pain.

Xavier got to his feet, wiping the sweat from his brow and took a deep breath centering himself again. All at once they heard new voices echoing in the trees. Bailey and the other deputies were here. He stepped back and looked for Hannah, who was standing off to the side with Lawson, his arm wrapped around her like he was trying to hold her back.

Cade and Aaron rushed up to stand watch over Sampson, waiting for Bailey and the deputies with her to make their way down to them.

"Looks like we missed all the fun," Bailey quipped as she pulled out cuffs and slapped them on Sampson's wrists. Xavier looked to the side and noticed Jed being picked up off the ground by another deputy from where Aaron had left him. Jed's face was bloody, too, so he and Aaron must have gone a few rounds before Aaron subdued him.

All at once, Xavier heard someone rushing toward him. He turned just in time to catch Hannah as she launched herself into his arms, wrapping herself around him and clinging on for dear life.

"Xavier!" Her cry was muffled from pressing her face into his neck.

He tightened his hold. "We're okay, Hannah. It's okay now." He pulled her back and kissed her forehead. He was still so angry he was vibrating with adrenaline at how horribly this all could have ended. But with Hannah safe and in his arms, the rage was starting to recede.

He pulled back slightly so he could gaze into her eyes for a moment. She was still so shaken, that much was obvious, but the first thing she had done was run to him for reassurance. She cared for him in a way nobody else ever had before.

She had seen the darkness in him, the battle he fought within, the part of him he kept hidden from his friends, and she hadn't run. She was still here, by his side and in his arms. She was brave enough to face his darkness and pull him back to the light. As long as she was by his side, he knew he would be okay.

"I'm so sorry," Hannah breathed. "I should never have let myself get taken. I should have—"

"It's okay," he murmured to her at once, smoothing a hand through her hair. "It's okay, Hannah, you have nothing to be sorry for. I should have done more to protect you. I should have listened to you when you said you had your doubts about Jed. I never should have let him get that close."

The two of them were talking over each other, spilling apologies faster than they could reply to them, until he kissed her again. She grasped him tight, like she was never going to let him go.

"We're safe," he promised her, planting a kiss against her temple. "I promise. We're safe."

She let out a long, shaky breath, but she seemed to believe him, managing to nod. With his arm around her waist, he steered her back toward the rest of the group.

"What happens now?" he asked Bailey.

"I'm passing this on to Willis," she explained. "With everything you gave him before, there's plenty to keep them locked up for now. And when you tell him the rest of the story, along with the damage to the lodge, what they did to Sarah and Hannah's kidnapping, the two of them are going to go away for a long, long time."

Xavier nodded slowly, taking the words in as she spoke. It almost felt too good to be true. This was it, he realized. The danger was gone. This was the last threat that had been pressing down on him for all this time. Now he could truly leave the past behind. Move on with the rest of his life and his future with the woman he loved.

"That sounds good. Thanks, Bailey."

"No problem, Xavier. We'll get these guys back to town and I'll tell Willis to contact you all at the lodge for statements later.

The sun was just starting to rise, and some of the light was beginning to filter through the trees. Hannah slipped her hand into his and squeezed it tight, seeming to need reassurance that he was right there with her and not sliding off into the nightmares that had plagued him for so long.

"You okay?" she asked him.

He nodded. It wasn't entirely true, but it was the closest he could come to the truth right now. He might not be all right in that moment, but for the first time in a long time, he knew he would be.

"We should get out of here," he told her, and she sighed in agreement, laying her head on his shoulder for a moment.

"Definitely," she agreed. "I want a hot shower. And a warm bed. And a huge meal. Not necessarily in that order."

He chuckled, already feeling some of the tension leaving his system. What was it about her that made everything easier, even a nightmare like this? Her softness, her kindness, her willingness to see the man beneath all the trauma and pain he had been through, beyond all the nightmares and horrors. She saw the person he wanted to be, the potential for who he could be, and it only made him even more certain that he would do everything he could to bring that man to life for her. Anything, as long as it meant they could be together and as long as he could make her happy.

The two of them followed the group out of the forest and into the sunlight beyond.

It was already shaping up to be another beautiful spring day.

Chapter Twenty-Six

"I really can't apologize enough," Xavier told Sarah for what had to be the hundredth time since their appointment had started.

She smiled at him kindly, shaking her head. "You have nothing to apologize for," she reminded him.

The two of them were meeting in her temporary office space while her original office was being repaired from all the destruction Jed had caused. In his fit of rage, Jed had pretty much torn apart the entire room, so it would be a while before she could feasibly work from that space again. She had too many patients needing help to take time off, and she had insisted on moving to a makeshift office in another part of the building and starting up her appointments again as normal.

Xavier was grateful for that. It had been nearly ten days since Jed had attacked him and taken Hannah, and he still felt unsettled sometimes. Being there in the middle of that shootout and feeling himself drawn back to all of the memories he had tried to leave behind was scary as hell.

Losing himself completely, forgetting where he was, not even being able to recognize his friends and allies—he never wanted that to happen again. So he was taking all the steps he could to help ensure he never lost himself to his past life again.

"We all made it out in one piece," Sarah reminded him. "That's what matters most."

"Yeah, we got lucky," Xavier agreed. "Though sometimes I can't help but think about how horribly wrong it all could have turned out."

"And how do you feel about the fact that it didn't turn out badly?" Sarah asked, gently steering the conversation back around to the focus of their appointment.

"I feel...grateful," he replied finally, letting out a long breath. "Extremely grateful that I didn't lose Hannah or anyone else. I don't think I could have survived it if I had. The guilt of harming one of my friends would have been it for me."

"Well, grateful is a great place to start. A good emotion to focus on," she agreed, jotting something down. "Has it brought up anything else you're struggling with right now?"

"I... When I was out there," he confessed. "In the middle of it, it was like my memories...fractured. Like everything that happened with Max was spilling over into the present moment, and I couldn't tell the difference between what had happened in the past and what was happening right in that moment."

Sarah nodded and wrote something else down on her pad. "The mind is a powerful thing. And sometimes, when we're reminded of those moments that have stayed in our memory, it can feel like they're happening all over again. It's the brain's way of trying to protect itself. You didn't want to have to face the possibility of losing the woman you love, so your brain put in place the memories that you'd already started to deal with."

"Makes sense," he agreed. He was still trying to wrap his head around the way all of this worked. He had spent so long avoiding these conversations, actually accepting this help was still foreign to him, but the more he learned, the clearer all of this became. Instead of being stuck under the control of the nightmares he'd had for so long, he could look at them a little more objectively and deal with them more clearly than he had before.

"And what about the dreams?" Sarah asked him. "I would expect you've been dealing with some of them lately."

"I have been dreaming about my brother," he admitted. "But not the same flashbacks I'd been having before. The ones from the last time I saw him alive."

"No?" she prompted him, sounding interested.

"I had this dream about the two of us racing across the field behind our house when we were young," he said, feeling a smile spread over his face. "To see who would make it to the edge of the woods first." Xavier briefly closed his eyes, pulling up the memory again. "It was so long ago, I'd almost forgotten we used to do that. And I always gave him a head start, but he still accused me of cheating, even though I mostly let him win." He smiled and shrugged, looking a little sheepish. "I didn't want to deal with him whining about how I cheated." He chuckled at the thought. "Max was always a sore loser. And slow, for the record. He never actually beat me."

Sarah laughed. "It's great that you're finally able to talk about your happier memories with your brother. And even better that you're not having the dreams about his passing anymore."

"You think so?" Xavier asked. Some part of him had felt guilty about the dreams turning from painful to happy, as though he should have had to contend with his failure to keep his brother safe a little longer.

"I know so," she replied.

"Why do you think it's happened? It seems wrong in some way that I've gone from reliving his death to memories of our childhood," he asked, frowning. He'd only just started therapy again. It seemed too soon to have made such huge steps forward and for his feelings of failure to suddenly be gone.

"I can't tell you the exact reason," she remarked. "But I can give you my theory, if you want."

"Go ahead," he replied, gesturing for her to keep talking.

"You've struggled for a long time feeling like you failed your brother," she explained. "Even though there was nothing more you could have done to help him. But now, this time, you saved *her*. And I think your mind knows on some level that he would be proud of you for that. Proud of both of you, actually. You're starting to forgive yourself, because this time, it went differently."

Xavier paused, taking it all in. It sounded right to him. His mind accepted that explanation. He hadn't been able to save Max, no matter how much he had wanted to, but he had been able to save Hannah. And maybe that was enough to start the process of forgiving himself. And letting him find some peace.

THAT EVENING, HANNAH SNUGGLED next to Xavier on one of the couches in front of the fireplace in the lodge's reception area. They had all decided on gathering in this room to warm themselves up after a long day of work putting the lodge back together. Sarah's office was the main focus, but Hannah and River had been out planting some more flowers, too. Her hands were still chilly as she pushed them into Xavier's and rested her head on his shoulder. Even though the spring days were warm, it still got chilly at night. Perfect for snuggling by the fire.

Opposite them, the rest of the space was filled with their friends—Cade and River, Bailey and Aaron, and Sarah and Lawson, wineglasses in hand and a quiet peace resting over all of them. After the chaos of the last several months, there was something distinctly precious about this time they had together, without having to look over their shoulders and worry about what was going to happen next.

As the season changed from winter to spring before their eyes, Xavier's mind had drifted to the future, too. There was so much he wanted to do, so much he wanted to try. Now that some of the weight of his past had been lifted off his shoulders, it felt like he could see a whole new future, something he had never let himself imagine before.

"Those flowers are already starting to bloom, Hannah," Bailey remarked as she peered out of the window beside her. "They're looking gorgeous. I can't wait to see how they'll look when summer comes."

"Yeah, everything looks better in summer," Aaron agreed, shooting Xavier a conspiratorial grin. He knew what Aaron was planning, because he had had come to Xavier to ask for help picking out the ring. He could have gone to Hannah, but he was worried she might spill the beans to Bailey before he was ready, and he wanted it to come as a complete surprise. Xavier knew Aaron could hardly wait to see the look on her face.

"Good time for a wedding, too," Aaron added as casually as he could.

Hannah frowned. "What do you mean, a wedding?"

Bailey's lips parted in surprise, but before she could say

anything else, Aaron handed his wine over to Xavier and dropped to one knee in front of Bailey.

Hannah's hand flew to her mouth, and River spluttered into her drink in shock.

"Bailey, our paths to each other haven't always been easy," Aaron began as he reached into his pocket to pull out a ring. "But all that matters to me is that our path to our future is one we embark on together." He popped open the box, showing off a glittering band with an oval-shaped diamond planted in the center.

Bailey's eyes nearly bugged out of her head.

"Will you marry me, Bailey?"

"Yes! Of course I will!" she exclaimed, almost dropping her wine as she sprang to her feet.

Aaron laughed and stood up to meet her, planting his lips against hers and pulling her into a warm embrace.

Hannah squeezed Xavier's hand gently as they watched the scene unfold in front of them, two of their friends dedicating themselves to one another.

"Now get that damn ring on my finger already," Bailey ordered him, and everyone laughed as he slipped the sparkly ring onto her finger. She gazed at it for a moment and then back to him, sinking into his arms again.

The rest of the evening was spent celebrating the newly engaged couple. Sarah went to the kitchen to dig out a bottle of champagne, and they shared it as they toasted to Aaron and Bailey's future happiness. It was a perfect evening, the antidote to everything they had been through with Sampson less than two weeks prior.

It was these nights at the lodge that Xavier lived for, surrounded by his friends, knowing he was safe…they all were safe…and there was nothing for him to worry about or fear any longer.

By the time the champagne was gone, he could tell Hannah was starting to get a little tipsy, and he led her outside so they could head back to their cabin. The two of them were living together now, as if he could spend a moment apart from her.

Even if his room hadn't been trashed, he would have wanted to wake up next to her every day. Their little coffee dates every morning gave him a reason to get out of bed, and eating dinner together at their tiny kitchen table was the perfect way to end each day. He couldn't ask for anything more.

He pulled her into his arms and planted his lips against hers in the cool evening air.

She giggled and smiled up at him, gazing at him with those beautiful eyes that still set his heart pounding in his chest. As he stared down at her, she cocked an eyebrow at him.

"Don't tell me that proposal has you feeling all romantic," she teased him.

"It's not that," he replied. "Just you."

He kissed her again, brushing his thumb over her cheek and pausing to take this moment in. There had been so many times where he had felt as though he would never feel true happiness again. Never be rid of the guilt weighing him down or the nightmares about his brother. But when he was with Hannah, it all seemed to fade away. He could just be there in the present with her.

He knew there was still a lot of work to be done when it came to healing himself entirely. But this? This was the start he needed. The reason he needed to keep going. To become the man she wanted him to be, the kind of man she could spend her life with. He would work every day of his life to make sure he got there.

"But there is something I want to tell you," he murmured. "Something I should have said a long time ago." He paused, looking down into her expectant eyes with a smile on his face. He wanted to linger in this moment forever. There were so many memories in his mind that he wished he could escape, but when he was with her, none of them seemed to matter. The only thing he cared about was her, and he wanted her to know just how deep his feelings for her ran.

She pushed her fingers into his hair, hand tracing the nape of his neck. He was sure she could tell what was on his mind. The two of them had felt this way about each other for so long now, but they hadn't actually spoken the words out loud yet. He needed her to hear it from him. Needed her to know.

"I love you," he told her softly, the words feeling right escaping his lips.

She smiled, that beautiful smile that seemed to light up the whole world around her, and stood on her tiptoes to plant her lips against his.

"I love you, too," she replied. "Now, let's get back to the cabin before I freeze out here."

"Hmm, I can think of a few ways to keep you warm," he remarked playfully, and she giggled.

"I bet you can," she replied. "Why don't you come show me?"

Taking his hand, she led him down the path toward their cabin, the flowers along the path just starting to come into bloom. Just like their love.

Epilogue

Hannah shivered as she stood next to the cold plunge tub. Why had she agreed to this again?

"You ready?" Xavier asked as he stood next to her in his swim trunks. The sight of him almost undressed was enough motivation to get her out of bed this early in the morning, but she wasn't sure anything could convince her to get into that water.

"No," she replied, and she reached out to slip her fingers into the tub. She snatched her hand back at once, letting out a cry. "Oh my God, it's so cold!" she protested. "You sure I can't just go have my morning coffee instead?"

"No, you promised," he reminded her, raising his eyebrows pointedly. "We have to test this out before any of the guests try it, right?"

"Right," she muttered, grimacing as she imagined submerging her whole body under the freezing water. "Tell me what it's supposed to help with again?"

"Reduces inflammation, increases circulation, improves metabolism and mood," he replied, ticking off the benefits on his fingers. He grinned at her. "You ready now?"

"Ugh, I guess so," she muttered, as she dropped the robe she had been hanging on to for dear life. She was in her one-piece swimsuit, and the warm summer that was starting to come in wasn't enough to keep her from shivering.

"You'll feel so good when you're out, I promise," he told her, grabbing her hand and helping her up the wooden steps to the tub.

"Three, two, one..." Xavier announced, and then the two of them both leaped into the water.

"Oh my God, no, no, no!" Hannah shrieked as soon as the freezing water hit her body. "No way!"

"It's not that bad," Xavier replied, but his teeth were already starting to chatter.

She laughed, even as the cold started to set in around her. "Yes, it is!" she protested. She was well aware that they were probably going to get into trouble for causing such a racket this early in the morning, but she didn't care. She curled her toes and tried to breathe, her body already crying at her to get out. It went completely against every part of her nature to sit here in freezing water. For goodness' sake, it went against human nature! She should have been stepping out of a hot shower right now, preparing a warm cup of coffee, not freezing her butt off in this tub.

"I bet I can last longer than you," he told her, and she narrowed her eyes at him. If he thought it was going to be that easy to beat her, he was wrong.

"Oh, yeah?" she replied, wrapping her arms around herself beneath the water. "Let's find out, huh?"

He knew there was no better way to get her to do something than to suggest she couldn't. She was stubborn right down to her bones. And she wasn't going anywhere.

"You can get out anytime you like," he teased her, even as his words started to shake from the cold.

"Oh yeah, so can you," she shot back. "You all right over there? Looks like you're struggling."

"I feel great," he replied, but he forced the words out through gritted teeth. His whole body was covered in goose bumps, and he was already glancing toward the spot where he had left his robe.

"Do you, now?" she asked him, nudging him with her foot under the water. "It's really cold in here. Nobody would blame you if you had to—"

But she couldn't even get the words out before he sprang from the water and grabbed his robe, wrapping it around himself quickly.

"Damn, that's cold!" he cried out, and she laughed and kicked her legs beneath the water.

"Really?" she replied, feigning innocence and trying to keep her own teeth from chattering. "I think it's just lovely in here." She counted out another ten seconds but then climbed out of the water, shivering wildly and slipping on her robe. "You know what, beating you really did improve my mood," she remarked as she reached for her shoes. "Maybe there's something to all of this after all."

"I should have known not to challenge you," he muttered, chuckling. "You never let yourself get beat."

"Exactly," she agreed, as she crouched down to slip on her flip-flops. These last few months had been some of the best of her life, partly because she had realized a strength in herself she had never noticed before.

She had started therapy at Xavier's request, after what she had been through at the hands of Jed and Sampson. She had been so focused on helping Xavier get back on his feet, she had found herself kept up late with nightmares and memories of her own.

Focusing on herself in therapy made all the difference, and she'd found herself better able to handle those dreams when they came around. As time passed, they were becoming less frequent and ferocious, and she knew it wouldn't be long until they all but vanished entirely.

It helped, of course, that Sampson and Jed had been locked up with the key pretty much thrown away. No court date had been set yet, as the state pulled together all of the evidence it needed to get them put away for life, but it was clear they weren't going to be getting out anytime soon. The horrors they had put her through, and the hardships they had caused for Xavier, were well and truly a thing of the past.

She hoped they would stay there, though she was sure she would have to testify against them when the case eventually went to trial. One of the reasons she was so determined to see her therapy through was so she'd be strong enough in her testimony to ensure they got a life sentence.

Seeing how much it had helped Xavier had also convinced her it was the right thing for her. It seemed nothing short of a miracle to Hannah that he had changed so much in these last few months, and she knew Sarah was a big part of that.

He had put in so much work, learning all these techniques to ground himself and pull himself out of a flashback when one hit him. She could only imagine how tough it had been to relive all those memories again in order to work through them.

But the person she had seen in the woods on that fateful day, she never laid eyes on again. The man who seemed so lost to his memories, to the bad dreams and his past, was gone now. When she looked at him, she saw his softness, his kindness—his dedication to making sure that nobody had to suffer the same way he had.

He had been an amazing support as she got back on her feet after the attack, and to the guests at the lodge, too. He understood so well what a lot of them had been through, and he did whatever he could to help them through it, encouraging them to get therapy and able to tell them exactly how it had helped him. His strength and kindness never failed to amaze her, and she was so proud to be able to call such a good man hers.

He talked a lot about his brother these days, which was such a nice change from before. For so long, he had hardly spoken Max's name out loud, but now, it was different. The happy memories he shared with her made her wish that she'd had a chance to know Max properly, but at least she could get to know him through his proud older brother's memories. That was something.

She had put up a picture of Max and Xavier as kids in their cabin, one that she'd dug up from his old room. It wasn't much, but it was some kind of reminder of him, of their happy times together.

She had never been happier, not in her whole life. Helping Bailey organize her wedding, coming up with fun wedding favors with River, watching the flowers she had planted bloom over the course of the summer, sharing the evenings with all of her friends, including her brother, who was totally accepting of her relationship with Xavier. It was everything she could have asked for, everything she could have dreamed of, and she wouldn't have changed a thing.

Well, maybe one thing. As she dried herself off, she pulled a face as she looked down at the flip-flops she'd brought with her.

"What's wrong?" Xavier asked, noticing her annoyance.

"Those things gave me blisters on the way out here," she complained. "It's going to hurt like hell getting back to the cabin to warm up. I should have brought something else with me."

"Well, maybe you can next time," he suggested.

She laughed. "Oh, you want a rematch already, huh?" she asked, pretending to square up to him.

He grinned and put his arms around her. "How about I carry you back?" he suggested.

She smiled, leaning into him. "I guess I could manage that," she agreed, and he swooped her up into his arms. "When did you become such a romantic?" she asked, and he lowered his mouth to hers.

For a moment, she forgot all about the bet he'd made and the fact she'd won. When he kissed her like that, nothing else in the world mattered to her.

"When I realized I could drop you back in the cold plunge tub," he murmured.

Her eyes widened. "Wait, what?"

But before she could get another word out, he dropped her back in the water—robe and all—and took off running.

"You're *so* dead!" she yelled after him, but she was laughing so much she could hardly get the words out. The freezing water rushed through her again, and she scrambled out as fast as she could. She took off her soaked robe and fished her flip-flops out of the water, then took off after him. She didn't care who saw her as she sprinted in the direction he had gone, robe and shoes in hand.

She saw him vanish down the path into the woods, just past the row of flowers she had planted before the first frost the year before. She put on a burst of speed, rushing to catch up with him, laughing so hard she could barely catch her breath.

When she finally caught up to him, he was already back at their cabin, sitting on the porch swing with a triumphant grin on his face.

"What took you so long?" he asked as nonchalantly as he could while still trying to catch his breath.

She matched his tone, stepping onto the porch. "Oh, I was just doing a little extra cold plunging. It has a lot of health benefits, you know."

"Does it?" He raised his eyebrows.

"Sure does. It reduces inflammation, increases circulation, improves metabolism and mood... I'm pretty much a champ at it."

He threw his head back and laughed. "Okay, champ, what do you say we warm up together in a hot shower? I hear that can have a few health benefits, too."

Hannah agreed enthusiastically, and as she followed him into their cabin, she realized that she was living her dream. She was safe, she was loved, and she was so incredibly happy.

She couldn't ask for anything more.

* * * * *

COMING SOON!

We really hope you enjoyed reading this book.
If you're looking for more romance
be sure to head to the shops when
new books are available on

Thursday 21st May

To see which titles are coming soon, please visit
millsandboon.co.uk/nextmonth

MILLS & BOON

FOUR BRAND NEW BOOKS FROM MILLS & BOON MODERN

Indulge in desire, drama, and breathtaking romance – where passion knows no bounds!

OUT NOW

Eight Modern stories published every month, find them all at:

millsandboon.co.uk

LET'S TALK
Romance

For exclusive extracts, competitions and special offers, find us online:

- **f** MillsandBoon
- **X** @MillsandBoon
- **O** @MillsandBoonUK
- **♪** @MillsandBoonUK

Get in touch on 01413 063 232

For all the latest titles coming soon, visit
millsandboon.co.uk/nextmonth